PRAISE FOR REBEKAH CRANE

June, Reimagined

"[T]he real love story here is between the protagonist and her authentic life . . . A sincere story about navigating life and love."

—*Kirkus Reviews*

Only the Pretty Lies

"Inspired by a true event, Crane (*The Infinite Pieces of Us*, 2018) earnestly explores how silence perpetuates racism and what it means to be antiracist . . . With countless quotable lines like 'Love is a human right, not a reward for good behavior,' and timely antiracism discussion, this is a YA novel with love and substance."

—*Booklist* (starred review)

"A naïve girl is forced to reconcile truths she thought she knew with the reality of the boy she loves. A romance that tackles serious issues . . ."

—*Kirkus Reviews*

Postcards for a Songbird

"An earnest exploration of the demise of a family, this book captures the sense of disconnect a teen can feel when buffeted by changing winds . . . The characters are well-developed, complex, and intriguing. A finely crafted story of the healing that can happen when family secrets rise to the surface."

—*Kirkus Reviews*

T0130915

"An enjoyable read. Wren's vulnerability and decision to no longer play it safe will engage readers."

—School Library Journal

The Infinite Pieces of Us

A *Seventeen* Best YA Book of 2018

"Crane has created an organic and dynamic friendship group. Esther's first-person narration, including her framing of existential questions as 'Complex Math Problems,' is honest and endearing. A compelling narrative about the power of friendship, faith, self-acceptance, and forgiveness."

—Kirkus Reviews

"Crane's latest is a breezy, voice-driven, and emotional read with a well-rounded cast of characters that walk that fine line between quirky and true to life . . . The novel stands out for its depiction of the American Southwest . . . Hand to fans of Jandy Nelson and Estelle Laure."

—Booklist

"[This] journey of self-discovery and new beginnings will resonate with readers seeking answers to life's big questions."

—School Library Journal

"*The Infinite Pieces of Us* tells a story of judgement, family, trust, identity, and new beginnings . . . a fresh take on teenage pregnancy . . . Crane creates relatable, diverse characters with varying socioeconomic backgrounds and sexualities that remind readers of the importance of getting to know people beyond the surface presentation."

—VOYA

The Upside of Falling Down

"[An] appealing love story that provides romantics with many swoon-worthy moments."

—*Publishers Weekly*

"Written with [an] unstoppable mix of sharp humor, detailed characters, and all-around charm, this story delivers a fresh and enticing take on first love—and one that will leave readers swooning."

—Jessica Park, author of *180 Seconds* and *Flat-Out Love*

"*The Upside of Falling Down* is a romantic new-adult celebration of all of the wild and amazing possibilities that open up when perfect plans go awry."

—*Foreword Magazine*

"Using the device of Clementine's amnesia, Crane explores themes of freedom and self-determination . . . Readers will respond to [Clementine's] testing of new waters. A light exploration of existential themes."

—*Kirkus Reviews*

"This quickly paced work will be enjoyed by teens interested in independence, love, self-discovery, and drama."

—*School Library Journal*

"First love, starting over, finding herself—the story is hopeful and romantic."

—*Denver Life*

The Odds of Loving Grover Cleveland

One of Bustle's Eight Best YA Books of December 2016

"Now that the title has captured our attention, I have even better news: No, this book isn't a history lesson about a president. Much more wonderfully, it centers on teenager Zander Osborne, who meets a boy named Grover Cleveland at a camp for at-risk youth. Together, the two and other kids who face bipolar disorder, anorexia, pathological lying, schizophrenia, and other obstacles use their group therapy sessions to break down and build themselves back up. And as Zander gets closer to Grover, she wonders if happiness is actually a possibility for her after all."

—Bustle

"The true beauty of Crane's book lies in the way she handles the ugly, painful details of real life, showing the glimmering humanity beneath the façades of even her most troubled characters . . . Crane shows, with enormous heart and wisdom, how even the unlikeliest of friendships can give us the strength we need to keep on fighting."

—RT Book Reviews

Last Call for Love

ALSO BY REBEKAH CRANE

Last Call for Love

a novel

REBEKAH CRANE

SKYSCAPE

Published by Skyscape, New York

www.apub.com

Amazon, the Amazon logo, and Skyscape are trademarks of Amazon.com, Inc., or its affiliates.

ISBN-13: 9781662513381 (hardcover)
ISBN-13: 9781662513398 (paperback)
ISBN-13: 9781662513404 (digital)

Cover design by Cassie Gonzales
Cover images: © Westend61 / Getty; © GoodStudio, © Amanita Silvicora, © Bibadash, © Ardea-studio / Shutterstock

Printed in the United States of America

First edition

For my parents, who taught me to always enter laughing

Of all the comrades that e're I had
they're sorry for my going away
and all the sweethearts that e're I had
they'd wish me one more day to stay
but since it falls unto my lot
that I should rise and you should not
I gently rise and softly call
good night and joy be to you all.

—*"The Parting Glass," traditional song*

1

Maeve Kaminski is a planner. Her mother likes to say that Maeve came into the world, saw what a mess it was, and has been trying to organize it ever since. It started with blocks when she was a baby. She'd spend hours ordering them by color and size. When most kids wanted a Barbie, Maeve wanted the house, so she could arrange all the little items inside, planning the living room, the bedroom, the closet.

By the time she was four, she was color-coordinating the bookshelf of board and picture books in her bedroom. At six, her favorite weekend activity was reorganizing the pantry. At eight, when most kids were begging for Harry Potter and iPods for Christmas, she wanted a datebook with rainbow-colored pens. The rosewood-pink leather-bound book with the year and her initials engraved in gold along the spine became Maeve's prized possession. She carried it around like most kids now carry their cell phones, pulling it out every chance she could to note each assignment, test, soccer game, birthday party, and school dance, each event written in its correlating color. School assignments in green. After-school activities in blue. Social events in pink. Every Christmas after that, Maeve received an identical new datebook with fresh pages for the year to come. As she got older, she added purple for dates. Red to monitor her period. Yellow for birthdays. She kept a list of all her crushes, written in orange, and then crossed them off in black when her affection eventually faded.

Now at twenty-four, Maeve has her datebooks all displayed on a bookshelf in chronological order. A solid collection, tracking all the important events of her life. "The Diaries of a Control Freak," her best friend and roommate, Sonya, says. But Maeve likes to see her life written out in a rainbow of colors, planned and organized. She wants to know what's coming. If a pantry is organized, you don't have to wonder what you need from the grocery store. If a desk is in order, you don't have to search for paper clips. When life falls to pieces, a well-organized person knows where the hell the parachute is.

Or so Maeve thought, until her proverbial parachute was stolen by a Midwestern heartthrob who never forgot Mother's Day and had a body like a Greek god. Now Maeve Kaminski is on a ferry bound for an Irish island, her life having made an unexpected U-turn just days ago, her existence now as cluttered as her best friend's closet.

It all started with Spencer Allen.

It was a typical Saturday evening after a long day in the bleachers at Wrigley Field. Maeve was dressed in her usual baseball attire—'47 Scrum Cubs T-shirt, cutoff jean shorts, and faded blue Cubs cap. She and Sonya had stumbled over to the Cubby Bear, which, as always after games, was packed with reveling, tipsy fans decked out in the team's gear. And there he was, wearing the same cap as Maeve, preppy baby-blue khaki shorts, canvas belt, and casual gray T-shirt. Soft brown eyes and sandy blond hair, ancestry from hardworking farmers in Germany or Sweden that made him tall and strong, melded with a Dutch grandmother whose influence softened and rounded his facial features. Maeve could have guessed he was into Big Ten football and chicken wings but worked out five days a week. Egocentric enough that he cared what others thought of his body, but not so much that it got in the way of having a good time.

"Nice hat," he had said, nodding toward Maeve's.

"Same to you." She raised her lite beer for a toast. "Are you from Chicago?"

"Michigan, actually. But I live here now. You?"

She told him about growing up a mile away from Wrigley Field.

"Nice. A city girl." They talked the rest of the evening about Maeve's childhood on the north side of Chicago, riding the L downtown by herself to the hospital where her mom, Maryann, worked. Sleepovers at her grandparents' house in Portage Park. Her parents taking her to Grant Park the night Obama won the presidency.

Spencer told her about his parents' divorce, his great-grandma's farm outside of Grand Rapids, his childhood dog, Pebbles.

"My sister named him," Spencer groaned. "He looked like a mop."

"I bet you cried like a baby when Pebbles died."

"Guilty. I have a little container of his ashes on my nightstand. But isn't that love?" He narrowed in on Maeve with such intensity that she felt it in her groin. "When you love someone, you can't let go. It physically hurts too much."

Maeve had never been in love before, and admitted as much.

"Sounds like something we need to remedy, Maeve Kaminski."

She liked the way he said her full name, as if etching it into his memory. He walked her home and didn't even try to come inside, instead promising to text on Monday.

"What time?" she asked, the question a test.

"Ten a.m." Then he sent her a calendar invite. *A calendar invite.* For a control freak like Maeve, that was almost as good as an orgasm.

And he did text at exactly ten on Monday. He picked her up at exactly seven on Friday for their first official date. Was never late. He always remembered important dates. Hell, he even reminded Maeve to schedule her annual. Spencer Allen may have been the only person more organized than Maeve. Unfortunately, for two years, he was meticulously planning her demise.

"I hate you, Spencer Allen," Maeve says aloud, as the ferry hits a substantial wave and lurches left, forcing her to grab the railing to steady herself as a rolling nausea rises within her. She will *not* allow herself to puke. That would just be too pitiful.

Seasickness has never been a problem on Lake Michigan, but the strait between Ireland's mainland and the southern island of Inishglass is rocky, the water churning and rolling like storm clouds below the boat.

"Keep your eye on the horizon. That'll hold your stomach steady. We're almost there." The older gentleman next to Maeve has a thick Irish brogue she can hardly understand, like the faint outline of a jetty through the thin layer of fog in the distance. The man is dressed in a pageboy hat, knee-length navy rain jacket, and muck boots. A perfect replica of a stock photo captioned "Irish farmer."

"My weather app said it was going to be nice today," Maeve says. "All sunshine. I planned accordingly."

The man laughs like this is the funniest thing he's ever heard. "Weather app? Won't get much use out of that here."

Maeve shows him the bright yellow suns stretching for hours, and the phone almost goes overboard when the ferry hits another wave. Again, the man laughs. Maeve feels like she might cry. And right then when her day can't get any worse, it starts to rain, but only on her, as if a single cloud hangs directly over her head. The man, who is dressed for rain, is completely dry. Maeve quickly retrieves her rain jacket from her backpack and slips it on.

"At least you didn't rely on that app of yours when it came to packing." The man points off the bow as the bright green of Inishglass breaks through the layer of fog and clouds, as though someone pulled back a stage curtain and before them is Brigadoon. "There she is," he says with affection. "I know you're not a local, which means you must be a tourist. Here to see if the rumors are true about our little island?"

Maeve has no idea what he's talking about, nor does she want to. The less time she spends here and the less she knows, the better. Not her usual approach, but she has her reasons.

"Just visiting for a few days," she says.

Inishglass is a patchwork of green rolling hills, intimidating jagged cliffs, and sandy beaches. If Maeve were here under different circumstances, and not on the verge of vomiting, she'd be snapping pictures like the rest of the tourists and promptly posting to Instagram. This is a moment for her, after all; she's never been out of the United States before today. If there was ever a time for social media, it's now. But Maeve's parents don't know she's left Chicago, let alone the country.

Not that she is doing anything wrong. She's twenty-four years old. She lives in an apartment she pays for. She has a job, and while being an inside sales rep for a cable company isn't her dream, it sustains her lifestyle. Ultimately, Maeve is an adult. Which is precisely why she has not told her parents about Spencer and instead plans to fix things herself.

"Well, if you ask me, there's no better pub on earth than the Moorings. My mother would come down from heaven and drag me out by my ears if she ever saw me in the Thatch. But that's how people on this island are. Loyal, with long histories and even longer memories, though no one is willing to fact-check, either."

Maeve is barely listening, too focused on keeping down the airplane chicken and rice that came with her economy seat.

As the ferry approaches land, people prepare to disembark, but the man next to Maeve doesn't move. He's been prattling on the past few minutes, Maeve only catching a word here and there, but now he examines her face intently and says, "You look familiar. Have we met before?"

That captures her attention. "This is my first time in Ireland."

"It's the freckles on your nose," he says, pointing at them. "And your eyes. You're Irish, for sure."

The boat staggers as it slows into the harbor, where a few other fishing boats are docked along the jetty. Maeve turns away from the man, uncomfortable under his stare.

"Polish," she says with a shrug. "Last name's Kaminski. I think it's time to go."

"My suggestion?" the man says with a wink. "Delete your weather app and embrace the unpredictability of the island. You'll have more fun." He walks away.

"Unpredictability is not really my specialty," Maeve admits under her breath. And she isn't here for fun. This is a business trip.

She reminds herself this will all be over soon. She will be back in her queen bed, in her garden apartment that smells like her favorite sandalwood and rose candle, in her beloved Chicago, before the end of the week. This speedy jaunt to Ireland will be a blip in her story. She is organizing the proverbial pantry, getting her life back on track. She will never again forget the parachute.

The rain over Maeve's head stops, and the sun breaks through the clouds. She shakes out her jacket before putting it back in her bag, wishing the nausea would disappear, too. The sun hangs low in the west, making its way toward America. If she could ride it home, she would.

Eager tourists file off the boat, but Maeve lingers, not confident her stomach can handle walking just yet. She's envious of everyone's excitement, their awe, their freedom, but mostly, their itineraries. The months of preparation they must have gone through to get here. Their confirmation numbers and planned tours and return flights. Maeve can't even go to a restaurant without first looking at the menu online, and now she's flown across the Atlantic without any idea of what's in store. Not her ideal, but she had no choice.

And then right as her self-loathing hits a pathetic low, her phone rings with a call from Sonya, offering the first stitch of relief since Maeve's flight left O'Hare yesterday afternoon, bound for Dublin.

"Top of the morning to ya!" Sonya yells.

"Your Irish accent is terrible. And it's evening here."

"Well, aren't you a bloody arsehole." Her accent is somewhere between cockney and East Indian, with a solid dose of flat, nasal Chicago.

"Did you google Irish phrases?"

"Maybe." Sonya switches back to her natural Midwestern accent. "Any word from He Who Must Not Be Named?" Sonya starts every conversation with this question, astounding Maeve with her optimism.

"Yes, after eight months of ghosting me, Spencer called to offer his condolences. Turns out, all this time, he was burning in hell. That's why he didn't call."

Sonya laughs.

"Tell me what you're doing right now," Maeve adds, needing a distraction from her seasickness.

"OK . . . don't kill me,"

And just like that, panic rattles her once again. "What?"

"I'm on my way to Homeslice for Bloody Marys." Quietly, like an afterthought she doesn't want Maeve to hear, Sonya adds, "With Melanie Kingston."

"Melanie Kingston? Who's—" And then Maeve remembers the girl that she and Sonya grew up with. A total snob whose mom invented a talking photo album back in the early 2000s, and when Oprah named it one of her "favorite things," Rachel Kingston became an overnight success and wrote a self-help book for entrepreneurial moms titled *Capture This Moment, Mommy: Manifest Your Future Now (Your Kids Will Thank You Later)*. Rachel now runs a mindfulness institute and retreat center. Melanie was the kid who knew your soft spot and smiled as she pressed on it with a manicured finger until it bruised.

"I ran into her last night at ROOF," Sonya explains. "I swear, she's changed."

"I've been gone for less than twenty-four hours, and you went to our favorite spot without me?" Maeve hears the music of the city playing behind Sonya. Horns, motorcycles, garbage trucks, barking dogs, angry bicyclists. What Maeve wouldn't give to be yelled at by a bike-delivery guy right now.

"We've been cooped up for months, Mae," Sonya says delicately. "Not that I'm complaining, but . . . it's June in Chicago." They have avoided the posh ROOF for months because of Maeve's lack of funds, and being the best friend she is, Sonya has spent most weekends in their apartment, drinking the cheapest jugs of wine they can find. No wonder Sonya broke out the second Maeve left.

"I'm sorry." Maeve puts her head down on the railing of the boat, her nausea worsening, though she's not sure whether it's seasickness or homesickness or lifesickness.

"Don't apologize for something you didn't do. You know who did this. This is his fault."

"I should have known better."

"Said every person who's ever ordered chicken wings on a first date. It happens to all of us. And in your defense, your chicken wing was really hot. A lot of people would risk getting sauce on their face for a bite of him."

Finally, a laugh. But right as Maeve is about to thank Sonya for being the best best friend a girl could have, the call drops. Maeve collects herself and exits the ferry. Just as she sets foot on the jetty, the phone rings again.

"You know you're the best damn friend a girl could ask for."

"Maeve Kaminski?" Not Sonya. The voice is male. "This is Konrad. I'm a collector with American Debt Services. I'm following up from a previous call last week. We have yet to receive payment from you."

Maeve holds the phone so tight her fingers ache. "I explained this to the last person who called. My identity was stolen."

"So eleven months ago, you didn't take a trip to Mexico where you racked up . . . fifteen thousand dollars of debt?"

"I did take the trip. But I didn't know I was spending the money."

"Sounds like too many margaritas."

The trip was Spencer's idea. They had been together for over a year, the longest relationship for either of them. He wanted to celebrate in a big way. *He* suggested Mexico and the five-star resort with a private plunge pool overlooking the ocean. And the snorkeling excursion. And the romantic beachside dinner with the mariachi band.

"That's not what—it was my boyfriend, Spencer. He spent the money. He bought the flights. He booked the trip. He's the one who owes you."

"But your name's on the card."

"He opened it without me knowing!"

"This sounds like a lovers' tiff. If your boyfriend spent the money in your name, tell him to pay you back."

"I would, if I knew where he was." Maeve hates how pathetic she must seem.

"Sounds like you're in a bit of a pickle."

"You have no idea, Konrad. If you knew everything that's happened, even you'd give me a break."

"Let me guess—this Spencer guy said he loved you."

"I really trusted him, Konrad."

That's the most shameful part. The debt is bad, but the fact that the little girl who loved to organize didn't see the mess all around her has Maeve doubting herself on a level she didn't think possible. If you don't have order, what do you have? A big fat mess. And Maeve hates messes.

Bottom line: she's a control freak who lost control.

"Why don't you just tell your mom what happened and ask for help?" Konrad suggests.

"There is no way I can tell my mom about this." Maeve takes in the foreign landscape, and her stomach knots, squeezing tighter.

"What about your dad?"

"That's . . . complicated, Konrad."

"I'm sure he'd understand. Dads love their little girls, right?"

"Well, asking him might be a bit of a problem."

"And why's that?"

Maeve may not be certain of much right now, but she's confident of this. "Because, Konrad. My dad is dead." Then she pukes into the harbor.

2

Maeve Kaminski has two dads.

One is the man who took her to her first day of kindergarten, who taught her to ride a bike, who bought her pads and gave her Advil and kept a secret stash of chocolate for when she got her period.

The other is listed on her birth certificate.

Keith Rothchild is the man who raised her.

Liam Doherty is the man who made her. They never met. He was a one-night stand, an unintentional sperm donor, found not at a bank but at a bar in Phuket. A chemically induced, blurred decision made by two consenting adults in their midtwenties, hopped up on mai tais. Maryann Kaminski had been on break before starting her residency. Maeve isn't quite sure why Liam was in Thailand. Maryann never said. And Maeve hadn't cared to ask.

Not that Maryann hated Liam for being estranged from his daughter. He had simply been a blip on her romantic radar. A speed bump on a detour she only followed for a block. Maeve had Keith, who came into her life at three months old, the only dad she's ever needed or wanted. As Maryann once said, "Parents are like cooks. Too many in the kitchen and you have a mess."

It should be clear by now how Maeve feels about a mess.

And then three weeks ago, she received an email at work from a Mr. O'Connor, a new associate at the law firm handling Liam Doherty's will. Liam had died of pancreatic cancer. Maeve was needed in Ireland, Mr. O'Connor insisted.

After Spencer, Maeve scarcely trusted the sun to rise, let alone an email from a stranger claiming to work for her deceased estranged father. She deleted it. Two days later, another email appeared. Again, she deleted it. Another few days passed before she received a third email, this time to her personal account, from Mr. O'Connor.

> Dear Ms. Doherty,
>
> It is important that you contact me regarding your father's estate. This is not a scam. Ask your boss. I would appreciate a timely response, as time, in this case, is of the essence.
>
> Regards,
> Eoin O'Connor

Maeve phoned her boss, Shira, who confirmed that Eoin O'Connor was indeed a real person who had found Maeve's work contact on LinkedIn and reached out to confirm her identity and employment.

"You gave him my personal email address? What about my privacy?"

Shira scoffed. "Like that exists anymore. Plus, he sounded sexy with the accent."

That was exactly what Maeve needed: another sexy guy out to swindle her. She emailed Eoin and thanked him for reaching out, but seeing as she never knew her father, she couldn't be of any help in the matter of his estate.

> Dear Ms. Doherty,
>
> Let me be clear, your father's death actually means quite a lot to you. He has left you an important

possession in his will. I cannot disclose the details of the inheritance in email. Liam gave specific instructions to handle this in person in Inishglass. The cost of your flight, transportation, and lodging will be covered. I have attached travel options below.

Please advise.

—Eoin O'Connor

His tone was more acerbic than Maeve liked.

Mr. O'Connor,

Please advise—my last name is Kaminski.

Maeve

He responded.

My apologies. You should consider a name change. Maeve goes well with Doherty. Please advise on travel plans.

Appalled, she wrote:

What kind of a name is Eoin? Who even knows how to pronounce that? Too many vowels. You should consider a name change. Maybe to Asshole. I bet people call you that all the time.

Unsurprisingly, he wrote back.

I assure you people in Ireland know how to pronounce Eoin. To you Americans, it's Owen. I will take
your idea into consideration, but it is worth mention-
ing Asshole and Eoin both have three vowels. Please
advise on travel plans.

—Eoin, the Asshole

He wasn't letting up, but Maeve had no intention of ever setting
foot in Ireland.

Owen,

I have a life. I can't just drop everything and come to
Ireland so you can give me a vase. I never knew my
father. I'm sure there's someone else who deserves
said possession much more than me. If not, you keep it.

Ms. Kaminski

Eoin then sent the email that changed everything.

Maeve Kaminski,

There is no one else. Liam was an only child and
very specific about his wishes. And we are not
talking about a vase. Your father has left you a substantial inheritance, the only stipulation being you
receive it in Ireland. Once again, please advise as
to your desired travel plans or we will be forced to
continue this snappish yet stimulating conversation
ad nauseam.

—Eoin O'Connor, Esq.

Substantial inheritance. Debt collectors had been calling for months, and Spencer was a ghost. The only upside was that Maryann and Keith had just left for a six-month cruise around the world, in celebration of their joint retirement, and Maeve had managed to hide her predicament from them before they left. If they knew, they would give her the money, bail her out with their hard-earned savings, and that was completely unacceptable. Not now, fresh into their retirement. Maeve made a commitment to herself that by the time Maryann and Keith got back to Chicago, her debt problem would be taken care of. Somehow. And until Eoin's email, she had still been searching for the answer. Then, it had appeared.

If flying thousands of miles, boarding two buses and a ferry, to end up on a small island off the coast of southern Ireland, barely the size of Lincoln Park and with one one-hundredth the inhabitants, could mean paying off the debt, Maeve would deal with the seasickness.

She agrees to pay a measly $50 of the $15,368 she owes—*Spencer owes*—to keep Konrad and American Debt Services off her back for another month, then lugs her suitcase up the jetty, feeling the weight of everything that has happened in her bones, desperate for a Tums and some water. At least the sky has cleared.

The island of Inishglass is straight out of *The Lord of the Rings*. Emerald-green hills. A jagged, rocky coastline. Dreamy rain that creates a fog over the mountains like a doorway into another realm. It's unlike anything Maeve has ever seen in person, so while her situation might be a mess, the backdrop is gorgeous. She can at least appreciate that.

The summer the girls were thirteen, Sonya went to India. When she landed in Mumbai, somehow her body remembered the air and the heat and the smells, down to her core, recognizing the place despite never having set foot there. Maeve waits to see if this will happen to her. Half her DNA is from here, after all. And she waits . . .

Nothing.

The harbor has mostly emptied of people, locals loading into cars and tourists filing into buses and cabs. Other than the parking area, it's just a dock and a single road that leads into the village. No shelter. No bar to belly up to and pass the time. Not even a vending machine where she could procure a soda to calm her belly.

Completely out of character, Maeve had done little research on the island. And though, after Eoin's emails, she was tempted to google every last detail on Liam Doherty, she had resisted. Hard. For twenty-four years, Liam had ignored his daughter, and in return, Maeve had done the same. In a way, Maeve has shown the most control in *not* googling Liam. It takes a lot of effort to avoid someone like she has, but secretly searching for Liam felt like a betrayal to the man who raised her. Keith deserves Maeve's loyalty. And if Maeve is going to accept whatever inheritance Liam has left her, she cannot get attached to it. She needs it to clear her debt. She must stay removed and unemotional. Sentimentality will only weaken her resolve. The more she knows about her father, the greater the threat of feelings getting involved. And she cannot let that happen again.

Ten minutes into her wait, the last ferry worker walks down the jetty toward the lone car in the lot. He notices Maeve.

"Are you alright, love? D'you need a lift?"

"Someone's coming to get me. He should be here any minute." She forces a calm smile, like it's no big deal that Eoin the Asshole is making her wait.

The man nods, and soon the place is deserted. Maeve checks her phone. With every passing minute, her anxiety ratchets up, swirling with leftover nausea from the ferry. But at ten in the evening, it's still light out, at least.

Finally fed up, she texts Eoin that she's arrived at the ferry dock and waiting, but her reception isn't good, and the message never goes through. Five minutes later, she tries again: Are you coming?

And again, no success. Without reception, she can't talk to Sonya or get on any socials or do, well . . . anything. In her anger she types: Owen, get your fat arse to the ferry dock asap, you twat. She sends it and

16

immediately regrets the text. Thankfully, this one doesn't go through either.

"He will be here," she says out loud. "He will not leave me stranded in a parking lot on some remote Irish island. I have not been bamboozled by a man *again*."

But another part of her brain speaks louder. She has placed her trust in Eoin, a stranger she only communicated with via email. Did she do the proper research? She had looked at the law firm's website, which could have been made by a third grader. Eoin wasn't on any socials. Maeve had been tempted to check dating apps. Sure, she has Eoin's number and email, but she knew Spencer's shoe size, what kind of shaving cream he liked, and the freckle on his left butt cheek. Hell, she knew his grandma's middle name!

But while she was falling in love, like a complete idiot, Spencer had been playing chess.

Maeve's chest squeezes, like a shirt being wrung out to dry. She paces the parking lot and contemplates hijacking one of the ferries back to the mainland, but beyond afternoons getting buzzed in the Play Pen, the notorious stretch of Lake Michigan in downtown Chicago where everyone parks their boats and parties in the summer, she has no boating experience.

She could always walk into town, but she has no idea how far it is, and with the fading daylight, she'll most definitely get caught in the dark. So with no other options, Maeve does the only thing that might calm a control freak's panicked mind. When life is a mess, grab a broom and get to work. She opens her suitcase, neatly organized in packing cubes, and dumps everything out onto the ground, to start folding and arranging them again.

She's deep into the work when the headlights appear down the road. The car stops in the parking lot, but the engine idles as a person steps out.

"Oh shite. Did your bag break?"

Maeve watches him approach. "You're late, Asshole."

"Sorry about that. Damn sheep wouldn't get off the road." Eoin kneels. "Let me help you."

Maeve stops him. "That won't be necessary." As much as it pains her, she shoves everything into the bag and closes it, cringing at the thought of wrinkled shirts.

Eoin helps her up, Maeve stumbling on unsteady feet due to adrenal overload and jet lag. "Bloody hell," he says in a muted Irish brogue. "You're completely knackered."

"Late *and* charming."

Eoin runs a hand through his hair. "I didn't mean that the way it came out. Let me start again." He holds out his hand. "Maeve Doherty, it's a pleasure to meet you."

Maeve is unsure she wants to take his hand, handsome as he might be. Eoin is shaving-cream-commercial attractive. Dark-blond hair with stormy hazel eyes. A chiseled chin line with skin free of blemishes or stubble. The kind of good-looking that only gets better with a close-up.

"It's Maeve *Kaminski*. And did you seriously blame *sheep*?"

"It's a legitimate defense on this island. There are more sheep here than people."

"Can we just get on with this?" She extends the handle on her roller bag, thinking of the clothes wrinkling inside it.

"Right. Let's get you settled. We can go through everything once you've had some time to adjust." Eoin takes the suitcase and moves toward the car.

Maeve stands still. "Time to adjust? I don't need to adjust. I came here because you said I had to. Now I want to know what this is all about."

"That might not be that easy."

Eoin's evasion, his lateness, and Maeve's lack of trust in anything right now are a lethal combination. Add in jet lag, and she's a powder keg that just met a spark. "I'm not going anywhere until you tell me what's going on!"

He beams with confidence, like he's entertained by her fury, which only stokes the blaze. "You don't like surprises, do you?" He examines Maeve like he's taking stock, judging her. "I bet you're one of those people who look at restaurant menus online before you go. You know what you're going to order before you set foot in the place."

"There's nothing wrong with a little preparation," Maeve huffs. Eoin laughs. "I doubt I can do that here, anyway. Is there reception anywhere on this island?"

"It's spotty. Locals would say it's part of the old-world charm."

"Well, I like new-world 5G."

"A little unplugging might be good for you. Help you"—again, Eoin's eyes scan her from head to toe—"relax."

"I don't need to relax."

He chuckles. "You might be surprised by this little island. It's one of the most visited destinations in all of Ireland."

"By sheep?"

"Come on, Kaminski. You obviously need sleep."

"Not until you tell me."

Eoin sighs like he's dealing with a petulant child. He approaches her, close enough that she can smell the mint and spice on his skin. "I wondered what you'd look like," he says sincerely. "You have his eyes. The same blue. Did you know that?"

Maryann has blond hair and brown eyes, the opposite of Maeve's chocolate-brown hair and blue eyes. Her nose is more pointed, whereas Maeve's slopes. Maeve has curves that her mother has more than once claimed to be jealous of. Maeve is organized; Maryann is a total pig, her bedroom always a minefield of clothes, her bathroom an explosion of lotion, hair accessories, and toothpaste. Maeve's bathroom drawers are full of perfectly configured containers, each with a distinct purpose: rubber bands, claw clips, bobby pins, scrunchies.

Has Maeve considered that she might look like her bio-dad? Not with any enthusiasm. She has always preferred to think of herself and her mom like batteries, a single unit with opposite charges. A yin and a yang.

"Please," Maeve says. "Just tell me what's going on."

Eoin hesitates. "It would be easier if I showed you." He holds out his hand.

Still Maeve doesn't move. She stares at it like it's a question she's unsure how to answer.

"You don't want to stay here all night, do you?" Eoin asks.

There is only one reasonable answer. Even Maeve can see that. She loads her bag into the back and climbs into the front seat, reveling in the plush leather and spacious legroom.

Eoin checks his phone, and a sly smile grows on his face. "A fat-arse twat, eh?"

"Crap." Maeve checks her messages, seeing that they *all* went through, finally.

"Relax, Kaminski. You're Irish. Taking the piss is in your blood. Looks like you got something else from your father."

"Let's not make assumptions. My mom is pretty damn funny." *For a doctor,* she thinks.

They start down the long winding road toward the village of Inishglass, passing farms and sheep along the way. *Lots* of sheep. So maybe Eoin wasn't lying. The hillside is barren of trees, just stone fences and fields in a whole spectrum of green. The car glides over the road, soothing Maeve. By the time they make it to the village, her eyes are at half-mast, jet lag smothering her body like a weighted blanket. Buildings move past in a blur of color, tightly packed, mostly closed for the night. Beyond that, Maeve's attention can't keep up, and soon, overwhelmed with brain fog and fatigue, she drifts off.

She wakes abruptly when the car stops, and for just a moment, she forgets where she is. Then reality dawns, slowly. Eoin. His car. Ireland. The ferry. Thank goodness her stomach has finally settled.

They're parked in front of a pub, the building white with black trim and a bright red door.

Maeve yawns. "I'm not really in the mood for a drink."

"That's good, because the place closed well over an hour ago."

She stretches her achy back. "Then why are we here?"

"Because you insisted," Eoin says.

"I did?" It's like her mind has been wiped. Nothing is clear.

"You wanted to know what Liam left you." He gestures toward the building. "Well . . ."

Maeve snaps to attention, wide awake. Two words dance through her mind: *substantial inheritance.* She can't believe this is happening, and yet she knows what Eoin is going to say before he says it.

"This is the Moorings. Your father left you his pub."

3

The mid-June evening at the Thatch is moving along like any other, just as Briggs Murphy had hoped. Then Brian Laughlin stands from his usual barstool, three in from the end, pint of Guinness in hand, and makes his way to the musicians playing in the corner.

Damn it, Briggs thinks.

Brian bends down to whisper in the guitarist's ear, who then whispers to the fiddler, who leans across the table to the frame-drum player, who nods at the woman playing the tin whistle.

What was a nondescript night will now be unforgettable.

Briggs is going to kill Brian Laughlin. He'd fire the musicians, but he only pays the players in free beer and chips. Plus, he needs them. It's tourist season. Fifteen minutes from last call, and Briggs foolishly thought he'd make it through the night unscathed.

From behind the bar, he's been chatting with a busty English woman in a hot-pink tank top announcing in silver lettering that she's part of the BRIDE SQUAD. The rest of the hen party—along with the bride, who's wearing a white veil and matching white tank top with the words OFF THE MARKET across her chest—is dispersed around the bar, standing out in their vibrant colors among the other patrons, who are mostly dressed in neutral tones, long sleeves, or fleece. More appropriate attire for the cool Irish evening. The hen party is dressed like this is

Temple Bar, Dublin's hot nightlife location, not a remote island off the southern coast of Ireland.

It took until five minutes ago for the well-endowed Brit to finally approach Briggs, though she'd been throwing him looks all night.

"So you, like . . . own this place?" she asks. Briggs keeps one eye on Brian, who's now circulating through the pub, quietly chatting with every local in attendance. No small feat, considering the large crowd. He wonders whether, across town, the Moorings is busting at the seams as well. Since Liam Doherty died, the place hasn't had the same fervor, understandably. Grief is a cloud that thins out only as time passes, never disappearing completely, and with Liam having passed away so recently, every local at the Moorings is under a thick blanket of gray. But the longer the pub stays in this state, the higher the probability that Briggs will have a problem on his hands this summer. The Moorings needs sunshine, which Ireland isn't exactly known for. Rumor has it, the light might come in the form of an American, but the island has yet to see her arrival. "You're Briggs Murphy?"

"Aye," Briggs says.

The Brit leans on the bar, accentuating her breasts, a move Briggs would commend and reciprocate with thankful glances if his attention had not been stolen by Brian.

"I've read about you." A twinkle sparks in her eyes.

"Best not to believe everything you read."

"The reviews are consistent," she counters. "Five stars across the board. A perfect track record for a man. A herculean feat, if you ask me. Most men can't find their way around a market, let alone a woman's body. But apparently, you have impeccable navigational skills."

Normally, Briggs would appreciate the innuendo, but suddenly he's not in the mood for games. Not with Brian halfway through the crowd, the inevitable now officially unstoppable. Damn those Yelp reviews that mention Briggs by name. As great as it is to have so many five-star reviews, Briggs is embarrassed at what women are willing to put on the internet, even if it is accurate. But that was the risk he took, sleeping with customers.

"I can't believe I'm meeting *the* Briggs Murphy in the flesh. You're just as I thought you'd be." She steps back to take him in, eyes roaming over his face and broad chest. Then she leans onto the bar on tiptoes to see the lower half of his body, her breasts pressed between her arms, practically falling out of her tank top. "Shame you're wearing pants."

"Damn food-safety laws."

She giggles. "I didn't picture you with a beard. It's quite nice."

He scratches at the thick stubble on his chin. "Thanks."

She leans in closer and whispers, "Do food-safety laws apply to the bathroom as well, because I'd be happy to take your pants off in there."

Only rarely will a patron be this forward, but then again, hen parties tend to bring out the immoral side, especially on a remote island that feels completely cut off from reality. The number of bachelor and bachelorette parties has increased over the years, with travel bloggers and social-media influencers writing about the island and its two infamous pubs.

Briggs doesn't respond. He has a hard time mustering any charm this late in the night. He hasn't even asked this woman's name, a mistake his father would chide him for. Always know your customer, whether local or tourist. A pub should feel like a home, and all the patrons, family members.

"This pub isn't just a place for people to get a pint," Joe Murphy would say. "It's the heart of the village. People come here when they're happy, sad, broken or whole, celebrating or mourning. They rely on our door to be open. And this pub, just like a heart, is built to hold it all. It's the best thing we offer to our patrons. Remember that, son."

Briggs usually does, but tonight, he's having a hard time with the suffocating crowd and Brian Fucking Laughlin.

The blond Brit takes a different tactic. "Is it true?" she asks.

"Is what true?"

"The feud between you and the Dohertys. Do you really hate each other? Like the Capulets and Montagues."

Briggs stumbles on his practiced line, his heart beginning to pound as Brian Laughlin returns to the musicians after rounding up the locals. He was so close to getting through the night without anyone acknowledging today's significance. If he could ring the last-call bell now, he would.

His silence lasts long enough that the other bartender, Briggs's roommate, Hugh Duffy, swoops in. "You know the Irish," Hugh says, in his American accent. "Their memories might be long, but they're not good with details."

The woman glances briefly at Hugh before looking back to Briggs. "So you don't even remember what you're fighting about?"

"Did the Capulets and Montagues?" Hugh counters.

"I can't remember Shakespeare that well," she admits.

"Spoiler. They didn't. That's why the story's a tragedy."

"Well then, whose pub opened first?"

Briggs answers, "The Thatch, of course."

"But you're a Murphy," she says, finally understanding how this all works. "So of course you'd say that. If I go to the Moorings, some Doherty would probably say the same thing."

What Doherty? Briggs thinks. That's the question everyone on Inishglass is asking themselves. Briggs and Hugh both shrug and speak their practiced line together. "You'll have to go to the Moorings and see for yourself."

The Murphys and Dohertys have had a silent agreement for decades. Once they got over their actual feud and realized it was better for business if they worked together, both pubs kept up the ruse, building a legend around their families, an ancient dispute between the only two pubs on the island. Inevitably tourists would want to visit both, to see which one they liked better. They'd travel back to wherever they came from, tell their friends about the famous rivalry, and the next year, Inishglass would see an uptick in tourists.

At least, that's how it used to work, back when Briggs's grandfather and father ran the pub, and word traveled like a game of telephone. Nowadays, it's Yelp or TripAdvisor or TikTok. The internet has done wonders for a business that relies on tourist season. It's also done wonders for Briggs's sex life, not that it needed help to begin with, as Hugh likes to point out.

"We're going to the Moorings tomorrow night," the Brit says and licks her lips. "But . . . I could be convinced otherwise."

Briggs usually appreciates a woman who wears her sexual intentions on her sleeve, or in this case, since her top has no sleeves, across her chest. Not tonight, though.

Out of the corner of his eye, Briggs sees Brian collecting the musicians in a huddle.

Bloody hell. It's happening, and Briggs can't stop it. Within minutes, every phone in this place will be aimed at Brian. Minutes after that, the videos will be posted on social media or texted to friends and family. Briggs should not complain. It's free marketing to people across the globe.

But he had one goal tonight. Make it through the evening on autopilot and into a woman's bed. Ignore his emotions and let his physical body carry him through the night. It was either that or get piss drunk, which is no longer an option. Briggs settled on the first, and until Brian stood up from his barstool, he was on track to accomplish his goals, the busty blond being his reward for survival.

Brian stands on top of a chair and hollers for the pub to quiet down. Even the Brit's attention is pulled away. The place quiets in a matter of seconds. Briggs feels his heart beat wildly in his chest. All he wants is fresh air. Forget the orgasm he'd planned to soothe his pain. A woman won't do. Not even his art studio will do tonight. Too many walls. He needs space. Air. All in short supply right now.

Five minutes until he can ring the last-call bell. But it's too late.

With the pub's complete attention on Brian, he speaks, loudly. "For those of you who don't know, you all have come to the Thatch on a very special night!"

A few locals pound on their tables and cheer, egging Brian on. Any tourists who hadn't already gotten their phones out do so now.

"Joe Murphy was the owner of this here fine establishment, and one of the best lads this island has ever known!" Brian continues, his voice growing in confidence. More cheers and pounding. Brian grins, face crinkled with decades of working his farm and spending nights at the pub.

He points at all the cameras, as if talking to each one like his own child. *Bloody hell,* Briggs thinks. Damn the Irish. Can't they ever do anything without putting on a show of it? "Today would have been Joe Murphy's sixty-second birthday. God rest his soul. He loved this place like he loved his family. With all his heart." Then Brian places a hand on his chest, closes his eyes, and pauses, like he's about to pray. When he looks around the room again, Brian's gaze lands on Briggs. "Am I right, lad?"

Briggs leans on the back bar, bottles of liquor stacked behind him on shelves. He crosses his arms over his chest and says, "Aye. My father was a great man."

"A great man!" Brian echoes. More pounding on the tables. More cheers. A truly idyllic Irish scene for the tourists. By the end of next week, the Thatch will have ten more five-star reviews about this moment alone.

But if Briggs could tear Brian down from his chair and toss his wrinkled ass out into the street, he would. Brian is just doing what he knows is best for the island, and if Joe were alive, he'd love the theatrics of it all. Any other night, Briggs would, too.

"Joe always ended the night with the same song, so it's only right that on his birthday, we should do the same. Now, I want everyone here to raise your glass!" Brian bellows. "To the *best* damn pub filled with the *best* damn people on the *best* damn island in Ireland! No matter what those bloody Dohertys say! To the Murphys and the Thatch!" The entire pub echoes his words, and he heaves his pint in the air, like it's a flag on a battlefield and he's claiming victory. Then on cue, the musicians strike up again and begin to play "The Parting Glass." Brian sings from his pedestal:

> Oh all the money that e'er I had,
> I spent it in good company.
> And all the harm that e'er I've done,
> Alas it was to none but me.

Briggs practically holds his breath as tourists gobble up the tear-jerking folk song that was Joe's favorite, so much so that it was played at his funeral ten years ago. This is why tourists come to Ireland, specifically Inishglass, a place known for two things: its vibrant green color, for which the island was named—*inish* meaning "island" and *glas* meaning "green" in Irish—and the rivalry between its only two pubs, the Thatch and the Moorings.

This scene will only help business, and it should make Briggs happy, but all he feels is sick to his stomach. He waits out the song, knowing he can't walk out of his own pub during his dead father's song, but unable to sing along, even as the pub overflows with the last refrain.

But since it falls unto my lot,
That I should rise and you should not,
I'll gently rise and softly call,
Good night and joy be to you all.

At last, the song comes to an end with an uproarious round of applause. Briggs forces a tight smile and tips his head appreciatively, every eye in the pub on this substantial man behind the bar, no longer the lanky eighteen-year-old boy who lost his father too young and too soon, but a handsome twenty-eight-year-old man and business owner.

Now the busty maid of honor in the hot-pink tank top gazes at Briggs with a new expression, a twinkle of emotional intrigue that kills any desire Briggs had. He doesn't do emotional. Not with women, at least. Not tonight. His only saving grace is the time. Finally, it's last call. Briggs rings the bell, and everyone moans.

"Sorry, but even the best nights must come to an end," Briggs announces. If he's speedy, he can be out the door by midnight. He busies himself refilling pints and drinks, a last round of shots for the hen party. Then he collects dirty glasses in the bus bin and takes it into the kitchen.

Safely hidden from the crowd, he makes himself an espresso and slams back the shot of rich, decadent coffee, hoping the relief of caffeine will loosen his tight jaw. He might hide in the kitchen until every last patron is gone, including Brian Laughlin. But his reprieve is cut short when Hugh bursts through the swinging kitchen doors and hollers, "Ooh wee! That is one fine set of cantaloupes!"

"Keep your voice down, Drongo. She'll hear you." Briggs sets his cup down. "And they're not cantaloupes. Cabbages at best."

Hugh considers that and agrees. Then he swats Briggs on the ass. "What the hell are you waiting for, Furphy? Get back out there and find out if those things are real!"

"Visual assessment: they're not." Briggs makes another espresso for Hugh, who's undoubtedly tipsy. "When was the last time you shagged something that wasn't your hand?"

"When was the last time you passed up the opportunity to inspect a fine set of bodacious fun bags? I can see the steam coming off that blond, and the weather definitely calls for oral sex. I get that you can bag any woman who sets foot on this island, and that must be a real burden for you, but come on, man. You owe it to your fellow brother who isn't lucky enough to be born with a brooding face and a beard that grows in evenly. You know the deal. It's your duty to take every opportunity and report back in detail."

"Your beard is atrocious. And I never tell you anything anyway."

"Don't I know it. You're sexy *and* a fucking gentleman. I'm basically Robin, and you're Batman. And you know what Batman does?"

"Flies around at night and fights crime."

"And gets laid by hot-ass English women with breasts the size of cantaloupes."

"Cabbages."

"We'll never know if you don't get back out there, Batman!"

Briggs hands the coffee to Hugh. "Don't worry, mate. Tourist season is just starting. There will be plenty of cabbages to come."

"No one comes to Ireland to shag an ugly *American* bartender," Hugh says.

"Don't say that." Briggs smirks. "You've been on this island so long, you almost sound Irish."

"Too bad looks aren't as transferable as accents. Women look at you and take off their clothes. Women look at me and just get confused." Indeed, Hugh Duffy is a bit of a conundrum, born to a large Irish American Catholic family with eight kids who favor their Chinese mother in appearance and not their redheaded father. Hugh stares down at his coffee and sways on his feet. "Do women use fruit when they talk about men?"

"What else is an eggplant emoji for?"

"Good point. What do you think I am? Squash, cucumber?"

"Baby carrot," Briggs says. He wiggles his pinkie at Hugh, who grabs it and twists. Briggs laughs and easily pulls his hand free.

"Come on, man," Hugh pleads. "I got drunk tonight for you. You owe me."

It's common for Briggs to be tipped in drinks, rather than money, and it would be rude to turn down a glass of whiskey from a tourist or a shot from a hen party. But he's not about to tell everyone in the pub that he's off the wagon indefinitely, knowing the news will circulate the entire island by morning. So Briggs accepts every last liquid tip, takes one sip, and then pawns off the rest on Hugh. "Fine," he says. "Celery. Now would you please drink the damn coffee so you can close this place up for me?"

Hugh's eyebrows pull tight. "What's up?"

After rooming for over half a decade, the two are fine-tuned to each other. Briggs is incapable of keeping anything from Hugh, even if he wants to. "I just need to get out of here. Get some air."

Hugh shoots back the espresso, wraps his arm around Briggs, and says, "Look. I know tonight can't be easy for you, especially after . . ." He scans the kitchen for eavesdropping employees, but it's only them and Finn, the pimply fifteen-year-old dishwasher whose ears are plugged with AirPods playing nineties grunge at top volume, as usual.

Briggs shrugs out of Hugh's embrace and picks up a clean rack of glassware. "I'm fine."

"You are so not fine." Hugh attempts to take the rack. "Let me carry that."

But Briggs shuffles out of his way. "I appreciate the concern, but I'd rather risk death than be treated like a fecking weakling for the rest of my life."

"Don't joke about that, bro," Hugh says seriously. "You could barely breathe a few days ago. Scared the shit out of me. You need to be careful."

"I am." In fact, Briggs has plenty of precautions in place to safeguard against pain. It's precisely why he won't get involved with a woman who wants more than sex. He sets down the glasses. "But I'm not taking up yoga, if that's what you're suggesting."

"I don't know . . ." Hugh claps him on the back. "Bendy chicks in tight pants."

"I don't need a yoga class to get a girl to bend over in front of me."

"Now, there's the guy I know!" Hugh pulls Briggs toward the kitchen door. "Come on. There's still time. I bet the blond is still here."

But Briggs stays. "She's all yours. I'm taking a walk."

"You know I'm not good with women."

"When are you going to get up the balls to ask a girl out?"

"Being the royal fuckup that I am," Hugh replies, "I have confidence issues, you know that. So probably never . . . or when that genie finally shows up and grants me my wish."

Briggs slips into his fleece jacket. "Don't you remember from *Aladdin*? Genies can't make people fall in love."

"No," Hugh says, picking up the rack of clean glasses. "But they can change celery into an eggplant."

Briggs chuckles.

"Hey," Hugh says, serious again. "History doesn't always repeat itself, Briggs. Your dad's story may have ended one way, but that's not going to happen with you."

Briggs opens the back door, feeling the cool, damp air on his face. Maybe Hugh is right. Maybe Briggs is destined for a different ending, but right now, he finds that hard to believe. Five days ago he was diagnosed with the same heart condition that killed his father.

4

Standing in front of the Moorings—a white building with its name in black lettering, its red door like a bright beacon drawing people inside—Maeve doesn't just need a drink. She needs a bottle. Because when nothing in life makes sense, there is only one thing to do.

Get drunk.

She catches very little of what Eoin tells her. Something about the Moorings having been owned by the Dohertys for generations. Something about it being a sort of destination for people when they visit the island. It's kind of what Ireland is known for, among other things like . . . green hills . . . and leprechauns. Maeve shakes her head, feeling sorely undereducated. That's what happens when you spend so much energy actively ignoring a place.

"Liam inherited the Moorings from his father, and he passed it to you," Eoin says.

Maeve is dumbstruck. Eoin keeps talking as if she knows Liam. Like they have a relationship. Like this place is *her* family history. But her family is from Chicago. And Polish! Maeve doesn't know how to make bangers and mash. Her *babcia* taught her to make pierogi. They celebrate Dyngus Day! Hell, her grandpa's favorite shirt says **YOU BET YOUR DUPA I'M POLISH!** And now she's supposed to start saying "Kiss me! I'm Irish!" just like that?

This wasn't supposed to happen. Liam gave up his parental rights. He chose not to have Maeve or Maryann in his life. But apparently, in death, he changed his mind.

"Now do you understand why you needed to come?" Eoin asks.

Maeve nods, but all she's thinking about is how desperately she needs vodka. She starts toward the red door, but Eoin grabs her arm.

"What are you doing, Kaminski?"

"Going inside."

"The pub's closed."

She turns to face him. "Who's going to stop me? It's mine, right?"

"Maybe sleep on the news. Come back in the morning."

Like Maeve could sleep right now. Her jet lag has dissipated, replaced by adrenaline. "I just want to see the place," she says. And then adds, "Alone." She doesn't need anyone witnessing her meltdown, and now that Maeve is in the village, the island doesn't feel so over-whelming. "You can go. I'll be fine. I'm an adult who lives in one of the biggest cities in the United States. I'll find my way. You can't get lost on an island, right?"

Eoin groans but doesn't fight her. "I have you booked at the Cabbage Patch. It's just down the road a bit. Run by a woman called Ivy. She's expecting you."

"Great. Just send me the address, and I promise I'll make it there."

"You can't trust reception on the island." Evidently not happy with the situation, Eoin takes Maeve's phone and types the direc-tions, rental instructions, and key codes into her notes. "I'll drop your bag off now and let Ivy know you're . . . taking a moment. It'll be waiting for you."

"Great."

But he doesn't leave. His jaw works like he's chewing his words before speaking them. "Listen, Kaminski . . ." He steps closer, words on the end of his tongue, and hands over the keys to the pub. "Just . . . call me. We have things to discuss."

And then Maeve is alone in front of the Moorings, the white building alight in the darkness. What she wouldn't give for Sonya to be here. Or her mom. But there's only one friend she'll find here tonight. Booze.

She puts the key into the red door and makes her way into the pub. The air inside is stale and heavy with the smell of barley and hops. She searches the wall for a light switch and finally finds one, illuminating the room with a dull yellow glow.

The pub is the kind of old that doesn't exist in the States. The floor is stone, each tile an earthy brown or black. Panels of dark wood cover the walls, decorated in alcohol advertisements and Irish paraphernalia. Heavy wood beams line the ceiling. In one corner is a fireplace with a stone facade. Next to it is a basket of firewood and peat. Wood tables line the walls, dining chairs with upholstered red cushions tucked underneath. A chalkboard rests next to the door, advertising "Daily Special: Seafood Chowder" and "Inishglass's Finest Fish and Chips. Locally Sourced!"

And there's the bar. Beer taps run along the front and in back. Shelves are covered in bottles of booze, including more than one vodka, exactly as Maeve had hoped. She pours a shot and drinks it straightaway, relishing the burn in the back of her throat. Then, for good measure, she takes two more.

The relief is almost instant. The tension in her neck loosens, just enough that she can breathe deeper. But the reprieve doesn't last. The longer she stands in the empty pub, the harder it is to believe she's here. In Ireland. On Inishglass. And she owns a goddamn pub! And can't even call Sonya to tell her about it!

Another shot goes down swiftly, then Maeve pours herself a pint of Carlsberg. No more appropriate time to double-fist drinks than when a girl finds out her estranged Irish father left her his pub, and she can't ask him why, because he's dead.

Maeve chugs half the pint. She should stop. A hangover tomorrow will not help her mental state. But she's standing behind a bar, with no cell reception, in an eerily quiet pub where Liam Doherty, a man who has only ever been an idea to her, stood, night after night, slinging pints and chatting up customers. The only way to melt herself is with alcohol. Lots of it.

And then Maeve remembers her downloaded playlist. She digs in her backpack for wireless earbuds. Sonya started the "Girl in a Room" playlist for Maeve years ago. Sonya is the kind of person who can sing at the top of her lungs, in a packed car with the windows rolled down, completely off tune, not caring what anyone thinks. Maeve prefers to do embarrassing things alone.

"That stick up your ass is going to collect barnacles. It's not good for you, Mae," Sonya once said to her, back in high school. "A girl needs to freak out sometimes. It's healthy."

The "Girl in a Room" playlist began for moments just like this.

Maeve scrolls to Walk the Moon's "Shut Up and Dance." The bright, upbeat opener begins, and immediately Maeve is fifteen again, back in her pristine bedroom with its color-coordinated closet and poster of Nick Jonas. The lyrics start, and she shakes her head, her hair swishing back and forth. The more she moves, the less she wants to cry. The more sweat on her forehead, the more she forgets where she is. The weight of anxiety drips from her fingers as her arms sway. By the time the chorus comes back around, Maeve is completely dissolved in the song, eyes closed, dancing, twisting in circles and flailing, her head spinning, sweat on her skin. She peels off her sweater and throws it across the room as she belts out the words. Her singing is as unimpressive as her dancing, but it doesn't matter. No one is around to witness this meltdown. The best messes are the kind you can clean up before anyone sees.

As the song builds to the end, Maeve gives everything she has, screaming the lyrics until she's hoarse, her body spinning, her mind a blur. These four blissful minutes of song are the best she's felt since she left the States, maybe the best she's felt in months. She's needed this freak-out desperately. After holding herself together, so long and so tightly, finally she's loose. And then her foot catches the leg of a table.

Maybe she was too loose.

Maeve opens her eyes, realizing just how dizzy she is. She stumbles. Hits another table. Grabs at a chair to steady herself, but her body is moving so fast and her head is so off-kilter, she knocks into the chair and fumbles back. The chair falls, Maeve quickly following suit. She's about to hit the cold stone floor when . . . she's caught.

Her immediate reaction is relief. To break her butt would have been the cyanide icing on a truly shitty day. But relief is soon replaced with deep, burning embarrassment. Someone was watching her dance routine and is now holding her sweaty, panting body in his arms.

The man says, in a soft Irish accent, "Should I get a spoon?"

"What?"

"Are you having a seizure?"

Maeve's first thought is that he is one of the most beautiful creatures she's ever seen. He is the definition of stunning. She's never seen a person who defines a word before. Her second thought: he saw her dancing . . . and singing . . . loudly. Oh God. She doesn't even do that in front of Sonya! Third thought: a bead of her sweat just dripped onto his sizable arm.

Maeve untangles herself and straightens out her T-shirt. "A seizure?"

He smiles broadly, clearly joking. "Anyone who says white girls can't dance hasn't met you."

Maeve hits a new level of mortification. The only solution: get this man out of the pub right now.

"We're closed," she says, collecting her earbuds from the floor.

"But the door was open."

She takes in the full size of this very tall, very broad man before her, dressed in jeans and a hunter-green fleece jacket, looking like a Patagonia model. "That doesn't mean you can just walk through any open door you want."

"But this is a pub. You're supposed to walk through the door. That's why it's red, so you can find it easily."

"Is that true?"

"I've never thought about it until now, but it makes sense, doesn't it?"

She points to the open door. "Please leave."

"But I just got here. I'm hoping there's a second act."

Maeve groans and walks behind the bar, needing a barrier between them.

Instead of following her instructions, the man takes a seat at one of the stools. "I have to thank you. I needed that."

Maeve grabs a rag and starts wiping down the clean bar top. "I'm glad my embarrassment entertains you."

He places a large, warm hand over hers. "Don't be embarrassed. Giving another person joy is one of the greatest gifts."

His hand feels really nice, but she pulls away. "Did you read that on a Hallmark card?"

He chuckles. "Jameson, please."

"I told you. We're closed."

"But I just saved your life. If I wasn't there to catch you, who knows what would have happened?" A good point, as infuriating as it might be. "Just one drink, Ferris. That's all I'm asking. And then I'll be on my way. It'll be like I was never here."

Maeve has two options: fight with this guy and delay his departure or just serve him the drink and be done with it. Judging by the fact he hasn't left yet, the latter seems more efficient. "Fine. One drink. But only if you promise to keep what you saw a secret. You can never tell anyone."

"A talent like that really should be shared." With a warm smile, he crosses his heart. "I promise. I won't tell a soul. Your secret's safe with me, Ferris."

She pours a stiff glass of Jameson and passes it to him. "Why do you keep calling me Ferris?"

"Your shirt." He points at her chest where **SAVE FERRIS** is written.

"This is from *Ferris Bueller's Day Off.*"

"Never seen it."

"What is wrong with you?" Maeve blurts. She is undoubtedly tipsy.

38

"Should you really be asking me that question when you were the one screaming and punching the air like a boxing bag just a few minutes ago?"

She straightens out her clothes and hair. "My name's Maeve. Not Ferris."

"Briggs." He extends his hand, swallowing hers in his own. "Can I ask you something, Maeve?" The faintest fine lines rim his dark-brown eyes, lines from smiling and sunshine, most likely. He's probably a few years older than she is: late twenties, maybe thirty. His short hair is a few shades lighter than his eyes, and unlike Eoin's clean-shaven face, Briggs has something between stubble and a beard, but well-groomed. Eoin had the look of a shaving-cream model, but Briggs looks like an adventure guide, maybe, or an arborist. A man who works with his hands and loves being outside.

Briggs takes a sip of his drink and leans his sizable forearms on the bar. "Why were you dancing?" he asks seriously.

It's not the question Maeve expects. "Can't a girl just dance?"

"Sure. But it's been my experience that when a woman dances like that, it's for a reason."

There's only steadiness in his gaze, no mockery. For just a second, Maeve seriously considers confessing her problems to this stranger, just to get them off her chest, but promptly thinks better of it. "You think you know women that well?"

Briggs sits back and crosses his arms. "I think I know pain that well."

That sucks all the wind out of Maeve's lungs. Damn. Who *is* this guy? She deflects his question with one of her own. "Why are you out drinking this late?"

"Can't a guy get a drink?"

"Sure, but it's been *my* experience that when a person drinks this late, it's for a reason."

Clearly impressed with her turning the tables on him, he says, "Tonight, I need the blur."

"From what?"

"Harsh reality." His intense expression pulls at Maeve's gut. He holds up his glass. "Drinking alone is kind of pathetic. Care to save me the embarrassment, Maeve?"

"I guess I should, since you saved me from breaking my tailbone."

She pours another pint, and Briggs raises his glass again. "To saving each other."

They toast. "To the blur," she adds, which makes Briggs's eyes twinkle further, enhancing his strikingly good looks.

Awkward silence follows, the kind that happens between strangers who have shared an intimate moment but who don't know what to do next. Briggs points at the dartboard in the corner. "Fancy a game?"

It's better than staring uncomfortably at each other, even with the nice view, so Maeve comes out from behind the bar, and they head over to the board. Briggs retrieves the darts and rolls them around in his hands.

"Let's make it interesting," he says. "Three darts. Three questions. The higher the individual points, the more personal the questions. And you must answer. No refusing."

"No way. I don't know you."

"Makes it that much better," Briggs says. "It's always easier to tell a stranger the truth. No consequences. Saying it to the people we love threatens us most."

He has a point. Isn't that why she hasn't told her parents about her debt *and* Liam's death? But like meeting a stranger on an airplane, Maeve feels completely comfortable, because come the end of the flight, they'll never see each other again.

"What if we hit the bull's-eye?" she asks.

"The ultimate confession. The harsh reality we don't want to tell anyone." Briggs lifts his glass, and Maeve considers the probability of his hitting a bull's-eye. But what does it matter? He doesn't know her. She could make up a confession, or tell him the truth and never see him again. It's a win-win. She agrees to the terms, and Briggs hands her three darts. "Ladies first."

Maeve aims and tosses. The dart lands in a single ring, the lowest possible points. There are plenty of mundane questions she could ask—where he's from, what he does for work—but most won't really tell her what she wants to know. Then it hits her. "What's your karaoke song?"

"That's your question?"

"The answer says a lot about a person."

Briggs raises an eyebrow. "Go on."

"Take any Adele song. Only a person with a gigantic ego and delusions of grandeur would pick one of hers. Or a man who sings Shania Twain's 'Man! I Feel Like a Woman.'" Maeve pretends to gag. "A horrible sense of humor, and he probably struggles with fears of inadequacy."

"You've really thought about this."

Maeve picks her sweater off the ground and folds it neatly. "Don't get me started on people who sing 'I Will Survive.' Desperate serial drunk dialers who can't get over their exes."

Maeve sets the sweater on the bar and checks her hair in one of the multiple mirrored signs on the wall. For near twenty hours of travel, she looks . . . alright. But then again, she's kind of drunk.

"Well, I wouldn't pick Adele, and I'm not a fan of country," Briggs says.

Maeve picks up the chair she knocked over and tucks it neatly under the table.

"And a drunk dial isn't my style," Briggs adds.

She notices a ring of moisture on the bar where he had set his glass, and she wipes it away. His attention follows her as she works.

"What is it then?" Maeve tosses the rag over her shoulder. "And don't say Oasis or I'll kick you out of this pub right now."

"Feck no," Briggs says in all seriousness.

This makes her chuckle. Maeve waits, her full attention on his answer.

"Miley Cyrus. 'Party in the U.S.A.'" This is so wholly unexpected that Maeve bursts out laughing. A warm feeling blooms in her chest for the first time since . . .

She sucks in a breath. *Wow.* Maeve hasn't felt this since Spencer.

"Now, give me your best psychoanalysis," Briggs says with a grin. "I can take it."

"Not telling." Maeve swallows down a heart hiccup and casually pulls her dart from the board.

"You have to."

"No, I don't. I asked a question. You answered. It's your turn to throw a dart."

Briggs groans playfully and takes his shot, hitting a triple ring—a good score, but not the bull's-eye. He narrows his eyes on Maeve and contemplates his question. "Why were you cleaning just now?"

"There was whiskey on the bar." But he isn't buying the answer, so Maeve adds, "I like a tidy space."

Briggs sits back on a table and crosses his arms. "I may not be Freud, but I know damn well there's more to it than that."

"Why docs there have to be more to it than that?"

"Because there always is."

Maeve considers this. "Having a clean space makes me feel in control. Is that what you want to hear?"

"It's better," he recognizes. "Why do you need to feel in control?"

"That's more than one question. It's my turn now." She walks toward him, but before she gets there, Briggs knocks over his drink.

"Oops." He shrugs with a smirk.

Maeve watches the whiskey spread across the table, her hand itching for the rag on her shoulder.

"It's fine," she says casually.

"Fine," Briggs echoes and hands her a dart. "Your shot, Maeve."

She aims at the board, but every few seconds, she glances at the whiskey flowing closer to the edge of the table. When it finally spills,

Maeve cringes, the sound of dripping magnified in her ears. She throws the dart and misses the board completely.

Briggs finds this utterly hilarious. Maeve can hardly breathe. She can't take it anymore and falls to her knees to clean the mess. But even with it all sopped up, she doesn't feel any better. She is suddenly too tired to stand, and on the verge of tears, completely embarrassed.

"Damn it." Briggs kneels. "I was only taking the piss."

"Well, you proved your point. I'm a freak. My closets are perfectly organized. The Container Store is my favorite place to shop. And I carry a datebook. A real leather-bound datebook with my initials engraved on the spine. And yes. The inside is color coordinated. Is that what you want to know?"

He lifts her chin, and something in his gentle gaze makes Maeve feel oddly . . . safe.

Briggs's voice is soft and low. "I'm sorry. I didn't mean to make you feel bad. Especially when this is the best I've felt all night. Thanks to you."

"Really?" Maeve has felt so useless for so many months that knowing she's helped someone, even the tiniest bit, makes her feel slightly less . . . pathetic. Maybe even capable. "I like your beard," she says, barely above a whisper. Why she chooses that compliment, in this moment, is beyond her, but "You're so gorgeous, I'd like to hang a poster of you on my wall" might be too much.

"My father always had a beard."

Had. Past tense. "Is your dad   " Briggs nods before Maeve can finish the question. "Mine, too." She feels instant guilt, knowing Keith would be hurt if he knew she called another man "dad." "Can I touch it?" Briggs places her hand on his cheek. Maeve rakes her nails along the coarse short hairs, mesmerized by the feeling on her fingers. "It's softer than I thought it would be."

"I hear it can be quite ticklish."

Her fingers skim his chin. "I've never kissed anyone with a beard."

"If you keep doing that, Maeve, you might just find out." They're so close that heat radiates between them, a pulse growing with each passing second, as if they're both in an alternate universe where time doesn't matter. Like they've known each other for years.

"I'm sorry about your dad," she says.

"I'm sorry about yours," he echoes.

"I didn't know him, actually." Their eyes haven't left each other. "Which is really confusing, because I don't know how to feel."

"Maybe it's a blessing," Briggs offers. "I know how I felt when I lost my father, and I wouldn't wish that pain on anyone."

His honesty draws Maeve further in, his mouth now inches from hers. "Just so we're clear . . ." she says.

One eyebrow lifts. "Yes?"

"We cannot kiss."

"Yes. Terrible idea. Horrible. Definitely a mistake."

"Huge mistake," she agrees.

This is a bad idea, and Maeve knows it. She's not in the right headspace, all jet-lagged in a foreign country, looking at the most gorgeous human being walking the planet, who just happened to save her from falling . . . in a pub she now owns. Maeve squeezes her eyes closed, forcing the moment to break.

She stands. "I need to close now." She goes behind the bar, every difficult step away from him like walking in sticky glue.

"At least let me help."

"As you now know, I like to clean." She offers a meek smile.

Briggs sets his empty glass on the bar. "Thanks for the blur, Maeve."

The way he says "tanks," instead of "thanks," might be the most adorable thing she's ever heard.

"Thanks for saving my life." She imitates his accent, which he evidently finds just as endearing. And again, Maeve feels a ridiculous amount of satisfaction. Instead of wallowing in her own misery, she managed to provide happiness and help. So she decides to confess one more thing. "I've never actually sung karaoke before. Only watched other people do it. I'm too scared everyone will laugh at me."

"If you did, what song would you sing?"

"That's the thing. I don't know."

Briggs grabs a napkin and asks for a pen. Maeve finds one by the till and hands it to him. When he's done writing, he gives her the napkin. "When you decide, let me know. I want to be there when you sing it."

On the napkin is his number and name: Briggs Murphy. She stares down at it as he walks toward the door.

When Eoin had first emailed, Sonya thought this trip to Ireland was a blessing. "It's just the break you need," she said. The word "break" carried two meanings—time away and a bit of good luck. "Try a different life on. See how it fits. Who knows? Maybe this lost half of you is just what you need to feel whole again."

Briggs is almost to the door when Maeve says, "Wait."

"Want to attempt the bull's-eye after all?"

Blood is pumping so fast in Maeve's veins that she feels it in her temples. Spencer stole more than money from her. He stole her trust. He made her scared of people in a way she'd never felt before. And she is sick of being scared, of suffering while Spencer is off scot-free, doing whatever the hell he wants.

Without another thought, she walks to Briggs and kisses him. Relief is instant, his warm mouth on hers tasting sweet and earthy, like whiskey and sex and masculinity.

Briggs pulls back. "I thought you said we can't kiss."

Shocked that she actually did it, Maeve says, "I'm sorry. I shouldn't have—"

But Briggs doesn't let her finish. His lips return to hers with fervor, like he's starving and Maeve is the only meal he wants. When his tongue slides into her mouth, her knees threaten to buckle. The contact, warm and wet, pulls deep at her belly, deliciously waking her up between her thighs.

Briggs's hands slide down her sides, grab her hips, and pull her closer. His tongue skims her lower lip, like he's licking the remains of a drink from her mouth, and Maeve gasps with pleasure before his mouth closes on hers again.

This kiss . . . she's never experienced anything like it. It's like they're caught in a tornado, swirling, their combined energy ratcheting up every inch of her body, sensation seeping into every pore. And then, right as she's about to throw caution out the pub window, the red door bursts open, bringing with it a blast of cool, humid air. Briggs and Maeve freeze, mid-embrace. An older woman walks into the pub dressed in flannel pajamas. She's maybe a few years younger than Maryann, with deep-red, curly hair hanging wild over her shoulders.

"What the hell is going on here?" she says.

The question is obviously rhetorical, but Maeve sputters, "A-actually—"

"You know you shouldn't be here," the woman says . . . to Briggs.

He straightens his clothes. "Now don't overreact. I was just walking by and saw the light on. I thought I'd check on the place."

"Is that what you're doing?"

"Honestly, Ivy." Briggs crosses his heart. "I came over to make sure nothing was wrong. The door was open, and I had a drink. That's all. Just being a good neighbor."

"You're not meant to be a good neighbor, Briggs. Remember? You're her enemy."

"Enemy?" Maeve interjects.

"Can't we let that go for one bloody night, Ivy?" Briggs says. "She just got here."

"No. We can't. This place is crawling with tourists. You'd do well to remember that."

"Wait," Maeve says to Briggs. "I thought *you* were a tourist."

"Is that what he told you?" Ivy says, her green-brown eyes sparkling with intrigue.

Briggs holds up his hands. "I never said that."

"I'm so confused." Maeve grabs her head, suddenly feeling all the alcohol.

"It's all right, love." Ivy touches her arm. "This has to be quite a shock. Which is why *you* shouldn't be here." Her words are directed at Briggs again. "When are you going to stop messing with every girl who comes to this island, Briggs? Even you know better than to go after a Doherty."

"I told you. I wanted to help," Briggs says, his jaw clenched tight. "I know a little something about what she's going through, Ivy."

Right then, Maeve remembers the directions Eoin gave her to the Cabbage Patch, owned by a person named Ivy.

"That still doesn't mean you should be here," Ivy counters. "Especially doing what you were doing. What if someone saw? How would you explain that?"

"Easy," Briggs says. "I was just playing a little joke on the new owner. A welcome present from the Murphys."

"A joke?" Maeve says. "Why the hell would you do that? And what do you mean you knew who I was?"

"Love," Ivy says in all seriousness. "Everyone on this island knows who you are."

"But . . . how?" Maeve turns to Briggs and points a finger in his face. "And why didn't you say you knew who I was? I thought you were a stranger."

"We *are* strangers," he says. "Just maybe not the kind you thought."

Frustration boiling over, Maeve points at the exit. "Leave." Briggs sputters, trying to explain himself further, but Maeve wants nothing to do with it. "The door is painted red for a reason," she snaps.

Briggs groans. "Fine." But before he goes, he picks up one last dart and throws it at the board. Bull's-eye. "Now we both owe each other," he says, and he walks out the door.

5

Briggs wakes at dawn, after a fitful sleep, and immediately wonders what the hell he was thinking.

The problem: he wasn't.

He knew better than to walk into the Moorings last night, no matter his excuses. He wasn't worried about getting caught, confident he could have spun the story, just like he told Ivy: Briggs Murphy seduces Liam Doherty's oblivious long-lost daughter. A better script to increase the popularity of the pubs has never been written, though the prank would be off-brand for Briggs. Much too cruel. He would never use sex as retaliation, his antics much tamer and innocent, like last year when he and Hugh broke into the Moorings and swapped the soap in the bathroom for glue. Any local would see straight through the seduction tale. Tourists, on the other hand, would love it.

But that's not why Briggs kissed her. He did it because . . . well, Briggs doesn't know why the hell he did it, which is the cause of his sleepless night. It must have been her suffering. He just couldn't stand the sight of it. He had to attempt to make her feel better at least. Or so he's telling himself this morning. Was the kiss his wisest decision? No. Was it a completely selfless act? No. But was it effective? Briggs would like to think so. Until it wasn't.

He won't consider what would have happened if Ivy hadn't shown up. He had let the situation get out of hand, too caught up in how good she tasted, her body too perfect in his hands.

Briggs launches himself out of bed. He needs to move. Ignore the images in his mind. He knew, when he saw that damn light on, that Liam's daughter would be inside. Since Liam's passing, everyone on the island has been wondering when she'd show up. Why it had to be yesterday of all days, Briggs won't begin to wonder.

And of course Liam Doherty's daughter is absolutely gorgeous, with big blue eyes that already feel permanently etched in Briggs's pounding, sleep-deprived brain. Of course she looked like a hilarious flopping fish dancing around the empty pub. Most women Briggs meets are painted and primed to look like magazine images. But Maeve was so uninhibited, which was just so damn . . . sexy. He had watched her through the window and laughed, from the bottom of his belly, something he'd thought impossible yesterday. Maybe that's why he did it. Because she made him laugh on a day he reserved for being bloody pissed off at the world. This year, even more so.

Briggs rubs a hand over his heart. He's always known it was broken, which is exactly why he avoided getting tested all these years, even after doctors told him that hypertrophic cardiomyopathy can be hereditary. He didn't need a doctor to confirm it. Was that classic avoidance? Sure. But Briggs managed the situation on his own, staying hyperattuned to any changes in his body, always taking precautions. His number-one rule: don't get too attached to life. It might end sooner than you think. Hence his lack of commitment when it comes to women. It's not that Briggs is a commitmentphobe. He's a realist. Objectively, if he can limit the amount of affection a person feels toward him, he can lessen their pain when he's gone. That was the only prescription Briggs needed.

And then last week, with Aoife, his friend of nearly twenty years, he fainted while running after her husky, Pema, who slipped her leash while tied up to one of the picnic benches outside the Thatch. Thank God Aoife had stopped by before the pub opened, so only she and Hugh witnessed Briggs's collapse. He had noted other symptoms in the last few months, more frequent heart palpitations and shortness of breath, but it was fainting in front of his two closest friends that forced a visit to the doctor in Cork to confirm what Briggs already knew. His recent diagnosis just solidified his decision-making all these years.

Now Briggs puts on his swim trunks and a hoodie, takes a piss, brushes his teeth, and slips into his worn-out trainers before sneaking down the stairs, instinctively skipping the very last step, like Joe Murphy had always done. Within seven minutes of waking, Briggs is in his Jeep, driving toward the ocean.

Since he came back to Inishglass five years ago, with Hugh in tow, Briggs rarely misses this daily routine. Even in December, when it's dark and cold, with sleeting rain, and he thinks his balls might turn into ice cubes and fall off. And he's not about to stop now.

Most days it takes eight minutes to get to his spot. From eyes open to the water, it's fifteen minutes total. At six in the morning, the roads are clear, with only the occasional sheep crossing. Thank goodness. After last night's kiss and the bloody image of Maeve as she frantically wiped the floor clean of whiskey *he* spilled, Briggs's body tingles with the need to jump, more than usual. She looked like a kicked puppy, and he had done it. Briggs would have licked the whiskey from the floor himself if it would have made her feel better. Instead, he licked something much more enjoyable.

He grips the steering wheel. Why the hell did he kiss her? She may have started it, but he went back for more, like an idiot. He prides himself on being decisive and in control. Last night was an eclipse, a brief blackout in judgment caused by a perfect storm of circumstance. That's the only way to explain the kiss.

Briggs accelerates, taking the windy road faster than his mother would approve, but having grown up on this island, he knows just how far he can push it. Hell, in his teen years he could take these turns at well over the speed limit, with two girls screaming in the back and his best friend hanging out the sunroof. But they were total idiots back then, with no concept of tragedy. Today, Briggs pushes it to eighty, but no higher.

When his destination comes into sight, he sighs with relief, and before the car is parked, he unbuckles his seat belt. Tire tracks are worn into the grass where Briggs parks each day, and he slides the Jeep Renegade perfectly into his spot. He's out of the car as fast as he can, sweatshirt thrown on the hood, trainers discarded on the ground, hands tingling like they always do the moment before he jumps. Briggs runs up to the edge of the water and leaps into the rough gray sea below.

~

Hugh is in the kitchen cooking when Briggs walks in. Hugh spins around, spatula in hand, and points it at Briggs's face, like a proper mother. "Under the circumstance, do you really think you should be plunging into freezing cold water, young man?"

Briggs plops into a seat at the kitchen table. "I hope you made coffee."

"We're out." Hugh turns back to the stove, breakfast sizzling in a skillet.

"Damn it." Briggs rubs a hand over his tired face.

"Is someone a wee bit cranky today? What happened, Furphy? I didn't hear you come in last night."

"That's because you were passed out on the couch."

"You can't blame me for being drunk on the job when you were the one giving me the drinks. Did you go back and find the blond Brit?"

Briggs had completely forgotten about her. "No," he says. He's not about to tell Hugh about Maeve. The American will ask endless questions. Briggs doesn't need that noise today. Better to keep the lone incident locked in a vault.

Hugh scoops the contents of the pan onto two plates and sets them on the table.

"What the hell is this?" Briggs looks down at the blob of white and green.

"Egg whites and spinach," Hugh says proudly. "The yolk is where all the cholesterol is."

Briggs pokes at the food. They've lived together for five years and mostly sustained themselves on frozen pizza, Indian takeout, and fish and chips from the pub. But since he collapsed, the fridge has been filled with tofu, vegetables, and kombucha.

Hugh takes a bite. "Hmm. Not bad."

"I don't believe you." Briggs leaves his plate untouched.

"No. For real, bro. The spinach really rounds out the dish. Very . . . earthy. You should try it."

"You've always been a terrible liar."

Hugh pokes at his plate but can't bring another bite to his mouth. He groans and drops his fork. "This tastes like slimy dirt. Healthy food blows."

"I appreciate the effort, mate, but I'd rather risk death than eat fecking tofu for the rest of my life."

"Don't joke," Hugh says seriously. "You have no idea how scary it was for me when you collapsed."

"I'm sorry *my* heart condition is so taxing for *you*." Briggs rolls his eyes and takes his untouched plate to the counter.

"I'm glad you're finally admitting to what a selfish bastard you've been. It's time to start thinking about someone other than yourself. I need you alive, bro. If I can't cling to your coattails, I'll actually have to grow up and take control of my life. Maybe even risk getting a real job or asking a woman out. Do you know how hard that will be for me? Balls don't just grow overnight. Cultivating insecurities like mine takes years of hard work and humiliation."

"You're right," Briggs says. "I should have been more thoughtful."

"Thank you." Hugh sets his plate down and claps Briggs on the back. "I accept your apology."

Briggs chuckles, shrugs out of Hugh's touch, and grabs his car keys.

"So does this mean you've decided?" Hugh asks.

"Decided on what?"

"Having heart surgery?"

"The only thing I've decided is that I need coffee. I'm going to Aoife's. You coming?"

Hugh snags the keys out of Briggs's hands. "The doctor said surgery is highly successful. It's an easy fix."

"When did open-heart surgery become an easy fix?"

"Point taken. I just mean there *is* a fix," Hugh says. "It isn't a death sentence."

This conversation would be exhausting no matter what, but without caffeine, Briggs feels drained and annoyed. He staves off Hugh with the only answer he can muster. "I can't do surgery until after tourist season, anyway. I can't be away from the pub that long." When Hugh starts to counter, Briggs cuts him off. "The doctor said it was fine to postpone as long as I take precautions and keep an eye on my symptoms. Which is exactly what I'm doing." He snatches the car keys back. "Now I'm going to get a bloody cup of coffee, which happens to be good for my heart. Are you coming?"

"Nah. I'm on a health kick. I'm gonna hit the gym before work."

"Is that code for masturbate?" Briggs says, halfway to the door.

"Don't underestimate it," Hugh says, dumping both plates of food into the garbage bin. "You'd be surprised how strong my wrists are."

Mettā Café is full of tourists when Briggs walks up. He parked three blocks away because the streets are so crowded this time of year, and while the island has grown to accommodate the rise in visitors, it's still an island, with limited space.

He's about to open the door to the café when he sees, sitting inside bent over her phone, the one person he was hoping to avoid. The fact that he knows Maeve simply by the top of her head and the way she shyly crosses her legs, like she doesn't want anyone to notice her, is concerning. But so is the fact that Briggs hasn't had a drop of coffee this morning. The conundrum pushes his patience, so he goes around to the back and enters through the kitchen door, knowing Aoife won't mind.

She has her arms full of dirty plates when Briggs sneaks inside, and he quickly helps her with the load, taking half and setting them in a bus bin. Aoife sets down her own stack and puts her hands on her hips. Colorful sleeve tattoos run down both her arms. Briggs has always admired Aoife's unconventional beauty, her bright blond pixie cut and endearing disregard for fashion, favoring flowy clothes one might find in an ashram.

"What girl are we avoiding this time, Briggs Murphy?" Aoife says, no formal greeting needed.

"Your café is too bloody popular. The line's out the door, and I'm having a caffeine emergency." Briggs snags a freshly baked scone from a tray.

Aoife throws a dish towel at him. "You're paying for that."

"Come to the pub later. I'll give you a free pint."

"I haven't paid for a pint since I was sixteen. And I drink wine. Which you well know."

"Well, then why are you complaining about the scone? You owe me. Mind getting a latte to wash it down?"

"Bugger off, you twat."

"Might I remind you, I know about the time you gave Harry O'Toole a hand job with olive oil."

Aoife gapes at him. "My hands were dry. I was being thoughtful. I would have chafed him otherwise, and it was all I could find."

Briggs chuckles, feeling lighter for the first time since he woke up. He should have come straight to the café. Aoife has a way of grounding him when he's untethered. Hell, she might be the only person Briggs would ever consider marrying, if the thought didn't disgust him so much. Too much like marrying his sister.

"Harry smelled like Italian food for a week," he says through a mouthful of scone.

"But my hands were smooth as silk." Aoife holds up all ten fingers and wiggles them with a laugh. Then she points at Briggs. "Don't think for a bloody second that sending me down memory lane will work. Out with it, Briggs."

"Can't a lad just get some coffee?"

"No. Now, who'd you shift this time?"

"No one. I swear."

But Aoife knows better, having been friends with Briggs since the dawn of his sexual existence. She stalks to the front of the kitchen and peeks into the dining room, which is decorated in what Aoife calls "anti-Irish charm." No bangers and mash or potpies on the menu, only baked goods, vegetarian dishes, and smoothies with ingredients like acai seed, tart cherry juice, and turmeric.

The tables and chairs are a mishmash of east Asian colors and designs, inspired by a trip Aoife took to India while studying Eastern philosophy at college. One wall is brick, decorated with plants. The window frames are painted in various bright colors—green, pink, yellow—so the café feels vibrantly alive. Dangling from the ceiling are at least fifty light bulbs in all different shapes, colors, and sizes. There's a Buddha shrine in the corner. Every morning at six thirty, Aoife offers a free meditation class, though Briggs has yet to attend, being too busy jumping into the ocean that time of day.

It only takes one glance around the room for Aoife to notice Maeve. She closes the door and glares at Briggs, slowly shaking her head. "I thought she looked familiar. The eyes . . . So Liam Doherty's daughter is finally here." Standing on her tiptoes, Aoife swats Briggs on his head. "What the bloody hell were you thinking?"

Briggs holds up his hands and backs away. "It was an accident!"

"You accidently screwed Liam Doherty's long-lost daughter?"

Briggs puts his finger up. "I didn't have sex with her. You know my rules, Aoife. I don't take advantage of vulnerable women. That's not my style."

"Then what the hell happened?"

"Let's just say I didn't make the best first impression."

Aoife pokes her head back out the kitchen door for another look. Maeve sits quietly in the corner. "I can't believe how much she looks like Liam," Aoife says, sadly.

As if Briggs could forget. Maeve has been etched in his mind all morning. He needs to get the hell out of the café. "Forget the coffee, Eef. I'll see you later."

But as he turns to go, she grabs his arm. "Like hell you're leaving. I don't care what you did to that poor girl to make her hate you, you need to fix it, Briggs. Now. We need her. Do you see all those tourists? They're here because of your families' feud. If she doesn't play along, if the feud dries up, they'll stop coming, and we're all screwed."

Briggs clenches his jaw, knowing Aoife is right. As much as he'd like to stay far away from Maeve Doherty, for reasons he is heartily trying to ignore, he has no choice but to put himself directly in her line of fire.

"Fix it, Murphy," Aoife insists.

"Fine," he groans. "I'll fix it."

"Thank you."

"Can I get a vat of coffee now?"

~

Five minutes later, Briggs sets a green smoothie aptly named Jet Lag Lube in front of Maeve. He plops himself in the seat across from her, his second large latte in hand. "Cat video?" he asks.

Maeve looks up from her phone, her blue eyes assaulting him. Briggs has to glance away to gather his composure.

"I don't watch cat videos," she says.

"Everyone watches cat videos. They're hilarious."

"I'm more of a dog person."

"I don't believe you."

"And why is that?" Maeve sits back in the seat.

"Dogs are messy. Too much shedding and slobber for you."

"Please." She holds up her hand. "I just ate." Then she starts to stand. "And now I'm leaving."

"But I brought you a smoothie." Briggs gestures to the green concoction.

"How do I know it's not poisoned?" Maeve rests her hands on the table, leans toward him, and says pointedly, "You are a Murphy, after all."

Try as he might, Briggs can't help but glance at her chest, which is at his eye level. *Grapefruits,* he thinks.

Get it together. He cannot think that way about this woman. Not because he's a gentleman, but because right now, accompanying that thought is a feeling, one that Briggs is wholly opposed to. One that he has tried all morning to ignore, claiming it's a figment of his imagination.

But he likes her. Holy hell. Briggs Murphy has a crush on Liam Doherty's daughter. Like a bloody thirteen-year-old boy who can't control his hormones.

Briggs clears his throat and forces his gaze away from Maeve's chest. "Ivy explained everything to you?"

Maeve crosses her arms. "Unlike some people, she told me the truth."

"I didn't lie to you, Maeve."

"I thought you were a tourist!" A few tables look in their direction, and she lowers her voice. "I thought I would never see you again. If I had known, I never would have—" She stops abruptly, biting back the words she was going to say.

"Never would have what?" Briggs goads her.

She sits down and states in a hushed tone, "You took advantage of me."

"Me?" Briggs rests back in his seat, ignoring the part of him that's happy she didn't walk away. "I believe you started things."

"You walked into my pub!" Again, she brings her voice back down to a whisper. "You knew who I was and conveniently failed to mention that our families are mortal enemies. You should have stopped me. You knew better. But you were trying to get the upper hand."

"And what about you?" Briggs counters.

"What about me?"

"You took advantage of *me*," he proclaims.

Maeve gasps. "What?"

"You just said you thought I was a tourist. You thought you'd never see me again. So you were clearly looking to take advantage of me sexually and then discard me."

"Don't say that word."

"What word? Sexually?"

Maeve shakes her head like her mind is an Etch A Sketch and she's attempting to wipe an image from it. She leans in. "You owe me an explanation."

He mimics her, leaning in, bringing them practically nose to nose. "You owe me a harsh reality," he counters.

They wait in silence, their faces so close that Briggs can feel the heat off her skin and smell her sweet, creamy perfume. Suddenly, his pants are too tight.

He grinds his teeth and sits back. "Will you please just drink the smoothie before it completely melts? It'll help your jet lag."

"Why should I believe that? You probably laced this thing with a roofie as a joke."

"I might not be who you thought I was," Briggs says, now utterly serious. "But that is despicable. I would never do that to a woman, or anyone else."

Maeve cowers back in her seat, lower lip nestled between her teeth, undoubtedly feeling guilty. "Why are you here?" she asks quietly. "Didn't you embarrass me enough last night?"

Bloody hell. That was the last thing he wanted to do. He wanted to make her feel better, and all he managed to do was make it worse. And now he can't explain himself because he'll sound like he kissed her for charity. She'll assume that he thinks she's pathetic. Not that his feelings matter. In fact, his feelings can't matter. It's best to ignore the whole lot of them and stick to business.

"You may hate me after last night," Briggs says, resting his elbows on the table. "But that doesn't change the fact that we have to work together. People come to Inishglass expecting a show from our families. It's imperative not only for both pubs, but for the whole island, that we give them what they want. Without a booming tourist season, most of these places would struggle to survive."

Maeve chews on that, her lip nestled in her teeth again, a move that is utterly adorable and infuriating. Briggs can't help but remember what that lip felt like in his teeth.

"A show?" she says.

"Aye. A good one at that."

Maeve nods and stands, her eyes glued to his face. She picks up the smoothie, now half-melted, and loudly announces, "A gift for you, Briggs Murphy! From the Dohertys!" Then she dumps the entire drink on his head and walks out of the café.

Briggs watches her leave. Aoife stands behind the counter, mouth agape.

"Well . . ." Briggs walks over to his friend, trailing green liquid behind him. "I don't think we have anything to worry about."

6

aeve storms out of Mettā Café feeling invigorated. If Briggs Murphy wants a show, she's happy to provide one, after what he did last night. Dumping the smoothie on his head is the least he deserves after tricking her. She seriously thought he cared. He sure as hell kissed her like he cared. Evidently, years of acting for tourists has its benefits. Maeve had had no idea Briggs was faking it or she *never* would have told him her karaoke secret.

Taking revenge now has nothing to do with being a Doherty, no matter what this business is between them and the Murphys. Maeve doesn't care about some ancient, Shakespearean feud between families she doesn't even know, whatever her genetics. She's a Kaminski, and she has no intention of staying on this island for any longer than she has to. She has a dentist appointment in July. She can't miss that. It's written in green pen in her datebook!

But it felt good to pretend, to see Briggs's face covered in green slime.

Maeve gets out her phone and wishes she could call Sonya, but it's the middle of the night in Chicago, and Sonya hoards beauty sleep like Maeve with multipurpose storage bins. Instead, she checks her connectivity—still catching the wireless from the café—and texts the only person who can expedite her exodus from Inishglass.

I need to see you.

Miss me already, Kaminski?

I'm not in the mood for banter, Eoin.

Hungover? Drinking alone is never a good idea.

She pauses, fingers over the keys, but Maeve is not about to tell him about Briggs.

Jet lag is a beyatch.

You have a filthy mouth, Kaminski.

Don't flirt with me.

You're the one who said you needed me. I'm just here to service you.

Stop.

Stop what?

No suggestive texts.

My text was innocent. Any inferred suggestion is reader error.

We need to talk.

Isn't that what we're doing?

In person.

Must be serious. Too bad I'm booked today.

Pilates and a facial?

So you noticed my toned abs?

I noticed nothing.

People underestimate the importance of a strong core.

Thank you, Tracy Anderson. Now, cancel your wax appointment. I need to see you.

Who waxes anymore when lasering is so effective? You're not my only client, Kaminski. It'll have to wait until tomorrow. I have an opening at one.

Thanks for squeezing me in.

I sense your sarcasm.

It's your fault I'm on this damn island, and now when I need you, you're busy! What the hell?

You know, most people spend a lot of money to come to this island.

Don't make me feel guilty.

I'm just saying . . . you could enjoy yourself. Just for the day.

Maeve groans at her phone. She tried that last night, and it backfired.

Tomorrow, Kaminski. The Moorings. 1 p.m. My advice—get some fresh air. A long walk is the best cure for jet lag.

Fine. Don't be late this time.

Sheep are unpredictable, Kaminski. Save yourself the heartache and lower your expectations.

Maeve rests back against the building, her adrenaline now waning, leaving her feeling tired again. She really could have used that smoothie.

For one glorious moment when she woke up this morning, Maeve forgot where she was. She pressed the crisp white bedsheets to her nose, enjoying the clean smell. The sunshine just starting to stream through the window. The crisp air and the smell of salt water. And then she remembered where she was, and the day has been on a downward slope since.

As it turns out, the Cabbage Patch is a field filled with eco-pods, round structures just big enough for two people. Maeve's has a double bed, small couch, kitchenette, small bathroom, and a TV. It's charming, neat, clean, and contained, just how Maeve likes her spaces. But the idea of spending the rest of the day in hers, surrounded by only her anxiety, feels claustrophobic.

This morning she dressed sensibly in black leggings, white crop top, and purple zip hoodie, with her raincoat stuffed in a sling backpack along with her planner. When her life is tossed in the air, a person can't go wrong with athletic casual. Oddly enough, she's dressed perfectly for the walk Eoin just suggested.

Then she has an idea. Briggs will be occupied with washing green smoothie out of his hair and clothes for the next hour at least. Maeve looks around for any spying eyes and then opens a browser on her phone and searches "The Thatch, Inishglass." An information page comes up right away, with location, address, phone number, website, hours of operation, pictures, and reviews.

As its name implies, the pub has a thatched roof. Unlike the Moorings's whitewashed exterior, black trim, and red door, the Thatch is a stone building with green trim and a door of the same color. Flower boxes line the windows, and Irish flags hang from either end of the building. It's utterly charming, and the reviews say as much. The Thatch has a 4.7-star rating. Maeve flips through the images of food and pints and locals playing music. The place looks delightful and cozy, as much as she hates to admit it. She skims the reviews, which gush about the authentic Irish atmosphere, the food—apparently the bangers and mash is to die for—and the local "trad music." Most of the reviews mention the Murphy-Doherty feud and the shenanigans between the two pubs.

Maeve laughs at a particularly funny one.

Nick P.
Cleveland, OH
6/14/2021

★ ★ ★ ★ ★

There is only one reason to come to this godfor-saken turd of an island Ireland shit out millions of years ago . . .

THE THATCH. I'd swim through a channel of used diapers and bologna. I'd walk across a moor of BO and dirty scalp mist. Do yourself a favor. Don't go to Ireland. It rains every fucking day here. But if you do find yourself on this floating fart pebble, take the ferry from Cork over to Inish-glass and go to the Thatch. Best pub in Ireland. And if anyone tells you different, tell them the Dohertys can go to hell.

Another five-star review lays out the feud perfectly. Maybe Maeve should have done a little research before coming here. A small failure, she now admits, but how was she supposed to know Liam came from a quasi-famous family on the world's smallest island.

Jessie V.
Brussels, Belgium
7/28/2019

⭐⭐⭐⭐⭐

Two households, both alike in dignity, on the fair island of Inishglass where we lay our scene . . .

Don't be fooled by this island's Irish charm, the rolling green fields and colorful pastel houses. Behind Inishglass's fair facade, an ancient feud rages between the Murphys and Dohertys.

Lucky for us, pints instead of pistols are their weapon of choice. These two families own the only two pubs on the island, and both offer everything a tourist could want to tickle their Irish fancy. Go to either for a drink, but stay for the high jinks. Just be alert. Before you sugar your tea at the Thatch, make sure a Doherty didn't sneak salt in that shaker. Sip your water carefully at the Moorings, a Murphy may have put vinegar in that glass. You can't be sure when a Murphy or Doherty will exact revenge, but one thing is certain—you'll have a jolly good time when they do.

And don't worry about a truce. In a feud that's lasted over two hundred years, it's not likely to end anytime soon.

Another review catches Maeve's attention, raising her heart rate a notch.

Christyn B.
San Francisco, CA
3/31/2021

★★★★★

No regrets.

It's a Saturday night like any other. You walk into a pub, survey the local beers on tap, find one that looks appealing, put on your lipstick, and hope the pint tastes as good as it looks. But on Inishglass, there is one beer that tastes exceptionally better than all the rest, and you can only find it at the Thatch. Strong and cool, this beer will leave you feeling lightheaded and satisfy your every craving. (Don't be afraid to ask. This pint is very giving.) I must say, I cried a little when the pint was done. I wish I could have this beer every damn night. I would drink it slowly. Savor every inch of it. Run my fingers down the sweaty glass and lick the foam from its rim.

If you find yourself in Inishglass, stop at the Thatch and savor the beer. Don't let the opportunity pass. You might wake up hungover and tired, but I promise, you'll be fully satisfied. Tell Briggs I sent you.

Maeve may not know Christyn, but she does not like her. And Christyn is not alone. As Maeve scrolls, she notices all the reviews written about Briggs, some more explicit than others. Some just mention what a kind person he is. Some describe him in detail, like he's the heartthrob in a romance novel. It's infuriating. At least Maeve wasn't the only person he fooled. In fact, she can't find a single review that speaks poorly about him. She has half a mind to leave one now, but that is too low for her, even with her bruised ego.

She opens a new browser and searches "The Moorings, Inishglass." As with the Thatch, there are thousands of reviews, averaging 4.5 stars. The Moorings doesn't have quite as many reviews, but it's not trailing by much. Maeve glances at the top review and stops still.

Gary M.
Fortrose, Scotland
5/1/2023

★★★★★

It's with a heavy heart that I report that Liam Doherty, owner of the Moorings, has passed away.

I was lucky enough to visit Inishglass a few months ago and returned last week with my girlfriend so she could experience the island and its famous feud. Unfortunately, the entire place was shut down, including both pubs. I'm leaving this five-star review because I've never seen what felt like an entire village mourning one person. The collective grief and love was overwhelming. Even a Murphy would have a hard time denying emotion. I only met Liam Doherty once, very briefly, but he must have been a great man. I can only hope that when I'm gone, I'm as missed as he is.

As to the future of the Moorings, no one on the island would say a word, which leads me to believe there's a story here, but we'll all have to wait and see.

Maeve closes the browser straightaway, feeling as though a boulder has been placed on her chest. She isn't prepared to read about Liam, not today at least. With everything else that's happened in the past twenty-four hours, it's just too much.

She needs a walk, and she knows her destination. As she's mapping the route, a short blond woman runs out of the café toward her, carrying a green smoothie. She's in a cropped white V-neck T-shirt and stretchy bell-bottoms, with colorful tattoos down both arms.

"Wait!" she hollers after Maeve. "Your Jet Lag Lube!" She shoves the smoothie into Maeve's hand. Startled, Maeve takes the drink and stares at the woman, who is maybe a few years older than her. "Brilliant move, by the way. Everyone inside is talking about it. They love the drama."

"Thanks," Maeve says, the word sounding more like a question than a statement.

"I promise, the drink works. I created it myself after a brutal flight home from Nepal." The woman holds out her hand, and they shake. "I'm Aoife, by the way. I own the café."

"Maeve. How did you know I'm jet-lagged?"

"I see it every day round here. You pick up on the signs."

"Do I look that bad?"

"No!" She laughs. "You look gorgeous. Better than most in your situation."

Aoife looks as though she didn't mean that last bit to slip out, and Maeve gathers that she isn't talking about Maeve's transatlantic flight. Aoife's looking at her the way the man on the ferry did—like Maeve is familiar.

The words of the review come back to her: *an entire village mourning one person.*

"Sorry about your loss," Aoife says quietly.

But Maeve can't accept her sympathy without feeling like a fraud. She didn't know Liam. It's wrong to claim the loss. She holds up the drink. "Thanks for the smoothie."

"My pleasure." Aoife smiles. "Can I see your cell?"

It's an odd question, but Maeve hands over her phone, not wanting to make a bad impression. Aoife touches the screen a few times and hands it back to Maeve.

"I put my number in your contacts, just in case."

Maeve looks down at the name: *Aoife Sheehan.*

"Are any names around here spelled phonetically?" Maeve jokes. "How is a person supposed to read that and know the pronunciation?"

"It's '*Ee*-fa.' That's the Irish for you." Aoife laughs as a group of tourists walks into the café. "I better dash. Call or text me if you need anything. I hold a meditation class here every morning at six thirty, right before we open. You should come."

"I've never meditated before."

Aoife shrugs. "Time for something new, maybe."

Maeve considers the idea and takes a sip of the smoothie. She practically moans at the taste. "Holy hell, this is good."

"Told you." Aoife winks. "Anything to help."

She disappears into the café as Maeve sucks down more of the smoothie. She doubts that Aoife offers her phone number and unlimited help to all the tourists who come into her restaurant, which means Aoife has one very distinct reason.

Liam.

Which leaves Maeve to wonder—why the hell did Liam tell everyone about her if he wanted nothing to do with her?

~

It doesn't take long to walk to the Thatch. With a few hours before it opens, and Briggs probably still cleaning smoothie out of his ears, Maeve trusts she won't run into anyone. Still, she's cautious, wearing sunglasses firmly fixed on her face and a hoodie pulled up over her head. Like the online pictures suggested, the place is quaint and well cared for. The outside looks like it belongs on @visitInishglass's Instagram. Picnic tables are lined up out front. Similar to Chicago, people in Ireland must take as much advantage as they can of warmer weather. Today, people are out riding bikes and strolling the beach. A few brave souls are even in the water, though none going farther than their knees. *Only a lunatic would fully submerge themselves,* Maeve thinks.

What's most noticeable about the pub is the banner hanging over the door, proudly announcing the Thatch as having been "Voted Best Pub in Inishglass!"

By whom? Maeve wonders. Briggs probably took the liberty of claiming the title without any formal vote, she reasons. Another convenient lie to benefit himself. How infuriating. But then why should she care? This is not her home. These are not her people. She is not involved in this feud. She will be gone from this island soon enough, and her time here will be a distant memory.

But that doesn't mean she isn't a little curious.

She takes one more careful glance around her, then climbs up onto one of the picnic benches and sneaks a peek in the window. The walls are painted a brick-red color and covered in a collage of signs, just like at the Moorings. A few large barrels are scattered around the center of the room, acting as tables. Banquette seating runs along one wall. There's no TV or games. It's simple, just a bar and seating, a place to come and uncomplicate your life.

Maeve imagines Briggs behind the bar, leaning on his elbows, a charming, concerned grin on his gorgeous face, coaxing out of each customer what ails them, so they'll keep coming back and buying more drinks. Like Yelp says, he makes people feel at home, giving them whatever they need. And according to the reviews, in some instances that's an amazing night of sex . . .

Maeve tries to push the memory of their kiss to the farthest recesses of her mind, but it comes back to her in a heat-filled rush, distracting her so much that when someone behind her says, "We don't open 'til noon," Maeve loses her balance and falls unceremoniously off the bench, knocking them both to the ground.

She jumps to her feet, apologizing profusely to the man she just squashed. He's dressed in a green-and-blue rugby shirt and a shit-eating grin. Maeve snatches her sunglasses from the ground, only to realize they broke in the fall. Her hood has fallen away as well. Her anonymity is gone.

"I could make an exception . . . just this once," the man says in an American accent.

Maeve brushes dirt from his sleeve. "I'm so sorry."

"Rough night?"

She runs her fingers through her hair. "Why do you say that?"

"Drinking before noon. It's either hair of the dog or still drunk from the night before."

Maeve laughs to hide her nerves, but her mind works in overdrive to find a way to escape the situation. Thank goodness Briggs didn't catch her. She decides to play tourist and hope that whoever this American is, he didn't know Liam. "I was just passing by and was intrigued. I'll be going now." She starts to walk away.

"Chicago. Definitely Chicago."

Maeve stops. "What?"

"That's where you're from."

"How did you know that?"

"One of my many talents." He brushes his shoulders off with an endearing smirk. "I can usually get the state, if not the city."

"That's . . . impressive."

He gestures toward the pub. "It's a skill I've honed while bartending and avoiding adulthood for many years."

"At least you're self-aware."

"If you understand your role, you can play it better." Maeve cocks an eyebrow. "Clever, with a crooked smile, a charming gap between his two front teeth, and a body not chiseled by the gods, but a perfect replica of an Idaho potato." He pats his stomach like he's just eaten Thanksgiving dinner.

"Is that your Tinder profile?"

"Romance book description, actually. Product of being raised around seven sisters. When most boys were reading *Playboy*, I was reading *Fifty Shades of Grey*, which is surprisingly like *Playboy*, but better."

"Wow. Seven sisters. I can't even imagine."

"Irish Catholics. We're like dogs. We come in litters."

"You're Irish?"

"Half. Dad's side. My mom's Chinese. What about you? Are you here to chase down your ancestry like most Americans?"

"Polish," Maeve says, not lying, but . . . omitting. "And an only child."

"If you want a sister, you're welcome to any of mine. Except Hailey."

They both chuckle. Maeve sees her opportunity for an exit. "Well, it was nice to meet you. Sorry I squashed you."

"Hugh Duffy, King of Useless Talents. And don't be sorry. It was oddly pleasurable," he says. After a pause, he adds, "I'm just waiting to see how long I have to stand here before you tell me your name. I'm in no rush. Take your time."

To lie would only make the situation worse, so Maeve hopes he'll forget her and never mention this incident to Briggs. "Maeve Kaminski."

"Maeve Kaminski from Chicago." He points to himself. "Hugh Duffy from Detroit. What are the odds? Two Midwesterners meeting in Ireland."

"I'd say pretty good this time of year."

Hugh chuckles. "Well, you might be Polish, but today you have the luck of the Irish. I know this place looks like it serves only warm Guinness, but I promise, I make the best damn Negroni you've ever had."

"How did you know I love a Negroni?"

Hugh extends his arms wide and winks. "King of Useless Talents. So what do you say?"

"I think ten thirty is a little early for a cocktail. But thanks."

"Are you sure you're Midwestern? We make a sport of day drinking."

"Some other time. I don't want to get you in trouble with your boss," Maeve says, turning toward the road back to the Cabbage Patch.

"If there's one thing Briggs isn't opposed to, it's bending the rules for a beautiful woman."

She stops. She can't help herself. "Briggs?"

"I know . . . he's a total fucker. Even the name is intriguing."

"You don't like him?"

"Unfortunately, I love the guy," Hugh says. "He's as good-looking as he is kind. It's offensive to the rest of us secondary characters." Maeve raises an eyebrow, frustratingly intrigued. "Alas, I've been cast as the goofy sidekick in life. The quirky roommate. The less attractive best friend who lives vicariously through his much hotter buddy's wild sex life. A self-deprecating guy with a longshot crush on a completely out-of-his-league woman who won't notice he exists until the end of the movie."

"You really have yourself nailed."

"I've had twenty-seven years of practice."

"And how would *Fifty Shades of Grey* describe this . . . Briggs?" The question comes out before Maeve can think any better of it, and she instantly regrets it.

"Viking in size and broodingly handsome, walks through life like a perfectly tailored Tom Ford suit," Hugh says. "He's basically James Bond. Every man wants to be him, and every woman wants to . . . well, you know."

"He sounds very on-brand for a man-whore."

"If only his conscience didn't get in the way. His heart is as big as his—"

Maeve's eyes grow wide. "I got it."

"But he's shit at making Negronis. So . . . how 'bout it?"

Maeve should have left already. In fact, she never should have come in the first place. "I think a nap will be better than a drink at this point. It was nice to meet you, Hugh Duffy."

As she walks away, he hollers after her. "Come back tonight and I'll make you that Negroni!"

"I'll think about it!" she calls back over her shoulder.

A bold-faced lie. Maeve will never set a foot inside the Thatch. Not tonight. Not ever. If there's a God in heaven, she will be long gone from this island before Hugh ever tells Briggs he met her.

7

Briggs is behind the bar at the Thatch, wiping glasses.

"I met a girl today," Hugh says.

Just from his friend's amusing tone, Briggs knows who it is.

"Midwestern smoke show. Brunette with blue eyes that turn soft body parts—"

"I get it." Briggs clenches his jaw.

"What have I told you about girls from middle America?"

"Ain't nothing average about them," Briggs says, poorly imitating an American accent.

"Fuck off. You even sound sexy with a bad Southern accent." Hugh fills a pint for a customer and sets it on the bar with a gap-toothed grin. He may complain about his empty bed most nights, but it's not for lack of charm. Hugh just isn't built for one-night stands. It's part of his appeal, which oddly enough could get him a lot of one-night stands. But being raised around seven sisters has instilled in him a respect for women that exceeds most men's. He may talk big, but it's just a cover. He's a romantic at heart, and it's one of the traits Briggs likes most about the guy.

Briggs recognizes a woman who appreciates a one-night stand, and for all her posturing last night, he knows Maeve isn't one of them. She may have allowed herself an impulsive moment, but deep down, that's not her. She toiled over that kiss too much, which only made Briggs want it more. Maeve would be perfect for Hugh, which gives Briggs the sudden urge to punch his best friend in the nose.

"I'm telling you, bro," Hugh continues. "This one was extra unique. She takes 'girl next door' to a whole other level."

Briggs contemplates smashing a whiskey bottle over Hugh's head. What the hell is wrong with him? He's acting like a schoolkid fighting with his friend over a crush. He takes a deep breath and files away another reason that Maeve Doherty is not good for him. Violence is the last thing his heart needs.

"So where'd you meet this girl?" Briggs asks, stretching away the tension in his neck.

Hugh claps him on the back. "She was poking around the pub. Peeking in the windows. She literally fell off the picnic bench, on top of me. That's a sign, right?"

That really gets Briggs's attention. "What?"

"Yeah. Like she was trying to break in. Hottest burglar I've ever seen."

A tiny, satisfied smile grows on Briggs's face. "Really?" He imagines Maeve snooping around the Thatch in her tight black pants, scoping out the competition. A bold move, he has to admit.

"She's a Negroni, man. All the way."

"You used the old 'I bet I can guess your favorite drink' line, eh?" Briggs carries three full pints to the end of the bar.

"Hell yeah, I did. And I was right. She's sweet, fruity, but a little bitter, which makes her interesting, so you keep coming back for more."

"You really need to get laid, mate."

"Well, Furphy, if you'd share the wealth, maybe I would."

"No, you wouldn't."

Hugh groans. "You're right. I need genuine commitment. God, I hate you."

Briggs rolls his eyes. Hugh may peg him as the handsome heart-breaker who won't settle down, but Briggs has never spent the night with a woman who hasn't consented to what they could offer each other.

Over all the years, he's seen enough customers to distinguish when a woman is looking for love and when she's looking for sex. He keeps his distance from the former. He's not in the market for love.

But he hasn't been able to get Maeve out of his mind all day, and that's a bloody problem. Even the incident at Mettā Café, which left him scrubbing green out of his clothes all morning, was kind of . . . adorable. He couldn't stop laughing about it. Hell, fighting with her was the most fun he's had in a while. Which is a huge problem for a guy who's fine with carnal attraction but draws the line at joy and laughter. Those are matters of the heart. Off limits.

The pub door opens, letting in a fresh wave of air and people. Hugh perks up.

"She's not coming, mate," Briggs says as he loads dirty glasses into a bin for the dishwasher, thankful Maeve can't set foot in his pub, offering his only reprieve.

"How the hell do you know?" Hugh says. "I told her to come in tonight. Maybe she likes chubby charmers."

"You're right. Maybe she does." Briggs picks up the bin and heads toward the kitchen.

"Wait." Hugh stops him. "Say that again."

"Maybe she does."

His jaw falls open. "No. Not fucking possible. You already met her!"

Briggs ignores him and disappears into the bustling kitchen. He checks in with the cooks, monitors orders, goes over next week's schedule in his office. Anything to avoid the bar. But eventually, he knows it's cruel to leave Hugh to manage the crowd alone.

Fifteen minutes later, he walks back out to the bar.

"Spill it," Hugh says, arms crossed.

Briggs slings a rag over his shoulder. "It's a small island. It's not that odd for us to meet the same person. Happens every day."

"Bullshit." Hugh pokes a finger in Briggs's face, which he swats away with too much vigor. "You don't make that face when we talk about girls."

"What face?"

"Like you want to rip off my balls." Hugh is now wearing a smartass grin. "I knew something was off this morning. She's the one who got your panties in a bunch!"

"I don't wear fecking panties." Briggs brushes past Hugh, bumping his shoulder. "And wipe that look off your ugly face."

Hugh follows him closely. "Redirecting unwanted feelings onto an innocent bystander. She must really be messing with you. This makes me so happy." He claps his hands like a puppet.

Briggs rounds on him and grabs his hands, squeezing. "I'm gonna kill you in your sleep."

But Hugh only smiles wider. Lucky for them both, Aoife walks into the pub, forcing Briggs to let go of Hugh's hands. He goes into the kitchen and retrieves the stool he saves just for Aoife, placing it at her usual spot at the end of the bar.

Before Aoife can sit down, Hugh blurts, "You're not going to believe what happened!"

Aoife lifts her arms in celebration. "You got your first pube!"

Hugh isn't fazed. "Briggs's panties are bunched so far up his ass, you'd think it was a thong. And it's about a girl!"

Aoife looks at Briggs. "You told him?"

"What?" Hugh exchanges glances with them both. "You already know?"

"She came into the café this morning, freshly jet-lagged. It was quite the scene. Did Briggs tell you about it?"

Briggs goes to the cooler for Aoife's bottle of wine—he's not about to offer Sancerre at an Irish pub—and pours a glass, which he sets in front of her with a heavy hand and a glare.

"Keep that to yourself, Eef."

"Absolutely not. It was brilliant. Everyone in town is buzzing about it. Quite the introduction, I'd say."

"What was brilliant?" Hugh asks, eyes alight.

Aoife sits back and crosses her arms, too satisfied with herself. "She dumped an entire smoothie on his head."

Hugh's jaw drops. "No way. Why the hell did she do that?"

Briggs stares daggers at Aoife.

"Because . . ." Aoife takes a dramatic pause. "She's Liam Doherty's daughter!"

Hugh lets loose with a gut-busting laugh that gathers the attention of most of the customers. "No fucking way!"

Briggs points at Aoife and mutters, "I'm kicking you out."

"No, you're not." She blows off the threat, knowing damn well Briggs would never. After twenty years of friendship, she's well acquainted with his programming and never hesitates to push every last button, all while wearing a warm smile. He won't do a bloody thing.

"Maeve Kaminski from Chicago is Liam Doherty's daughter?" Hugh repeats, keeled over from laughter. "I can't believe it."

Briggs grabs the back of his shirt and yanks him up. He muscles Hugh into the bar and points a finger in his face, but he says nothing. What is he going to say? He lets go of Hugh's shirt. "Keep your voice down."

"When have we ever done that when it comes to the Dohertys?"

"She doesn't need a bunch of people swarming the Moorings, gawking at her. She just got here."

Hugh sees right through the excuse. "No way. That's not why."

"Her father just died," Briggs presses. "She needs space, Hugh. Best we leave her alone for now."

Hugh claps Briggs on the back. "You son of a bitch. After all these years, it's finally happened."

"What the hell are you talking about?"

"You like her," Hugh whispers in his ear.

"Ah, for feck's sake." Briggs shoves him away.

Hugh sidles up to Aoife. "He likes her."

"He sure does," she agrees.

"Both of you." Briggs points an angry finger at them. "Out."

"It's like all my dreams are coming true," Hugh says, starry-eyed. "This is everything I've ever wanted. Briggs finally likes a girl, and it turns out, he can't touch her. Who do I congratulate for writing this script?"

"Shakespeare," Aoife offers and takes a sip of wine.

"I do not like her," Briggs says through tight teeth.

"Sure," Hugh says. "And I don't like pizza."

Aoife rolls her eyes. "God, you've always been a terrible liar."

"So, she's like . . . here to stay, right?" Hugh asks. "The Moorings is hers now. She's the only Doherty left."

"She could always sell." Aoife glances at Briggs, clocking his reaction.

"She can't do that," Hugh counters.

Briggs wipes down the bar. "If she owns the place, she can do whatever she wants."

"But the Murphy–Doherty feud is legend. You can't have one without the other. The Thatch isn't the Thatch without the Moorings. She's gotta know that, right?"

"I don't know what she knows. Our conversation was cut short when she dumped a smoothie on my head."

"I really wish I had gotten a picture," Aoife says.

"Well, there's an easy solution to the problem." Hugh pulls his phone from his back pocket. "Let's look her up."

Briggs rounds on him and takes the phone. "Don't you dare."

"Or I could just text her and ask?" Aoife has her phone out, and she flashes Maeve's contact at Hugh and Briggs.

"How the hell did you get that?" Briggs asks.

Aoife answers coolly. "She's new in town, so I gave her my number in case she needs anything."

"Bloody hell." Briggs shakes his head.

"Can I get her contact?" Hugh pleads.

"Absolutely not." Briggs reaches for Aoife.

She swats his hand away. "Calm down. I would never. And I'm not about to ask what her plan is. It's personal. We just met. That would be rude. But . . . there's no harm in looking her up on social media." She leans back with a grin.

Hugh moves hurriedly to Aoife's side, leaving Briggs behind the bar. "Where should we start? Google? TikTok? Tinder?"

"*Not* Tinder," Briggs says strongly.

"Instagram," Aoife says. She types into the phone, focused on the screen.

Briggs squeezes the bridge of his nose like he's coming down with a headache. "I don't have time for this. I've got a pub to run."

"You better get back to work then," Aoife says casually. "We've got this covered."

"You're about three seconds away from getting fired," Briggs snaps at Hugh.

"Go for it, bro. I bet Maeve would love an experienced bartender to help her through this tough transition at the Moorings."

Briggs snarls and turns, but he only makes it three steps before Aoife says, "Found her." And like Pavlov's dog, he's right back where he was just standing. Jesus Christ, he hates that his stomach just flipped. That there's a catalog of pictures of Maeve online. That he might have to break his policy of no social media.

"Shite. Her page is private," Aoife says. "I'll send her a follow request."

"Don't—"

"Already done. And . . . she accepted."

"Already?" Briggs says.

"This is better than my first hand job." Hugh leans over Aoife's shoulder to see the page. "Yep, that's the girl I met. God, I can't believe I didn't put the pieces together. She looks just like Liam."

Briggs grips the edge of the bar, too damn intrigued for his own good.

"This is odd," Aoife says.

"What?" Briggs hates that he jumped so fast at the statement.

"There's a gap in her posts."

"What the hell does that mean?"

"The dates," Aoife explains. "She didn't post for over a year. The page goes from May 2021 to just a few months ago."

"What the hell is odd about it?" Briggs snaps. "Maybe she got sick of posting for a while."

Aoife and Hugh both glare at him.

"I broke up with social media once," Hugh says. "It lasted five hours before I was back on TikTok watching dance videos."

Aoife gasps and points at her phone. "I know what happened!"

"What?" Briggs asks, hating that he cares so much, wishing he could snatch the phone from Aoife's hands.

"She deleted the pictures from that year."

Aoife and Hugh glance at each other, eyes sparkling like they just discovered the identity of Jack the Ripper. Then they look at Briggs and simultaneously say, "A breakup."

Briggs's entire body constricts.

"It's the only explanation," Aoife says. "Someone broke her heart, and she deleted the evidence that he ever existed. Damn. It must have been bad."

"You're totally right," Hugh says, his gaze softening. "Poor baby. Now I like her even more."

Briggs can't take it. "Put the goddamn phone down," he begs Aoife, rubbing his chest with his palm.

She tracks his movement and finally concedes, then drinks the last of her wine and passes the glass back to Briggs. "I should go home anyway. The café is insanity these days. Can't afford to feel like boiled shite tomorrow." She stands and heads toward the bathroom.

Clearly disappointed that their fun is over, Hugh yields, too, and heads back around the bar. "I guess I'll get back to work, boss."

Briggs and Hugh fall into rhythm, pouring drinks and charming patrons, but Briggs's mind continues to spin on Maeve and the

Moorings. He hadn't considered that she might sell the pub. For both families, that's never been an option, but Maeve wasn't raised here. The Moorings could mean nothing to her. Either way, Briggs has a problem. If she stays, Briggs's crush might grow worse. If she sells, the Thatch could be ruined. Hell, the whole island would be affected. If they don't have tourists . . .

Briggs is deep in thought when Aoife comes out of the bathroom and pulls him aside, careful that Hugh can't overhear.

"Please, Aoife, I don't want—"

"This isn't about her," she says quietly. "I saw Eoin this afternoon."

"That vampire showed his face outside during the day? I'm surprised he didn't combust. Did he speak to you?"

Aoife shakes her head. "He didn't see me. I just hate that he has me feeling like I'm eighteen again, with something to hide."

Briggs shakes his head. "You can't let him do that to you."

"I know. I just don't understand why he's back after all this time."

"Running from another burning bridge, no doubt. He's not our concern anymore. I wouldn't be surprised if he left the island by July."

"You're right." Aoife pulls out her phone and checks the time. "Will you come to meditation tomorrow morning?"

"I'll think about it."

"You always say that."

"And I always do." Briggs exaggerates a smile, knowing damn well he has no intention of going.

"It'll help. I promise. Especially with your—" She eyes his chest, knowing she's sworn to secrecy on the subject, especially in the pub.

"I'll think about it," he says gently.

She kisses him on the cheek, and right then, the pub door flies open. A customer runs inside, yelling, "She took it! I saw her do it! And now she's getting away!"

Briggs, Hugh, and Aoife all run toward the young man, not from the island, whose face is lit up with excitement like he just saw Santa Claus.

"What are you talking about, mate?" Briggs asks. The noise in the pub is down to a dull chatter of whispers.

"The sign," he says. "She stole the sign!"

Everyone funnels out into the night, drinks in hand. In the distance, the culprit speeds away on a bike, the "Voted Best Pub in Inishglass!" banner flapping behind her. Briggs watches in amazement, and damn it if he doesn't smile, just a little.

"Who was that?" the young man asks.

Hugh pats Briggs on the shoulder, beaming. "Looks like you have your work cut out for you."

Briggs looks at the gathered crowd, his face wiped clean of amusement, and growls loudly, "Those bloody Dohertys!"

8

The banner is false advertising, that's all there is to it. It needed to be taken down.

Maeve would swear under oath she didn't go on an evening bike ride *intending* to steal the sign. Sonya hadn't returned her texts or snaps. The eco-pod was too quiet, and Maeve was too alone. The only interaction she'd had was Aoife's Instagram request—she considered ignoring it, but Aoife had been so kind and thoughtful, and the smoothie really did help her jet lag—and there's only so long a person can stare at the ceiling before she goes crazy. Then she remembered the e-bikes Ivy offers to guests at the Cabbage Patch. It started off innocently, a way to burn energy in the hope of then falling asleep. An island doesn't have that many places a person could go. She was bound to ride past the Thatch at some point.

The pub was bursting with people. Maeve felt its vibrancy from outside, and yet she wasn't allowed in. Her loneliness hit a new low. And that damn sign. It was total bullshit. There was no vote. Briggs was crowning *himself* king. She couldn't stand for it. Stealing the sign was her parting gift. She may not want the Moorings, but she wasn't going to let the Thatch lie so blatantly. It's a matter of principle. She thought the coast was clear, until that kid came out of nowhere. At that point, there was no choice but to finish the job and get away as fast as she could.

Now, as she waits outside the Moorings in daylight, the sign is neatly folded in Maeve's backpack. She'll take it back to the States as a souvenir, proof that she got a little crazy while in Ireland.

Maeve takes a few pictures of the pub, knowing that Sonya will want digital documentation of everything. If only she had a picture of Briggs. Then again, she isn't sure she wants his image on her phone. In a weak moment, she might look at it, like she did with pictures of Zac Efron when she was in junior high. A ridiculous, unattainable heart-throb fantasy.

"On time, as requested." Eoin climbs out of his car in a fitted blue button-down, slim dark jeans, and a pair of unscuffed Nikes. Maeve snaps a picture of him before he can protest. He's metropolitan and smooth, a contrast to the rough, rocky island, and he stands out. "You're welcome to use that picture however you'd like," he says, and winks.

Sweet Jesus, does this guy ever turn it off? "No sheep today, Asshole?"

"Just trying to keep my client happy."

"Good. Because I need help, and you're the only person who can help me."

"I can do a lot of things for you, Kaminski. But I usually like to buy a woman a drink before we get down to the dirty stuff. How about it?" Eoin gestures toward the pub. "I hear they sell drinks here."

"You're one of the most unprofessional people I've ever met."

"Thanks for the compliment." Eoin's hand settles on Maeve's back, and he guides her through the red door.

Inside, nothing has changed. Already, half of the tables are filled with lunch customers. Soon the place will be crawling with people. Maeve recognizes the man from the ferry at the bar. He catches her eye, and she gives him a small wave. Immediately, he is out of his seat and coming toward her.

"I'll grab us a table," Eoin says, and scoots away.

The ferry passenger wags a finger at Maeve, a broad grin on his face. "I knew I recognized you. You have your father's eyes. Why didn't you tell me you're Liam Doherty's daughter?"

"I didn't want to cause a fuss . . . or puke on you," Maeve says quietly. "And if you would . . ." She's about to ask him not to draw attention to her when he cuts her off and announces her arrival to the whole damn pub. The place lights up like he's just announced free beer for everyone. For the next ten minutes, Maeve is passed around and introduced to more people than she can keep straight. The only name she retains is Derry, the man from the ferry, because it rhymes. Apparently, he's a fisherman and provides all the local fish on the menu at the Moorings.

"Your father was my number-one customer for thirty years. Bought anything we caught, even when the pub didn't need it, just to keep me in business," he explains. "We all heard about what you did last night. Your father would be damn proud."

With everyone's attention on her, Maeve draws a complete blank. What did she do last night?

"The sign!" Derry announces. "Bloody brilliant!"

Maeve downplays the move. "I just don't think it's right to advertise a lie."

The next thing she knows, a pint is shoved into her hand, and Derry yells, "The Thatch has met its match in Maeve Doherty!"

The sheer enthusiasm is so contagious that Maeve doesn't bother correcting her name. She finds herself chanting along, clinking glasses, celebrating like they just won a battle. And while she knows it's all for show, and that Derry is just doing his part to keep up the charade of the feud, it's hard not to get caught up in the ridiculous fun of it.

Eventually Eoin pulls Maeve from the crowd, proclaiming that she needs space to eat so she can keep up her strength for battle. No one argues, and Maeve and Eoin settle themselves into a corner table.

"What's this about a sign?" Eoin asks. Apparently, he's the only person in town who hasn't heard.

Maeve takes a sip and says, "I may have stolen something from the Thatch. It was an impulse grab. It just kind of . . . happened."

"Really?"

Maeve prefers to avoid an interrogation. "You know, you could have warned me what I was walking into, Asshole. 'By the way, you own a pub, and your family is in a Shakespearean feud with another family on the island, but it's all fake, so just play along.' Kind of an important detail."

"You asked me to leave you alone." Eoin sits back, his arms crossed over his chest. "I just followed my client's instructions."

"Whatever. I'm not here to argue. We have business to discuss."

"Sounds serious. But I can't do business until we've eaten. I ordered you the fish and chips. Hope that's OK."

"What did you get?"

"A salad. Dressing on the side. I have a figure to maintain." Eoin displays his sculpted chest like it's a work of art.

"You dress like you walked out of the pages of *GQ*." She points at his cocktail. "You drink old-fashioneds. You avoid people at all costs. And I'm guessing you carry earbuds on you at all times."

"And?"

"You're obviously a city boy, Asshole! Why do you live here?"

"An old-fashioned is whiskey."

"Trendy whiskey."

"Fine." Eoin rests his elbows on the table. "You got me. I'm new here. In an old sort of way."

"Meaning?" Maeve pushes her pint to the side and mimics his pose.

"I grew up here. Left when I went to uni. Did some time in London after that. Recently started working for a firm in Cork that just so happened to be handling your father's estate. They needed someone who knew the island, and I volunteered."

He relaxes back in his seat again, but Maeve isn't completely convinced he's sharing the whole story. She's about to pry further when a server delivers her fish and chips and his salad. Her hunger beats out her curiosity, and Maeve eats nearly her entire meal. Fifteen minutes later and sufficiently stuffed, she sits back and notices Derry glancing in her direction every few seconds. She gives him two thumbs up, and a blush blooms on his wrinkled cheeks. And right then, for the first time, Maeve feels bad for what she is about to do. She can't stay on this island. She can't give up her life in Chicago for a place she doesn't know. She cannot, after twenty-four years as a Kaminski, suddenly become Maeve Doherty, even if it has been a bit fun to pretend.

"OK, Asshole. This can't wait any longer," she says.

Eoin raises a hand to stop her, noting the serious tone. "Let's take this conversation outside."

The day has clouded over, but the green hills are vibrant. The cool June air is edged with salt and earth. Maeve takes a picture, but it doesn't capture the magnitude of the scene. One has to be here, in person. Since she arrived, her skin has been brighter and rosier, even with the jet lag. She hadn't noticed how sallow she'd gotten from months of hiding in her garden apartment, drinking bad wine, unable to go out because she's broke.

She follows Eoin down the road toward the sea. "Look, I appreciate what Liam was trying to do, leaving me the pub."

"And what was he trying to do?"

"To make up for the fact that he wasn't in my life. But he really doesn't need to. I never felt abandoned. I have two amazing parents. Liam had nothing to feel guilty about. So while I appreciate the gesture, I can't take it. This place isn't my home."

"What are you saying, Kaminski?"

Maeve takes a deep breath. "I want to sell the pub."

Eoin's head bobs. "Liam thought you might say that." He reaches into his back pocket and pulls out an envelope.

"What is this?"

"Honestly, I don't know. Liam instructed me not to open it but, in the event you want to sell, to give you the envelope and say you have his blessing, contingent on the completion of what's inside." He hands Maeve the sealed envelope.

Maeve is cautious as she peels back the flap. How many surprises are in store for her on this tiny island? Inside is a single piece of paper. Written in neat, masculine block letters is a list.

1. KNIT AN ARAN CABLE SCARF
2. WIN THE ANNUAL FOOTBALL ROUNDERS GRUDGE MATCH
3. VISIT CAIRN ISLAND

"What does this mean?" Maeve shows Eoin the list.

"It means . . . to sell the pub, you have to complete the list."

"Can Liam do that?"

"Technically, yes."

Maeve reads it again. The three items seem random, disjointed. "Knit an Aran cable scarf? But I don't know how to knit. And what is the Annual Football Rounders Grudge Match?"

"It's a ridiculous island tradition." Eoin shakes his head. "Football rounders is a game. You call it kickball in the States."

"I have to play kickball?"

"Not just play, Kaminski. You have to win. And there are only two teams that ever play in the *grudge* match."

Maeve gasps. "Dohertys and Murphys!"

"A real tourist trap, if you ask me. But it's the biggest event of the summer. Same time every year. First weekend in July."

"July!" Any panic Maeve had managed to stave off now ignites with a fury. "I can't stay here that long. I have things to do. I have a dentist appointment and . . . work!"

"If you want to sell the pub, you don't have a choice."

But she had a *plan*. Tell Eoin she wants to sell the pub. Leave the details to him. Go back to Chicago, collect her inheritance when the place sells, and pay off her debt, with money to spare. Enough for her and Sonya to go out any night they want, Maeve's treat.

"Who normally wins?" Maeve asks. When Eoin doesn't say, the answer becomes clear. Damn Briggs Murphy! "When was the last time the Dohertys won?"

"I believe it was over five years ago."

Maeve's head falls to her hands in an avalanche of dread. Normally, she loves a good list. She never goes to the grocery store without one. To-do lists, wish lists, packing lists . . . But lists are meant to clarify and organize. They give structure and reduce stress. This one, however, does not. And the most frustrating part is that the person who could answer all her questions is gone.

"I don't have enough clothes to be here until July. Or a place to stay. I can't just leave my life. I have a job! An apartment! I'll miss the Chicago Pride Parade! I *can't* miss the Pride Parade!"

"Calm down, Kaminski." Eoin grabs her shoulders and tells her to breathe. "Ivy has you booked for the whole summer, free of charge. And as for clothes, I've always found them highly overrated."

"Why would Liam do this?" Maeve exclaims. "Why would he ruin my life after he wanted nothing to do with it?"

"Maybe he didn't think he was ruining your life. Maybe he was dying, and this was his way of making up for choices he regretted."

That stabs through Maeve's self-loathing and pouting. She deflates, her anxiety now making her want to cry. But for herself? Or Liam?

"There *is* another choice," Eoin offers. "Don't sell the pub. Then the list means nothing."

"I *have* to sell." But she can't admit that she's in debt because she fell in love with the wrong guy. It's too pathetic. "Ireland isn't my home."

"Well . . . then I suggest you start on the list."

Three tasks. Three seemingly harmless acts, but they feel like mines rigged to blow up her life. "This last one," Maeve says. "What is Cairn Island?"

Eoin points off the coast to a tiny island, like a broken piece of Inishglass perched a mile or so away. "That's Cairn Island."

"It's not that far." Maeve pulls on Eoin's arm. "We could go there now!"

"And how do you suggest we get out there, Kaminski? Swim?"

"Isn't there a ferry or something?"

"Ferries don't go there."

"But I took one to this island. Can't we use the same one?"

"That's not how it works."

"Then we'll borrow one."

Eoin's eyebrows rise. "Do you know how to drive a boat?"

"No. Don't you?"

"Do I look like I know how to drive a boat?" In truth, Eoin looks like he's used to being driven, most likely in a big black SUV with tinted windows. "Do you see that water?" He points at the angry whitecaps between Inishglass and Cairn Island. "It'll eat us alive. And even *if* we made it, and that's a big if, where would we dock the boat?"

"But I have to go. It's on the list." She points to it.

"My suggestion: start with a safer activity, like knitting. At least that won't kill you." Maeve's shoulders slump at the sarcasm, and Eoin laughs. "Come on, Kaminski. I'll let you buy me another drink. Take a day to adjust. You can start on this list tomorrow."

Standing outside the Moorings, Maeve assesses this place that she had no clue existed, and that now runs her life. This island she never intended to visit, now her home for the foreseeable future. If she wants to clear her debt and get back to her life, her only choice is to settle in and work her way through this. And if that's the case . . .

Maeve opens her backpack and pulls out the stolen banner. "Hey, Asshole," she says. "I'm gonna need your help hanging this up."

9

Rohan G.
Yorkshire, England
6/20/2023

★★★★★

DING-DONG. There's a new dish in town and she's yummy.

Forget what you've heard about bland American food. This eye candy is so flavorful, your tongue will long for the taste even after you're done for the night. And don't gobble the whole meal in one bite. She's meant to be savored. If you're one of the lucky blokes who gets a seat at the bar, congratulations, mate. You just won the lottery. Too bad that's as close as you'll get to actually consuming this meal yourself. She's impossible to reach, but worth the try.

Long-short: Don't waste your time at the Thatch.
It's a sausage party over there. The best meal in
town is at the Moorings. She's worth a return trip
to Inishglass just for a second bite.

Hugh runs behind Briggs at the crack of dawn, panting and cursing the fact that, in a moment of weakness after a few pints—tips for Briggs that were handed off to Hugh—he asked his "much healthier and more-in-shape prick of a roommate" to train him.

Last year at the Annual Football Rounders Grudge Match, Hugh embarrassed himself when he was dragged off the field crying after tearing both quads. Having not sprinted since junior high, he had kicked the ball—barely making it to the pitcher's mound, though Briggs won't remind him of that—and taken off like a shot, his legs wholly unprepared. Not only was Hugh tagged out by Mary Kelly Shanahan, a seventy-year-old with bad eyesight and an artificial hip, but he then collapsed onto the field, midway to first base, hollering in pain, feeling like his muscles were torn from the bone and unable to move. Briggs had carried him to the sideline, where Aoife came to the rescue with ice to soothe his wounds and beer for his bruised ego.

The crowd loved it, and Briggs has made sure never to let Hugh live it down. Last night, Hugh realized the game was less than a month away and swore this year would be different. And since Briggs is only able to coach, relegated to the sidelines due to his broken heart, Hugh is even more determined not to make a complete ass of himself again.

"Tomorrow morning! Six o'clock!" Hugh announced with a slight slur as he marched up to bed. "Prepare yourself for spandex!"

Briggs leisurely bikes ahead of Hugh, laughing at his American friend whose legs are like logs, whose stomach is like a barrel with last night's beer still sloshing around inside as he tries to keep up.

"You're pedaling too fast." Hugh pants. "Slow way the hell down."

"If I go any slower, I'll fall over."

Briggs swerves the bike back and forth along the empty road lead-
ing into town, the chilly early-morning air perfect for a run. What he
wouldn't give to hop off the bike and race Hugh down the road, goading
him the entire way, but doctor's orders are doctor's orders, and as much
as Briggs wants to ignore his cardiologist, he can't. He was sure, when
he left Hugh sound asleep, that this morning's training session wouldn't
happen, but Hugh is here, indeed clad in spandex and sweating like
he's in a sauna.

"Did you read the new reviews?" Hugh prods. "Five in the past
three days."

He isn't talking about the Thatch, and he knows damn well that
Briggs has read the reviews. But Briggs has no interest in talking about
them, for two reasons. First, he can't talk about Maeve without feeling
giddy. It's a real problem. It's hard enough pretending that he's upset
with every person who asks about the damn stolen sign, when Maeve's
theft only made him like her more. Second problem: each new review
was written by a man. He'd be a hypocrite to complain, but inside he's
burning over it.

"We're not the only people she's impressed," Hugh says, wheezing.
"Not that I'd expect anything less. You'd have to be blind not to notice
her, and even then, she's got this awkward charm."

"It's called being a control freak." Briggs says it like an insult and
instantly wants to take it back. He will not be the boy who pushes his
crush on the playground. "She's gutsy, which can be appealing."

"Appealing?" Hugh says as he catches up. "That's one way to put it.
Have you thought about your revenge?"

"Revenge?"

"She stole our sign, Furphy! People expect a good retaliation."

Briggs has spent so much energy *not* thinking about Maeve that
he hasn't considered payback. He looks at his struggling roommate. It's
too damn early to be talking about this. Briggs needs coffee first. He
changes subjects. "Did you use a stick of butter to get those clothes on?"

"Don't body-shame me, Furphy. How far have we gone?"

Briggs checks his phone. "Barely a kilometer."

"That's it?" Hugh groans and falls back. "My calves are on fire, and my sweat tastes like Guinness."

"Whose fault is that?"

"Yours! I'm drinking for two, like a pregnant woman," Hugh complains. "And come on, man! You're supposed to help me."

"How would you like me to do that?"

"Distract me from running."

"How?"

"By talking about your feelings? Particularly toward an American hottie with an ass—"

"Enough!" Briggs takes out his phone and plays "Eye of the Tiger." "This is all the motivation you'll get from me today."

Hugh groans again, but after seven years of friendship, he knows when he's pushed a subject far enough.

They met in Australia, two travelers running from the past, Briggs from his grief over his father and Hugh from his failure, after just one year, out of Western Michigan University. He never should have been there in the first place, he confessed to Briggs, but after his seven sisters successfully graduated from college, he didn't want to let his parents down by *not* trying, so he forced his way out by failing every class except for Modern Dance.

Hugh couldn't face going home to his family's disappointment, so he took the leftover money he'd saved from a summer landscaping gig and bought a one-way ticket to Australia, where he was determined to find himself. He found Briggs instead, bartending at the Gaelic Club when Hugh came in for a job.

"Have you noticed how Aussies shorten every word? They're the tallest people in the world, with the shortest vocabulary," Hugh said, a few weeks into his bartending gig. "It's like they're either in a hurry or they don't give a shit about the English language, and they're like, 'Screw you. You want me to call it an avocado. Now, I'm calling it an avo. Breakfast is now brekkie. I'm defo gonna have a bikkie in the arvo after my smoko but before my tea. I hope I don't liquid laugh, but if I do, I'll take a sickie. No wukkas!' They're all a bunch of giant badasses. I swear I only understand fifty percent of what they're saying, but I'm too scared to ask, so I just pretend I know. What's a sky gator anyway?"

"Airplane," Briggs said. "You'll get the hang of it, mate."

"Yesterday, Tracie told me not to be such a drongo, and I was like, 'What does that mean,' and she said not to worry about it, so of course I looked up it up, and now everyone is calling me Drongo instead of Hugh. As if I need a reminder of what an idiot I am! I thought Australia would be easy for an American, but it turns out I suck at English, too! I'm a failure no matter where I go."

Briggs patted Hugh on the back as his head fell to the bar. "Cheer up, mate. At least she didn't call you a bogan."

"Why do they call you Furphy?"

"My surname's Murphy." Briggs turned from Hugh, but even then, Hugh knew when Briggs was hiding something.

"What does it mean?" he pressed. When Briggs wouldn't come out with it, Hugh went straight for guilt. "Help me out, man. I'm dying here."

"A furphy is a rumor. A story someone says is true, but no one believes."

"So why do they call you that?"

Briggs played it off casually. "When I first started here, someone told a story about me that no one believed."

"What was the story?"

"It was stupid." Briggs tried to walk away, but Hugh stepped in front of him, trapping him behind the bar. Briggs stepped back and cocked his head.

"Tell me," Hugh said.

"It's stupid."

"You already said that. But is it true?"

Briggs refused to answer. He wasn't the type to kiss and tell, even about pleasuring a particular girl eight times in one night. Hugh would have to inquire elsewhere, which he did. When he returned to the bar, he grabbed Briggs by the shoulders and yelled, in his face, "Eight times, Furphy! I didn't even think that was possible!"

For the next two years, they were the bartending duo of Drongo and Furphy, a local attraction in Sydney. Work long nights, sleep away the day, rinse and repeat, until Briggs couldn't take his guilt anymore. Peggy Murphy had encouraged him to take some time off after university, before coming back to Inishglass to run the Thatch, which Briggs had always planned to do. While he knew his mum would never directly ask him to come home, he felt the pressure mounting every month. Peggy, who was not an Inishglass native, had married into the Thatch, and though it may have become part of her legacy, she had still compromised to live on a small island, and Briggs knew it.

When he eventually told Hugh that he had to go home, Hugh said, "I've never been to Ireland before. Need a bartender?"

And that was that. Five years on the island, and Hugh has been the best friend Briggs never knew he needed. Looking back, he's not sure how he would have survived without Hugh.

"Fine, if you won't talk to me about Maeve," Hugh says, somehow keeping up his run, "I still have something to tell you, Furphy. I'm going home at the end of summer."

Shocked, Briggs turns, and the handlebars follow, throwing the bike off balance and tossing him to the ground.

Hugh slows to a halt. "Shit, man. Are you OK?"

He attempts to help his friend up, his calves start to cramp, and he falls next to Briggs, clutching his muscles and writhing in pain.

"This is why I don't work out!" he hollers. "My body rejects exercise! I can't do this!"

"You're just dehydrated." Briggs chuckles and hands Hugh the water bottle that spilled to the ground in the fall. "You're capable of more than you think, Drongo."

"If the bar is low, it's easy to jump over." Hugh dumps half the bottle on his sweaty head.

Hugh has always used excuses and humor to cover his insecurities, but when the man decides to dig down and really try, the sky's the limit. Briggs is confident in that. After all, Hugh dug in with Briggs, and the Thatch. Neither would be the same without him.

"You're really leaving? When did you decide this?"

"A few weeks ago. I didn't want to tell you right then because . . . you know . . . your heart and all. I thought you had enough on your plate." Hugh scoots closer to Briggs. "But my sister's getting married in September. I was planning to go home for the wedding, and then it hit me. I'm twenty-seven, Furphy. That's almost thirty. *Thirty*. Fuck, when my parents were thirty, they had three kids."

"Comparison is the thief of joy, mate. Isn't that what Aoife's always saying? You're not your parents."

"No, but I can't stay here bartending my whole life, either." Quickly he adds, "It's different for you. You *own* the pub. As much as I love being Diongo to your Furphy, you can't give me what I want for the rest of my life . . . like matrimonial love and biweekly orgasms. This is *your* family's legacy. Not mine. I've ridden your gravy train long enough."

"You know that's not how I see it."

"I know." Hugh twists a blade of grass between his fingers. "But if I'm honest, I've used our friendship to justify not making difficult decisions for my life, like what the hell I want to be when I grow up. And it turns out, at thirty, you're grown up. It's kind of now or never."

Hugh's confession hits Briggs between the eyes. Has he done the same? Used Hugh to justify not making difficult decisions? Briggs is older, not by much, but still. And yet, he never planned on a life of matrimonial bliss. As for orgasms . . . those aren't hard to come by.

"What are you going to do?" he asks.

"I've thought about it," Hugh says, "and I can't do a desk job. I like moving while I work." Briggs glares at Hugh's calves and cocks an eye. "Fuck you. Within reason. I reached out to a guy from my home-town who's an electrician. Apparently, the trades need young people. He promised me an apprenticeship after I take the classes and do some training. I can't believe I'm saying this about hard work, but . . . I'm excited about it."

Briggs pats him on the back. "As you should be, Drongo. You'll be grand. He's lucky to have you." The prospect of being alone in his house sits uncomfortably with Briggs, who's appreciated the noise of another person for five years, but this is the right move for Hugh. It was bound to happen. Briggs wasn't naive enough to think their lives would stay the same forever. Five years just went by so fast.

"What about you, Furphy?"

"What about me?"

"Even Batman considers a different life every now and then."

"The pub is my life."

"No," Hugh says. "It's *part* of your life."

"I can't leave, nor do I want to. This is my home."

"There's plenty you can do on the island without leaving home."

"And I do plenty."

Hugh shakes his head. "Don't I know it. Your house has thin walls. But I know you. Eventually, you won't be satisfied with a life of cold plunging, banging tourists, and pouring pints."

"It's worked so far." He stands and picks his bike off the ground.

Hugh follows, brushing dirt from his spandex. "What about your art?"

The question surprises Briggs. "What about it?"

"I don't know . . ." Hugh says sarcastically. "Maybe it's time to show it to people."

It's not a hobby Briggs shares with most. But four years ago, when he bought an old barn from a neighbor to refurbish into a studio, he came clean to Hugh. Now the place is littered in canvases, not that Briggs has ever considered showing them. He just likes painting. He has no interest in making money or being critiqued. That would take the joy out of it.

"No way," Briggs says. He gets on the bike and starts pedaling toward town.

Hugh groans and runs after him. "Why not?"

"My work isn't for mass consumption."

"But it's good."

"You have to say that, or I'll kick you out."

"When have I ever said anything that isn't true?"

As frustrating as Hugh's perpetual honesty can be, he has a point. "And where would I display it?"

Again, Hugh takes a mocking tone. "I don't know . . . maybe a place with walls where loads of people congregate on a daily basis and drink too much."

"The Thatch?" Briggs laughs at the idea of his artwork hanging in the pub.

"You own the place."

"I can't change it."

Hugh catches up to the bike, sweating again. "Why not?"

"People expect an Irish pub to look a certain way. It's best for business."

"You always say that, but that's bullshit, man."

Now in town, Briggs skids to a stop and steps off the bike. "What does that mean?"

Hugh clutches his side. "You know . . . exactly what . . . I mean. You're scared . . . *Damn it!* I hate running!"

Briggs wants to bite back at his friend, but the words get caught in his throat. Because it's true. God, he hates Hugh sometimes.

Hugh clasps Briggs on the back, using him as a prop to hold himself up. "Love is honesty, bro, and after all these years, you deserve nothing less, so here's the bottom line. You're a great guy."

"Thanks, mate."

"I'm not done yet. You're a great guy. There aren't many people out there like you."

"Thanks—"

"I'm not done!" Hugh takes a deep breath. "There aren't many people out there like you, which means the world deserves more from you. You're being selfish, keeping it to yourself. You think you're protecting people from suffering, but all you're really doing is depriving this shitty world of an A-plus person. You should be making lots of babies and raising them to be just like you. Isn't it better to leave the world better *because* you existed than leave it with nothing because you were too scared to love someone and actually make an impression on this spinning beach ball?"

"Did you rehearse this speech?"

"Maybe. Friends don't let friends piss away their life. How'd I do?"

Briggs bobs his head. "You could have stopped at 'You're a great guy,' and I would have liked it a lot better. And the earth is an oblate spheroid, not a perfect sphere."

"Piss off." Hugh slaps him on the shoulder. "Your heart condition isn't a death sentence. Have the surgery and move on. Share your artwork. Fall in love. And live happily ever after."

Briggs acknowledges the suggestion, but it's not that simple. Surgery or not, life isn't guaranteed to last. How can he make babies knowing that he might leave them without a father one day?

They're half a block from Mettā Café when Hugh says, "I need to carb load. Let's go to Aoife's and make her make us breakfast."

Briggs isn't hungry, but could go for a large coffee. He rests his bike against the building, next to a baby-blue e-bike cruiser, as Hugh opens the door.

Hugh gestures into the café. "Furphy first."

Briggs steps inside, expecting patrons and the delicious smell of coffee. Instead, he's confronted with sandalwood incense, wind-chiming spa music, and round cushions spread around the floor. He looks at his watch. It's six thirty. The café opens at seven.

Holy hell. Meditation class.

And sitting right there, practically at his feet, is Maeve.

When Briggs looks back for Hugh, he's disappeared . . . along with Briggs's bike.

10

When a girl emails her boss that she'll need the rest of the summer off to go to Ireland, that girl gets fired. In a single week, Maeve Kaminski has gained a pub and lost control of her life. And to top it off, on an island full of wool, there is only one knitting shop, aptly named Stitches and Bitches, which has been inconveniently closed for five days while the owners are away on holiday in Scotland, according to the sign.

So Maeve did what any logical twenty-four-year-old control freak would do. The first day, she bought cleaning supplies, a block of cheddar cheese, crackers, and ice cream, and threw herself a pity party. The next day, her fingers aching from scrubbing, she binged every season of *Bridgerton*. The following day, she couldn't stand herself anymore and decided to get to work. If knitting wasn't an option, she'd move down the list. She needs to build a winning kickball team. And the most logical place to find players . . . the Moorings.

For three days now, Maeve has tucked herself behind the bar, chatting up locals and tourists alike. And while she hasn't completed a single item on Liam's list, if she's being honest, the pub has been not only a great distraction from the garbage fire that is her life, but kind of fun, too. Maeve likes the social aspect of bartending, which is imperative since Sonya still hasn't called her back. Also, the story of her stealing the Thatch banner has made Maeve even more of a celebrity, especially now that it hangs proudly over the Moorings's door. To safeguard it from

Briggs, she brings it in every night and hides it under the bar, only to hoist it proudly again the next day.

Until yesterday, when Aoife texted her, Maeve hadn't thought about online reviews.

5 new reviews in a week! That might be a record! Aoife wrote.

Too intrigued, Maeve checked, and while she was embarrassed that a few mentioned or implied her specifically, she was also thrilled to be catching up to the Thatch. If all else is falling apart, at least she is gaining on Briggs.

Take that, Murphy!

The two women chatted back and forth. Aoife asked lots of questions. How was Maeve doing? Does she like being on the island? Has she adjusted to the time change? Does she need anything? Aoife shared, too. Apparently, she makes her own face and body oil, soaps, and bath salts out of seaweed she collects herself.

An ancient family tradition, she texted. Packed with vitamins, minerals, and plant magic!

Aoife intrigues Maeve, mostly because of her overwhelming kindness, but also because deep down, Maeve wishes she were into plant magic, beyond natural cleaning products.

Come to meditation tomorrow and I'll give you a bag of goodies.

Wanting to make a friend, Maeve said yes.

Which is why she has dragged herself out of bed after a late shift at the Moorings to sit on a cushion and try not to fall back asleep.

Maeve props the baby-blue e-bike outside of Mettā Café and races into the restaurant, worried she's late. On her way out the door, she ran into Ivy, who was out throwing a ball for her tireless black lab, Murray. They exchanged pleasantries, commenting on how early they were up and about. When Ivy threw the ball again, Maeve noted the distance, the impressive speed, the sheer athleticism . . . and she had an idea.

"I bet you could throw a ball clear across, say . . . a kickball pitch," Maeve suggested, which sparked a broad grin on Ivy's face.

"Indeed, I could."

"Is your leg as good as your arm?"

"Better," Ivy said. "I played football at university. You should see my instep kick."

With Ivy, the Moorings's kickball team is almost complete. As for one of the final positions, Maeve has a certain person in mind, but she'll need to be strategic in her approach.

The tables and chairs in the café have been pushed back along the walls to make space in the middle for round meditation cushions. They're lined up in neat rows, blankets underneath, like little relaxation pods on the floor. Incense burns in the corner, and mellow, spa-like music plays over the speakers. The crowd is bigger than Maeve thought it would be.

She tries to blend in and not draw attention to herself, especially because she's sweating slightly from the speedy bike ride. Having never been to a meditation class, Maeve dressed in leggings and an oversized Nirvana T-shirt, a proud vintage item from Maryann's younger years. She finished the outfit with her hot-pink Converse. Cute and comfortable, with just enough brightness to counter the black.

But as sweat drips down Maeve's cheek, Aoife approaches, looking like a hippie pixie in search of higher consciousness. Maeve herself looks like a drowned rat in a grunge-band concert souvenir, and she worries she might be in over her head. Thirty minutes alone with her wandering thoughts? Maeve has kept herself busy this past week so she can avoid doing just that. Add that her pores are spouting water like a drinking fountain and Maeve is now righteously nervous.

"You came!" Aoife says, bounding over to Maeve dressed in flowy black pants, white crop top, oversized cardigan, and multicolored beaded bracelets stacked on her wrist. She has a crystal hanging around her neck. No doubt she knows about auras and chakras. She's probably danced naked around a fire in some pagan ceremony and done ayahuasca. Whereas Maeve most recently ordered a folding board from Amazon so her garments are neatly put away in her drawer with as few wrinkles as possible. Maeve seriously considered packing it, but Sonya refused to let her.

"As promised!" Maeve manages a smile. "But looks like you might be full."

"Don't be silly. There's plenty of room." Aoife guides her to a nearby unclaimed cushion. "Take a seat here and we'll get started."

"But—"

Aoife is gone before Maeve can ask her how one meditates in the first place. She has no choice but to sit down and wing it. Not Maeve's strong suit. In fact, she's never even worn that kind of suit.

Sonya made her go to a yoga class once where the teacher encouraged them to make noise while they practiced. People moaned and exhaled loudly. At one point, someone wailed. Maeve, on the other hand, didn't make a sound, too worried it would be the wrong sound or done at the wrong time and people would stare at her. At one point, the teacher had them flop around to "release stuck energy." The students jumped, flapped their arms, and shook their heads, Sonya included, and Maeve just stood there watching them all move. She swayed a little, bobbed her head from side to side, but she wasn't about to let it all go. That is strictly reserved for when she's alone in her bedroom dancing.

Aoife asks everyone to find their cushions. Maeve takes a deep breath of the incense as she sits, then crosses her legs, uncrosses, recrosses.

Then right as Aoife says, "Welcome—" the café door bursts open, and all the students turn toward the noise. Briggs stands there, stoic, taking up the entire doorway. The sight of him actually steals Maeve's breath. Holy hell, even at the crack of dawn, dressed in joggers and a T-shirt, the man is stunning. A breeze blows through the door, and his fresh salty scent invades Maeve's whole being.

Aoife approaches him with a knowing twinkle in her eye and whispers, "What a surprise."

"Quite," he says quietly, with a tight, forced smile.

Aoife points to the cushion beside Maeve and shrugs. "Only seat left."

Briggs sneers and says, "No more bloody Sancerre for you."

"You wouldn't do that to me." Aoife blows off the threat like it's dust.

Briggs plops himself on the cushion. "Gah. You know I wouldn't."

Given the way he follows her instruction without pushback, and the intimate nature of their interaction, Maeve realizes that Briggs and Aoife are friends. Of course they are. They both grew up on the island. How did she not consider this before?

Maeve ties her sweaty hair into a topknot, actively ignoring Briggs and hoping that any smell she's producing is masked by the incense.

Briggs shifts around on his cushion, like a giant trying to get comfortable on a mushroom top. When his leg brushes Maeve's, she says, "Would you please stay in your designated space?"

"I can't help it. These blasted cushions aren't built for people my size."

Maeve rolls her eyes. "You just love excuses."

"It's the truth."

"Like you know what that is."

Aoife clears her throat at the front of the room. "If you two could please put your feelings aside for the duration of the class, that would be much appreciated."

"Sorry," they mumble together.

Maeve closes her eyes, adjusts her seat, and tries to ignore the overwhelming man next to her, whose body heat is slowly warming her own space and delightfully jumbling her stomach.

"By the way, I want my sign back," Briggs whispers.

"Absolutely not." Maeve sits up straighter, resolve on display.

"You know, I could have you arrested for stealing."

"I doubt the police care about a ten-dollar VistaPrint banner."

"I worked hard on that," Briggs groans.

Maeve turns toward him. "Well, I could sue you for false advertising."

"It's not false advertising."

Maeve gapes at him. "There was never a vote. You made it up!"

"I didn't need a vote. The reviews speak for themselves. The Thatch has a higher online rating than the Moorings. That's all the proof I need."

"Well, check again," Maeve says with a cocky smirk. "Because the evidence has shifted in my direction."

Briggs clenches his jaw and leans in closer. "Just give me back my sign."

She reciprocates, coming almost nose to nose with him. "You want it, Briggs Murphy? Come and get it!"

They sit, deadlocked, breathing heavily, their faces so close that Maeve can smell his toothpaste.

"Are you two done now?" Aoife asks.

They turn to find the entire room staring at them, wide-eyed, transfixed.

Aoife shrugs. "That's just what happens when you put a Doherty and a Murphy in the same class. Let me remind you that we're here to meditate, not fight. Now, can you two control yourselves until the end of class?"

The scene couldn't have been better scripted. Maeve can already imagine the chatter. By the time she gets to the pub this afternoon, news of this fight will be all over the island.

"Sorry, Eef," Briggs says, all warmth and charm. "We won't interrupt again."

Maeve shoots him an annoyed look. *He* started it. "Yeah, sorry. Not another word," she says, doing her best to sound remorseful, though really she liked fighting with Briggs. It was . . . fun. Invigorating. Maeve hasn't felt this revved in months.

They settle back onto their cushions, and Aoife starts the class with the chime of the tingsha bells. She instructs the students to sit with their backs straight but not rigid, upright but not forced. Eyes closed or hold a soft gaze. Then all they're supposed to do is breathe.

Maeve follows instructions, and for the first part of class, it goes well. She inhales and exhales and tries to ignore Briggs. Then about five minutes in, she gets antsy. Her toes tingle. Her stomach growls. Her nose itches. She loses concentration on her breathing. Her thoughts start to spin, and what she feared would happen happens. For a week, she's avoided reality, treating this whole excursion to Ireland like it's a play and she's just acting out a part. But what about her life in the States? Nothing on Liam's list has been accomplished yet. She's no closer to returning home than she was a week ago. And what if she loses the kickball game? What if she can't sell the pub? What if she can't pay off her debt and she's right back where she started, but *without* a job?

Maeve's breath picks up and becomes shallow. Anxiety swarms in her belly. Holy hell, she's going to have a panic attack in meditation class. How insulting to Aoife!

"Maeve," Briggs whispers. "Just breathe."

"I can't." She wheezes and shifts, pulling at the neck of her T-shirt. "I'm no good at this."

Briggs lays his hand on her leg. "You're OK. Just focus on my hand."

She tries, desperate for anything to stop the fear. She concentrates on the warmth of his skin, the size of his palm, each individual finger and where it rests on her thigh. She homes in so acutely that she swears she can feel his fingerprints.

"Good. Now just watch your thoughts come and go," Briggs offers. "Just let them be."

"Easier said than done," Maeve says.

"I know this is hard for you. You want to clean up your thoughts. But don't." His hand hasn't left her leg. His thumb gently moves back and forth on her thigh, soothing her. "Pretend they're a movie. Just watch what happens, like your mind is a theater and you're in the audience."

Maeve's thoughts continue to bounce, like a rock rolling down a hill and catching more momentum as it goes. But the second she starts to panic again, she focuses on Briggs's hand. It becomes her safe place. There she can relax and let her thoughts go instead of attempting to tame them. Gradually, she settles into the theater of her mind, watching as thoughts and images come and go. And then one daydream rises to capture her attention.

Maeve hasn't allowed herself to think much about their kiss, but with Briggs next to her, his hand on her thigh, he is the movie she turns on. She relives every detail. His tongue as it glided across her lower lip, teasing her mouth open. His hands, hungry for her body, lifting her closer to him, desperate to be devoured. And that was just a kiss. Maeve's mind drifts further, wondering, wandering, imagining the potential, until she's one big warm sensation, so wrapped up in the fantasy she barely hears Aoife ring the bell to end the meditation. Briggs takes his hand off her thigh, and Maeve's eyes fly open. The fantasy was so real, it was almost tangible.

"Are you OK?" Briggs asks. "You look flushed."

That was so not what you're supposed to do in meditation. With your enemy!

Maeve scrambles to her feet. "I have to go."

She bolts outside and jumps on her e-bike. She needs a shower. Preferably cold. She'll apologize to Aoife later, after she's calmed down. Maeve rides straight back to the eco-pod and promptly texts Eoin: What is long and hard that a Polish girl gets on her wedding night?

He replies right away: Please advise.

A new last name.

Why can't you borrow money from a leprechaun?

Maeve types back: Why?

Because they're always a little short.

If you were singing karaoke, what song would you pick?

Eoin's response comes back quickly: Wonderwall.
Maeve cringes. I need to schedule another meeting. Tomorrow 6 p.m. The Moorings. I hope you like potatoes.

Please tell me potato is code for something else.

Is that a yes?

How could I say no?

~

Stitches and Bitches is a complete mess. After this morning's meditation debacle, it's just what Maeve needs.

The store has multiple shelves of yarn, some organized by color, others mismatched and stuffed to the gills. Pattern books are displayed next to lotions and knickknacks. Off-putting headless mannequins model scarves and sweaters. There is no cohesive structure, and Maeve starts to hum at the potential, like when she walks into Maryann's disheveled closet.

The store is open but quiet at nine in the morning, which is perfect. Maeve doubts that Briggs frequents the place, which means it's another refuge. She pretends to shop, but then she can't take it anymore and starts deconstructing a display table: a bin of crocheted coasters, smelly candles, books, colorful yarn bags, fake felt-made flowers, pattern packets, and a basket of scrunchies. Nothing is displayed properly. It's like a poorly planned garage sale.

She clears the table and starts from scratch. Books as the centerpiece, stacked neatly, with one displayed on top. The bags become the backdrop, interspersed with the candles. She's organizing the scrunchies by color when a woman comes barreling in from the back of the store.

"What the hell are you doing?" she says in a thick New York accent. Her gray hair is cut bluntly, just above her chin. She looks to be about sixty, maybe sixty-five, and round in the hips.

"You're back," Maeve says, startled and excited. "How was Scotland?"

"I asked you a question first. What the hell are you doing?"

"Reorganizing the table. Do you like it?" Maeve asks hopefully.

"It was fine the way it was. Put it back."

"But now people can see exactly what you're selling."

"Are you telling me how to run my shop?"

"No! I just thought I'd help."

"We don't need help." The woman examines the table. "What happened to the flowers?"

"I thought they went better over here." Maeve gestures to the checkout counter.

"Well, they don't."

"Trust me. I'm good at this kind of thing. You should see my mom's pantry. It's color coordinated."

"Something is very wrong with you," the woman says, pointing a finger in Maeve's face.

"I'm aware."

Another woman emerges from the back and says, "Barb, how many times have I told you not to be such a bitch? You scare people away."

Barb calls over her shoulder. "I named this place Stitches and Bitches, Linda. It's not false advertising. People know precisely what they're getting."

Linda looks at Maeve apologetically. "I'm sorry. Something happens to women when they turn sixty."

"Yeah," Barb says. "They stop giving a shit. You should try it."

"I'm not sixty yet." Linda's accent matches Barb's. Her long black hair is highlighted with heavy streaks of gray. She gives Barb a smartass grin.

"Maybe just give a few more . . . shits," Maeve offers gently. "Since this is a store, and you want to sell things." To make her point, she walks to another display table that resembles the bric-a-brac section of a Goodwill. "Most people don't want to hunt through clutter, so each display should play into the others. Put a sweater next to a book about knitting sweaters, next to candles that smell like evergreen trees and campfires. Then people will buy all three."

"So my store is a goddamn mess," Barb says. "Is that what you're saying?"

"No!" Maeve backtracks, remembering that this woman might be the only person who can teach her to knit. "I just got carried away. It felt good to fix something. I'm sorry."

Barb raises her hand. "Don't say sorry. Women apologize too much."

Linda throws her hands up. "Jesus, Barb. You're confusing the girl. First, you're yelling at her, now you're giving her a feminist empowerment speech."

"It's my fault," Maeve says. "I shouldn't have touched the table."

"The girl has a point, Barb. This place looks like my grandmother's basement. We could use her help."

"Really?" Maeve says. "I'd be happy to."

Barb isn't convinced. "Aren't you a tourist?"

"Not exactly," Maeve offers.

Recognition dawns on Barb's face, and she points a wagging finger at Maeve. "Liam Doherty's daughter. I heard you were in town."

Maeve is unsure whether Barb is happy about that. She could be Team Murphy, after all.

"If I let you help around the store, what do you want in return?" Barb asks.

"Could you be more cynical?" Linda says.

"I'm a New Yorker," Barb counters. "I know better than to think anyone does anything out of the goodness of their heart."

"I thought we moved here to increase our faith in humanity."

"*You* moved here to do that," Barb says. "I moved here because I can't live without you." It's an oddly sweet moment, despite Barb's jackhammer tone. "So what do you want, Doherty?"

"My last name is Kaminski. And actually—"

"I knew it!" Barb throws her hands up.

"I need to learn to knit," Maeve says. "An Aran cable scarf, to be exact."

Barb's gaze narrows. "Aran cable?"

"Yes."

"Have you ever knit before?"

"Never."

"That's a difficult stitch for a beginner. Too bad I don't offer private lessons to strangers," Barb says. "YouTube it."

"Barb!" Linda scolds.

"Store policy," Barb states, crossing her arms.

Maeve offers her most endearing smile. "Well, maybe I could become . . . not a stranger, if you let me fix up the store. We could get to know each other."

"It's not a bad idea," Linda says.

Barb assesses Maeve from head to toe. "I had cancer, you know." She reaches into her shirt, pulls out her breasts, and puts them in Maeve's hands. Once her shock dwindles, Maeve realizes she's holding prostheses. "Double mastectomy. Three years ago. Go ahead. Check them out."

"It's like the early eighties again. Everyone in town has felt your boobs," Linda says with another eye roll. "And you wonder why I wouldn't commit to you back then."

"I was drunk for the entirety of the eighties."

"A slutty drunk. There wasn't a girl in Hoboken you didn't sleep with."

"Nor a bump of coke I didn't snort." Barb gestures around the room. "Now I'm a sober, monogamous yarn-store owner in Ireland. Go figure."

"Put your boobs away," Linda says. "You're making the girl uncomfortable."

Barb grabs them and shoves them back into her shirt. "Just don't get in anyone's way."

Maeve perks up. "You mean I can—"

"Yeah, yeah, you can organize the store." Barb starts collecting items from different shelves. "But you don't get any freebies." She hands a load of knitting supplies to Maeve and a bag to put them in. "These will get you started."

"So you'll teach me?"

"Not yet. I still don't know you. But best to be prepared." She rings up Maeve's items and gestures to the felt flowers that Maeve moved next to the register. "They look good here."

"I won't disappoint you. I promise."

As Maeve is about to leave, Barb offers a last piece of advice. "You need one more thing to knit, Maeve."

"What?" She looks around the store.

"Courage," Barb says, in all seriousness. "If knitting were easy, we'd all make our own clothes."

"Poetic," Linda says.

"Well, you didn't marry me because I'm Yeats."

"No," Linda says. "Yeats had a way with words. You're much more talented with your mouth."

Maeve leaves feeling accomplished, one step closer to completing Liam's list. She heads to the Moorings. She has an idea and wants to get started on it right away. But when she shows up, the red door is unlocked. She tentatively steps inside, offering a bashful "Hello?" She flips on the lights and gasps. The place is covered in toilet paper. It's a disaster zone, and Maeve can't help but chuckle. Then she remembers the banner and races behind the bar.

It's gone.

She takes pictures of the toilet paper as evidence, which she plans to show every patron who enters the pub. Then she puts her earbuds in and spends the next two hours cleaning. Most people would be furious. Most people would curse the vandal who did this. Maeve can't help but smile.

Briggs gave her a mess to clean. And it's exactly what she needed.

~

The next night Eoin walks into the pub, shakes rain from his jacket, and looks around for Maeve. "What happened to the banner, Kaminski? Lost it already?"

She won't deign to answer, knowing everyone in town is buzzing about the sign being back outside the Thatch, in plain view.

"'Wonderwall'? Seriously, Asshole?" she says from behind the bar. He's five minutes late, but she lets it slide. "I saved you a stool."

Eoin takes his perch. "What's wrong with that song? Oasis is classic."

"What isn't wrong with it?" Only an egomaniac with delusions of grandeur would pick one of the most overplayed karaoke songs. And nobody except the Gallagher brothers can sing it. So either Eoin thinks he's as good as the Gallaghers, which Maeve highly doubts, or he picked the song because he secretly thinks he's above everyone. And while Eoin can be charmingly arrogant and overtly sexual, it's always seemed in good humor to Maeve, not complete self-interest. "Wonderwall" just seems out of character. But then again, maybe she has him pegged wrong. She's made mistakes with men before.

"Did you plan this meeting just to insult my karaoke pick?"

She hands him an old-fashioned. "Why did you leave London?"

"Why do you care, Kaminski?"

"Isn't that what friends do? They care about each other?"

"Friends?" Eoin takes a sip of his drink. "That's a term we haven't used before."

"Well, maybe we should."

Eoin regards Maeve intensely with his piercing eyes. He'd be intimidating if he weren't on her side. "Fine. I left London because of a girl." He crosses his arms over his chest and sits back. "There. I said it."

"What happened?"

"Classic story. We fell in love. She broke my heart. Left me for another bloke. After that, the city wasn't the same." He takes another gulp. "So I left, heartbroken, and went back to Cork. I just wanted to be someplace familiar. Satisfied?"

Maeve comes around the bar and, without thinking, hugs Eoin, a move that startles them both. His expensive cologne smells good as she presses her nose into his shoulder. Eoin isn't soft. His chest is solid, his arms strong. Like hugging a statue. It's the opposite of Briggs, who, while just as strong, sort of melted around Maeve. When he placed his hand on her thigh during meditation, it was heavy but soft, like a weighted blanket. Eoin is more like a boulder. When Maeve realizes she's comparing the two men, she immediately stops the hug, blushing.

"What was that for?" Eoin asks.

"I'm Midwestern. We hug."

Eoin lifts his glass. "I'm Irish. We drink and hide our emotions with sarcasm and dark humor."

Maeve chuckles. "At least we know who we are."

Eoin whispers, "Are you sure about that, Kaminski? You look pretty damn natural behind that bar."

"Really?" And then almost straightaway, Maeve wants to take it back. Because it doesn't matter. No matter how much fun she's had, she's not staying here. She can't. "Don't answer that." She goes back behind the bar and takes a few orders, filling pints, making drinks, and chatting up customers.

When she gets back to Eoin, his drink is empty and he's perusing the menu. "So, what are you buying me tonight?"

Maeve leans her elbows on the bar. "How about a new item we're testing out." Eoin sets down the menu, intrigued. The idea hit Maeve earlier in the week, when she was texting with Aoife. She *does* have an old family tradition, it's just not Irish. But luckily the main ingredient is in abundance here. "I figured I'd throw the competition for a loop. It doesn't make sense for both pubs to serve the same Irish food. Let's give customers something they can only get here."

"Spoken like a proper business owner." Eoin leans in. "Are you sure you haven't changed your mind, Kaminski? Because I've been doing some work on that front. I have a mate in London who works for a restaurant conglomerate. I reached out to him, and he's intrigued. But I don't want to string him along if you're not in."

"No," Maeve says. Unfortunately, she cannot change her mind about selling. One week of fun doesn't justify turning one's life upside down, especially when fifteen thousand dollars of debt hangs over her head. "I haven't changed my mind."

"Good." Eoin hands his empty glass to Maeve for a refill. "Now what's this new item?"

She stands up tall. "I think you're gonna like it."

~

"Fecking hell. Those are brilliant." Eoin doesn't just eat his entire portion of pierogi. He demolishes them and practically licks the plate. He leans back in his seat and rests his hands on his stomach. "Where did you learn to make that culinary orgasm?"

The pierogi recipe is Maeve's grandma's, passed down from generation to generation. Maeve describes her grandparents' small brick house in Portage Park, with its cement stoop, small backyard, and the rickety old metal swing set they bought when she was born. "I have such a vivid image of Babcia standing at the stove, apron on, covered in flour, trying to get me to pay attention to her cooking, when all I wanted to do was clean up."

"You obviously absorbed something. Your granny would be proud."

Maeve beams, knowing her grandma would get a kick out of her pierogi being on the menu at any restaurant. Too bad she can't tell her, seeing as no one in her family knows she's in Ireland.

She makes Eoin another drink and hands it to him. "What about you?" she asks. "What's your family like?"

"Parents are divorced. Mum lives in Dublin by my sister and her kids. Da moved to Portugal years ago and lives there with his new wife and kids. I'm the only one still in the area."

"Does that bother you about your dad?"

"That he abandoned his wife and kids and started a new life with a younger woman?" Eoin gives a sly grin. "No. Completely fine with it. Haven't spent years in therapy unwinding my daddy issues."

Maeve chuckles. "At least I'm not the only one with daddy issues."

"You are a unique, beautiful butterfly, but . . . harsh reality, Kaminski—everyone has some kind of family drama or trauma."

"Harsh reality?" she repeats. Maeve hadn't considered that Briggs and Eoin might know each other. They might even be . . . friends. But Eoin would have mentioned that, right? Plus, he hasn't said anything about going to the Thatch. People on this island pick sides, at least for the summer, and he's undoubtedly on hers. She doesn't notice she's staring at the dartboard until Eoin interrupts her reverie.

"Please tell me you're not into bar games, Kaminski."

"I'm Midwestern. We love bar games."

"And hugs, apparently." Eoin gets a naughty glimmer in his eyes.

Maeve ignores it. "You're so competitive, I thought you'd love a good game."

"True," Eoin agrees. "I just prefer more of a challenge."

"Like, I don't know . . ." Maeve shrugs and feigns innocence. "Pitching in a kickball game?"

Eoin clicks his tongue. "So the pierogi were just a coercion tactic. Well played, Kaminski."

"So you'll do it?"

"I don't know . . ."

"Please, Asshole," she begs, leaning toward him on the bar.

"If you want a favor, it usually comes with a price."

Maeve groans. "Can't you do this pro bono?"

"Sorry. I don't do that kind of work."

"Isn't the glory of winning enough? I need a strong pitcher if I'm gonna beat Briggs."

Eoin stiffens, a sudden sense of iciness rolling off his skin. So she was right. They aren't friends after all.

"You've met Briggs, eh?" he asks. "What'd you think of him?"

Maeve plays it cool, not only for Eoin but for the rest of the ears that might be listening. "Just what I expected. An arrogant liar who's only out for himself and his pub."

Eoin narrows an intimidating eye on Maeve, as if searching for a lie. He shifts and leans in close, gesturing for Maeve to do the same. "Listen to me, Kaminski," he says softly. "If Briggs ever finds out you want to sell the Moorings, he'll turn the whole island against you. Take it from me. He's ruined lives before, and he'll do it again."

"You sound like you know from personal experience."

"Just trust me. Stay away from him." Eoin sits back, his casual demeanor returned. "I'll play on your stupid team. Time the Murphys know what it feels like to lose." He stands and slings on his raincoat. "And put the pierogi on the menu. They're a sure hit. Boosted revenue always looks good."

"Thank you," Maeve says, relieved.

Eoin slugs back the rest of his drink and sets the glass on the bar. "Just remember, if something happens, you're the one who wanted me on your team."

She rolls her eyes dramatically. "It's a kickball game. What could go wrong?"

"Have you learned nothing over the past week?"

11

Forget his heart problem, Briggs has clearly lost his goddamn mind. What person leaves a mess as a thoughtful gesture? Or flirts with a woman by toilet-papering her pub? An idiot. That's who.

Within a week, the man who knew all the right moves with women now only makes the wrong ones. No wonder Maeve ran out of Aoife's class so quickly, leaving behind her sweet scent and a perfect print of her ass on the meditation pillow.

He never should have put his hand on her thigh. He knew it was risky, and if his damn mind had been working, he never would have done it. But sitting there, it was all thoughts of her, and when her anxiety ratcheted, he felt it. He couldn't just let her struggle. He had to *do* something. But holy hell, if touching her didn't super-charge his body. He is no stranger to physical contact, but this was next level. So simple and yet so powerful.

It's not like Briggs doesn't know that kind of magnetic connection exists. He saw it with his parents. He just never thought he'd experience it. In fact, he was determined not to, hence his current frustration. Not only is he an idiot, he's an idiot who can't rid himself of this crush.

Briggs stands in front of an empty canvas, staring, with no idea what to paint. Art has always been his release, a way to settle his mind. But he can't find that space when his whole body wants Maeve. And it goes well beyond carnal attraction. Sure, he's dying to see Maeve naked. To touch her in just the right way, to make her quiver. But it's the laughing and banter and fighting, too. The Murphy-Doherty feud has always been an act that Briggs puts up with for the sake of the island, but with Maeve to spar with, he actually looks forward to it.

Which is why it's so concerning that, five days after he stole back the banner and toilet-papered her pub, she's done nothing. Every day he sees that damn banner at the Thatch, Briggs grows more worried. The toilet-paper mess was a mistake, and every day that Maeve doesn't retaliate, he regrets it more.

Briggs paces his studio, shaking his hands out at his sides, chiding himself.

When he bought the barn four years ago, he spent a year fixing it up, replacing rotted boards, insulating the walls, cleaning, and adding electrical, Wi-Fi, and a new coat of paint. The studio still smells slightly of farm animals and gasoline, but it looks like an artist's living room, with a large oriental rug, wood-burning stove, hand-me-down couch, chairs, table, speakers, and an espresso machine. One wall displays a giant collage: a poster of the Beatles' *Abbey Road*, an article from the *Irish Times* about the rivalry between the Thatch and the Moorings, a picture of Hugh and Briggs behind the bar in Australia, and images by other artists who inspire him—Rothko, Van Gogh, Richter, Matisse, Klimt—all covered in rainbow speckles of acrylic paint. On that wall he tacks his works in progress. When he finishes one, he builds a custom wooden frame for it. Art isn't just about the image, Briggs knows. It's the process, creating the entire piece, over time, down to the placement of staples.

Peggy Murphy introduced Briggs to art. She moved to Inishglass from Cork, a concession made when she married the love of her life. But deep down, Briggs's mother has always been a city girl. At every opportunity—school breaks, quiet winter months—she'd scrape together what she could and take the family to Paris, London, Barcelona, Vienna, Budapest, Florence, even New York. But it was in Amsterdam, at the Van Gogh Museum, where Briggs fell in love with art. Van Gogh's painted emotions, his vibrant yet tortured self-portraits, how he captured not just landscapes but the *feel* of a cold winter day. Peggy had to drag Briggs out of the place. He saw Klimt in Vienna and Matisse at the Met. Everywhere they went he ingested as much art as he could, until one birthday Peggy bought him his own supplies. Briggs resisted at first, claiming to be a viewer and not a creator. But the longer the supplies sat in his bedroom, the more they taunted him, until one day he splattered some paint on a canvas. The adrenaline rush was better than anything he'd experienced on a football pitch. Anxiety and passion blended, part torture, part ecstasy. He had to fight the demon in his brain that told him he was shit. He had to be willing to mess up, only to start over, undaunted. He had to trust when a piece was done.

Painting was what Briggs had missed most in Australia. He took some supplies with him, just a few brushes, a small set of acrylics, and blank postcards. These he'd painted and sent to Peggy, who has them framed and hanging in her new house in Cork. But when Briggs returned to the island, he wanted a proper studio. Hugh suggested one of the rooms in the house, but Briggs couldn't do it. Nothing has changed in his parents' house since he grew up there. Peggy took a lot of personal items with her to Cork, but what was left he can't seem to get rid of. So he can't stay in his parents' bedroom, the largest, and instead opts for his childhood bedroom. Hugh has Briggs's sister Isla's old room, still painted pink. And yet, while Briggs hasn't succeeded in making the house fully his own, selling it would feel like betrayal. So it stays, just as it is.

The freedom he needed to paint wasn't available at the house, so Briggs bought the barn. Some days, he wishes he lived here. Occasionally he opts for the barn couch instead of his bed at home.

He stands back, hands linked behind his head, and stares in frustration. His attention drifts to the bottom corner of the collage wall, to the last Murphy family photo before Joe died. The family is posed in the living room, wearing paper crowns from Christmas crackers. Joe had set a timer on the camera and raced back to get into position, but no one knew when exactly the photo would take. Isla was seven, sitting on

Briggs's lap, hitting him over the head as he tickled her, cringing from her blows. Joe is kissing Peggy on the temple, and Peggy is yelling at Isla not to hit her brother. Cecelia, who is two years older than Briggs and was at university going through an existential crisis at the time, is off in the corner, thoroughly annoyed, bright pink paper crown crooked on her angry blue hair. Joe took one look at the photo and called it "perfect." He sent it out as a "Happy New Year!" card to all their friends the next week. It was the last year that a card would go out with the whole family on it.

Of all the art Briggs has seen and made, that imperfect-perfect photo is his favorite masterpiece.

A knock on the barn door relieves Briggs from his thoughts. He sets the paintbrush down and answers the door.

It's Aoife, holding a tray of scones. "It's been five days," she says.

Briggs blocks the doorway with his arm. Aoife rolls her eyes and dodges underneath before he can stop her. "Five days since what?"

"Since you've responded to my texts. You're ghosting me, Briggs Murphy."

"Clearly not, seeing as you're standing in front of me right now."

"You know what I mean."

"That's what happens when your best friends trick you. I'm protesting."

"That's why I brought a peace offering." Aoife sets the scones down on the table and heaves herself onto the couch.

"You and Hugh set me up, Eef."

"You make it sound like we did something bad, when I know you enjoyed it. Now make me an espresso. I'm exhausted. Is it busier this year? I swear it wasn't this crowded last June."

Briggs groans, but he can't refuse Aoife, so he starts the coffee machine. "We had the same conversation last year. And the year before that." He takes the small container of milk from the minifridge and warms it, just how Aoife likes it.

"It's going to be total madness for the football rounders game. I'm not going to get a wink of sleep that week."

"If this is you trying to get out of playing, tough shit. After what you pulled, you owe me." Briggs hands her the steaming mug and grabs a scone. He takes a bite. Of course, Aoife brought strawberry and cream—his favorite. "Damn it," he says with his mouth full. "Un-fecking-fair. You know me too well."

"I knew you'd forgive me." Aoife smiles and sips her coffee.

If Hugh knows the general outline of Briggs, Aoife could write the Wikipedia page. Hugh would say Briggs has big feet; Aoife knows the size. Hugh knows that Briggs paints; Aoife would say that his work leans toward impressionism, using mostly acrylic paint, but sometimes he changes things up with watercolors or spray paint. She's perceptive. She catalogs information for later. She's a woman.

"Have you ever had pierogi?" she asks Briggs.

He cocks an eyebrow at her. "Why?"

"That's all I've heard about this week. Apparently, they're the hot new menu item at the Moorings. They can't keep them in stock. They've sold out the past two days. *Before* dinner."

Briggs perks up. For all of Aoife's talk about how busy things are, the past two days at the Thatch have been oddly slow during lunchtime.

"It must be her, right?" Aoife says. "I know we think of her as a Doherty, but her last name is Kaminski. That's Polish."

So maybe Maeve *is* retaliating. She's changed the game on him. And bloody hell, if it doesn't make him happy. His chest might burst. But this poses a new problem. Maybe she did like the toilet-paper mess. Maybe he wasn't out of line when he touched her. Maybe . . .

He stops his thoughts. No matter which way he slices it, Maeve Kaminski is a problem. End of story.

"Do you think she's staying after all?" Aoife asks.

Briggs rests back in the chair, attempting to keep composure. "It's none of my business."

"Like hell it isn't! It's all our business!"

"The girl can do what she wants. We'll find a way to survive."

"Will we?" Aoife shoots daggers at Briggs. "You're telling me you'll be just fine if she up and disappears one day. You won't care at all?"

"We'll figure it out," he says coolly.

"Oh, just admit it! You like her!"

But Briggs will not concede that easily. "So? It's no secret I like women."

"Will you stop being so stubborn?" Exasperated, Aoife sets her mug down with a thump. "You're not your father, Briggs. You're not going to die like he did."

Even after all the work he's done to come to terms with Joe Murphy's death, the image of his lifeless father, a man whose mere presence had once filled a room to capacity, will never leave Briggs. From the time he was little, he was Joe's spitting image, a smaller version of a man larger than life. They walked the same. Talked the same. Hell, Briggs's habit of skipping the bottom step for luck felt practically innate.

"Have you considered," he challenges Aoife, "that liking Maeve causes a wee bit of a problem for everyone on the island? It's kind of important that we remain mortal enemies."

"So we create a new story." Aoife brightens. "A better one. What if Romeo and Juliet had a happily ever after? People would eat that up."

"It's not that easy."

"Yes, it is," Aoife presses.

"No, it's not!" Briggs hates that he raises his voice, but now everything he's locked inside himself since Maeve arrived comes spewing out. "Happily ever after? That's bullshit, Eef. My parents sure as hell didn't have one. My mum could barely get out of bed for months after my father died. You call that happy? Sometimes walking away *is* an act of love. Have you considered that?"

He takes a breath, relieved to have that off his chest. Briggs has thought over the situation like an algebra problem, always coming to the same answer. Pleasure only lasts so long. Pain lingers longer. Now, maybe Aoife and Hugh will stop sticking their noses in his business and leave him the hell alone.

"I admire you, Briggs," Aoife says, standing. "You've always been on the right side of the story. Never the villain. But you might be the biggest fecking eejit I've ever met. I've let this stupid crusade of yours go on for too bloody long. I should have nipped it in the bud years ago, but it never mattered. Until now. What the hell is wrong with you? Thinking you have power over someone's suffering isn't only arrogant, it's fecking insulting. I hate to break it to you, but people will be bloody sad. That's just life. Refusing to love isn't going to change it. It's only going to make it harder." She points at him. "You want the harsh reality? You're scared. That's why you haven't scheduled your surgery. That's why you're pushing Maeve away. Fate isn't to blame. You are. If your da had the opportunity to change his fate, he sure as hell would have taken it, even with the risks. You want to honor the man? Make him proud? Love someone, like he did. Joe wouldn't have pushed his feelings away. He would have held on with all his might, and not because love is some magical elixir that takes the pain away, but because love makes pain worth it. Happily ever after doesn't mean you won't suffer. It means you'll find a way to endure it. Your mum would marry your da again, even knowing his fate."

Aoife's words are a gut punch. Briggs wants to yell at her for conjuring his dead father and using the man against him, but he . . . can't. It's the truth, and it hits him square in the chest, right through his broken heart. He exhales, shaking his head, "I just   don't know what to do, Eef."

"I'll tell you what you do," she says. "You *try*. Because if you let her go, I promise, someone else will have her."

The thought of that tightens his hands into fists. "I hate when you're right."

"I'm always right." Aoife loops her arm around him.

They stand in front of the collage wall that Briggs has always considered his greatest masterpiece. When he dies, people will see this wall, more than any of his other paintings, and know the man who made it. But lately, it's felt like there's an important piece missing.

"Thanks for kicking the emotional shit out of me," Briggs says. "I needed it."

"You saved me once, remember? It's only right I repay the debt by saving you from your stupid-arse self now."

Briggs isn't sure this feels like saving—more like Aoife dropping him out at sea and telling him to swim to shore. "I didn't save you," Briggs says. "I did what any person would do for a friend in need."

"And I'm forever grateful." Aoife grabs him by the shoulders and turns him to face her. "Which is why I've waited to tell you something else I found out. Just remember to breathe."

A waterfall of tension rolls down Briggs's spine. "What is it?"

"You're already breathing hard."

"Just spit it out, Eef."

She holds his gaze. "It's not just a coincidence that Eoin came back to the island right after Liam Doherty died. He's handling Liam's estate."

"Why would Liam do that?"

"No one knows. But now it's in Eoin's hands."

Briggs starts to pace, working through this new information. How could he have been so stupid? So blind? He thought if he just ignored that bottom feeder, Eoin O'Connor would eventually disappear, like he always has, but apparently nothing about the man has changed. Cunning moves, expertly hidden under overt charm. Eoin's always been this way, ever since they were little. In primary school he'd tape "spank me" signs on kids' butts or lay plastic wrap across the toilet in the teachers' bathroom or glue a quid to the ground and just watch people try to pick it up. All harmless, back then. Funny even. But in secondary school, Eoin was the one whispering nasty comments under his breath during a football match to raze the other team. He cheated on tests and girlfriends. Briggs still saw it as funny or inconsequential, fooled by Eoin's freewheeling charm and breezy demeanor. Until Aoife. After what Eoin did to her, Briggs saw him for the selfish dick he really was, willing to do anything, hurt anyone, for his own benefit. A classic narcissist, he'll create havoc for Maeve and convince her it's her fault, then leave her high and dry.

"Damn it." Briggs clasps his hands behind his head, attempting to breathe like Aoife instructed. If he warns Maeve about Eoin, it'll appear suspicious. For all she knows, Eoin's helping her. Who's to say she'd even listen to Briggs? Eoin could spin it as just another Murphy trick.

"Have you seen Maeve today?" he asks Aoife.

"She's probably at the knitting shop. She goes there every morning, right at nine. That woman keeps a strict schedule. It's impressive."

Briggs grabs his car keys, his blank canvas forgotten. "Thanks, Eef."

She shrugs. "I've been waiting ten years for this. Now, Briggs Murphy, we're finally even."

12

Sonya finally calls as Maeve is almost to Stitches and Bitches. She leaps off her bike, tossing it on the ground, and answers her FaceTime, out of breath. Just seeing her best friend's face—her long black hair, brown eyes, the scar on the top of her forehead from falling off the monkey bars in elementary school—gives Maeve an ache of homesickness she hasn't felt much in recent days, probably due to how busy she's been at the pub.

"I'm apologizing now if we get cut off. The reception on this island is—"

Sonya's raspy voice cuts Maeve off. "Mae, I'm in love."

Not the words Maeve was expecting. She leans on the outside of the building, panting. "With who?"

Wherever Sonya is, it's not their apartment in Lakeview, with its constantly dripping faucet, cracked paint, and mismatched but well-organized decor. This place is high-end, something Eoin would like.

Sonya brings the phone closer to her face. "OK. Don't kill me."

"Why would I do that?"

"Because . . ." Sonya pauses. "It's Melanie."

Maeve is so confused, she blanks on who Melanie is. And then it registers, and she blurts, "You're in love with Melanie Kingston?!"

Sonya glances around. "Keep it down. She's sleeping."

None of this makes sense. Maeve must be hallucinating. She wants to grab Sonya's face through the phone and make her explain. "But

Melanie's not gay!" Sonya cannot be in love with the mean girl they couldn't stand in high school. Melanie made everyone's life miserable, and she took pleasure in it. How the hell did this happen?

"I assure you, Mae. She very much is. She just wasn't out in high school because she knew her mom would capitalize on having a queer kid. Make a big deal on social media and use it to her advantage for her business. So Melanie played straight."

"More like played bitch."

"Please don't call her that, Mae. You know people do extreme things when they have to deny who they are. But she's not mean like we thought. She's . . . wonderful. She asked me out because she's had a crush on me since high school. Can you believe that? *High school.*"

Maeve cannot believe *anything* coming out of her best friend's mouth. "Was she flirting when she called you a Paki?"

"She didn't mean it." Sonya's voice rises and she catches herself, lowering it to a whisper. "She was angry because I was out, and she couldn't be. So she took it out on me."

"By *hurting* you." Maeve still can't believe what she's hearing.

"She's different. You have to trust me." Sonya then tells how they talked for hours, about everything, at brunch recently. Melanie apologized, explained, begged Sonya's forgiveness. Next thing she knew, they were back at Melanie's house, having the most amazing, intimate sex she'd ever had. They've spent every day together since.

"Is this why you haven't called me in almost two weeks?"

"I wanted to tell you in person. I thought you'd be home by now. And I didn't want to stress you out while you were dealing with . . . everything. It felt unfair to rub my happiness in your face when you're struggling with so much."

This gives Maeve pause. *Has* she been struggling? She's been busy, but she's also had more fun since she got to Ireland than all of last year.

"I'm telling you, Mae. When I'm not with Melanie, it physically hurts. I mean, that's love, right?"

"It's hardly been two weeks. People don't fall in love that fast."

"I wasn't aware there was a timeline," Sonya snaps.

"Fine. Maybe there isn't. But how do you know you can trust her?"

"I just know I can."

"Melanie could be lying about all of this. She could just be using you. Last time we saw her, she was a real-life Regina George, but she never got hit by a bus."

"I can't believe you, Mae. After all the months I spent supporting you after Spencer. Staying home every weekend. Giving up my life so you didn't feel so shitty about yours."

"I'm just trying to protect you," Maeve pleads.

"No, you're not," Sonya states. "This isn't about me. You're doing this because of Spencer. You got screwed over, and you want the same to happen to me so you won't feel so shitty. So you're not alone. You're just jealous."

"Jealous?" Maeve can't believe that just came out of Sonya's mouth.

"Yeah. Jealous. I'm in love with someone who accepts me for who I am, who I can be completely myself with, who I trust, and you can't have that because you're too scared to let anyone that close to you. To see the real you. Hell, you love karaoke and yet you won't even get up and sing because you're scared of what people will think."

"I can't believe you'd throw that in my face!"

"Perfection doesn't beget love, Mae. Honesty does. Spencer may be a fucking asshole, but don't kid yourself. You never let him in. He never knew the real you because you wouldn't show him. Your relationship was doomed from the start. You may want to hide in your room and dance for no one, but I don't. I'd rather risk getting laughed at. Or getting hurt. At least I know I tried. It's better than ending up alone with only my regrets."

Maeve can barely breathe.

Sonya rubs her face. "Look, I'm tired. I need to go back to bed."

"Back to Melanie?" Maeve snaps.

"After all these years of friendship, can't you just trust that I'm making the right decision and support me? I thought you'd be happy for me, Mae. All I want for you is love. Real love. It might not be pretty and perfect all the time, but it's honest, and that makes it worth the ugly parts. Can't you want that for me, too?" But Maeve can't say it. She can't say anything, even when Sonya's bottom lip starts to quiver. "Fine. Whatever. I just wanted to tell you I'm moving out."

"What?"

"Melanie asked me to move in with her. I'll cover my portion of rent until you can find another roommate. It's what I want, Mae. Not that you care about that."

"You're just going to leave? Just like that?"

"At some point, we all have to move on. We can't live in our garden apartment forever."

Sonya hangs up, and Maeve rests against the building, stunned, replaying the conversation over and over, every word imprinting on her skin like the lash of a whip. *You're too scared to let anyone that close to you. I'd rather risk getting laughed at. Or getting hurt. At least I know I tried. It's better than ending up alone with only my regrets.*

Maeve whimpers, her face in her hands. Sonya just served up a sucker punch to the gut and walked away. She didn't ask about Ireland or Liam at all. Maeve didn't get to tell her all the good things that have happened. She wanted to tell Sonya about dumping the smoothie on Briggs's head and stealing his banner. And the pierogi! They're a hit! People love them. Maeve can't make them fast enough. She wanted to tell Sonya about Barb and Linda, and the kickball game! Maeve has a full team now. Even Derry and his son are playing for the Moorings. Barb is their unofficial coach, barking orders at practice. And they're not half-bad. The Moorings might actually win.

Maeve's backpack, and the datebook, pens, and knitting supplies, are scattered on the ground. She scrambles to pick them up now, placing each one back in the bag in its ordered spot.

Perfection doesn't beget love, Mae. Honesty does.

Maeve slumps to the ground, her cheeks wet with tears.

"Bloody hell, Maeve?" Briggs kneels in front of her. "Are you OK?"

Oh great, he witnessed her meltdown. She was too busy losing her shit to notice who might be watching. "I'm fine," she lies, wiping her tears away.

You're too scared to let anyone that close to you.

Nausea bubbles in Maeve's belly. She pivots, word vomit exploding, uncontrolled, maybe for the first time in her life. "You know what? No. I'm not fine. I'm so . . . scared. My whole life I've fought to keep everything in order. Minimize the surprises, and you minimize pain. But people fuck you over and people leave and people die. There's nothing I can do about it, and I hate that. So I just hold on tighter. Control more. Keep the mess to a minimum. Organize and reorganize. But it's useless. And I'm so tired." Her head falls to her hands. "I'm just a control freak who's destined to end up alone with her color-coordinated closet and bleached white hand towels."

"Give me your hand," Briggs says, his palm extended. He helps Maeve off the ground and picks up her backpack. "I'm taking you somewhere."

"You are?"

"Unless you don't want to come with me?" Briggs holds her gaze, his question genuine. But Maeve can't think of anyone she would rather spend the day with. From that first night, Briggs planted something deep inside Maeve that she can't get rid of. She stole the sign *hoping* he would catch her. She's played the pub rivalry game *because* of him. Everything she's done has been to *keep* herself in his path, even when she's denied it. The moment he stepped through that pub door, something shifted in Maeve. Maybe it's because Briggs is the only person who's ever seen her dance like that, but with him, she's more herself than ever before. And she genuinely likes who she is.

"Is that a good idea, though?" Maeve glances around for any lingering eyes, but miraculously, the street is quiet.

Briggs smiles. "I promise. Where we're going, no one will see us."

Maeve stands at the shore, looking down at the blue-gray water three feet below. "You jump into this every morning?"

Briggs mimics her stance, gaze trained downward. "I don't usually look before I do it. I just . . . jump."

"Even in the winter?"

"In the winter I don't jump. It's more of a . . . slither."

"You're nuts."

"Would you believe me if I said it's the best rush you'll ever have?" Then he amends. "Well, one of them, at least."

Maeve chuckles at the innuendo. "It looks really cold."

"I'm not going to lie. It is. But it's not as bad as you think. You just have to ignore the part of your mind that tells you to panic, and trust that you'll be OK. You can handle this."

Briggs wasn't lying when he said no one would see them. This secluded part of the island is down a dirt road that looks like it leads to private property. Along parts of the coast, the ocean can be rough, with whitecaps and gray seas, but here the water is calm and crystal blue. Maeve can see all the way to the bottom. Far off, large rocks jut out of the water, covered in bright green grass.

"You can't think about it too much," Briggs says. "Just trust yourself, and do it."

"It's deep enough?"

"How about this . . ." Briggs peels off his T-shirt. "I'll do it with you." He starts to unbuckle his pants, but Maeve stops him, her heart in her throat.

"First tell me *why* you do this every morning. And don't say because it feels good."

Briggs pauses, his attention on Maeve, like he's debating whether to answer honestly or give some bullshit superficial answer. An answer Eoin would give. "As a sort of test," he says. "To remind myself I can handle whatever is down there." He exhales and squats to sit on the edge.

Maeve follows suit. The day has warmed some, but it's by no means hot. Maybe seventy degrees.

"After my father died and I was done with uni," Briggs says, "I left Ireland for a few years, went to Australia, thought I could run away from all the sadness. Turns out, grief isn't like a sweater. You can't leave it behind in a drawer. It comes with you wherever you go. When I came back, it was just as suffocating as when I left. The second I set foot on the island, I felt this overwhelming pain, because I knew no matter where I went, no matter how hard I looked, I'd never see my father here again. There wasn't a place in the entire world that didn't remind me of his infinite absence. And then one day, I was standing right here, feeling so overwhelmed and lonely, and I thought, this feeling will never go away, and I just . . . jumped."

Maeve gasps. "Just like that?"

Briggs nods, a small grin on his face. "The water was so shocking, I couldn't think of anything but the cold and getting the hell out as fast as possible. But I forced myself to stay in. To calm down. To trust that I could handle it. It felt like I was in the water forever, when really it was probably a minute, but when I got out, this rush came over me. I had stayed when I wanted to run. I felt utterly alive for the first time since he died. And then just as quickly, every emotion, every memory I'd been fighting back for so long, hit me all at once. I sat in my car, wet and cold, and cried. But the next day, I came back and did it again. And the next. And the next. Until one day I wasn't counting the seconds until I got out. I had come to a kind of peace with the water. And all of a sudden, it was like I could hold my grief instead of drowning in it." Briggs turns from the water to Maeve. "You're not a freak, Maeve. Everyone handles suffering differently. Sometimes we just need to do something to remind ourselves that *feeling* broken doesn't actually mean we are."

"Why did you tell me all of this?" she asks sincerely.

"Because I hate that you think I'm a liar. And the best way to prove I'm not is to be honest now. So there it is." Briggs shrugs.

"I don't think you're a liar," Maeve says quietly. "You may have omitted some details . . . but I've known liars, and you're not one."

"So you forgive me?" Briggs asks.

"I don't know . . ." She grins, unable to resist his sculpted chest, her fingers itching to touch him. "If I forgive you, do we have to stop fighting?"

"Feck no," Briggs says. "What fun would that be?"

"Good." Maeve removes her shoes. She stands and takes off her shirt, then her pants, until she's standing next to Briggs in only her black bra and underwear.

"Bloody hell," Briggs says, scanning her body, his eyes hungry.

"You didn't expect me to jump in with my clothes on, did you? Now, are you with me or not?"

Briggs grits his teeth. "Problem is . . . I hadn't considered that part, and now that I'm seeing it in real time, I'm having a bit of a reaction that I wish I could hide." He glances down to his pants.

Maeve smirks. "Do you want me to turn around?"

"I appreciate the offer, but it won't help. It might make matters worse seeing the whole picture. I just don't want to make you uncomfortable."

But Maeve feels the opposite of that. This might be the most relaxed she's ever felt. And to show him, she pulls Briggs up from his seat so he's standing in all his glory, right in front of her. She steps closer. They're almost touching. "Sounds like you need a cold shower, Briggs Murphy."

He pulls in a ragged breath. "Not just cold. Bloody freezing."

Maeve unbuttons the top of his pants. "There's only one solution then." She unzips his fly. "And for the record, I'm far from uncomfortable. I'm flattered, really."

Briggs inhales through tight teeth. "Maeve, I'm trying to be a gentleman and control myself, but since we're being honest with each other, I have to tell you that if your hand stays on my zipper one more second, I'll be forced to eat your knickers off with my teeth."

Maeve bursts into laughter that fills her up to her earlobes with happiness. "Tempting . . ." She giggles, stepping back with a wide grin. "Rain check?"

"Name the date and time, and I'll be there."

"How orderly of you. Now you're turning *me* on," she jokes. She takes one last glance at the water and then holds out her hand to Briggs. "On the count of three."

Briggs pulls off his pants and tosses them. Maeve can't help but sneak a peek at his raw maleness, her stomach somersaulting. "The key is to remain calm," he says.

"One . . . ," Maeve says.

"Fight the body's urge to constrict."

"Two . . ."

"When you hit the water, you'll want to gasp. Don't, or you'll take in a bunch of water. Cover your mouth. Are you scared?"

Maeve doesn't answer but says, "Three."

And they leap.

They hit the cold water, and Maeve's lungs instantly squeeze. She gasps and takes in a mouthful of salt water. Her feet never find the bottom, so she kicks toward the surface. When her head emerges, Maeve breathes, but it feels like she's sucking through a straw. She's never felt this kind of cold. Chicago winters are brutal, but this is different. It's everywhere. She's completely exposed, completely immersed.

Briggs is next to her, treading, salt water dripping from his eyelashes and beard, his face beaming. Everything in Maeve wants to get out of the water. Every alarm in her brain is going off, but she stays. Trusts herself to know she's OK.

What feels like an eternity lasts, in reality, about thirty seconds. Maeve finally succumbs and climbs out, her whole body buzzing, teeth chattering, skin covered in goosebumps. She's pretty sure her lips are blue. And it's all amazing.

Briggs grabs towels from his Jeep and wraps one around Maeve. "Do you want to get in the car? I can turn the heat on."

"No." She's freezing, but she wants to stay outside. She turns her face toward the spotty sun, feeling its warmth on her cheeks.

Maeve spent months hiding in her garden apartment, half-underground, worried and ashamed, feeling violated, her trust in people completely obliterated. But the worst part was losing trust in herself. Feeling that something about her *allowed* Spencer to take advantage of her. That she should have been better. That *she* was the problem. Of all the girls in the bar that night, he knew she was the one he could take advantage of.

She smiles at Briggs. "I just jumped into freezing cold water and survived."

"You sure as hell did."

"I want to do it again."

"Maybe when you're not so blue." His fingers touch her bottom lip. "You need body heat." He opens his towel and envelops her in his arms, her face to his warm chest. "Better?"

"A little. But we should probably stay like this for a while." Out here, away from town and all the eyes, she feels freer. Gutsy, even. She nuzzles her nose into his chest, right between his pecs, and takes a deep breath of salt water and masculinity. Her lips brush his skin, and a noise comes from deep in Briggs's throat.

"Maeve . . ." His face is tense, his jaw working as she looks up at him. "I think we should go."

"But I'm not warm yet." Her hands reach around his back, her fingers pressing into his spine.

"You're on a high. You're running on adrenaline."

"So?"

"I don't want you to do something you'll regret."

"What about you?" she counters. "You jumped, too."

Briggs holds her gaze, steady and fierce. "I threatened to eat your knickers off well before we jumped."

Maeve's bottom lip nestles between her teeth. This isn't some feral need induced by a natural high. She's wanted him from the start. That hasn't changed. She runs a hand down his chest to the waistband of his boxers. "I am of sound mind. I promise."

Briggs steps back, his eyes no less hungry but his jaw tight. "Damn it." He paces. "I don't know how to do this."

Maeve hugs her towel around herself. "It's OK. You don't have to."

"No." Briggs presses her against the Jeep, his hand on her face, forcing Maeve to look up at him. The intensity in his gaze reaches into the bottom of her belly and squeezes. "I want you, Maeve. From the first night I saw you. More than any other woman in my entire life. I am dying to devour you. Inch by inch. I can barely think of anything *but* you. These two weeks have been torture." His forehead falls. "But I can't mess this up. I need to get my head on straight first. What's happening between us is new to me. There's a lot at stake. But one thing I do know is you deserve better than the back seat of my car. At the very least, I owe you a bed." He peels himself from her, taking her breath away. "Tomorrow, I'm leaving for a week to visit my mum in Cork. But I'll be home in time for the football rounders game. I think a little space is a good thing. For both of us."

As much as Maeve wants to ignore his reasoning, she knows he's right. This day has been a complete turnabout. But what happens when they return to town? And what is Maeve thinking, when she has every intention of leaving the island? They both need time to process, as much as she'd like to ignore reality and have sex in his Jeep right now. But a week on the island without him? That sits sour in her stomach. She gathers what strength she has and, with wobbly legs, puts her clothes on.

Back in town, Briggs drops her off on a quiet side street by Stitches and Bitches, hiding her from anyone who might see, though the scandal of it could be good for both their businesses. They agree to take the week for themselves. No communication. Clear their minds.

"But just so you're aware, Briggs," Maeve says before she exits the Jeep. "Just because I like you doesn't mean I'm gonna go easy on you now."

"You like me?" he says brightly, like an innocent schoolboy, and damn, it only makes him sexier.

"See you in a week, Murphy."

But as he pulls away and the teasing fades, a heaviness settles on Maeve. One week on the island without him. It's ridiculous to miss someone she hardly knows. Sure, they had a magical day together, maybe the best of her life, but it was one day. Then again, she knows damn well that a single moment can alter a person's life forever. And that might scare her most of all.

13

Emily K.
Salt Lake City, UT
7/14/2022

★★★★★

How is this spectacle not televised?

The Super Bowl. Monaco Grand Prix. Tour de France. March Madness. The World Cup. DON'T WASTE YOUR TIME. If there is one sporting event you attend anywhere in the world, make it the Annual Football Rounders Grudge Match on Inishglass in Ireland. Never heard of it? Imagine a kickball game at Woodstock. This is a full-on experience. You'll laugh, you'll cry, you'll cheer, and then you'll party your ass off with strangers who will quickly become your best friends by dawn. You'll wake up covered in face paint and glitter with seventy new contacts in your phone. Your voice will be hoarse. Your legs will hurt from dancing. And if you pick the right team to root for, you'll wake up a winner.

Don't come from a loving family and always wanted to be a part of one? The Annual Football Rounders Grudge Match is a lovefest (for everyone whose last name isn't Murphy or Doherty). Come to Inishglass the first weekend in July and they'll welcome you with open arms.

SIDE NOTE: How is there not a reality show about the Murphys and Dohertys? It's the ancient grudge of *Romeo and Juliet* meets the hotness of Kardashians with the antics of *The Parent Trap*. If any Hollywood producer reads this review, contact me. People would *so* want to watch these two families go at it. Not only are they pretty, they're pretty brutal.

The ferry ride back to Inishglass is smooth this July afternoon. The calm before the storm, Briggs thinks, as he stands on the packed deck of the boat, looking at the island, knowing it's filled to capacity with visitors for the Annual Football Rounders Grudge Match. Even now, people on the boat recognize him as a local celebrity, offering him good luck, a few women attempting to pass him their numbers.

The weather for tomorrow's game seems favorable, but apps can never be trusted when it comes to Inishglass. A sunny day can turn stormy in a matter of minutes.

Last year at this time, on the same ferry ride after visiting Peggy Murphy, Briggs wanted to turn around and avoid the damn event all together. It might be good for every business on the island, but the pageantry of it all is exhausting work. Briggs is comfortable being on display behind the bar, but not in front of hundreds of spectators. Years past, the only time he's managed to catch a break from the crowds is his morning plunge.

Briggs grips the railing, his knuckles white, willing the boat to pick up speed. His doctor told him not to run, but hell, if he could, he'd sprint across the water, find Maeve, fling her over his shoulder, and disappear into his art studio for a week. It took herculean effort to control himself that day at the shore. So much had shifted for him in just a matter of weeks. It was disorienting. First his heart diagnosis, then his father's birthday, and then Maeve appears. Briggs had to clear his mind, and his trip to the mainland was an experiment. Would distance diminish his desire?

His findings: he's a goddamn idiot who should have shagged her while he had the chance. Instead, he gave himself the worst case of self-inflicted blue balls known to man.

It took approximately ten minutes on the mainland to realize his mistake, but he couldn't skip the trip, it being his mum's birthday and all. So Briggs made use of his time in Cork and went to see his cardiologist. His surgery is now scheduled for this fall, after the busy summer months. He's not looking forward to having his chest cracked open, his heart stopped, and a chunk taken out. In fact, he is downright terrified. But Aoife was right: if Joe had had this opportunity, he wouldn't have let stubborn fear get in the way. If Briggs really wants to be like his father, maybe he needs to start loving people like Joe did.

Every night he was away, Briggs wanted to text Maeve. Even Peggy noticed how distracted and skittish he was. His stomach was in knots, his thoughts preoccupied with worry . . . like a goddamn teenager in love for the first time. He replayed his day with Maeve over and over. He should have shown her how much he wants her. With his hands and mouth and . . . every other part of him. Instead, he tried to be a goddamn gentleman.

Now, as the island grows bigger, so do his nerves. A week was too much time to think. Why in the hell would she ever want to get involved with a rough Irish pub owner whose longest relationship is with his idiot roommate, and whose life is so dull that the highlight of his day is jumping into the ocean?

Maeve is a city girl, used to museums and fancy hotel bars and live theater. Could she be satisfied with a small island in Ireland whose only theater performance is the primary school's Christmas pageant? Maeve hasn't experienced winter here, either. Gale-force winds, air so cold and damp your toes never warm, more darkness than sunlight. And the island gets quiet, people either leaving in search of better weather or shut in, huddled by their fires. Chicago may have terrible winters, but at least in a city that size, people have ways to distract themselves. American football games, indoor concerts, shopping. On Inishglass, you have no choice but to hunker down and wait.

What happens when Maeve misses public transportation and stores that sell nonwoolen clothing? Her favorite drink is a goddamn Negroni, for God's sake! And who says she plans to stay? Maybe this is just a summer fling. In the end, he may have to let her go no matter what, and that guts him.

The questions are bloody insufferable!

Briggs looks down at the gray-blue water, wishing he could jump in and clear his racing thoughts. Ever since he returned to the island years ago, his life has been defined. Each day starts with a jump and ends either in a stranger's bed or alone in his own. Now he wants Maeve in the bed with him. He wants to wake up and not leap out, but linger, spreading her legs, sinking himself deep into her until she's satisfied. He wants to make her coffee. He wants to paint for her. He wants to eat pierogi and sing karaoke and be the reason her color-coordinated datebook is full. He wants her to be his proper girlfriend.

What the hell has happened to Briggs Murphy?

The ferry is not moving fast enough. Briggs is tempted to threaten Nigel, the captain. Move quicker or he'll bar him from the Thatch for the rest of his God-given days. But then again, Briggs can't just drive over to the Moorings, walk right in, and profess his feelings. There's no hiding for the next few days. Even now, he feels all the eyes on him. And a lot can change in a week, especially with Eoin around.

Maybe it was a mistake not warning Maeve about Eoin, but Briggs didn't want that rat infiltrating their perfect day. Bringing Eoin up would have soured everything and potentially made Maeve not trust Briggs.

"I can't believe it's been a year since I was here."

Isla's voice pulls his attention from the water and his aggravation. She's changed significantly since her first year at university, slightly taller and more confident. Briggs's shy baby sister stands almost six feet, her curly auburn hair now long and wavy. The sporty teenager who never wore makeup and constantly had a sprinkle of pimples on her forehead is now clear skinned, and Isla has traded her joggers for jeans, though she remains forever a sneakerhead.

Peggy suggested Isla come back to Inishglass, stay at the house for the summer, and work at the pub. Briggs couldn't say no. When a mum recommends something, she's really insisting. No is not an option. Of course, right when Briggs wants his first proper girlfriend, his sister moves in.

"Are you sure it's OK I'm coming to stay? You look . . . gassy." Isla makes a pinched face. "Like you're holding in a huge fart." Isla's outward appearance is more refined, but she's still just as uncivilized.

"I'm not gassy," Briggs chuckles.

"Then what is it?" She nudges him.

But Briggs is not about to tell Isla about Maeve. His little sister is a direct line to his mother, who has been concerned about her only son's noncommittal ways for years. Not yet, at least. If Peggy knew he was gobsmacked, she'd be on the next ferry to the island, diamond ring in her pocket.

"Busy weekend," he says. "That's all."

"Don't worry, bro," Isla says in an American accent, smacking him on the back. "You brought back a ringer."

Briggs glances at his stunning sister and pictures her behind the bar at the Thatch, knowing that for all the women he's slept with, there are plenty of men trying for the same thing. "By the way, you're in the dish pit this summer."

"What? I thought—"

"I can't give family special treatment. You start at the bottom and work your way up. It's only fair."

"But my shoes. I can't get them dirty." She wiggles a foot at him.

"The island is covered with thousands of years of piled shite. You're bound to get some on your shoes."

Isla groans.

Briggs smiles to himself as the ferry finally pulls into port. They grab their bags and head down the jetty. People wish him good luck at the game, and a few snap not-so-covert photos. Briggs can hear giggling as he and Isla head toward his Jeep.

Hugh waits in the driver's seat with the window rolled down. He eyes Isla and looks curiously at Briggs. "When I said bring back a souvenir, I thought you'd get me a snow globe or a collectible spoon or something." He smiles widely and extends his hand through the window to Isla. "Hugh Duffy, at your service."

Briggs swats Hugh's hand away and opens the trunk. "You're an eejit."

Then it apparently dawns on Hugh who the redhead is, and his jaw falls open. He hangs halfway out the window to check out Isla's pristine baby-pink crocheted Chuck Taylor platforms. "I should have known by the shoes," he says. "Damn, someone call the fire department, cuz Isla Murphy is back, and she's smokin' hot!"

As Isla models the trainers for Hugh, Briggs climbs into the passenger seat and whacks Hugh on the back of the head.

"Ouch, man, what the hell was that for?"

"Just a preview of what I'll do if you ever touch her," Briggs says, buckling his seat belt.

Last Call for Love

Isla climbs into the back seat, feigning annoyance, and leans between the two men in the front, resting her elbows on the center console. "When you started at the pub, did he make you wash dishes?"

"Fuck no," Hugh says, pulling out of the parking lot.

Isla glares at her brother. "I didn't bring my best pair of Air Force Ones to be stuck in the dish pit all summer. Those deserve an audience."

"It's dish pit or a one-way ticket back to Cork," Briggs insists.

"You know . . . I don't have to work at the pub. I bet Aoife would give me a job."

Damn his stubborn little sister. Briggs has no doubt that Aoife would hire Isla in a second. "Fine. Busser." Isla celebrates with air punches. Briggs adds, "But you're not working behind the bar."

"Whatever. Anything is better than dish pit."

"So how long are you here?" Hugh says.

"'Til I head to uni in the fall." Isla sits back, satisfied with her victory.

"So . . . did Briggs tell you?" Hugh asks.

"Tell me what?"

"The Moorings has a new owner." He levels a glare at Briggs, landing a jab of his own.

"Oh, feck, I totally forgot Liam Doherty died. Mum mentioned it, but I was deep in finals. So who is it?"

"His daughter, Maeve," Hugh says.

Briggs feels Isla's attention on him. "Liam had a daughter? I don't remember her."

"Estranged daughter," Hugh clarifies. "She'd never been to the island before."

"Well, what's she like?" Isla presses.

"Yeah, Briggs, what's she like?" Hugh nudges him with his elbow.

Briggs can't speak about Maeve. His emotions will show, and the last thing Isla needs is more ammunition. She'll use it to her advantage and threaten to tell Peggy if he doesn't make her bartender. And Hugh

151

is enjoying this too much, wearing a shit-eating grin like a well-tailored suit.

"Well . . . ?" Isla waits.

"She's . . ." Briggs settles on the only safe word he can think of. "American."

"And speaking of the American," Hugh adds. "There's something you both need to see."

Hugh pulls up in front of the Moorings, which is due to open in an hour, just like the Thatch. People are already queueing outside. Briggs looks aghast.

"Whoa," Isla says, leaning forward.

"It's the pierogi, bro," Hugh says. "This has been happening all week. And she started an Instagram page for the pub. She posts a count-down on the pierogi in her story. Scarcity Marketing 101. It's fucking brilliant. There's even a hashtag. Irelandsmostwantedpotato. She already has a thousand followers."

"Is that a lot?" Briggs asks.

"Compared to how many we have? Yes."

"Well, how many do we have?"

"Let me see . . ." Hugh pulls out his phone and shows his Instagram to Briggs. "*None*. The Thatch doesn't have an account! She's changed the game on us. She took it to the web, and now she's kicking our ass."

Isla sits back and smiles. "This summer just got so much better. I can't wait to meet her."

"What do we do?" Briggs begs. Part of him is dying to leap out of the car, knowing Maeve is so close, just inside the pub. Jesus, he needs to get control of himself. He needs to play the part of a feuding Murphy this weekend, not a lovesick puppy.

"I had an idea while you were gone, but we need to act fast." Hugh puts the Jeep in drive and heads toward the Thatch, which appears oddly deserted. The "Voted Best Pub in Inishglass!" banner is still on display, but compared to a thousand followers on Instagram, who cares?

When they arrive, Briggs notices that the stand-alone supply shed next to the pub has been completely whitewashed.

"Who the hell did that?" he asks, getting out of the Jeep and slamming the door.

"Me, actually," Hugh says. "That's what I wanted to show you."

"You painted my shed *white*?" Briggs snaps.

"No. I primed it. *You're* going to paint it."

"Why the feck would I paint on a perfectly good shed?"

"Uh-oh," Isla says, enjoying Briggs's discomfort too much. "I changed the toilet-paper brand once, and Briggs had a total meltdown."

"To make an Instagram wall, Furphy," Hugh explains. "It's the best way to drum up a following! People will take pictures in front of it and tag the pub!"

"Explain to me what an Instagram wall is," Briggs says through tight teeth.

Isla shakes her head in disbelief. "You're the oldest twenty-eight-year-old on the planet. It's a mural where people take cool photos and post them to their socials."

"Hashtag fuck yeah." Hugh and Isla high-five. "It's free advertising, bro. A cool-ass mural painted by the owner himself. Customers will post that shit all day long, and you don't have to do a damn thing but paint it. People will spread the word *for* you. If Maeve has the pierogi, we have this. Hashtag the Thatch."

"Hashtag coolest pub in Ireland," Isla says.

"Hashtag get beer here."

"Hashtag shut the feck up," Briggs snaps. He stares at the shed. Can he really paint a piece the whole town will see? More than the whole town . . . the internet?

"Maeve bested us with food," Hugh admits. "We can't compete with those pierogi. But you have talents, too. Time to show one of them off."

"I think the wall is brilliant," Isla proclaims. "A marriage of modern and traditional."

"What the hell am I supposed to paint?" Briggs begs.

"That, my friend, is up to you. But you better do it fast. We're not dealing with Liam Doherty anymore."

"She sounds fierce," Isla says. "I'm gonna love her."

"You wouldn't be the only one," Hugh says.

Briggs groans. "We'll deal with this after the weekend. There's nothing we can do now."

"There is one thing we could do," Hugh says. "We need our first picture on Instagram. Something to get us started. And what's better than a pic of two smokin' hot Murphys?"

"Just make sure you get my shoes," Isla says, popping a pose.

Briggs might be asked at least fifty times a night for his picture, and he knows he's all over social media, but this is different.

"Come on, man," Hugh says. "Do it for the Thatch."

If this is where the game is now played, he has no choice. Briggs poses with Isla in front of the pub. Hugh edits the photo and starts typing. He shows Briggs what he's written.

@thethatchinishglass We beg to differ, @themooringsinishglass. We have #irelandsmostwantedpotato. And his name is Briggs Murphy. #thethatch #downwiththedohertys

Isla laughs and smacks her brother on the back. "Welcome to the internet, bro."

Hugh shrugs. "What can I say? Sex sells."

14

On the day of the Football Rounders Grudge Match, Maeve wakes at five in the morning and can't get back to sleep. Last night, the pub was the busiest she's seen yet. She was on her feet for twelve hours straight. People were lined up at the door before the place opened. They sold out of pierogi at 3:27 p.m. She posted a picture on Instagram of the last plate and the happy tourists who got it.

She thought of the idea earlier in the week. People were coming in only to be disappointed when the pierogi sold out. She needed a way to let customers know. Then Dylan, one of the longtime bartenders, suggested a countdown board outside the restaurant. But Maeve wanted people to have quicker access to the information. And if there's one thing everyone is almost always guaranteed to have on their person, it's a phone. She started an Instagram page for the Moorings and told customers to spread the word. She had no idea the pub would get so many followers so fast. And while she thought it might help control the flow of people coming in for pierogi, it only increased demand. Her economics professor would be so proud of her.

Maeve was sure she'd sleep like the dead last night, but here she is, eyes wide open, her chest buzzing with nerves. She's not worried about winning the kickball game. Her team has practiced for weeks now. Barb hasn't let anyone slack, making them run sprints until they want to puke. Winning isn't on Maeve's mind. Liam's list isn't either. Maeve hasn't had a single knitting lesson, not that Barb has offered. She's spent most days and nights at the pub. There's been no time for anything else.

No, what has her anxious is the same thing that has distracted her all week. Made her stomach hurt so much she's hardly eaten. Made her smile until her face hurts. Maeve Kaminski has a behemoth-sized crush on Briggs Murphy. She likes him. Like, *likes* him.

She thought she'd come to her senses while he was gone. Logically, it's crazy to get involved, knowing she'll eventually leave. But what felt crazier, what made her sick to her stomach, was the thought of letting him go. And for what? To go home, where she has no job and no room-mate, and hide in her basement apartment until the Moorings sells and she can pay off her debt? She had been in a hurry to complete Liam's list, but now she doesn't see the point. Maryann and Keith won't be home until the fall, so Maeve has no reason to go back to Chicago until then. Why not nurse a crush on the most gorgeous man she has ever seen? For once, Maeve isn't making a list of the reasons why she shouldn't do something. She's making a list of the reasons why she should.

She rolls over and picks up the napkin with his number. Technically, since he's back on the island, their week of silence is over. She could text him right now. But then again, *he* hasn't texted her, which could be for the obvious reason that they're both slammed at work. Or it could be that he changed his mind about her. After all, Briggs said he was scared. Said he needed to think. Said it was best if they didn't talk. He should be the one to break the silence, right? Or is he waiting for her? Does she text him now, or wait until they're face-to-face at the game?

Maeve groans into her pillow. She feels like a thirteen-year-old waiting for her crush to pass her a note in study hall. She pulls herself out of bed. She can't lie around or she'll go crazy. There is one other option: chance a run-in before the game. She doesn't want to go to his plunge spot, fearing it'll come off as stalkerish, so the next best option is Aoife's meditation class. Maeve dresses quickly, heads out the door, and gets on her bike.

She is almost to the café when it starts to rain. In her distraction, she forgot a rain jacket, so by the time she walks in, she is drenched. The place is packed. She casually glances around, hoping to find Briggs, but there's no sign of him. Aoife finds her instead and examines the puddle collecting on the floor.

"It's raining," Maeve says with a shrug.

"I see that."

"And I forgot my raincoat."

"I see that, too."

"I'm just here to meditate," Maeve rambles. "With people . . . all . . . people. No one in particular. You know . . . get my head straight before the big game. Not that it's not on straight. I am perfectly fine. Totally focused. Not distracted at all."

Aoife wraps her arm around Maeve and guides her toward the kitchen. "Why don't you grab a change of clothes? I keep some in my office. Class doesn't start for ten minutes. Grab a cup of tea, too."

"Tea is good. I like tea."

"I'll save you a cushion next to . . . people. If anyone in particular shows up." Aoife winks.

Maeve gets a cup of green tea and finds a change of clothes in Aoife's office. She only looks half-ridiculous in a white T-shirt, knotted at the side to cinch her waist, and stretchy bell-bottom pants with a bold pattern. But now that she's finally dry, with warm liquid in her belly, Maeve's nerves calm. She sits at Aoife's desk, taking a few minutes to collect herself, examining knickknacks and smelling a scented candle. A framed abstract painting of what seems to be mountains and a forest at sunset is displayed on the desk, the colors bold in places, soft in others. The frame is undoubtedly handmade. It is so Aoife, like the artist captured her essence in an abstract. Maeve tries to find the artist's signature, but there isn't one.

Right then, Aoife's phone, which is sitting on the desk, chimes with a text, reminding Maeve that she has a class to get to. She presses the screen to check the time and sees Briggs's name. Her stomach drops.

She shouldn't read it, but who doesn't read a text when it's right in front of them?

I'm such a fecking eejit. I made a huge mistake with Maeve. It won't happen again.

Maeve flips the phone over and sits back, frozen with shock. And then to add insult to injury, her own phone buzzes with a text from Dylan. It's a screenshot from Instagram.

Look at this! The Thatch is on Insta now, too. And they stole our hashtag!

The picture is of Briggs and a gorgeous redhead, standing in front of the Thatch. Maeve reads the caption and gasps. It's a double slap in the face. Not only is Briggs posed with another girl, but he stole her hashtag!

Maeve's chest actually aches. Evidently Briggs came to his senses while in Cork, and this is his way of telling her. But can she be mad at him? He asked for time to think, knowing she might not like the decision he came to. He made no promises. She was the one who pressed him to get physical, and he stopped it. Briggs has done nothing wrong. So why is Maeve's heart breaking?

She changes back into her wet clothes and sends Aoife an apology text for skipping class, giving an excuse about the game. She needs to get back to her eco-pod and regroup. She's going to win this grudge match if it's the last thing she does.

~

Maeve is kicking a ball against the outside of the eco-pod, the afternoon having warmed and turned sunny, when Eoin's car pulls up.

"Nice form," he says as he gets out. He wears his black team T-shirt, **THE MOORINGS** written in white block letters across his chest, and a snug pair of athletic shorts that accent his well-defined legs. On the back is written **DOHERTY** and his jersey number. Unsurprisingly, Eoin picked the number 1. "Need help stretching? I'm happy to bend you any way you want."

Maeve kicks the ball at the wall, hard. "Why is everything you say laced with sexual innuendo?"

"The better question is: Why is your mind so dirty you think everything I say is laced with sexual innuendo?" She picks up the ball with a groan. "What's got you down, Kaminski? You always find me charming."

"Not always. Just . . . sometimes."

Eoin takes the ball. "Come on, out with it," he says.

They volley the ball back and forth in silence for a while. Finally, Maeve says, "Did you know Liam?"

"Honestly?"

"Are you ever not honest?"

Eoin cocks an eyebrow. "In law, there's a lot of gray when it comes to the truth."

"Then yes, honestly."

"No, I didn't know Liam. We met toward the end so he could make sure I knew his wishes, but that was the extent of it. And by then . . . well, he wasn't the man he used to be."

"What about when you were younger?"

"He was the old twat who wouldn't let me drink when I was underage."

Maeve laughs. "I bet you were an ass to him."

"Total shit," Eoin says. "What teenager isn't a narcissistic prick when they can't get what they want?" He kicks the ball to her. "Where the hell is this coming from, Kaminski?"

Maeve stops the ball and stares at the ground, poking her sneaker into the grass. "It just kind of hit me today that he's not here."

"He hasn't been here the whole time."

"I know," she says, swallowing a lump in her throat. "But today . . . for the first time . . . I wanted him here."

As Maeve was getting dressed, putting on her team Doherty shirt, she actually felt like one. Like the name on her back wasn't a stranger to her anymore. And she missed Liam. Or the idea of him. She missed everything she'll never know about him. She missed . . . the relationship they could have had.

And then she felt instantly guilty. Keith is the world's best dad. He never treated her like she wasn't his. He let her paint his nails and put makeup on him.

Maeve's face falls to her hands. She waits for a sarcastic comment from Eoin, but instead, he hugs her, and it hits Maeve how badly she needs to be embraced. She just feels so . . . heavy today. She melts into Eoin, happy to be held. She hadn't expected to care about this place, or Liam, or anyone for that matter. This was supposed to be a transaction. She was supposed to get a fucking vase and move on with her life. Now, she'll never be able to do that. And that reality sits on her chest like a boulder. She needs to walk away, but every day she stays, leaving becomes harder to fathom.

"Kaminski . . ." Eoin lifts her chin.

His clean-cut face is blurry through her tears. But she wants Briggs's beard. She wants to look at a different face right now. To feel different arms holding her. And then, before she realizes it's happening, Eoin kisses her, and her brain is too foggy, and her body just reacts. But when Eoin's tongue slips past her lips, she snaps out of it.

What the hell is happening?

She pushes Eoin back. "What was that for?"

He smiles. "You seemed like you needed a little distraction."

"Is that how you distract all your clients?"

"I believe you were the one who said we were friends." Eoin laughs. He puts his arm around her and guides her toward his car. "Don't worry about today, Kaminski. You have me on your team. I only know how to win. Now let's go do this for Liam."

But after that kiss, Maeve starts to think he's only out for himself. Something else is at play here, and it has nothing to do with kickball.

~

Maryann has a framed picture from Maeve's first Cubs game. Maryann, Keith, Maeve, and her grandparents are posed in front of Wrigley Field under the iconic red "Home of the Cubs" sign. They're all in matching blue-and-red Cubs gear. Wrigleyville looked different back then. The neighborhood wasn't fancy like it is now. Dive bars serving Old Style, Budweiser, and loud music had lined the streets instead of restaurants with manicured patios and sleek furniture, serving wine and draft IPA.

Maeve remembers the day well. The energy of the crowd. The taste of the hot dog. The sunburn she got. The ubiquitous smells of popcorn and beer. Chicago might be the most lively city in the world in the summertime. But her most vivid memory is when the Cubs won the game and the entire ballpark sang "Go, Cubs, Go" at the top of its lungs. The excitement of tens of thousands of people shook the stadium, and she knew, even as a little kid, that she was experiencing a special moment. Something that only happens in Chicago. In that moment, everyone felt like family. It was impossible to feel alone.

When Maeve steps out of Eoin's car, she gets the same sense. This isn't just a kickball game. This is a festival. A celebration of the entire village of Inishglass. A celebration of family, where every person in attendance is an extended member. The soccer field is swarming with people, drinking, chatting, laughing. A band plays traditional Irish music. Kids run around, chasing each other and eating sweets, sporting T-shirts and signs in support of either the Murphys or the Dohertys. It's a gigantic family reunion.

"Let's get a drink," Eoin says and grabs her hand.

"Barb won't like that."

"Who cares? I've let that bitchy Yank boss me around for weeks. It's time to have some fun."

Maeve releases herself from his grasp, put off by his acerbic tone. "I don't want a drink."

"Come on, Kaminski. Look around. It's a party." But Maeve refuses, crossing her arms. Eoin softens. "The looser you are, the better chance we have at winning. That's the ultimate goal here, right? You need to win this game. A drink will help your nerves."

But suddenly, after weeks of trusting Eoin, Maeve . . . doesn't. Not after that kiss. It wasn't organic. It felt calculated.

"So will stretching," she says.

"How about both?" And before Maeve can protest again, Eoin heads toward one of the drink stands. Maeve makes her way to the Doherty side of the field, where a tent with a banner that says **THE MOORINGS** serves as a makeshift dugout along the first-base line. An identical one along the third-base line advertises **THE THATCH**. The soccer field has been transformed into a kickball diamond, with white lines marking the baselines and pitcher's mound. Three identically dressed referees confer by home plate.

Seeing her team warming up in uniform fills Maeve with so much love, she can barely contain herself. These people have embraced her without question. It's not just Briggs who's made an impression on her. It's this whole place. And that scares the shit out of her. But now is not the time. She needs to stretch and focus. As she heads toward the dugout, Briggs intercepts her.

"Hiya . . ."

Maeve whips around at the sound of his gruff voice, her stomach dropping. They're completely exposed, which seems to dawn on Briggs as he glances around at the growing number of people taking their seats for the game. His navy-blue T-shirt boasts **THE THATCH** in kelly-green lettering.

Briggs clears his throat, steps back from Maeve, and holds out his hand. "I just wanted to say good luck."

She stares at his open palm. "Is that all?" Immediately she wants to take it back.

Just then Eoin sidles up next to Maeve, a drink in one hand, and drapes his free arm over her shoulder. "Already playing dirty and the game hasn't even started," he says to Briggs. "Typical Murphy."

"Get the fuck out of here and go back to the hole you crawled out of, O'Connor."

"Easy, Murph. No need to get out your pistols. I'm just here to support my friend. Can't abandon my team now." Eoin gestures to **THE MOORINGS** on his shirt. "She needs me."

Tension pulses in Briggs's neck. "Stay the hell away from her."

Eoin acts shocked. "She asked me to be on her team, Briggs. Buttered me up with dinner and everything. I tried to say no . . . but she just looked so cute, begging."

Briggs lunges at Eoin so fast that Maeve doesn't have time to think. She jumps in between the two men, each double her size. Eoin throws his drink to the ground, and an elbow—Maeve isn't sure whose—connects with her shoulder, shoving her away as the men raise fists. She stumbles back, grabbing her stung arm, and loses her balance, hitting the ground on her left side. Luckily, she manages to brace herself before her head hits.

Briggs is reaching for her, speaking, but she can't hear, his attention not on Eoin.

In that split second of distraction, Eoin lands a punch across Briggs's cheek, but he scarcely reacts, his focus only on Maeve. People rush the field, and right as Briggs is about to pull Maeve up off the ground, Hugh pulls him back. Barb and Dylan drag Eoin back toward the dugout, telling him to cool down.

The crowd is enthralled, as if both sides brilliantly planned the scene to rile them up before the main event. No doubt, someone is posting photos or video to social media right now.

Maeve picks herself up, her shoulder sore, her shorts wet from spilled beer and damp grass.

"Maeve—" Briggs pleads, but the redhead that Maeve saw in the Instagram photo steps between them, grabs Briggs's face, and examines his bruised cheek.

"He needs ice," she says to Hugh, in a sweet Irish lilt.

Maeve turns her back on Briggs and walks away, unable to stomach any of this, trying to shake it off, ignoring the stares and chants of the crowd. She needs this win. Get through this game. Check an item off the list. That is the only goal.

For the next half hour, Maeve ignores Eoin, Briggs, her nerves, and the growing crowd. But she can't shake the feeling that Eoin and Briggs's fight is just the beginning of something brewing. The people, the noise, even the air is frenetic.

Barb interrupts Maeve's stretching routine to hand her a water bottle. "Most people are grossly dehydrated. Drink this."

Maeve takes it and slugs down a gulp.

Barb stares out at the field, her eyes narrowed in thought. "Liam loved this game. Looked forward to it every year."

"He did?"

Barb nods. "He was terrible, too. Not an athletic bone in his body. This one time he was up to kick and full-on missed the ball. His legs flew up in the air like a cartoon, and he landed on his back in front of everyone. And you know what he did?"

"What?"

"Laughed his goddamn ass off." Barb's face lights up at the memory, and for a second, Maeve thinks she might actually cry. "Then he got up and took a bow. The crowd loved it. He understood why they were there."

"Why?"

"Why does anyone go to a game? To feel a part of something," Barb says. "That's what all these people want. Hell, that's what everyone wants."

Maeve chews on that for a minute. Isn't that what she's found at the Moorings? On Inishglass?

"When Liam was diagnosed with cancer, he made up a mantra for the end of his life," Barb continues. "'Enter laughing.' If you walked into his pub with anything but a smile on your face and a funny story to tell, he'd make you turn around and try again. I'm not saying he didn't have bad days, but we have a choice about how we live, and if we're lucky, how we die. His hip was never the same after he missed that damn kick, but he never told that part of the story. Never focused on it."

The dull ache of grief settles in Maeve's bones once again, grief for a father she'll never know. "Why are you telling me this, Barb?"

"When Liam told me he was giving the pub to you, I wasn't sure what to expect. But what you've done there, in such a short time, *and* pulling together this kickball team . . . It's more than impressive. Some might call it a miracle."

The compliment is so shocking that Maeve manages only a sputtering thank-you.

"I have no doubt we can win this game. Just think about *how* you want to do that. This game is your legacy now." Barb lets that sit for a beat before adding, "And Monday, I'll teach you to knit. Nine a.m. Meet me at the store. Don't be late. And take the day off. This might take a while. Got it?"

Maeve nods.

Barb glares lasers at Eoin. "And be careful with that one. There's only one thing he likes more than power."

"What's that?" Maeve asks.

"Himself."

As if Eoin can tell they're talking about him, he glances toward them.

"What's your karaoke song?" Maeve asks Barb.

"'Come to My Window,'" Barb says without hesitation. "Melissa Etheridge. Best love song ever made. Linda and I danced to it at our wedding."

The perfect pick. "Watch out, Barb. I'm gonna start thinking you're a softy."

"Love doesn't make you soft, kid. It makes you strong." She smacks Maeve on the back. "Now drink that damn water and let's win this game."

Then she blows her whistle, and the night begins.

~

Maeve and Briggs walk to the pitcher's mound from their respective sides for the coin toss. People cheer: *Murphy! Doherty! Murphy! Doherty!*

"Just a reminder of the rules," says the referee with short curly black hair and brown eyes. "This is a seven-inning game. Ten people are allowed on the field. You get one base on an overthrow. No head shots." Briggs and Maeve both nod. The ref produces a coin. "The Thatch won last year, so Briggs, you get to call it."

"Tails," he says.

The ref flips the coin, which lands heads up. "Heads it is." The ref looks to Maeve. "Do you want to kick or field first?"

"Field," she says, as Barb instructed.

The ref yells to the spectators, "The Moorings will take the field!"

Both teams begin to move, and another cheer erupts from the crowd.

"Good luck." Briggs holds out his hand for Maeve to shake. His cheek is red and a little puffy, but the damage makes him sexier, which is downright obnoxious. Everything in Maeve wants to heal his cheek with a kiss.

"I'm half-Irish," Maeve says with confidence. "I've got some luck of my own." And she walks away, the crowd cheering her on.

~

At the top of the second inning, with two outs and the Thatch up by one run, Aoife comes up to the plate for the first time. Eoin is pitching. Briggs stands on the sideline coaching, his arms crossed tightly over his chest. He's not playing, which seems odd to Maeve, considering that he's the biggest person on his team by far. No doubt he could kick the ball deep. She had assumed he'd be the Thatch's star player, but he's just coaching, like Barb, though he doesn't seem pleased about it.

Maeve is at center field, just to the right of the pitcher. Aoife gives her a little wave and an apologetic smile as she walks to the plate in jean shorts, her team T-shirt cut to the midriff, her toned stomach showing, and her tattoos on display. On her feet, she wears a pair of beat-up red Converse.

"Still as gorgeous as ever," Eoin says from the pitcher's mound. "I always loved you in red."

"You loved me weak," Aoife counters. Her tone is sweet, almost musical, as usual, but her eyes carry none of it.

Eoin chuckles. "Still can't let the past go."

"Some scars never leave you," Aoife deadpans.

"Remember what I told you, Eef," Briggs calls from the sidelines.

"Still doing whatever Briggs says?" Eoin tosses the ball in the air. "I thought you'd be done with that by now."

"Just throw the ball, Eoin," Maeve says, uncomfortable with whatever veiled conversation they're having.

"Don't worry, Kaminski. Aoife likes it when I tease her. Always has." He undresses Aoife intimately with his eyes, and embarrassment blooms on her face, which only seems to please Eoin more. The move is so violating, so arrogant. Briggs looks like he's about to launch himself onto the field. Maeve is appalled that Eoin would do this in front of a crowd and yanks him by the arm to the sideline.

"What the hell are you doing?" she snaps.

"I'm just playing the game," he says, too casually.

"By embarrassing Aoife?"

"No," he says. "By getting under her skin. Plant doubt, and people mess up."

"You're acting like this is a trial you need to win. It's just a game."

Eoin holds her gaze. "You asked me to be on this team because I'm a winner, and you desperately need that. This is how we do it."

"Not by playing dirty." Maeve takes the ball from him. "I'm pitching from now on. You play center field." She walks toward the mound.

"Don't be like that, Kaminski!" Eoin yells. "You like it when I'm dirty!"

Every muscle in Maeve's body clenches. But he's right about one thing. She wants to win, not to check off an item on the list anymore, but in honor of Liam. She will never meet her biological dad, never touch his face, smell his clothes, hear him laugh. A month ago, none of this mattered, but now it hurts, somewhere deep inside that Maeve didn't even know existed. If she will never be able to touch or hold or hear Liam, the least she can do is win this game. Liam would have wanted it. And since Eoin is the best player on the team, Maeve can't kick him off. But she doesn't have to let him lead.

She lines up at the pitcher's mound and glances at Barb, who nods, pleased.

With a deep breath, Maeve rolls the ball to Aoife. Aoife sends the ball soaring into right field and mouths "sorry" as she takes off to first base. She rounds the bases for a home run, right behind her teammates from second and third base.

Eoin snickers. "You won't win playing like that, Kaminski."

~

In the bottom of the third inning, Linda gets a three-run home run. The Moorings inches closer to the Thatch, now only two runs behind, but then in the top of the fifth, a player for the Thatch sends a ball so far into the outfield that it takes several minutes to retrieve it and start play again. By the top of the seventh, the crowd is antsy, anxiously awaiting a big finish and the party that follows. Hugh comes up to the plate for the Thatch.

Eoin walks up to Maeve and says, "He's got a good kick, but he's not a fast runner. Put some spin on the ball so if he kicks it, it won't travel far, and we can get him out at first base."

Since Maeve took over as pitcher, Eoin's been quietly playing midfield like a good teammate, which makes Maeve more nervous than when he was being verbose. But she does as he says, and the play goes better than expected. Hugh is tagged out at first base, and the player forced to second gets hit with the ball as she's running. A double play.

The Moorings side explodes in celebration. Eoin grabs Maeve in a surprising hug and spins her around. As he sets her down, his hand comes to her face, and he rubs his thumb across her cheek. "Just a bit of dirt."

The crowd watches the intimate moment with collective awe. It all happens so quickly that Maeve doesn't have time to stop it. She is instantly embarrassed. Not only is Eoin giving the crowd the wrong idea, but he's undermining her authority. And then to push it just a little farther, he says loudly, "Keep making those plays, and I'll have no choice but to kiss you again!"

All the air leaves Maeve's lungs. It feels as though the whole world is staring at her. Eoin knows damn well she didn't initiate that kiss and never would have. Whatever show he's putting on—for the crowd, for Briggs—she did not agree to it.

Briggs is on his sideline, fists clenched, jaw tight. Maeve can't say anything to him with everyone's attention on her, and even if Briggs may have changed his mind about her, she hates the idea of him thinking she would ever go for Eoin.

A tidal wave of shame, regret, grief, loneliness, every emotion she's staved off for the past month, pummels her flat. It's the final straw. She's drowning. She can no longer hold herself together. She calls a time-out and runs off the field as fast as she can.

15

B riggs is going to kill Eoin O'Connor. Every ounce of his body wants to charge the field and destroy him. Ten years of pent-up anger pushes on Briggs's chest. He could do it, too. Eoin may appear strong, but he's a coward who only ever gets the upper hand with cheap shots. One on one, undistracted, Briggs could finish him.

Eoin is the only person on the planet who infuriates Briggs to the level of physical violence. Adrenaline swirls uncontrolled through his body. His heart pounds. For months, Eoin has hidden out in town like the snake he is, cunningly planning his attack. How did Briggs not see this coming? Of course, Eoin would use a stage like the game to assert his influence. That's always been his way. He places himself in a position where he appears blameless. To everyone watching, he's just trying to win for the Dohertys, but he is burrowing under Briggs's skin, hoping he'll take the bait. Then when it's over, and Eoin is bloodied and bruised, he'll say he was just playing the game and that Briggs's lack of control, his temper, his violence, instigated the fight.

"You need to calm down," Isla whispers. "It's not good for you to get riled up."

But Briggs can't. He should have warned Maeve about Eoin. Who cares if she hated him for it. At least he would have tried. But it's Aoife's story to tell—*her* secret. Hell, Briggs should have taken care of Eoin ten years ago, when Aoife first showed up on his doorstep, panicked and abandoned. Briggs had played into Eoin's hands back then, too.

And now here he is again, on a grand stage, hoping Briggs will take the fucking bait.

But right when Briggs's anger is ready to erupt, Maeve runs off the field, and instead of charging Eoin, Briggs takes off after her, worried she'll disappear. His heart hiccups at the unreasonable thought. This is a goddamn island. He'd search every nook and gully until he found her. But he runs as hard as he can after her, ignoring his doctor's orders, unwilling to let one more minute pass without telling her what a goddamn idiot he is.

Maeve races around the vendor tents and toward the stage where the postgame band and DJ will play tonight, when Inishglass will turn into a raging party, welcoming the summer season well into the early morning. With the noise of the crowd diminishing, Briggs yells after her, but that only causes her to speed up, which makes him work even harder.

"Fecking hell, Maeve! Would you slow down! I'm not supposed to run!"

Maeve stops. They're behind the stage now, out of view of everything and everyone. The only noise is their breathing. "Why can't you run?" she asks, confusion in her eyes. "Is that why you're not playing?"

Briggs bends over, catching his breath, hand to his pounding heart, willing it to keep working. His vision splotches with spots, his head feels light. "Doctor's orders," he pants.

"Doctor's orders? What does that mean? What's wrong?"

Briggs shakes his head. This isn't how he wanted to tell her. If he had it his way, he wouldn't admit to his heart condition at all. He'd have the surgery without her knowing. He doesn't want her to worry about him. He never wants to be the cause of concern, but he can't lie to her. He promised honesty, and that's what she'll get.

"Harsh reality, Maeve. I have a broken heart."

She steps closer to him and reaches her hand out, then pulls it back. "What do you mean, a broken heart?"

"Hypertrophic cardiomyopathy. That's the technical term for it." He gives her space, though it's the opposite of what he wants. "The condition is hereditary."

Maeve's hand comes to her mouth. "Your dad . . ."

Briggs nods. "I found out right before you showed up. Shit timing, really. Though a part of me has always known, I think."

"Why didn't you tell me?" she begs. Then she casts her eyes downward. "I take that back. You don't owe me an explanation."

"I think I do." But when he tries to approach her, Maeve backs away.

"No. You don't."

"What's going on?" Briggs asks.

Maeve looks up at him, resolve on her face. "If you changed your mind, it's OK, but you could have just told me."

Briggs sputters, thrown off guard. "What the hell are you talking about? Changed my mind?"

"Your Instagram post was pretty damn clear. I got the message."

"What message?"

"The redhead, Briggs."

Briggs is confused. Redhead? And then it hits him. Isla.

"You basically advertised yourself with another woman," Maeve adds.

Briggs chuckles to himself. He's going to kill Hugh. He points at Maeve and says, "Well, what about you?"

"What about me?"

"I leave you for a week and you kiss Eoin Fecking O'Connor!"

Maeve gasps. "I didn't kiss him! He kissed me! Without my permission! And I totally pushed him away."

"Tomato, tomahto, Maeve." He crosses his arms.

She groans and gets in his face. "Well, you stole my hashtag!"

"You don't own the hashtag!" Briggs says. "I can use whatever the hell I want!"

"How typical," Maeve snaps. "Taking what you want. Which apparently is a redhead with really good taste in shoes!"

Briggs groans. "That redhead is my baby sister!"

Maeve steps back, shocked. "What?" She gulps.

"Isla's working at the pub this summer. I brought her back with me."

Maeve's eyes grow wide. "Why didn't you tell me?"

"I tried, but Eoin Fecking O'Connor got in the bloody way." Briggs rubs his bruised cheek. Maeve focuses on the ground, her snark turning to sheepishness. "Why don't you trust me, Maeve?"

"Because . . ." She shakes her head. "You said you needed space to think. A lot can happen with . . . space and . . . thinking. What felt like a good idea one day can become a mistake the next."

Briggs runs a hand over his face. "Damn it. Maeve, look at me."

"I can't. Just say what you came to say, so we can get back to the game."

"Fine." Briggs groans. "You're right. I made a very bad mistake. One I greatly regret. I should have acted differently."

"That's all you had to say. Let's get back to the game now."

But when she turns, Briggs grabs her arm and yanks her to him. She gasps as he holds her so close, consumed by her sweet smell.

"The mistake I made was thinking I could ignore my feelings for you," Briggs confesses. "The mistake I made was thinking my life would be better without you. The mistake I made was not telling you sooner, and wasting all this bloody time fighting when we could be fucking! And for the record, the only thing that's changed since I left is how badly I want you!"

"You do?"

Briggs groans and drops his forehead to Maeve's. "Infuriatingly so." He runs his hands down the length of her body, aching for her, reveling in the closeness. "We started all wrong that first night. I should have told you the truth about me, but I thought if you knew who I was, you'd kick me out of the pub, and I'd lose the one chance I had to meet you without the baggage of my last name. It was a mistake, but I promise, from this moment forward, I will never intentionally hurt you, Maeve Kaminski. Trust me. Can you do that? Can we start again, right now?"

Her eyes penetrate deep into his, holding his gaze. She nods, and overwhelming relief rolls through him. She sinks into his body, through his tough exterior, rooting herself into the deepest part of him. And Briggs knows, no matter what happens, she will be a part of him forever.

Maeve links her arms around his neck and pulls him close. "We don't have to stop fighting, right? I kind of like that part."

He chuckles. "Hell no. You're gorgeous when you're angry."

Maeve blushes. "So . . . how should we mark this new beginning?"

"Well, I had a lot of time to think this past week, and I came up with a few ideas."

"I hope you wrote them down."

"Oh, believe me. I could never forget these. They were very vivid in my mind."

"Really?" Maeve's hand trails down his chest, plays with the waistband of his joggers.

Briggs closes his eyes, attempting to control himself. "We have a game to play, Maeve."

"Game? What game?"

"You're trying to distract me so I lose focus, but it won't work."

"I would never do that." Her hand brushes the bulge between his legs, ever so lightly, coaxing a moan out of him.

Briggs's head falls to her shoulder, his jaw clenched in restraint. "The Moorings hasn't won since I took over five years ago. I'm not giving up the title that easily."

Maeve leans into him, pressing her hips where her hand was, and whispers, "I don't want you to give it up. I want a dirty, sweaty fight 'til the end. And then I'm gonna tear it out of your hands fair and square."

"God, you turn me on when you talk like that." Briggs's mind could not be farther from kickball. It's been weeks since he touched another body, and his hands tingle with need. "Don't get your hopes up, Maeve. We're up five runs. It would take a miracle."

She brings her mouth to his ear, and her breath warms his skin. "I've come back from worse."

Briggs can't stand it anymore. He grabs her ass, pulling her hips to his, wishing he could wrap her legs around his waist and drive himself so deep into her that she moans for the whole crowd to hear.

And then, in the distance, a whistle blows, signaling the end of the time-out.

Maeve peels herself away. "See you on the pitch, Murphy." She saunters back toward the field, all confidence. "I'm looking forward to kicking your ass."

Briggs breathes heavily, pulsing with a carnal desire like he's never felt. His head falls to his chest. "We're fucked."

~

Watching Maeve celebrate her win was almost as satisfying as watching Eoin's face when she sidelined him for the rest of the game. True to her word, the Moorings came back to kick the Thatch's ass in the final inning, Maeve herself clinching the victory with a grand-slam home-run kick. Fans rushed the field, and Maeve was hoisted on the shoulders of her teammates—all but Eoin, who disappeared immediately after the game. Briggs made a proper show of utter disappointment, but inside, as she ran the bases, arms raised in victory, face brighter than he'd ever seen, he actually thought that he could love this woman. One day. The idea was altogether terrifying and yet, for the first time in his life, a real possibility.

The sun has almost set now, and the sky is dusty rose and orange. Briggs has settled into one of the picnic benches on the outskirts of the main stage area, nursing a beer while keeping one eye on Maeve. Aoife finds him tucked away from the festivities, a glass of wine in her hand and a half-cocked smile on her face.

"Hiding from the shame of your loss?" she asks as she sits down.

"Aye, tragic."

Over her cropped Thatch T-shirt, she now wears a black Mettā Café hoodie, the evening having grown chilly. "If you're supposed to look pissed, you're doing a shite job of it. You've been giving her the glad eye all night."

"Maybe I'm plotting my revenge."

"More like plotting your marriage."

"Piss off." Briggs takes a sip of his beer. Aoife clocks his intake. "Don't worry," he assures her. "The doc said I could have limited alcohol. This is the only one I plan to have. It'll look odd if I don't."

Aoife smiles. "So you're doing the surgery?"

Briggs nods. "You know, this is all your fault. A month ago, my feelings were contained. Now, they're fecking everywhere."

Briggs realizes he can feel his craving for Maeve even in his fingertips. It's as if he kept his life contained to a box, and she has opened the lid, but the feelings didn't come out in solid pieces he could put back if he needed to. Maeve has turned him into vapor, expanding him beyond what he ever imagined.

"That's what love is, eejit," Aoife says.

Briggs considers her use of the word "love." He won't refute it, though Aoife's saying it doesn't make him any more comfortable with it. Seeing his unease, she lays a hand on his.

"People have the wrong idea about love," she says. "They think it makes you a sappy pushover, but it's the opposite. Love gives you a backbone. Why do you think I named my café after it?"

"That's what mettā means? I thought you made the word up."

She punches him in the shoulder. "I've had to listen to you and Hugh talk about food, sex, and sport for years, and now we finally get to talk about our feelings. You owe me, Briggs Murphy."

She has a point, but Briggs can't talk about Maeve yet, not when it's all so fresh, so he offers something else to appease his friend. "I'm sad Hugh is leaving."

"Sad." Aoife nods. "That's an emotion. I'll take it."

"I got kind of used to his odor in the house."

Aoife chuckles. "Maybe it's time to sell the place?" That gets his attention. "Be honest. You don't like living there."

Briggs has never actually said as much to Aoife, but she's right. He has never felt comfortable in his parents' house. Joe and Peggy's dreams were built and lost there. Briggs only moved in because getting rid of the place felt wrong. But he's much more at home in his art studio.

Hugh and Isla emerge from the vendor tents, their faces painted. Sparkly purple butterfly wings bloom around Hugh's eyes, and Isla looks like a fairy princess, with sparkles around her cheeks and a silver and baby-blue crown across her forehead. She carries a stuffed bear nearly her own size.

"Check out what we won!" she yells at Briggs.

"How many times did it take you, Tinker Bell?" Briggs asks Hugh with a knowing look.

"Fuck off." And then sheepishly, Hugh admits, "Thirty-seven times. And these are butterfly wings. Tinker Bell is a fairy, dummy."

"Your Disney knowledge astounds me."

"You know what else is astounding? We might not be losers after all." Hugh pulls up the Thatch's Instagram page. In one day, it's acquired five hundred new followers. Hugh pulls Briggs up from his seat. "Now come on. I saw a photo booth with our names on it."

Briggs sits back down. "No."

"But it's my last grudge match, Furphy! We need to document the moment."

"Your stay on the island has been well documented by the smell you're leaving in my house."

"Don't forget the stained sheets," Hugh adds.

"I might burn the place to the ground after you leave."

"Not a bad idea." Hugh shrugs. "Easier than cleaning. Now get up and let's take some wacky pictures."

Briggs shows Hugh his phone. "We walk around with cameras all the time. Who needs a photo booth?"

This time Isla pulls her brother up. "You can't say no."

Briggs groans and looks to Aoife for support, but she's on her feet and finishing her glass of wine. "Fine. But no tarot card readings."

"We'll see . . ." Isla links her arm through his.

"Where'd you get that wine, by the way?" Briggs asks Aoife as they walk toward the bustling tents.

She tosses him a casual glance. "I broke into your pub and poured myself a glass."

~

An hour later, after visiting nearly every vendor and playing nearly every game, along with multiple sessions in the photo booth, Briggs stands outside the tarot card tent, a Batman mask painted on his face. His phone chimes.

You never told me your ideas.

He stares down at Maeve's text like an infatuated teenager who's been desperately waiting all night for this.

He chuckles. Let's just say they all included Ireland's Most Wanted Potato.

She sends back a laughing emoji. I'm calling in my rain check for you eating my clothes off.

I was hoping you might.

Name the time and place and I'll be there, fully dressed.

Briggs sends the address and tells her to meet him in an hour. Don't be late, and prepare to stay all night. This might take a while.

He shoves the phone into his pocket and peeks inside the tent, where Isla, Aoife, and Hugh are huddled around the tarot reader, enthralled. He sends a text to Isla and Hugh that he's spending the night at the art studio. He has no interest in knowing his future. He made the mistake of believing he was destined for a certain life before, and he won't do that again.

~

Exactly an hour later, as Briggs waits in the studio, nervously fixing the pillows on the couch, the mugs on the counter, then cursing himself for being ridiculous, there's a knock at the door.

Maeve stands outside, bottom lip nestled between her teeth. Seeing her eases the annoying pressure in Briggs's chest. She wears a cropped white long-sleeved shirt that shows a sliver of her stomach, and a pair of jeans that hugs her hips perfectly. How he went the past few hours without touching her is suddenly unfathomable, but Briggs contains himself, inhaling deeply.

He takes a minute just to look at her, like he would a piece of art, examining the details. What drew him to Van Gogh was the artist's use of color in his self-portraits, infusing greens, pinks, blues, and yellow in small strokes that are artistically vibrant and yet wholly human. To Briggs, Van Gogh not only managed to paint a human face accurately, but he captured the experience of being human, the flashes of light among the darkness.

Maeve is one such light. Briggs saw it radiating from her that first night, and only now does he realize just how dark he had become.

"Well, this is unexpected," Maeve says. "I thought you invited me over for sex. You should have told me we were fighting crime. I'd have brought my Lasso of Truth." Briggs is confused until she adds, "Is the Batmobile parked out back?"

"Shite." Briggs touches his face, remembering the painted mask.

She chuckles and breezes past him into the studio. The wood-burning stove warms the room. A fresh canvas hangs on the collage wall. Maeve glances back at Briggs with an awed expression. "You're an artist?"

"I don't know if I would call myself that. I like to paint."

"But you have an art studio."

"Aye, I do."

"And those look like paintings." She walks over and thumbs through the finished canvases. Briggs's stomach constricts, worried she'll think they're all shit. "And these are a lot of art supplies." She admires the bins of paints, brushes, scissors, stacks of art magazines, and Briggs's collection of coffee table books on Matisse and Van Gogh and Klimt. Maeve faces him, hands on her hips. "Harsh reality, Briggs Murphy. You're an artist."

The word has never come out of Briggs's mouth easily. In the past, impostor syndrome would have prompted him to downplay his abilities.

"I need to hear you say it," Maeve demands cheekily.

"I'm an artist, Maeve," he says, feeling the truth of it for the first time.

She moves to the collage wall, examining the artwork, taking her time, like each is a puzzle piece in the mystery of who he is. She kneels low, where his family picture is mounted.

"The redhead . . ." She points at a young Isla and smiles, sheepishly. Then Maeve's attention moves to Joe. "I wish I could see his full face," she says, "and yet I love that I can't because he's kissing your mom."

"That's why I love it, too."

Maeve stands. "Thank you for showing me this."

Briggs knows she means more than just the picture. Letting her into the studio feels as intimate as letting her walk through his mind. He stands next to her. "I was hoping you could help me with something. I need to add a piece to my collage."

A spark of panic hits Maeve, evident in her eyes, and the confidence she had moments ago vanishes. "But I'm not an artist."

"You don't need to be an artist to help me."

She steps back, wringing her hands. "I can't."

"Yes, you can."

"No," she says in a pinched voice. "You don't understand. I physically can't." She gestures to the canvas. "That right there terrifies me."

"It's a canvas, Maeve. It doesn't bite."

"A *blank* canvas. I need lines to fill. I can handle an empty bookshelf because I know what to put on it. Same with a closet. An empty datebook is full of detailed potential. So many squares and lines. Even an empty room has boundaries. But that—" She points at the off-white rectangle.

He cocks an eyebrow at her. "I thought you might say that."

"Is this when you tell me to just try?"

Briggs lifts her chin. "No."

"I know . . . I have problems."

He holds both sides of her face. "Problems to some are talents to others."

"Are you disappointed?"

"Disappointed?" *I'm fecking infatuated with you,* he thinks. "I'm the furthest from disappointed. But do you trust me?"

"Yes," Maeve says without hesitation.

"OK. Pick a color." He gestures to the bins of paint.

"Any color?"

"Pick one that speaks to you."

That doesn't seem to sit well with her, but Maeve agrees and begins to rummage around the bins. Eventually, she settles on a light violet and hands it to Briggs. He's not sure how many bottles of that color he's bought, but it's his most frequently used hue. There isn't a painting he's done that hasn't included it. He tries not to read into this, but it's impossible not to consider the coincidence of her picking his favorite.

"Let me see your hand," he says. He turns her palm face up and traces the lines and fingerprints that mark her skin as all her own. "This might be a little cold. Just hold still." He then puts a dollop of light violet in the center of her palm. Then with a brush, he slowly spreads the paint from the center outward until it covers her hand. Maeve watches, biting her lower lip. *Just wait,* Briggs thinks. This is only the beginning.

He walks her over to the collage, and they stand admiring it. Briggs has long felt like a piece was missing, but he could never figure out what. He places her palm right above the photo of his family and holds it there, letting the paint etch her uniqueness on the collage.

"I have a question for you," he says.

Maeve grins as he pulls her hand away. She glances down at the mess of paint on her fingers and palm.

"Will you be my girlfriend, Maeve Kaminski?"

She laughs at the innocence of the question and throws her arms around his neck. "How could I turn down Ireland's *second* most wanted potato?"

"I'd wait on that declaration. You haven't tasted both yet."

Maeve releases herself. "My turn." She goes to the sink, washes her hand, and returns with a damp washcloth. She stands on the couch, eye level with Briggs. "You make the mess. I clean it up." She runs the warm cloth over his cheekbones and eyebrows, leisurely yet meticulously wiping the Batman mask from his skin. "I've cleaned a lot of things . . ." She tilts her head, focused but gentle. "But I think you're my favorite."

The warmth of the cloth and Maeve's sweet voice are so calming that Briggs closes his eyes, soaking in her touch. Her fingers graze his face, making sure every last speck of paint is cleared away.

She leans into his ear and whispers softly, "All clean." Then she runs her tongue along his earlobe.

A fragment of Briggs's resolve crumbles away, and he moans her name. Maeve's mouth moves down his neck, her tongue licking his skin, tasting him like he was a sip of coffee in the morning, slow and indulgent.

"Maeve, I need to apologize to you."

She pulls back slightly. "For what?"

"Because I promised you a bed. Will a couch do?"

She laughs. "You could have fucked me up against that car and I would have been fine with it."

He nudges her back onto the couch, and she lands with a giggle. Then he bends down and takes the bottom of her shirt in his mouth, nipping at her belly and making her laugh more. He slowly pulls her shirt from her body, taking his time, soaking in the sight of her breasts. He nibbles at her bra, teasing her nipples. As desperate as he is to disrobe and devour her, Briggs restrains himself. He kneels between her legs, his mouth coming to her stomach as she lies back, watching him crawl up her belly, his tongue making a trail to her breast. He reaches behind her and unclasps her bra, tossing it to the side, then takes one breast in his mouth, sucking and swirling his tongue until she moans. Then he moves to the other one, teasing it as she arches her back, her hips pressing up into him.

"Not yet, Maeve," he says as he reaches for the button of her jeans. "I'm still working my way through these clothes." He slides them off, adding them to the pile. Black lace panties greet him, and he nips at the fabric.

Maeve squirms with delight. She lifts her hips, inviting more, pressing herself into his touch. Briggs slides a finger inside her, prompting a low pant of approval, and by God, it's everything he's wanted and more. He circles her, enjoying the rise he induces, the heat in her cheeks and between her legs, bringing her closer and closer to climax.

Then he delicately shimmies the panties over her ass and down her legs. Maeve is completely exposed, vulnerable before him, legs wide, nipples tight, her pale skin practically glowing in the dim studio light.

"Now don't move, Maeve."

Briggs begins at her toes, his tongue unhurriedly licking its way up her calf, knee, inner thigh. As he gets closer to the sensitive area between her legs, her breath gets faster. When his tongue lightly touches her, she melts back into the couch with a deep moan, giving herself over. He's never tasted anything better as he swirls the apex of her being, coaxes more heat, egging her on to come.

Maeve pants and grips the couch. "Briggs, I want you."

"You have me," he reminds her.

"No. I want you inside of me. Now." She looks at him like she might break, a craving in her gaze that makes his whole body throb.

She reaches down and strokes him, a deep growl rumbling from the back of his throat.

"Do we need protection?" he asks. "I was just tested at the doctor, and everything came back grand."

"Same. And I have an IUD."

He's never undressed so fast. And when she guides him between her legs, they both gasp. He thrusts himself into her, the ache he felt now calming to warmth.

"More," she says, grabbing his hips and pulling him deeper into her, another gasp escaping her lips.

"This is what I thought about, Maeve. Every goddamn second of every goddamn day." He watches her pleasure rise with every drive of his hips, his muscles tensing as he goes deeper and deeper.

Maeve grabs his shoulders, her eyes squeezed closed, and begs him not to stop. As if he could. As if, from this moment forward, he could ever stop consuming her, tasting her, loving her. Briggs has never felt this with another human being, and now that he has it, he can't let it go.

"I want all of you," he pants, his body on the edge of release. "Every last broken piece."

Maeve's fingernails dig into his skin as she gasps, balanced on the same edge as Briggs. He drives himself into her one last time and they both let go at last, their mutual ecstasy releasing in simultaneous cries.

As they lie on the couch after, naked and wrapped in each other's arms, Maeve rests her head on Briggs's beating heart. With her here, he's not so afraid of it. How could he have considered *not* doing surgery? How could he have played with fire for so many years? No more. He's fixing his broken heart. He has to. He has too much to live for.

"You win," Maeve says with a tired smile. "Your potato is better. But don't you dare tell anyone I said that."

16

Jen H.
Avon Lake, OH
7/15/2023

★★★★★

IRELAND'S MOST WANTED POTATO?

This little island feud is now a global debate, thanks
to social media. And I, for one, can't get enough.
Is it the pierogi or the person? Both are quite the
dish, but almost impossible to taste. For one, your
only hope is to get in line early because they sell
out fast. And as for the other . . . if you can find a
way behind his bar, you're a lucky woman. Bottom
line: There's a potato to satisfy everyone's craving
on Inishglass, but you need to be cunning to get it.
And trying for both is the best part.

~

Nila N.
Paris, France
7/8/2023

★ ★ ★ ★ ★

Umm, hello?! Am I the only one who noticed this?

If you were lucky enough to be in Inishglass this past weekend, you witnessed one helluva grudge match. After a five-year slump, the Moorings finally beat the Thatch in a surprising victory, but that wasn't the best part of the game. This year's fights weren't like the past (and I've been three times). There was a new tension on the field and dare I say it was . . . sexual.

Maybe I'm crazy. But isn't it a little suspicious that a Murphy and a Doherty disappeared during that kickball game . . . together? Forget #irelandsmostwantedpotato. I'd like to know #whathappenedduringtimeout

And Emily K. from Salt Lake—I'm with you. How is this not a TV show????

At precisely nine in the morning, Maeve is about to walk into Stitches and Bitches when Barb bursts out the door and snaps, "What the hell happened?"

"But I'm on time!" Maeve says, adjusting the knitting bag slung over her shoulder.

"Have you read the recent reviews?"

"No. I've been . . . busy."

Barb points at Maeve's face. "Exactly." She puts on the reading glasses that dangle from her neck, and leans in close. "With whom?"

Maeve gasps. "How did you know?"

"Please. I was a high school teacher for twenty-five years. I know the look." Barb wags her finger at Maeve. "For the love of God, please tell me it isn't that lawyer. I warned you about him."

"No! Definitely not him," she insists. Maeve can't believe she ever entertained the idea that Eoin might be a decent human being. Barb waits expectantly, tapping her foot. There is no way she's going to let this go. "Fine. I'll tell you, but you have to keep it a secret."

"You're seriously asking a sixty-year-old lesbian if she can keep a secret?"

Solid point. Maeve tells her about Briggs, starting from the beginning but leaving out the intimate details. Those she keeps for herself, stored like bubbly, fizzy soda coursing through her veins, making her skin buzz and her head light and her feet practically float off the ground.

Maeve fully expects Barb to yell that it's a terrible idea to get involved with a Murphy, seeing as they're supposed to be enemies. Instead, she says, "It's brilliant."

"Really?" Maeve can't believe it. "But the feud? We're supposed to hate each other."

"But now you're like leprechauns. People will want to catch you together to prove you exist. Liam would love this."

Maeve never thought about it that way. "He would?" She can't explain why Barb's reaction makes her so happy, but it does, even as a part of her is jealous that Barb knew Liam and Maeve never will.

Barb asks pointedly, "Does this mean you're staying on the island?"

Behind Barb, the rainbow window display that Maeve composed from bundles of yarn, with a pot of gold yarn balls at the bottom, still celebrates Pride Month. She's been so busy at the pub that she hasn't had time to redecorate yet.

It hit her yesterday that Chicago's Pride Parade was two weeks ago. She and Sonya have never missed it before. Every year the Boystown neighborhood transforms into a huge festival with food, vendors, music, and the best drag show you'll ever see. On Sunday of the big weekend, Maeve and Sonya park themselves on Broadway, mimosas in water bottles, and watch the parade, anxiously awaiting the ROTC—Righteously Outrageous Twirling Corps—a group of male performers doing synchronized military-mixed-with-dance routines that bring down the house. It's Chicago at its best: summer, sunshine, and a good show. But this year, what used to feel so pivotal to Maeve now feels, not completely expired, but dated.

But to stay in Inishglass? How could she abandon her family in the States for a birth father she never knew? It would be like saying to them, "Thanks for raising me all those years, but now I'm moving to Ireland to be a Doherty because Briggs Murphy asked me to be his girlfriend, and he's really talented with his potato."

When she thinks about going back, though, a knot tugs at her belly, and her whole body winds tight.

"Don't answer that," Linda says, coming up behind her wife. "God, you're nosy, Barb. That's none of our business."

"I had an idea for July," Maeve says, gesturing to the window.

Barb stops her. "You're not coming inside today."

"But my lesson?"

She takes Maeve by the arm and drags her away. "We're not doing our lesson here."

"Then where?"

Barb stops and looks Maeve dead in the eyes. "Well, now it's my turn to tell you something."

~

"I thought you said I was supposed to take the day off," Maeve protests. They're standing outside of the Moorings, the pub still closed this early in the day.

Barb takes a set of keys out of her purse and walks to the back of the building.

"Where are you going?" Maeve scampers to catch up with her. Barb stops at a door Maeve has never noticed before.

Maeve expects a storage closet, but instead there's a staircase that leads to the upper level of the pub, which Maeve has never explored.

"What's up there?" she asks.

Barb groans. "Has anyone ever told you, you ask a lot of questions?"

"I don't like surprises," Maeve admits.

Barb softens and lays a comforting hand on Maeve's shoulder. "Sometimes you just have to take a deep breath, walk up the damn steps, and trust that whatever is waiting for you at the top, you can handle it. There's a reason I brought you here now and not a month ago."

"But I thought we were knitting?"

"Do you honestly think Liam cared if you learned to knit?"

The pieces come together then. Liam didn't want her to learn to knit a stupid scarf. He wanted Maeve to go to Stitches and Bitches and run into Barb.

Maeve gazes up the staircase and slowly takes one step, then another, over and over, until she's at the top. She has to grab the wall to steady herself as she realizes that she's standing in Liam Doherty's home.

The walls are white, the A-frame ceiling outlined in dark wood beams like downstairs. Multiple windows allow the daylight in. Sitting in the middle of the empty room is a large box with Maeve's name on it.

"Liam and I met in grief counseling," Barb says, coming up behind Maeve. "I was a year in remission, and while I was happy to be alive, I hated my new body. I hated that I was scared that the cancer might come back, even though everyone expected me to be happy because

I was alive. Linda heard about the group from a person in town and forced me to go. I asked her what the hell I was grieving over, and she said, 'You lost your boobs, Barb! It's OK to cry about it!'" She chuckles, her attention on the box. "I swear fate brought me to that first meeting so I could meet Liam."

"Was he there because of cancer, too?"

Barb shakes her head. "That would come later."

"Then why?" Maeve asks.

Barb's eyes are softer than Maeve has ever seen. "He was grieving you, honey." The words suck the wind out of Maeve's lungs. "He didn't want you coming up here until you were ready. For that." She points at the box. "Look inside, Maeve."

"I don't know if I can." But when Maeve steps away, Barb stops her with a gentle hand.

"You just walked up the stairs. Don't stop now. You can do this, or I wouldn't have brought you here." She nudges Maeve forward.

Maeve kneels before the box, touching her name, written in the same handwriting as the list. When Barb heads toward the stairs, Maeve stops her. "You're not leaving, are you?"

"This is between you and your father."

"But where are the rest of his things? Is this all that's left?"

Barb points to the box. "Liam only wanted to save what was most important to him. Everything else he donated."

"Wait, Barb." Maeve stands. "This apartment . . ."

"It's part of the pub, so it's yours . . ." Barb holds Maeve's gaze, like she knows ownership isn't as easy as handing over some keys. "If you want it."

"Wait," Maeve begs again. "Will you still teach me how to knit?"

Barb grins, and Maeve can see the young girl Barb was in the eighties, dancing on bars, falling in love with Linda. "It would be an honor." Then she leaves Maeve alone with the box.

How long Maeve sits staring at it, she doesn't know. Seconds, minutes, hours . . . she traces her name over and over, willing herself the guts to pull back the tape and confront what's inside.

She wants Briggs here. She wants him to hold her and tell her it's going to be alright, that she can handle whatever is in the box. But this is between her and Liam. She owes her father this moment. Just the two of them.

Her heart pounds so boldly in her chest that she can hear it as she peels back a corner of the tape, then hesitates. Her hands are shaking, and she pulls in a deep breath to steady herself. Then another.

Why didn't he reach out to her before he died? Why wait until there was no chance they could ever know each other? Sadness and longing fill her bones, making her body heavy. No matter what's in this box, she'll never be able to talk to Liam about it. Never be able to thank him or hug him or yell at him or cry on his shoulder. Or share a pint at the pub together. She'll never get to see him grow old. Why did he bring her here if he knew he wouldn't be around to witness it? There must be a reason.

At that, she musters the courage to pull the tape away.

Maeve first sees an envelope with her name on it, just like the one that held the list. She opens it, running her finger along the sealed flap and pulling a thick letter free.

Before she reads it, she needs another breath. Then gradually she unfolds the paper, a sad smile growing at Liam's recognizable handwriting.

> *Dear Maeve,*
> *Well, if you've gotten this far, you've met Barb. Let me guess, she pulled out her boobs the first time you met. She did the same to me. I thought she was taking the piss until she reached into her shirt and actually did it. It took me a bit to understand she was testing me. If I was going to be her friend, I had to be able to handle the ugly side of life. As it turned out, it was my life that got a lot messier. But we'll get to that part. Just know this—there are a lot of friends who will go through life with you. There are*

only a few who will sit next to you while you die. Barb sat next to me.

If I learned one thing in grief counseling, it's that we all mourn differently. Barb hides her sadness in thorns, so only the bravest get close to her. So if you're reading this now, you must be brave. Know that, wherever I am, I'm proud of you.

But enough of that. The Irish aren't known for being sentimental, and I won't start now. This letter isn't meant to make you sad. I have some explaining to do, and this is my attempt. I wish I could have done this in person, but time ran out on me. I hope you don't mind if I play my dad card here and tell you not to make the mistake I did. I'm not talking about the mistake of giving you up, though I have regretted that for many years. No, the biggest mistake I made was thinking I had more time. And when I realized I didn't, it was too late.

But none of this makes sense to you, so let me start at the beginning of a story I'm sure you know by now. I met your mum during a year-long holiday, having made a deal with my father, after my mother died suddenly in a car accident, that I could travel the world for 365 days, and the 366th I would take over the Moorings. He needed me more than ever to help run the family business, now that it was just him and he was getting older.

I met Maryann on day thirty-seven in Phuket. I liked her Midwest accent and short blond hair. I liked that she would stop our conversation if there was a good song playing in the bar and sing along at the top of her lungs. I admired that. I've always had a bit of stage fright. Even now, knowing people have to cheer for me (because what kind of arsehole would boo a dying man), the thought of singing in front of a crowd makes my palms sweat. We shared drinks and laughs and eventually ended up in bed together. She was moving on the next day with a group of Germans to visit Chiang Mai. I was headed to Vietnam with some folks I met from Canada. We went our separate ways, and that was that.

I didn't know her middle name. I didn't know her favorite color. She mentioned medical school, but I had no idea what kind of doctor she planned to be. That's not to say I couldn't have asked—I just didn't care to, because we were only meant for one night.

I explain all of this not so you'll forgive me, but so you know the truth. I was not prepared to be a father. I was not thinking about babies when Maryann and I got together. I was only thinking of myself.

Six months later I opened Maryann's email that said she was pregnant. She had sent it four months earlier, but I had ignored it, assuming it was a note to keep in touch. I almost deleted it. At the time, I was in Nepal. I had moved on from Thailand, my night with Maryann, and the Canadians, and I was having so much fun, I didn't want to look backward or forward. But there was a reason I didn't delete the email, as much as I wanted to convince myself otherwise. I knew deep down that if Maryann was reaching out, it wasn't to say hello. So I finally opened it.

Here I must admit something, and I'm terrified to do it. You'd think death would make this easier. By the time you read this, I'll be gone. I'll never feel your anger. I'll never hear your hateful words. But please know, I wish I could. Not having those things has been my punishment for the past twenty-four years. What I would have given for you to yell at me face-to-face.

I read the email. She was pregnant. I deleted it. Maryann told me she was having our baby, and I erased you. Why? Because I was a selfish coward. Because I wanted to stay in Nepal. Because I convinced myself I wasn't the father. I told myself Maryann had slept with other men, one of the German blokes she traveled with, and it was a mistake. Even if I was the father, Maryann and I weren't in love. She wasn't going to move to Ireland, and I couldn't move to the States. As the only Doherty child, I had a family obligation. The Moorings would pass to me. I had known since I was little what my future would be, and if I couldn't leave Ireland and Maryann couldn't leave the States, there was no point in acknowledging that I was your father. I made every excuse I could, and then I pressed delete. I had 173 days left before I had to be home. The world owed me those days. The world owed me that this was all a mistake. That's what I told myself. Once I got home, I'd contact Maryann, and she'd tell me she had been wrong. The baby was someone else's, and she'd apologize for ever sending the email. That was the bargain I struck with myself that day.

I knew you had been born by the time I went back to Ireland. I knew I had lied to myself. I had done something despicable. I knew Maryann didn't just deserve a response, she deserved a man to be the father of her baby, not a selfish child. I was so far from what you needed.

I still did nothing, again choosing myself over you. About a month after I got home, Maryann sent me another email. I expected her to curse me for ignoring her. Instead, she said she had met a man called Keith Rothchild, and she was in love with him. More importantly, he loved you. He changed your diapers and rocked you to sleep and did all the things I wouldn't do. He was who you needed. A proper father.

"When we met in Thailand, you said you felt trapped in a future you had no say in. I won't do that to you. Maeve has everything she needs now. Keith and I will do all we can to give her a good life. You don't ever have to worry about her. You're free, Liam. I say that with no animosity, only love. I hope you find happiness."

Those were her exact words. I deserved none of her kindness, and yet your mother offered me an abundance. She didn't have to tell me about Keith. She didn't have to put my name on the birth certificate. She didn't have to let me off the hook. She owed me nothing, and yet she gave me everything.

Knowing I had Maryann's blessing, I assumed I'd move on. She had freed me from any obligation. And you had a mother and a father now. And then on your first birthday, I found myself in Cork. I can't remember why I was there, but I wandered into a children's shop and saw this small stuffed elephant. I love elephants. Always have. Seeing the stuffed animal, I was reminded of an elephant sanctuary I'd visited in Thailand. And suddenly, I had this overwhelming need to tell you about it. And then just as quickly, I realized I couldn't. In fact, I would never share that memory with you.

On a whim, I bought the elephant and thought I'd send it to Maryann as a birthday gift for you. But once I got home, I came to my senses. I had no right to interfere in your lives, no matter how innocent the gift felt. Not after what I'd done.

But the next year, as your birthday approached, I found myself noting the day weeks in advance. I started searching shops for a gift. When I found a small jigsaw puzzle of Ireland, perfect for a toddler, I bought it. This time I wrapped it up and left it out on the table for a week as I debated whether to send it. In the end, I didn't.

Come your third birthday, I searched the internet for the perfect gift. I researched best presents for three-year-olds. I read up on your development and settled on a book to help encourage you to start reading early. Once again, I set the wrapped present out on the table, this time with the other gifts I had bought, thinking I'd send the whole lot.

I didn't. But I didn't stop buying you birthday presents either. On your fifth birthday, I came clean to my father about you. I told him everything I'd done. I expected him to be furious, but instead he reinforced that I made the right decision (though went about it the wrong way). In his estimation, by giving you up, I had given you the greatest gift I could—two loving parents. He patted me on the shoulder and said one day I'd have a family of my own. "When the time is right," he said.

But when you turned ten and I bought you nail polish, I was still single. Thirty-six years old. Thought I had time. On your fifteenth birthday (a Coach purse), I was forty-one and your grandfather was just starting to show signs of what would a few years later deteriorate into Alzheimer's. When you turned eighteen, the legal drinking age in Ireland, I threw a party at the pub in celebration. We had so much fun that the next year I did it again. And soon it became tradition. We even sang you "Happy Birthday." In an odd way, you gave this island a reason to gather. You created a closer bond for us all, simply by existing in the world.

And every year, I bought you a gift, wrapped it up, and set it out on the table with the others. Every year, I considered sending them. And every year, I didn't.

Two months before your twenty-fourth birthday, I was diagnosed with pancreatic cancer. I knew this would be the last birthday present I'd ever buy you, the last birthday party I'd ever throw. Everyone on the island came. The Moorings was packed full. It was one of the best nights of my life. This pub that had felt like a prison when I was younger turned out to be my paradise, and the people in it my family. To have them all together was as good as seeing my own funeral. Again, you had given me a gift simply by existing.

I thought one last time about contacting you, but it would have been unfair. How could I come into your life as mine was ending? How could I ask you to love a dying man when I hadn't loved you when your life began?

Well . . . if you're reading this, you know how my story ends. I'm sorry I never sent the birthday gifts, Maeve. Forgive me. I thought I'd have more time. They're yours now. This is my small offering in return for the abundance of love your existence granted me.

Love,

Liam

As she looks into the box, Maeve can barely see through the tears pooling in her eyes. Inside are the wrapped presents, just as Liam said. On top, with a red bow around its neck, is the elephant. Maeve presses the soft stuffed animal to her nose, hoping that maybe it'll smell like Liam. But she can't tell.

Now it makes sense why everyone on the island knew her. Every birthday she celebrated in America, he celebrated here. People she didn't know were gathering because of her. And now all that's left is this box in an empty apartment. The vacancy of it all physically hurts.

Maeve sets the elephant aside and texts Briggs.

I'm moving.

He responds right away. Maeve, where the hell are you?

At the pub. Second floor.

Don't move. I'm coming.

When Briggs races up the stairs fifteen minutes later, Maeve is still sitting among the pile of presents spread around her. He appears in the doorway, out of breath. "What do you mean, you're moving?"

"You're not supposed to run," she squeaks.

"Answer my question. Are you leaving?"

"I can't stay at Ivy's anymore."

"That's not an answer."

"Liam lived here," she says. Briggs nods, because of course he knows where Liam lived. "Did you ever go to one of my birthday parties?" He nods slowly. "The last one?"

"No one missed that one."

"So you knew my birthday before you knew me," she says.

"Aye. November fifteen."

"I don't know yours."

"April nine," he says.

Maeve picks up the final birthday present. "He bought me a planner."

"Maeve . . ."

She flips through the crisp, blank pages. "It has organized tabs and color-coded stickers." Briggs kneels in front of her, and the last dam holding back her tears finally breaks. "Do you think he somehow knew?" she whimpers. "Like somewhere deep down, he knew me?"

Briggs wipes a tear from her cheek. "I don't know. Maybe."

"He gave me all of this, and I can't even thank him, Briggs. I just feel so . . ." She sighs, her body unbelievably heavy. "Broken."

"Oh, love." He scoops her up off the ground, and she clings to him, stuffing her face into the nook of his neck, smelling his familiar scent of salt water and earth. She grabs at his shirt, pulling him as close as possible, wrapping her legs around his waist. If she could melt into him, she would.

"He's gone, Briggs. I'll never get him back." Every emotion Maeve has ignored from the time she set foot in Ireland rushes her at once. The ghost of Liam fills the space all around her, which echoes with her unanswered questions.

Briggs holds her tightly, as if he can hold her together as she falls apart. His warm breath on her skin is her only comfort.

"This hurts so bad," she sobs.

He kisses her neck, her cheeks, her eyelids, soaking up her tears, replacing the pain with remnants of him. Only when his mouth comes to hers does she feel the smallest ease in her heart's pain. She dissolves into the kiss, searching for relief, trying to pull it from Briggs's body.

She takes off his shirt, and then her own. Tiny pins prick her skin, and she clings to Briggs again, needing his warmth, his touch.

"Maeve . . . ," he whispers.

"Please, Briggs," she begs, her lips warm and swollen with need. "Just make this go away for a little while. I know it's not right to run from it, but I can't handle all of this. Make me feel good so it hurts less."

He obliges, filling the emptiness with his body, easing the pain with pleasure, until the presents and the ghost of Liam fade and Maeve is left shaking, not with sadness, but anticipation.

"I know you want me to make this pain go away," Briggs says, his grasp never faltering. Maeve's fingers claw at his bare back, desperate for him to continue. "But you don't need to be afraid, because it hurts for the best reason. You didn't get to know the man, but he loved you with all his heart."

Maeve cries out, feeling her whole being release. Sadness, joy, long-ing, passion, pain mingle in one burst. Tears pour in waves that she couldn't stop if she tried, from her chin to her chest, too many for

Briggs to make disappear. He holds her to him as she cries. This apartment is so empty, so vacant, like no one ever lived here. Like Liam never existed.

"Don't let go," she whispers.

"I won't."

They stay in each other's arms until Maeve finds the strength to hand Briggs the letter and say, "Liam said he was proud of me."

~

Aoife knocks on Maeve's eco-pod that night, carrying a canvas bag. She pulls out a bottle of white wine. "A little birdie told me you might need this."

Knowing Briggs talked to Aoife makes Maeve smile until her cheeks hurt, and after all her crying today, smiling feels pretty damn good. Aoife marches straight into the pod and opens the bottle.

Maeve goes to get glasses, but Aoife produces another bottle from her bag and says, "Why dirty dishes when we each can have our own?"

They toast with a laugh, and then Aoife dumps the rest of the bag onto the bed.

"Holy hell." Maeve examines the impressive booty.

"You can't have a proper girls' night without the essentials." Aoife has them covered: nail polish, homemade seaweed face masks, wax strips, candy and chips of all kinds, even a DVD of *Sweet Home Alabama*. "It's been a while since I had a proper girls' night. I may have gone a little overboard."

Maeve picks up the wax strips. "I definitely need wine before we attempt this."

Aoife relaxes back on the couch. "God, it feels good to have a girlfriend. To Hugh and Briggs, girl talk is a deep discussion about breast size and comparable fruit." Then she eyes Maeve. "Not that Briggs has done that with you."

Maeve examines her chest. "What do you think? Grapefruit?"

Aoife busts out laughing. "Definitely."

Maeve grabs her phone and sends Briggs a text with two grapefruit emojis and a question mark, then shows it to Aoife.

She laughs louder. "He's going to kill me."

"Not if he ever wants to touch my grapefruits again," Maeve says, inducing another fit of giggles. God, she needed this. Living with Sonya for two years, Maeve got used to having a girlfriend around. She's missed that. She picks up the magenta nail polish and taps it against her palm. "I better paint your nails before I get too drunk."

Two hours later, *Sweet Home Alabama* is over. Most of the wine is gone. Maeve's face is covered in a seaweed mask that makes her look like Michael Myers from the *Halloween* movies. Aoife applies a wax strip to her leg.

"Can I ask you something . . . personal?" Maeve says, the wine having loosened her tongue.

"Oranges at best." Aoife displays her chest with a smile. "But probably lemons."

"Don't sell yourself short. Oranges, for sure." Maeve blows on her painted nails. Unsurprisingly, Aoife cares little for staying in the lines. Polish sticks to Maeve's skin and cuticles. In the past, she would have raced for the nail polish remover, but seeing the mess now, knowing that Aoife made it, only makes her smile. She sips her wine, her tongue practically numb from all the candy they've eaten. "So . . . what's the story with Eoin?"

Aoife's attention drifts up from Maeve's leg. "Well, shite. If I'd known you were going to ask me that, I would have brought another bottle."

"Never mind. You don't have to tell me."

"No," Aoife says. She settles back on the couch and places the open bag of Hunky Dory Cheddar Cheese and Onion chips on her stomach. "Classic story, really. Girl falls in love with boy. Boy falls in love with girl. Girl gets pregnant. Boy decides he doesn't love her anymore."

"Pregnant?" Maeve sits up straight.

Aoife nods. "Summer before we all left for uni. I told Eoin, think-ing he'd help—we were supposedly in love—and instead he yelled at me for screwing up his future. I was panicked, so I went to Briggs, hoping he could talk some sense into his best friend . . ."

"Best friend?" Maeve blurts.

Aoife nods. "From the time they were little. It was always Briggs and Eoin getting into trouble, and because they're both gorgeous and charming, they got away with it."

"Briggs didn't tell me any of this."

"Don't blame him, he did it to protect me," Aoife says. "Plus, he was worried that if he told you, you'd go straight to Eoin, and Eoin would manipulate the story, like he always does. Then you'd trust Briggs even less."

Maeve sits back, realizing that she would have played right into Eoin's hands. "So what happened when you told Briggs you were pregnant?"

"He went to Eoin, of course, but that only made it worse. Eoin claimed I was telling everyone on the island, trying to trap him into being a father so he couldn't dump me when he went to uni. All I really wanted was help."

"What did you do?"

"I couldn't think straight. It was Briggs who came up with the solution. I couldn't have a baby at eighteen. I knew that. His older sister, Cecelia, was in England at the time, so we told everyone we were going to visit her for a week, and . . . I had an abortion. We came home and pretended it never happened." Aoife shakes her head. "You'd think Eoin would have been pleased. Briggs solved his problem. But Eoin hated that Briggs sided with me, so he told everyone on the island that we were having an affair. I was a cheater, and Briggs was a horrible friend. In the end, we looked like the villains, and Eoin looked like the brokenhearted victim."

"What a fucking asshole."

"Among other things." Aoife chuckles.

Maeve shakes her head and grabs a handful of chips out of the bag on Aoife's stomach. "I can't believe I trusted him."

"Don't blame yourself. He hides it well. Rumor has it he left London after he was caught cheating with his boss's wife. He got blackballed there, so he ran back to Cork to hide out for a while."

"Really?" Maeve recalls the brokenhearted story Eoin told her about the girl. He had failed to mention she was his boss's wife.

"I actually owe you," Aoife says. "I've been waiting ten years to return Briggs's favor. Thanks to you, I finally got my chance."

Maeve eyes Aoife, confused.

"Who do you think was responsible for talking some sense into him?" Aoife explains. "He didn't abandon me when I needed him, and I wasn't going to let him walk away from the best thing that's ever happened to him."

The best thing that's ever happened. That takes Maeve's breath away. She goes to swig another gulp of wine, but her bottle is empty. "Thanks for telling me about Eoin," she says.

"That's what girls' night is for, right?" Aoife smiles and sets the chips on the table. "Now, I think it's time."

Aoife pulls the wax from Maeve's leg, inducing a loud yelp.

"Sorry!" Aoife says, giggling. "It's best if you don't see it coming."

They fall over in a fit of laughter fueled by wine and honesty. But too soon, the ache in Maeve's chest from early in the day is back, and she fears tears coming on again. She glances at the clock. It's almost eleven. Aoife notices the change and offers to bring Maeve to Briggs's house.

Within minutes, they are on their e-bikes. Briggs's house is dark, but the back door is open. Maeve flips on the kitchen light and slowly makes her way upstairs. With the lack of furniture and personal decorations, the house looks practically unoccupied. Upstairs Briggs's room smells like him—salt water and earth. The bed is neatly made, and a few articles of clothing are cast on the dresser. His swim trunks hang drying on a hook. Just being here calms Maeve down, and she crawls into his bed, pulling the comforter up to her nose and inhaling all that is Briggs.

She must have drifted off to sleep, because the next thing she knows, Briggs is whispering her name, his gentle fingers on her cheek.

"Maeve, what the hell are you doing here? I thought you were with Aoife."

She smells hops and barley on his skin. "I was. But then I came here."

"How was girls' night?"

Maeve holds up a finger. "Cardinal rule of girls' night. No one talks about girls' night." Briggs chuckles, and Maeve yawns. "Thank you," she says.

"For what?"

For sending me Aoife. For being my boyfriend. For this. For existing, she thinks.

"You promised me a bed," she says.

"That's right. I did." He takes off his shirt, his muscles lovely in the moonlight coming in the window, and climbs in, curling his body around Maeve's. She rests her head on his chest and listens to his heartbeat.

"Briggs?"

"Maeve?"

She props herself up on her elbow, takes his hand, and places it on her breast. "Grapefruits, right?"

He laughs. "I think I need a closer inspection."

17

Maeve doesn't like coffee, but Briggs has lined up a tasting bar in the back of Mettā Café, hell-bent on convincing her otherwise.

"Nope. It's gross." She sets down a small paper cup of vanilla soy latte. Briggs growls and pins her between his arms, his hands on either side of her on the table. She spins around so they're face-to-face, those bright eyes getting him even at this early hour. "Just give up, boyfriend. I'm never going to like coffee. I'm a green-tea girl."

He clenches his jaw. "Green tea is piss water, Maeve."

"Coffee is liquid rubber, Briggs."

He leans in, close to her face. "You'll pay for that."

She smiles. "Are we fighting?"

"You bet your perfect arse we are." Briggs pushes the paper coffee cups off the table, making a mess, picks her up by her ass, and sets her where the coffee was. "I'll give you the choice of punishment. Fingers or mouth?"

Maeve giggles, her gaze warm with anticipation. "I think I can handle both," she says confidently.

"You asked for it." He goes at her then, tickling her sides and making her cackle. He lifts her shirt and blows a raspberry on her stomach while his fingers continue to play her sides like a piano. Maeve can't get a word out, gasping for air between fits of laughter. She wiggles like a worm underneath him.

Three weeks they've been sneaking around the island together, and Briggs has never been happier. His bed smells like Maeve. When he gets home from the pub and finds her under the covers, his whole body relaxes. He's taken to climbing back in bed after his morning plunge. Maeve's warm body nuzzles into his side. She plays with his beard and tells him he smells like salt water. Her feet coil around his cold ones. He has no idea what he did before meeting Maeve, how he spent his time.

Maeve has single-handedly reorganized his life, and now he can't imagine his days without her. He can't believe it, but Briggs Murphy actually likes being someone's boyfriend.

"Oi!" Aoife yells, coming back into the kitchen. "I know this place is called 'The Love Café,' but for feck's sake, keep it down. People are getting suspicious. And clean up this mess."

Maeve jumps down from the table and grabs a rag, apologizing.

Briggs starts to pick up the cups. "We're leaving anyway."

Maeve freezes, her wide eyes penetrating his. "We are?"

He nods, pleased with himself. "I'm taking you to the mainland today."

Something like panic flashes across Maeve's face, and she flinches. The café door chimes with more customers, and Aoife gives them another warning look before heading back up front for the morning rush.

"But we have to work," Maeve says.

"Best part of owning our own pubs, love. We don't have to request time off. They'll survive without us for twenty-four hours."

The Moorings and the Thatch aren't just surviving, they're thriving. The Thatch has made more money in the past two months than it did all last summer. As much as Briggs doesn't want to admit it, Hugh was right about social media. It's bolstered business exponentially, and with very little effort. Hundreds of times a day, people pose in front of the Instagram wall Briggs painted with hearts in every color of the rainbow. A tribute to his dad. People love it almost as much as they love Maeve's pierogi. Inishglass is seeing more day-trip visitors than ever before, many of them coming just to take pictures in front of the pubs and buy a T-shirt at one of the local shops, which now carry Team Doherty and Team Murphy souvenirs.

The only downside is the increased attention that Briggs and Maeve receive, which is why he thought she would be excited for a day away from the chaos. But her body seems rigid in a way that he hasn't seen in weeks.

Maeve wrings her hands. "But how can we get off the island without anyone seeing?"

"Derry offered to take us."

"Derry?" she says.

"I asked if he'd be willing to take us over on one of his fishing boats. He was more than happy to. In fact, I think he has a bit of a crush on you." But Briggs's levity only seems to make Maeve heavier. "What is it, love? You don't have to worry about the locals. We're in this together, remember? They'll keep our secret."

She picks at her chipped nail polish from girls' night, weeks ago. "It's just . . . this will be my first time off the island since I arrived."

Briggs grabs her face, trying to focus Maeve's scattered attention. "Exactly. We can actually act like a couple. In public. We don't have to worry about who might see us and take a picture. I can kiss you all I want, wherever I want. Imagine the possibilities." He nips at her neck and whispers, "Aren't you sick of this place yet?"

"I don't know what I am." Maeve peels away from him and starts to pace. She runs her fingers through her hair, anxiety rolling off her like a wave.

Briggs grabs her by the hips to make her stop. "Talk to me, Maeve."

She chews on her bottom lip, like she's tasting the words before she says them. "It's just . . . what if . . . what if . . . I change?"

He cocks his head. "Change?"

She shows him her fingernails. "This would never happen if I was in Chicago. There are five manicure shops within two blocks of my apartment, Briggs. The second that one of my nails chipped, I would have gone running to one."

"So?"

"But here . . ." She gets her planner out of her bag and shows him the blank pages. "I haven't written in my planner all week."

"You're right," he says, touching her cheek. "I should have told you about my idea, so you could be prepared. I'm sorry."

"That's not it." She leans into his touch and pinches her eyes closed. "I like who I am *here*. On the island. But what if it doesn't last? What if I set foot on the mainland, and the spell breaks, and I go back to the control freak I was?"

"Maeve . . ." Briggs rubs a thumb over her cheek. "I hate to break it to you, but you're still a control freak. Last night, you ordered me a folding board."

She slaps him on the arm and then holds him close again. Briggs's entire body sighs. He tries to ignore the nagging voice in the back of his head reminding him that Maeve has a life in the States. They don't talk about it. They don't talk about her family and friends. She hasn't mentioned Sonya since their fight. They talk about the future in terms of weeks, not months or years. Briggs doesn't have the guts to ask her about the long term, but soon he'll be forced to. For now, he has encased them in a fragile bubble that he knows damn well could break at any second.

"The folding board is gonna change your life," she says. "I promise." She buries her nose in his chest, and Briggs savors the warmth of her breath on his heart.

"Does this mean you'll come with me today? Because I have something special planned."

She nods in agreement, but a tension remains in the air. "I have something for you, too," she says, reaching into her bag and retrieving what appears to be a long piece of a mangled sweater, possibly eaten by wild dogs.

Briggs hesitates as she places it in his hands, unsure what he's supposed to do with it.

"It's an Aran scarf. I knitted it myself. Well . . . kind of. Barb helped me cast on, but then I did the rest. It's the first thing I've ever made. Do you like it?"

Briggs examines its full hideousness. "I love it." He wraps it around his neck. "I've never worn a scarf before."

"Barb's going to teach me how to knit hats," Maeve says proudly. "Any preference on color?"

Briggs shakes his head, his neck already itching from the poky wool. "As long as it's made by you, I don't care what color it is."

~

By midmorning, Maeve and Briggs are on one of Derry's fishing boats, headed to the mainland. They stand on deck, enjoying the dry, warm day, though Maeve hugs her arms tightly around herself.

"Are you cold?" Briggs asks, tugging at the creation around his neck. "I have a scarf you can wear if you need it." Maeve chuckles and shakes her head, her hair tangling around her face, her attention on the island as it disappears. Briggs can tell she's nervous, so he gets her AirPods out of her bag and says, "I have an idea. Close your eyes."

Maeve obliges, and he plugs her ears. For a moment, he just stares at her. It hit him the night after Maeve showed up in his bed after girls' night. Briggs Murphy is in love. He hasn't been able to say the words, but he feels it in his bones, so much so that it worries him. The emotional walls that he'd built have crumbled, and now he's completely exposed. When he drives out to the water each morning, he panics about losing her. Then he jumps, reminding himself to let go of it, to prove he can handle whatever might happen. He's experienced loss before. And when he gets home each morning and finds Maeve in his bed, relief overwhelms him.

He opens Maeve's music app, finds the song he's looking for, and presses play. She immediately smiles and opens her eyes as "Shut Up and Dance" begins.

Briggs takes one earbud out. "I'll be here if you fall."

Finally, a small smile. Maeve drifts into the song, her eyes closing again. Her shoulders start to move back and forth, her head swiveling, loosening up her muscles, letting the tension go. Months ago, she wouldn't have dared to dance out in the open, with people around. But now, her knees bouncing, her head bobbing—nothing too overt—Maeve looks freer than the scared American Briggs met that first night.

As the island fades into the distance, Maeve's phone rings. Her eyes fly open, and she grabs the phone from him, checks the caller ID, and declines the call. The tension is back.

"Who was that?" Briggs asks.

"Spam." She puts the phone back in her bag and takes the earbuds out. Clearly the call rattled her, and Briggs wants to push her for more information. If she would tell him, maybe he could help. But she wraps her arms around her waist and says, "I'm a little cold. Can we go inside?"

They spend the rest of the ride in the enclosed cockpit with Derry, Maeve too quiet for Briggs's liking. Once on the mainland, they make a plan with Derry for their return trip later in the day. Briggs rents a car, and they're ready to start on the road toward Cork.

"Well, you got me off the island," Maeve says. "Now are you going to tell me where we're going?"

Briggs trails his lips up her neck to her ear, and goosebumps form on her skin. "No."

~

"I can't believe you're still wearing that hideous thing." Maeve pulls at the scarf around Briggs's neck.

He swats her hand away. "Hold your tongue. My girlfriend made this for me."

They stop at a red light. Maeve grabs either end of the scarf and pulls his face to her for a kiss. Briggs growls as her tongue slides along his bottom lip.

"Maybe we should just go to a hotel?" she says against his mouth.

"I didn't bring you to the mainland so we could hide away in a hotel. Plus, where I'm taking you is better. Now close your eyes. We're almost there."

She does as he instructs with a groan, resting her head back on the seat. Fifteen minutes later they pull into a parking lot.

"OK. You can look now," Briggs says.

Slowly and with a tense face, Maeve opens her eyes. It takes a second to register just where they are, and then she turns to him, mouth wide open.

"Oh my God." She jumps out of the car and slams the door. Briggs follows, pleased with her reaction. "Oh my God!"

Maeve stands frozen, staring at the Organised Store, filled with every item a person could need to *Home Edit* a new apartment.

Three weeks ago, when Maeve texted Briggs that she was moving, he thought his heart would give out. The panic squeezed his chest so violently that he lost his breath. When he found her on Liam's floor, surrounded by gifts, his relief was like a tidal wave.

Since that day, she's spent hours furnishing Liam's apartment from hand-me-down items accumulated on the island. She's taken to the task like she did Stitches and Bitches, making sure everything is coordinated and pleasing, though she refused to let anyone see the place. Then three days ago, she announced that she's throwing a housewarming party next week, when the place will be done. Like tiny breadcrumbs, Briggs took the news and stacked it with the rest of the evidence he's silently collected that indicates Maeve isn't leaving anytime soon.

"You found me a Container Store," Maeve says. "It's control-freak heaven."

"I figured the new place could use some drawer organizers and colorful chip clips."

She launches herself at Briggs, wrapping her legs around his waist and almost knocking him to the ground. She peppers kisses all over his face before landing one on his lips. "Thank you, Briggs."

The words "I love you" are on the tip of his tongue, but Briggs restrains himself and simply nods.

She takes his hand and yanks him toward the store. "This is gonna be so much fun!"

Two hours later, their shopping cart is overflowing. Maeve has gone up and down every row, picking out different items for the closets, drawers, bathroom. The store stocks wicker baskets, plastic baskets, racks, storage containers, clips, labels—everything she'll need to put the final touches on Liam's place. Watching her shop was everything Briggs had hoped. Her glow has returned. Maeve stands tall, her shoulders back, a captivating smile on her face. He can see her head spinning with ideas, and holy hell, if her joy doesn't infuse into him. Briggs hates shopping, but today, with Maeve, he's enjoying watching her scrutinize every item, picking through aisles of boxes that to him all seem the same. But mostly he's enjoying touching her in public, being her boyfriend in front of people. Briggs Murphy is damn proud he gets to love her.

Maeve reaches up on tiptoes for yet another container, some round spinning contraption, but she can't reach it. Briggs manages it easily.

"And what the hell is this one, exactly?" he asks, giving it a twirl.

"A lazy Susan. It's for organizing condiments." Briggs narrows his eyes, and Maeve snatches it from him. "Don't even think about using them at the pub. I saw it first."

Cart full, they line up at the cashier and begin to unload. When they're halfway through, Maeve stops and examines all that she's picked out, her bottom lip tucked in her teeth.

"You know what . . . I don't need the lazy Susan." She reaches to take it back. "Or the pantry canisters. Or a tea storage box. Am I really going to use that? I mean, how much tea does a person need . . ."

She starts to put items back in the cart, her joy replaced by anxiety yet again.

Briggs stops her, taking her by the chin. "What is it?" And there goes that bottom lip again, stuck between her teeth. "If you keep chewing that lip, I'm gonna get jealous. That's my job."

Maeve grins, but it doesn't reach her eyes. She glances at the items. "I can't buy all this."

"Because you won't use it?"

"No, I'll definitely use it. I just . . . can't afford it," she mumbles.

"I asked you here on a date, Maeve. It's only right I pay."

"But—"

He won't let her refuse him. Instead, Briggs kisses her to stop her from saying anything else, relishing that he can do it in public. Then he starts unloading what she's put back in the cart onto the checkout counter.

After they've loaded everything into the car, Maeve turns to Briggs in the front seat. "What now? Target? Crate and Barrel?"

"Now," he says, "I show you off to Cork."

They head to Fitzgerald Park first and spend a few hours walking the grounds, hand in hand, watching people in the gardens. They get brunch at the SpitJack, Briggs's favorite restaurant in the city, where they both order the SpitJack Classic, a twist on eggs Benedict, and Bloody Marys. (Briggs takes his virgin.) They stroll through the English Market and finally end up at Costigan's Pub.

"So . . . ," Briggs asks as they sip their pints. "Have you enjoyed our first date so far?"

It dawned on him last week that while he and Maeve had spent nearly every day together, they had yet to go on a proper date because, well . . . they can't on the island. Not this time of year.

"I don't have a lot of experience when it comes to these things, so I'm open to feedback," Briggs jests. Maeve chuckles, and then her eyes well with tears. Panicked, Briggs reaches for her hand. "What is it, Maeve? Did I mess up somehow?"

"No!" She focuses on her lap.

"Are you not having fun?"

"Today is so perfect, I don't want it to end," she says between sobs.

"Then . . . why are you crying?"

Maeve fumbles for the right words. "It's not you . . . it's me. I have to tell you something."

Briggs takes a breath to calm his racing heart. Every beat echoes in his chest like a drum. She's going to tell him she's leaving. That's what her anxiety has been about all day. Bloody hell, how could he have been so naive?

"Look at me, Maeve," he pleads. And again, the words "I love you" are on his tongue. But how can he say them now?

Then it's like she snaps out of whatever trance she was in. "It's just . . . I found out recently that my grandpa is alive."

Briggs exhales, and he swears his heart does, too. "Bloody hell, Maeve. I thought you were about to tell me something bad." He relaxes in his seat and waits for her to continue.

"I'm sorry. I thought both of Liam's parents were dead, but Barb told me my grandpa is actually in a nursing home that specializes in Alzheimer's. Here in Cork. She and Linda visit him twice a month. Being here, knowing he is, too . . . I've been thinking about him all day."

No wonder she's seemed distracted. Finally, her behavior makes sense.

"I'm well aware he won't know who I am," she continues. "Barb said he doesn't even remember Liam, or that he died, but . . . I want to see him, Briggs. Is that crazy?"

"Not crazy." Briggs touches her cheek, and she leans into his palm. "But why didn't you just tell me?"

"Because I didn't want to ruin our date. You planned it so well, and I didn't want to mess it all up."

"I like your mess, remember? But are you absolutely sure you want to do this? You might not like what you see. It might hurt more afterward."

"I know." Maeve winces. "But . . . I'd rather meet him and deal with the pain than have the regret of wondering what it would have been like. It's a piece of Liam I actually get to see alive. A piece of . . . me."

Every time Driggs thinks he can't admire Maeve any more, she says something like that. "You might be the bravest person I know."

She brushes off the comment. "You jump into ice water every day, and I won't set foot in a grocery store without a detailed list, or I'll have a panic attack."

"That's complete shite," Briggs says. "I don't jump because I'm brave. I jump because I'm scared out of my head, and I hate the feeling. But you . . . for all your packing squares and monthly planners and chip clips, you walk into chaos well."

"Colored pens help." She smiles.

He returns the grin. "Do you know the name of the place?"

Thanks to Barb, she does. They finish their pints and drive to meet Niall Doherty.

The nursing home is a sprawling property on the outside of Cork, surrounded by mature blooming gardens and pathways that wind around the estate. Patients and visitors stroll the grounds, enjoying the midsummer sun.

At the front desk, Maeve asks about Niall. If she's nervous, she doesn't show it. When she introduces herself as his granddaughter, Briggs's heart squeezes.

"Well, that's obvious," the nurse says with a friendly smile. She escorts Maeve and Briggs to Niall's room.

It's small, a cross between a hospital room and an apartment. Niall sits in a wheelchair, perched by the window. When the nurse announces that he has a visitor, Niall turns, and Maeve sucks in a breath. Niall has the same crystal-blue eyes as his granddaughter.

They wait to see what will happen next, but Niall just turns back toward the window. The nurse had tried to prepare them for Niall's failing condition. Communicating is difficult at this stage, she warned, almost nonexistent. And he can't move much.

"What should I do?" Maeve asks.

"Just sit with him," the nurse suggests. "He'll like that."

Maeve moves toward her grandfather and pulls up a chair. Briggs lingers in the back of the room, giving her space. Before she sits down, she glances back at him. He gives her an encouraging nod.

The nurse leaves them, and for a while nothing is said. Niall and Maeve look out the window at the courtyard.

Maeve finally says, "It's a nice day outside. Why don't we take a walk?" She covers Niall in a blanket, his body frail and thin, blue veins lining his hands. She wheels her grandfather through the hallway and out into the courtyard, picking a bench under the shade of a tree. Briggs hangs back, present but not wanting to interfere. They sit in silence, a lost look in Niall's eyes. The longer they sit, the more evident it is to Briggs that Maeve is struggling. Maybe this really was a bad idea. She was gutted after reading Liam's letter, and this is no better. Niall can't give her answers. Can't tell her stories. Won't remember that she visited.

But right when Briggs decides it might be best to leave and spare Maeve any more heartache, Niall turns to her. Their eyes meet. He places a hand on Maeve's and says, "I know you." He seems to light up, as if snapped out of a trance. Briggs doesn't dare move.

"Hi, Grandpa," Maeve whispers, tears already collecting on her cheeks.

Niall smiles at her. "Liam said you might come."

She gasps and clasps her hand over her mouth. And then as quickly as it happened, Niall's clarity ends. The veil comes down over his eyes again. Maeve puts her head on his shoulder, tears running down her cheeks, and the two of them sit in silence until a nurse tells them it's time to head back inside.

Briggs doesn't say a word when they leave. He didn't want to interrupt Maeve, but now they're too late to meet Derry. It would be treacherous to sail back to Inishglass in the dark. They'll have to wait until the morning.

Now in the car, Maeve says quietly, "Do you think he really knew me?"

Briggs wants to tell her yes, but he can't lie to her. "I don't know, love. Maybe."

She turns to him, emotionally overwhelmed, like the day he found her surrounded by Liam's presents. Damn it. He wanted today to be a good memory. One they would remember fondly for years to come. And now he can't even get her back to the island.

But her hand lands gently on his, and a smile slowly grows on her face. "That was one of the most amazing experiences of my life, Briggs. And it's because of you. Niall may not remember me, but I will never forget this day. It felt like . . ." She searches for the right words. "Like Liam was there. I know it doesn't make any sense. I didn't know him. But I swear I could . . . feel him. Do you think that's possible?"

After Briggs's father died, he begged for a sign that Joe Murphy hadn't completely left the Earth. None came. Weeks, months, years went by without even a dream of his father. And then one day, Briggs was walking to the pub and heard his father's voice. He whipped around, startled, thinking Joe was behind him. He heard the voice again, but he couldn't explain it. It wasn't conjured from his own imagination. It *was* Joe. He's never told anyone about the experience, and still today, as he tries to describe it to Maeve, it remains inexplicable, mysterious.

"Maybe it really was him," she says. "And maybe Liam was there today."

"Maybe."

She settles back in her seat, seemingly more serene than she's been all day. "Today was perfect."

An idea comes to Briggs, and he asks Maeve if she can handle one more adventure. He knows of a place they can sleep tonight.

"One of the best views in the city," he says.

In Cork city center, they pull up in front of a three-story town house, blue with white-trimmed windows lined with colorful flower boxes. They walk up to the front door, and Maeve looks adorably pinched, fighting her need to know, to plan, to prepare. But right as Briggs is about to open the front door of his mother's home, Peggy Murphy comes barreling out and almost runs into her son.

"Mum," Briggs says as he stumbles back.

"Briggs," Peggy says at the same time. Usually more chaotic, her shoulder-length curly auburn hair is styled. Her face, normally bare, has a touch of light makeup. "What are you doing here?"

Normally, Peggy delights in seeing her son, but tonight, she seems nervous. Something is off. Briggs takes in the scene—her bag, the makeup, the nice clothes. "Are you . . . going on a date?"

"Don't give me that look." Peggy feigns annoyance. "I'm fifty-seven years old. I don't need permission from my kids to spend the night with my boyfriend."

"You're spending the bloody night? And since when do you have a boyfriend!"

Peggy adjusts the overnight bag on her shoulder. "Don't look so shocked. I'm not that old. And what the hell are you doing here, anyway?"

Briggs introduces Maeve and explains the situation broadly. Peggy does a terrible job trying to act like she has no idea that Briggs is dating Liam Doherty's daughter, when he knows damn well that Isla hasn't missed relaying a single detail.

"So the rumors are true?" Peggy asks with a broad smile. "God, your father would get a kick out of this. Even he couldn't have seen this one coming."

"It's nice to meet you, Mrs. Murphy," Maeve says bashfully. When she moves to shake hands, Peggy snatches her into a hug.

"Guest bed is made, and there's wine in the kitchen," Peggy says with a wink. "And next time, Briggs, maybe call before you come. For both our sakes." She adjusts the overnight bag slung over her shoulder, and Briggs cringes at the thought of what his mother will be doing later on.

He knew she dated. Hell, he was happy for her when she finally put herself out there, five years after Joe's death. But Isla had conveniently forgotten to mention an actual boyfriend, a fact that he plans to bring up with her once he's back on the island.

But on the bright side, he and Maeve have the house to themselves, not a bad turn of events. He guides her inside. The downstairs has a living room, dining area, and kitchen, all neatly decorated in modern furnishings.

Maeve takes it all in, as if absorbing the first floor one breath at a time. Framed on the fireplace mantel in the living room is the first painting Briggs ever made. She homes in on it immediately.

Briggs scratches the back of his neck as she examines the stick figure of his father. The whole body is painted in yellow, with a sprinkling of brown across the face where Joe's beard was. A green square serves as a jumper, and for pants Briggs painted two long rectangles of dark blue. The eyes are brown, the lips are red. No nose, those being too hard to paint at five. But his mom's favorite part is the arm that holds the pint and looks like it grows from Joe's ribs instead of his shoulder.

Maeve picks up the painting. "This is my new favorite."

She walks into the kitchen like it's her own and rummages around the cabinets, pouring a glass of wine for herself and a glass of water for Briggs.

"I'm glad we're stuck for the night," she says. "I guess there are advantages to being late . . . sometimes."

They continue the tour, making their way to the second floor where Peggy and Isla have bedrooms. Maeve stops to admire Isla's shoe collection, and finally heads up to the third level, which boasts a guest bedroom and a terrace. The evening is warm, and Maeve leans on the railing, gazing out at the city around them.

Briggs stands next to her, resting his forearms on the railing, and chances a question he hasn't dared ask until now. "Do you miss Chicago?"

Maeve nods, and then shakes her head, and then shrugs. "I don't know. I miss Chicago like you miss your dad. I miss how I used to love it."

That he understands.

Maeve takes a sip of wine, the setting sun making her skin glow and her eyes sparkle. Seeing her like that, radiant in the fading light, has Briggs's fingers itching to capture the moment on canvas. "Don't move," he says, disappearing inside to search for art supplies. When he comes back, Maeve is right where he left her. She laughs at the markers and construction paper in his hands, art supplies lying around for when his nieces come into town.

Briggs shrugs. "It was all I could find."

He gets to work drawing her in the dimming light. His attention roams every inch of her, taking in her curves, her legs, her lips. Maeve is the most relaxed she's been all day.

When he's done, Briggs hands her the drawing. The laughter that booms from the back of her throat echoes across all of Cork.

The stick figure has long brown hair, red lips, and blue eyes. One arm juts out from her ribs, holding a glass of wine. "Like I said," Briggs teases. "I don't do portraits often, but I think this one's pretty damn close."

Maeve throws herself at him, nuzzling her face in the nook of his neck. "I'll cherish it forever," she whispers.

Finally, the words that have been building up all day gush out. "I love you, Maeve."

Maeve lets go of him. "What?"

He's surprisingly calm when he repeats the words. "I love you. I'm not asking you to say it back. I just need you to know how I feel."

Maeve blinks, her eyes wide, as if calibrating what he's just said. "Thanks for telling me," she says casually, as if he just told her he wanted Indian food for dinner.

They stare at each other, gobsmacked, and then burst out laughing. Briggs grabs her around the waist and throws her over his shoulder in a fireman's carry. "Well, this deserves a proper fucking."

He lays her down on the guest bed and strips her clothes off as she giggles. How he lasted all day without licking her from top to bottom seems unfathomable now that she's naked before him. His tongue teases the softness between her legs as he slides his fingers inside her. Her back arches, her breath catches, and every time she says his name, he grows harder, knowing she wants him. And now that he's told her how he feels about her, Briggs feels more like himself than ever before. Like his love for Maeve fills in for his shortcomings and makes him a better person.

"I'm going to do this to you for as long as you'll have me," he says, and they both gasp in relief as he slides inside her. She grinds her hips into his, panting his name, pulling him closer. "This is just the beginning of our story, Maeve, but if my heart gives out tomorrow, at least I know that every last beat of it went into loving you."

He ignores the hiccup in his chest at his own words. The tightness that, over the past few weeks, has gotten worse. The fact that walking up the three flights of stairs earlier made his head light and his vision speckle with stars. And as they unravel together, Briggs says a little prayer, asking for more time and yet knowing prayers like those usually go unanswered.

18

Anna F.
New York, NY
8/3/2023

★★★

Where's all the drama????

Popped over to Inishglass last week after following the Thatch and Moorings on Insta, hoping for a
giant slice of drama pie. NOTHING. Briggs Murphy
wasn't even there. Neither was the Doherty girl. I
feel like I bought tickets to a Broadway show and
saw the understudies.
I will say, though, it is a little odd that they were
gone at the same time. Maybe the conspiracy the-
ory about those two is true. Is there a secret no one
on Inishglass wants us to know?
SIDENOTE: Had a great smoothie at Mettā Café. If
you're on the island, go there. That place is dope.

Maeve meets Derry at the fishing dock, without Briggs. The day is warmer than usual, with thin clouds hanging in the sky. The air is eerily still, like it's conserving its energy before unleashing a storm, which everyone on the island is predicting for this evening. Even the water is calm along the coast, small ripples, nothing like the usual churning whitecaps and stormy gray. Far out on the horizon, there's no hint of the onslaught anticipated for Inishglass. It's the literal calm before the storm, and the weather couldn't be better, which is exactly why Derry said they needed to do this today.

After Derry took Briggs and Maeve to the mainland, Maeve realized the person she needed to get her to Cairn Island had been in front of her the whole time. A slightly more precarious trip, since there is no dock to pull into, meaning that Derry will have to anchor off the island and send Maeve in on a dinghy, so they had to have a calm day.

Now that it's finally happening, Maeve's nerves are at an all-time high, and not because of the weather, though Derry assured Maeve that if they get their timing right, that won't be an issue. It's not the sea or storm she's worried about. It's what's on the island that has her stomach in knots. Maeve has come to realize that Liam's items aren't arbitrary. There's something out on Cairn Island that he needed her to see, but what, she hasn't a clue. She just knows she has to see it—and not to complete the list, not because she needs to sell the pub or because Konrad from American Debt Services has called her every day for a week asking for payment.

She's doing this for Liam.

Maeve has made her decision. She's staying in Ireland. When she dares to entertain the idea of leaving, her body seizes up. Her heart squeezes, her muscles grow tense, her stomach turns into a tight knot that won't relax no matter how many breaths she takes. How could she deny what her body is telling her? And while she doesn't want to hurt Maryann and Keith, what's worse? Abandoning her family or abandoning herself?

As she walks down the dock toward Derry's boat, her phone chimes with a text.

Watch out for the sharks today.

Maeve laughs at Briggs's text, happiness welling to the top of her head.

She replies, I didn't know there are sharks in Ireland!

Eoin?

Good point.

Just . . . be careful.

You're cute when you're worried. But it's just fishing. You're the one who jumps into the ocean every morning. WITH SHARKS.

Bloody hell, it's sexy when you're right. Just wear a life jacket for feck's sake. And let me know you made it back.

I will. Promise.

A few seconds go by as she waits, watching the typing bubbles, for Briggs's next text. They disappear, but then they're back, and a moment later his text comes through.

I love you.

Seeing the words induces a pinch of guilt in Maeve, who told Briggs that Derry invited her for a fishing "ride along." She knew that telling him she was going to Cairn Island would only incur an onslaught of questions, and after he's been so open and honest with her, how could she let him down and admit she's kept things from him? She should have told him everything weeks ago, but back then, Maeve didn't know what she was going to do. She had no idea she was going to fall in love with this place, let alone with Briggs. The past few weeks have been like a dream, and she's treated it as such. She has lived in an alternate universe, actively avoiding her life in Chicago, her parents, her debt, Sonya. She avoided telling Briggs the truth because she didn't want to make a mess of everything. And now that she's waited, she only looks more guilty. So she panicked and lied about today, as well.

But she does love Briggs. The oddest thing happened when he said those three words. Standing on the terrace of his mom's townhome, at that moment, everything was . . . right. Maeve didn't have to think. Didn't have to plan. She felt her whole body, so solidly, right then. It was like placing the last piece in a puzzle, completing the picture.

Turns out, in Ireland, Maeve found what she didn't even know was lost.

Herself.

But she has to talk to Maryann and Keith first, come clean about Liam and Spencer and the debt. She plans to after the party tomorrow. She just needs another day of living in this dream. And then she'll talk to Briggs, tell him everything, make him understand why she did what she did, and then tackle him to the ground and not only tell him how much she loves him, but show him, too. Maeve hearts his text and puts her phone in her pocket.

Derry is clad in rubber overalls and a rain jacket. He stands on the deck of his boat, which is outfitted with multiple fishing lines and nets. A dinghy with oars is hooked to the back. The plan is to get as close to the island as possible and drop anchor. From there, she'll row to shore. Derry helps Maeve aboard and hands her a life jacket that smells strongly of fish and salt water. She loops it around her neck, takes a picture for Briggs, and tries to send it, unsure whether it will go through. As the motors flare, Maeve asks Derry, "Have you ever seen a shark out here?"

"A few." He winks. "But don't worry about them."

"They won't eat me?" she jokes.

"Oh, they'd eat you if they could. But if you fall overboard, you'll be so hypothermic by the time they get to you, you won't notice."

"You're taking the piss, aren't you?"

"Best to stay on board and not find out." Derry winks again, cheeky old man. Derry's son Mikey—the spitting image of the fisherman with rosy cheeks, freckled fair skin, and kind eyes—tells Maeve to head up to the captain's deck while they push off from the dock, which she gladly does.

Twenty minutes later, Derry anchors the boat about fifty yards off the island. Not wanting to send her alone, he asks Mikey to accompany Maeve, and they climb into the dinghy. Once in the small, vulnerable craft, Maeve understands why they had to do this today. Normally, the waves would demolish it, but today they glide through the calm surf like a duck on a pond.

The island is shaped like a butte, rocky cliffs rising to a flat, green expanse at the top. The beach is part sand, part rock. Maeve takes off her shoes and socks, rolls up her pants, and helps Mikey drag the dinghy out of the water. The cliff to the top of the butte is intimidating, and somehow Maeve knows whatever she's searching for is at the top.

As she dries her feet and puts her shoes back on, Mikey says, "There's a trail to the top just that way." He points to her left.

"Have you been out here before?"

"Only once. A few months ago." The hesitation in his voice stops Maeve from asking any more questions. Probably best not to know. Mikey looks out at the horizon and says they have an hour before the wind is supposed to pick up and they need to be back on the fishing boat. Maeve thanks him and checks her phone. There's no service on the island. Her text to Briggs never went through. With only an hour, she sets out.

The trail is a series of steep switchbacks. At times, Maeve crawls on hands and knees, dirt embedding itself under her nails and scuffing the knees of her jeans. It takes ten minutes of sweat-inducing work to get to the top. By the time she does, she's out of breath, dirty, and chilled.

But once her body calms and she takes in the expansive view, awe returns. All of Inishglass is spread out before her, the rolling green hills for which it's named, the tangly roads and patchwork fields. The view is gorgeous, better than any you'd get from a ferry. Maeve is struck by the place all over again, but this time because it is her home. Just thinking the word causes a wave of relief to wash over her, like nothing she's ever felt before. Her frustration dissipates. If she had time to sit down and just stare at her island, she would. But with every passing minute, her time is running out. She needs to find what she's looking for, and fast. Trouble is, she has no idea what that is.

Maeve takes an organized approach, starting her search at the outside of the butte and working her way in. The ground is uneven, and she has to watch her step while staying on guard for anything unusual. But nothing stands out. It's all just green grass, rocks, and peaty earth.

Maeve closes her eyes. Out here, the air smells fresh like Briggs, earth and salt water. Maeve can't imagine going back to the bus fumes and exhaust of the city. And yet, that girl is still in her. The one who was lulled to sleep by the rumble of the L train, who learned to ride a bike in the alley behind her house, whose collection of takeout menus filled two kitchen drawers (alphabetized and categorized, of course). For a second Maeve wonders if she's just fooling herself. Can she really give up that life for a small island with one Indian takeaway joint that doesn't even deliver?

She opens her eyes again, and every doubt evaporates when she sees her island. Then she notices a crop of ordered stones, different from all the other scattered, rough ones. These are smooth and placed in a line. Maeve races over, feeling time slipping away from her.

Everything stops when she sees what they are. The air stills as Maeve looks down at the neat rows of graves cut in perfect rectangles. Each has a cross, an inscribed name, and dates.

George Ronan Doherty, January 17, 1915–May 29, 1996
Grace Mary Doherty, July 31, 1918–August 3, 1994
Doherty . . . Doherty . . . Doherty . . .

Each one a relative.

Judy Catherine Clare Doherty, March 4, 1940–October 16, 1997

Her grandmother. And then Maeve falls to her knees in front of the newest stone, not yet weather-beaten like the rest.

Liam Niall Doherty, November 23, 1973–April 29, 2023

Mikey's words come back to her. He was here, just once, a few months ago. That explains the hesitation on his face. Maeve's finger traces the letters and numbers on the headstone.

"Hi, Dad," she whispers. "I made it."

A gust of wind picks up, sending ripples over the water below, and just like Briggs described, Maeve hears a voice that she has never heard before, one that is wholly not her own.

"Thank you," Liam says, from somewhere out at sea, far over the horizon, the words echoing in Maeve's heart.

~

The storm blows in with gale-force winds and sheets of rain, knocking out power across the island. The pubs close, as do all the other establishments, and people hunker down to wait out the worst of it. Maeve is packing up the eco-pod in candlelight when there's a knock at the door. Briggs stands outside, soaked from head to toe.

"What are you doing here?" She guides him inside.

"I tried to call, but nothing's going through. I was worried since I hadn't heard from you."

"But I texted." She grabs her phone to show Briggs, but it never went through. She and Derry had returned to Inishglass right as the rain started, and the weather turned so quickly, even Derry seemed nervous as the sea kicked up and waves hit the stern, splashing the deck as ominous clouds trailed them the entire way back to Inishglass.

Maeve had gone straight to the pub, which had already shut down for lack of power. She returned to the eco-pod and ran into Ivy, who gave her candles, a flashlight, and a bottle of wine, which is now open on the counter, half-drunk. "Storm essentials," Ivy called them. Maeve immediately jumped in the shower and has been packing ever since.

"I'm sorry," she says. "Do you want a drink?"

Briggs shakes his head and exhales. "No. Don't be sorry. It's the storm. It's making me irrationally worried."

"You're pretty cute when you irrationally worry."

"It's not a look I'm used to, honestly." He runs his fingers through his wet hair, his stress palpable.

Maeve places a hand on his chest, feeling the heavy beat of his heart. "Don't worry. The sharks didn't get me."

Briggs bows his head like he's exhausted. "Feck, Maeve. What have you done to me?"

"I could ask the same of you," she whispers. With Briggs here, the violent storm outside disappears, and everything settles. For just a moment, all Maeve's confessions sit on the tip of her tongue, ready to tumble out. She needs to tell him, should have told him already. The mounting pressure sits on her chest like a boulder, but how can she unburden herself tonight, when Briggs is already out of sorts? She can't, so she holds in all that she wants to say. Just a little longer.

Briggs runs his hands up and down Maeve's arms, as if reminding himself that she's here in front of him, solid and breathing.

"Do you ever visit your dad's grave?" she asks.

He shakes his head. "My mum and sisters do. They find it comforting." He exhales a long, shaky breath. "Not me. All I think about when I'm there is what a big man he was, and what a small box he ended up in."

Maeve has come to know one thing about grief—it never goes away. It just changes outfits. One day grief dresses up as sadness. The next it's masquerading as joy. The next it's a dull anxiety in the back of the throat. Humans think death is final, but it's one of the longest relationships a person will ever have. Joe Murphy may have died ten years ago, but Briggs will live with his ghost for the rest of his life, just like Maeve will live with Liam's.

Briggs steps back from her and paces, clenching and releasing his fists. Maeve has never seen him like this, all tightly coiled like he's about to burst. She moves closer, wanting to soothe his unease, but he holds up a hand to stop her. "I never wanted this, Maeve."

His words steal her breath. "What?"

"I tried to stop it from the start."

"I know," she whispers.

"I was perfectly fine before you came to this damn island." He finally meets her eye, his expression intense and strained. Maeve's heart is wild in her chest. Whatever he needs to say is growing bigger with every passing silent second, sucking the air out of the room.

"Why are you saying this, Briggs?"

"I don't know if I can do this, Maeve. I'm so fecking scared."

He rubs his hand over his head as she attempts to digest the bomb he's just dropped. Water has collected on the floor, and Maeve does the one thing she can think of to calm the pounding in her ears, the fuzz in her brain. She grabs a towel and starts wiping, frantically trying to fix the mess.

Briggs drops to his knees next to her and grabs her hands, but she can't look at him. "Damn it, Maeve. I'm not saying this the right way."

"It's OK." She shakes her head, refusing to cry. "I'm just glad you're telling me now. Better to back out before . . ." Before she upends her whole life. Before she attempts to make this dream a reality. She knew better. It felt like a dream for a reason: because it's not real. How could it be? People don't fall in love like they have. There's no logic to it. Only frenzy. You can't navigate a whirlwind. Eventually you'll end up lost. What's that famous quote? "A goal without a plan is just a wish." She's been living in a wish, but she knows that wishes are just vapor. No structure. That can't be sustainable, right? No wonder Briggs is coming to his senses.

"That's not what I'm saying." Briggs holds her tightly. "When I hadn't heard from you, the thoughts that went through my head . . . I was out of my mind. You're all I want, Maeve. And the worst part is, I know we won't last. No matter what. One day I will lose you. It could be tomorrow. It could be in eighty years. And I'm trying, with everything in me, not to run from that, but damn it, it's hard. I don't know how to hold you lightly, knowing that at any second this could all end."

"You don't think I'm scared, too?" she counters. "You made a mess of my life, Briggs Murphy. You're the last thing I expected when I showed up on this island. But—harsh reality—it happened. *We* happened."

He shakes his head. "I never wanted to be a 'we.'"

"Well, I never wanted a mess. But you spilled that damn drink and changed my life."

At that, the coil wrapping Briggs loosens. His mouth slackens, and one end curls up ever so slightly. "I knew the second I saw you, flopping around like a fish out of water." He takes her face in his hands, his thumb caressing her cheek as he inhales deeply. "Maeve, I'm gonna mess this up over and over again. I'm gonna make mistakes. I'm gonna say the wrong thing and freak out when you don't call, but I promise, I will work every day to be a better man than the day before. I will work at holding you lightly, so I don't suffocate you. I don't want to be the man I was before you. That man didn't deserve you, and I want to be the one who does." He reaches toward his pocket. "I know what I'm about to do is crazy. I have no idea how we'll make it work, but I've come to realize that's love. Trying every damn day to build a life with no guarantees, other than that you'll do it together for as long as you can."

It dawns on Maeve that Briggs is about to pull out a ring, a diamond ring for a very specific purpose. She can't let that happen. Not yet.

"Wait." She stops his hand, and Briggs's eyes go wide. She hasn't told him everything yet. Hell, she hasn't spoken to Maryann and Keith. They don't know she's in Ireland. They don't know Briggs exists. How can she say yes when her parents think she's still in Chicago? She's too far gone, and none of it will be rectified tonight.

"Do you not want—"

"No," she says quickly. "I mean . . . yes. I want you. And I want you to ask your question. But I need more time. Forty-eight hours. Just until after the party."

Briggs exhales again, his taut shoulders releasing. "The party . . . right."

To reassure him, Maeve grabs her planner, turning to two days from now. She writes in bright purple: *Meeting with Briggs Murphy.*

"Does ten a.m. work?" She taps the page with the pen.

Briggs considers for a moment. "I think I can shuffle things around."

"Now don't be late." Maeve wags a finger at him. "We have a few things to discuss."

Briggs takes her by the hips and pulls her toward him, his body relaxed and playful once again. "I love it when you talk organization."

"How many hours should I block off?" she jokes, pressing into him. "One? Two?"

He takes the planner and crosses out the whole day. "I plan to take my time celebrating." Then he tosses the planner to the side as Maeve wraps her arms around his neck. All feels right again. Maybe Maeve was wrong. Even a whirlwind has form. Maybe crazy love has a plan after all. "You've got forty-eight hours, Maeve."

"Is that a threat?" she postures.

"It's a fecking promise."

He kisses her to seal that promise, and her hands run through his damp hair as she savors the taste. She strips Briggs out of his wet clothes and stands back to admire the man that's all hers.

"If you keep looking at me like that, I'll be forced to mess up this clean room," he says.

Maeve's suitcase is open on the bed, the clothes neatly organized in packing cubes. She pushes it onto the floor and lies down. "Do your worst, Briggs Murphy."

~

Liam's apartment is perfect. Every item is where Maeve wants it to be. She adjusts the navy and cream throw pillows decorating the matching couch, slicing her hand down the middle to create the perfect V. The stick figure that Briggs drew of Maeve is framed on the mantel, making her smile now when she passes it. Next to it is the elephant, a red bow still around its neck.

The dining table is set for eight: Barb, Linda, Derry, Hugh, Aoife, Isla, Briggs, and Maeve. In the next room, the bed is made. The bathroom is stocked with toiletries. The only thing Maeve didn't have time to unpack was her bag, because she spent all morning prepping pierogi, which are lined on the kitchen counter and ready to be boiled. She stands back to admire the apartment. This is not what she planned for her life. It's better.

Now that the power is back on, Maeve needs to shower and change into fresh clothes. Downstairs the pub is bustling again. Tomorrow, she'll be back behind the bar, but tonight is reserved for Liam.

The storm ended early this morning, though it took a few hours for the island's power to be restored. Outside, the sky is clear blue, no lingering evidence of last night's destruction except pools of leftover rain on the pavement and in the fields. This evening, cooler air coasts through the open windows, filling the apartment with the fresh scent of the earth after a hearty downpour.

Maeve showers quickly, then picks through the clothes in her bag, settling on a lavender crop sweater and jeans. She adds the pearl earrings Liam bought for her eighteenth birthday. With her hair done, it's nearly time for the guests to arrive. Maeve lights the sandalwood and rose candle (bought for her fourteenth birthday) and attempts to play Spotify on the wireless speakers (her twenty-second birthday present), but the Wi-Fi has been iffy the past few hours.

What shocked Maeve most about Liam's gifts was their accuracy. Of all the candle scents, he picked sandalwood, her favorite. Maeve had always borrowed Maryann's pearl earrings, never her diamonds, for formal occasions like school dances and family weddings, preferring the softer look. When she was eight, she was obsessed with Taylor Swift's album *Fearless*. She watched the "You Belong with Me" video on repeat. Maryann got her the album poster for her eighth birthday, along with a T-shirt. That year Liam got Maeve an iPod Nano, which she charged a few weeks ago. One album was loaded on the device: *Fearless*. That might be easily explained; Maeve wasn't the only young girl obsessed with Taylor Swift, and it was the best-selling album for kids her age at the time. Maybe for everyone. Liam could have googled "best gifts for eight-year-old girls" and taken a chance that Maeve wasn't any different than most. But then there's the elephant . . .

It's her favorite animal. When three of them died at Lincoln Park Zoo, Maeve started a petition to ban elephant exhibits in northern states. She walked up and down her street in Chicago, rang every apartment buzzer, and collected over one hundred signatures. A few people even gave her money, which she donated to the International Elephant Foundation. She was five years old. She had elephant sheets and a bedspread and an elephant shower curtain. When she had to pick an animal for a first-grade report, she picked the elephant. She researched the different species—African savanna, African forest, and Asian—and could recite a list of their differences. African elephants are bigger and both males and females grow tusks, whereas only male Asian elephants grow tusks. African elephants have a flat head; Asian elephants have two cranial bumps. They have a different number of toenails and different coloring on their trunks and ears. And then there are Borneo pygmy elephants, the smallest in the world, and Maeve's particular favorite.

She got a perfect score on the assignment, and for Christmas, Maryann and Keith adopted a Borneo pygmy from the World Wildlife Fund for her. She hung its picture and adoption certificate on her bedroom wall and told everyone she had a pet elephant named Bubbles. The day she read Liam's letter, she checked the tag on the stuffed elephant: Bubbles.

Maeve didn't have the words to tell Briggs all of this when he found her. How can any of it be explained? How can a man she's never met know her? Maybe it's all coincidence. She's not the only one who loves elephants and pearls and sandalwood and Taylor Swift. But she's choosing to believe in magic.

When the first guest knocks right at seven, she knows it's Briggs. He wouldn't be late. But as she goes to answer it, her phone chimes with multiple text messages and music starts to play over the speakers, a sign that the Wi-Fi has finally kicked back on. Maeve forgoes the phone for the door. The most important people tonight will be here in person.

Briggs is wearing a baseball cap and hoodie, pulled over his head to hide his face like a celebrity attempting to avoid paparazzi. He peels them off, displaying the scarf Maeve knit, and kisses her on the cheek.

"I cannot believe you wore that," she says. "It's hideous." But when she attempts to pull it from his neck, he stops her.

"I hope you're making a matching hat. Winter will be here before we know it."

Hugh, Aoife, and Isla file in after Briggs, bearing housewarming gifts, which Maeve chastises them for buying.

Isla hands her a wrapped box. "Open it," she says with a wide smile. Maeve gives it a little shake, suspecting what's inside, then neatly pulls back the paper, flips the lid open, and reveals a pair of pristine white Air Force Ones. "Classics," Isla says. "Every closet needs a pair."

Maeve knows just where she'll put them in her closet, but for now she immediately puts them on, modeling the shoes for Isla.

"Brilliant," she says and smiles. While the two of them haven't spent much time together, Maeve likes Isla. Like Briggs, his beautiful little sister has spunk. She doesn't let Briggs get away with anything. She fights back. And while she may keep her shoes clean, her room is a mess. There's a story there, Maeve can tell. Maeve thanks Isla with a long hug. Tomorrow she'll be Isla's future sister-in-law. The thought ignites a whole new round of butterflies.

Aoife hands Maeve a heavy round pillow with a bow tied around it. "It's a meditation cushion. I expect to see you both in class on a regular basis, considering I'm the reason you can't wipe those goofy smiles off your faces."

"You? What about me? It was a group effort," Hugh says. "I almost died that morning running." He hands Maeve a grocery bag. Inside is gin, Campari, sweet vermouth, and some oranges. "Everything you need for the perfect Negroni, since I won't be here to make them for you myself."

Briggs won't let it show just how sad he is that Hugh is leaving, but Maeve knows. She gives Hugh a long hug and whispers, "Thank you."

When he pulls back, Hugh looks at Briggs. "You're right. Definitely grapefruits."

Briggs yanks Maeve away from Hugh with a threat to keep his hands off, and they all bust up laughing. Briggs's gift is last, but Maeve can tell from the wrapping that it's a painting.

"Did you hear the news?" Hugh asks her, slapping Briggs on the back.

"What?" she says.

"Furphy's finally doing an art show at the pub."

Briggs shrugs off Hugh's hand. "It's not a feeking art show. I'm running out of space in my studio, so I figured I'd hang a few at the pub."

"Sounds like an art show to me," Aoife says, which gets her a glare in response.

"I wish I could see it," Maeve says.

Briggs kisses her on the temple. "I'll give you a private tour."

Maeve opens his present, expecting one of his pastoral paintings, but instead she finds a self-portrait, identical to the one on the mantel, except that this stick figure holds a whiskey instead of wine.

"It's perfect," she says. She places it next to his other drawing and steps back to admire them both. "Now the room is complete."

Barb, Linda, and Derry arrive, and what was an empty space a month ago is now full. It's exactly what Maeve wanted. Hugh breaks into the Negroni ingredients and starts making drinks while Maeve gets to cooking the pierogi.

At one point, between the music, laughter, and talking, the apartment is so full that Maeve is almost overwhelmed. For so many months she hid in her garden apartment, spending time only with Sonya, scared to put herself out there, scared to leave her protective bubble, worried there was something wrong with her. And now, to have all this feels almost impossible.

Briggs comes up behind her at the stove and pins her between his arms. "I have an important question for you," he whispers, nipping at her earlobe and sending warm goosebumps down her arms.

"I thought questions were on hold until tomorrow."

"This one I need to know before then."

"Really?" Maeve spins toward him, spoon in hand. Her phone chimes with two more text messages. It hasn't been this active since she's been on the island, but after the storm, it must be catching up on old texts that never came through.

"I've wanted to ask this for a while now," he says. "The answer says a lot about you, so choose wisely."

Maeve cocks an eyebrow at him. "Go on."

He leans down to her ear, his breath light on her skin. "What's your karaoke song?"

A few weeks ago, at Mettā Café, Maeve heard it, and she knew right away that the song was hers. No one else at the party knows that hidden in the corner is a karaoke machine she plans to pull out after dinner. Tonight, she'll sing it in front of everyone. Maeve backs away from Briggs with a cocky grin. "Almost time to eat."

"Fecking tease." He grabs her ass in delicious retaliation.

Everyone takes seats at the table as Maeve browns the pierogi in the skillet until they're perfectly crisp. Babcia would be so proud. She would get such a kick out of knowing that her pierogi are a huge hit in Ireland. They even have a hashtag! Maeve has the inclination to send Babcia a picture, but Babcia's terrible with her phone. When Maeve sends her a text, she calls complaining that she can't read it because the font size on her phone is meant for young people and she's an old fart. Her words, not Maeve's. Maeve has tried to explain that she can make it larger, but Babcia has no interest. Maeve can't believe it's been over two months since she talked to her.

With the pierogi perfectly plated, just a sprinkle of chives on top, Maeve turns to serve her guests. She hears the first-floor door open and someone start up the steps. She counts the guests to see who is missing, but they're all here. She tries to remember who she might have mentioned the party to, but there's no way she did. Briggs's and her relationship is the best-kept secret on the island. The only people who know are in this apartment. And no one else would just walk in without knocking, like they owned the place.

Except . . .

Maeve thinks Eoin's name as he appears in the doorway. "Well, look at this. Seems like we've crashed quite the party. I must have missed my invitation."

The plate slips from Maeve's hands, falls to the floor, and shatters. She drops to her knees to pick up the mess, and Aoife and Linda immediately jump in to help her. Dinner is ruined.

Briggs stands from his seat, anger in his eyes. "What the fuck are you doing here, O'Connor?"

"Calm down, Murphy. God, you always were a hothead. I'm just as surprised to see you."

Maeve glances up from her spot on the ground, hands covered in butter and potatoes, attempting not to cut herself on the broken porcelain. "What are you doing here, Eoin?"

"You didn't get my email?" he says, sounding shocked but knowing full well that the island's internet has been down for almost twenty-four hours.

"I wasn't sure I was going to make it with the storm," says a man that Maeve finally notices standing behind Eoin. He speaks in a posh British accent and looks around the apartment like it's a piece of art. "And I thought England had shitty weather. Ireland's bloody dreadful."

"This is Henry," Eoin says. "He's the one I told you about."

"Told me about?" Maeve asks, confused.

"God, Kaminski. You really have been distracted." Eoin glances at Briggs, who is doing everything in his power to remain calm. She wipes her hands, and as she's about to grab her phone from the counter, Eoin adds, "We discussed this in detail. He's my mate from London."

Maeve is still trying to piece together what the hell he's talking about when she sees six missed texts on her phone. Five from her mom and one from Sonya.

Shit. She quickly pulls up Sonya's text.

I think I messed up. CALL ME. Maryann knows.

Her stomach sinks as Henry, now in the living room, says, "Love the place."

Maeve doesn't know what to deal with first: the messages or the situation in front of her. She doesn't remember Eoin ever talking about a friend from England, but whoever this Henry is, it's not her concern. Maeve opts for her mom's texts.

Honey, call me. I'm concerned.

I just got a voice mail from Konrad. Who is he and why is he calling me? He said something about a debt? What is going on?

OK. Now I'm worried. I'm calling Sonya. Where are you?

YOU'RE IN IRELAND?!

I spoke with Konrad. I don't know what to say. How could you keep this from me? Keith and I are back in Chicago. Come home NOW.

"I wasn't convinced when Eoin proposed the location," Henry says. "A pub on a remote Irish island? It's a crazy investment, but then I did my research. Not only is this place an Irish wet dream, but you've made it a social-media sensation. I couldn't believe the online presence. The number of reviews. And the whole hashtag Irelandsmostwantedpotato dispute? Brilliant. People love family drama. Look at Harry and William. Meghan and Kate. We'll need the pierogi recipe, of course, and rights to the Doherty name, but well done, you. I should be thanking my lucky stars that Eoin contacted me first, so I can get in before the other potential buyers."

That's when Maeve remembers. The restaurateur friend *in London* who might be interested in buying the Moorings. Her stomach sinks. There is no time to salvage the situation. No time to halt the breakdown about to take place.

"Potential buyers?" Briggs says.

Maeve needs a pause button. Her life is coming down around her, and she can't stop it.

"Kaminski didn't tell you?" Eoin asks, as if Briggs is pathetic, as if Eoin and Maeve have had multiple secret conversations about selling the pub. That might have been true, but they haven't talked about it for weeks now. Not since the kickball game. Eoin had gone silent, and Maeve thought they were done. She figured he knew he lost and was licking his wounds.

How could she have been so stupid? After everything Aoife told her about him.

"We'll have to remodel a bit, of course," Henry says, walking around the apartment with an inspector's eye. "But this second level is perfect. More tables means more customers."

Like a cunning animal who knows when he has his prey backed into a corner, Eoin's face blooms into a malicious snarl. This whole situation was a planned attack.

"If you can't tell, Maeve's selling the pub, mate," Eoin says casually. "You didn't honestly think she'd keep the place, did you?"

Briggs's jaw works, bloodlust written all over his face. Aoife steps in front of him and says, "Fuck off, Eoin."

"Dirty talk has always been your specialty. Glad to see nothing's changed."

Briggs tries to leap forward, but Hugh grabs his arm. "Bro, you have to calm down."

This isn't good for Briggs's heart, not that Eoin knows or cares.

Maeve steps forward and points at the door. "Eoin, get out."

"But I thought this is what you wanted," he says innocently. "I mean, that's why you finished the list, right?"

"What list?" Briggs snaps.

"Liam's list of requirements that she has to complete before she sells," Eoin says matter-of-factly. "It's the only reason she stuck around the island in the first place. She's been begging for me to send her home this whole time. But rules are rules, right, Kaminski?"

"What list?" Briggs growls, this time at Maeve.

"What was it, Kaminski?" Eoin says. "Learn to knit some kind of scarf . . . win the football rounders game, which was brilliant by the way, though I was upset not to be a part of it." Maeve cringes as he ticks off on his fingers. "And Derry told me yesterday you made it to Cairn Island. Congratulations. I didn't think you'd check that one off so easily, but I shouldn't have underestimated you. You've got guts, Kaminski. You work hard when you need to. You got the pub revenue up, just like I suggested. I knew the pierogi would be a hit. You could teach a class in scarcity marketing. And taking the pub to social media. Brilliant. And from what I read recently, there are rumors of a secret romance between you and Murphy. A cunning move. Nothing draws people in like forbidden love. It's a little too *Romeo and Juliet* for me, but people like that sort of romantic shite, and if it brings visitors to the island and into the pub, who cares, right? Money is money, no matter how you get it."

Maeve is too stunned to counter this speech. In one swoop, Eoin has managed to make everything that Maeve has done seem like a calculated plan to sell the Moorings. Even her relationship with Briggs looks like a deception.

"Congratulations, Kaminski," Eoin concludes smugly. "Now you can get the hell off this island, just like you wanted."

"We can iron out the details once I get back to London," Henry says, oblivious to the mess around him. "But I think I can speak for my partners when I say we'll take it. You've got yourself a deal."

Henry extends his hand, offering Maeve the solution to all her problems, but she's frozen. She thought she had time to explain, thought she had time to clean up her mess and fix the situation without hurting anyone. But she was wrong. Again.

But right as she's about to bat away Henry's hand and unleash her anger on Eoin, Briggs turns to her and says, "And you called me the liar." He storms out of the apartment.

Isla throws Maeve an apologetic look and chases after him, Aoife on her tail, calling his name. Hugh lingers to finish the last swig of his Negroni, then glances down to Eoin's crotch and says, "Baby fucking carrot." And then he's gone, too.

Barb, Linda, and Derry are left at the table. Maeve falls into one of the vacant seats, phone in her hand, tears welling in her eyes.

Derry puts a hand on Maeve's shoulder, worry across his wrinkled brow, his eyes laden with guilt. "I think this was all my fault. I mentioned the party to Eoin. I thought he'd be invited since he's your friend."

"Should I book your ticket home, Kaminski?" Eoin asks, pleased.

Right then, Maeve's phone rings. She picks it up.

Maryann doesn't bother with hello. "You have some explaining to do. Get your ass home. Now."

19

Briggs sits at the edge of the water, feet dangling into the ocean. He can't feel his toes or calves anymore. He's been up all night and sitting here since five in the morning, wishing he could just jump and rid himself of the terrible feeling in his gut. But he hasn't moved. It's now well past nine. For the first time in years, Briggs simply sits on the edge and waits.

He knew this would happen. For as much as he wanted to believe otherwise, logic whispered in the back of his mind these past two months. No wonder he was so terrified the other night. He knew this was coming. He just didn't want to admit it. Why the hell would Maeve stay in Inishglass? She has a life and a family in America. As pissed as he was last night when Eoin sauntered in like the asshole he is, a part of Briggs wasn't surprised when he heard the news that Maeve wants to sell the pub. Why hold on to a family relic that means nothing to her? Seeing what he wanted to see, Briggs may have convinced himself that she cared, that she felt a connection to the Dohertys, but that doesn't change the reality. He wanted to believe the dream he had concocted, but believing something doesn't make it true.

Last night, he had to leave. One second more in that apartment with Eoin and he would have gotten violent. Too many years of pent-up frustration with that prick would have reared its ugly head. He didn't want to do that to Maeve, not when she spent so much time fixing the place up. Not in front of her friends. Eoin wanted Briggs to look like an animal, like the villain. Beating Eoin to a bloody pulp would have played right into his hands.

Briggs rubs a hand over his tense brow, seeing the past couple of months clearly. How could he have not recognized that there was more at play? Just a few days ago, Maeve said she was going fishing with Derry, when really she was going to Cairn Island for some blasted list. He had sensed she was keeping something from him, but he didn't have the guts to ask. What an idiot.

He clenches his hands together until half-moons form on his palms. Had their day in Cork been a part of it, too? Was visiting Niall part of the list? It makes Briggs sick to think about it.

God, he wishes he could jump into the water and forget about her. But he can't shake her off like a shirt at the end of the night. He can't rinse her from his skin like soap. He can't fuck away the feel of her, no matter how many women he invites into his bed.

Lost in furious thought, Briggs doesn't hear Hugh approach until he sits down, out of breath and sweaty.

"Well, that was one way to get me to run." Hugh exhales an exaggerated breath.

"You didn't need to come here."

"Piss off. Yes, I did."

"No. You didn't. I'd rather be alone."

"So, we're back to this. How typical."

"What the hell does that mean?"

"This is just so predictable, Furphy."

"Watch what you say, mate. I'm in the mood to pound something."

"Hit me all you want. It won't solve your problem."

"Do you have anything useful to say, or did you run all the way here to piss in my wounds?"

"Your wounds?"

"Yeah, my wounds," Briggs snaps.

Hugh chuckles. "You know . . . I thought you finally got it, bro, but you haven't changed at all."

"Got what?"

"You hoard pain like it's fucking money. The more you have, the more careless you get to be. Pain gives you all the excuse you need to dick around. Travel the world. Shag anyone you want. Never make a commitment. Hell, you wouldn't even decorate your own damn house! And then Maeve came along, and I thought you finally snapped out of it. Grew the fuck up."

"Don't talk to me about growing up when you've lived in my sister's bedroom for the past five years. For free."

"Of course I'm not grown up. That's not my role here. I'm the fuckup. The drifter. The last kid that parents neglect because they're over all the parenting. No one expects great things from me, and for a while, that gave me every excuse not to give a damn, just like pain gives you all the excuses you need. But now it's just old. It's fine if no one else cares what I do, but *I* need to care. At the very least, I need to respect myself. I need to give a shit about me because I have to live with myself, just like you have to live with yourself. And it feels better to care, Furphy. It feels good to try. Not caring is actually really exhausting. I'm tired of meeting everyone's low expectations. I'm tired of being predictable. I thought you were, too. I thought we were in this whole 'grow the fuck up' thing together. You're better than this, man. Why are you giving Eoin what he wants?"

"What the hell is that supposed to mean?"

"He set you up, and you fell for it. I'm an idiot, and I saw it coming! Last night was so well staged, I thought I was watching a goddamn nineties sitcom. And you played right into his hands, like you haven't read this script a million times. It's always the same with assholes. You don't think that was calculated? Eoin knew exactly what you were going to do. And just like he wanted, you left her. You didn't even let her explain!"

How could he have played into Eoin's hands yet again? How many times has Aoife told him to let go of the past, but he never did? He let it fester until it became poison. Aoife had warned him, and now he's living it.

"I didn't want to get blood on the carpet," Briggs says through clenched teeth. "And explain what? She's selling the pub."

"She didn't say that, dummy. Eoin did. And if she *is* selling the pub, which you have no real proof of, have you considered that there's most likely a very good reason?"

The more logic Hugh throws in his face, the more Briggs feels like he's being slapped repeatedly. His body actually aches from the verbal beatdown.

"You're taking the word of an arrogant son of a bitch who's notorious for twisting a situation for his own benefit," Hugh continues, "over this woman who has spent the past month fucking your brains out and making you smile like a goddamn idiot. You say you love her, but you took the word of your enemy over hers. You didn't even stick around long enough to let her talk. So she didn't tell you everything up front. So she has a past and a few secrets. Don't we all? Her life was turned upside down in a matter of months, and you're pissed she didn't tell you everything? She's been a little busy, bro, running a pub and fighting with you. And you haven't helped."

"What do you mean I haven't helped?"

Hugh looks agog. "Um . . . you're about as fragile as a porcelain doll right now. My sisters went through puberty with fewer emotional outbursts than you've had in the past two months. Combined. And may I remind you, there are seven of them."

Briggs sputters over what to say, wanting to bite back at Hugh but unable to justify it.

Hugh pats Briggs's knee. "It's OK, man. I get it. No one's blaming you. You pulled an emotional one-eighty in a matter of days for this girl. Hell, you fell in love. That'll trip up the best of us. You're bound to be . . . overly sensitive. But consider her perspective. Maybe she just didn't want to rock the boat by dumping a bunch of baggage in your lap right now."

Briggs wants desperately to counter him, but when Hugh puts it like that, it makes complete sense. He replays scenes from the past few months, seeing them from Maeve's perspective. He's been all over the board with her. And two nights ago, during the storm . . . Briggs rubs his forehead. He was a basket case. Bloody hell, what has he done?

"I'm gonna ask you something, and I want you to seriously think about the answer," Hugh says. "Do you *really* love her? I mean, *love* her. Not just love fucking her. I mean when she's old and wrinkly and your dick can't get hard anymore. When her tits are down to her knees and her mind is gone, and your ass is so saggy, it practically drags on the floor. Do. You. Love. Her?"

When they visited Niall Doherty, Briggs observed the old man, his mind gone, unable to remember that his wife was dead, let alone what it felt like to love her. And Briggs had faltered, for just a second, slipping back into his old self, seeing the uselessness of it all. He imagined Maeve in the same chair, vacant eyes, spending every day staring out a window, waiting for the end. All those years loving a person, only to forget them. Life could be brutal. Life could mangle a person beyond recognition. And then, Niall looked at Maeve, and Briggs knew that life could be beautiful, too. It could offer moments that take your breath away. Briggs would rather die tomorrow loving Maeve than live a lifetime screwing beautiful women only to go to bed alone.

"You know I love her," he says.

"Well, last night, it didn't seem like it," Hugh says. "You left her. With Eoin. You handed her over to your enemy without a look back. And now you're sitting here brooding because you think she doesn't love you. But a man in love would have stayed, Briggs. Love doesn't make you run. It makes you dig your heels in. So maybe the problem isn't Maeve selling the pub. Maybe the problem is *you*."

Each word sinks in like nails, deeper and deeper, until all Briggs can do is yell, *"Fuck!"*

Every word Hugh said is true. Briggs feels it to his core. His heart begins to pound. How could he have been so stupid? When he found

Maeve crumpled on the apartment floor, his only thought had been to help her. Why didn't he do that last night? She needed him, to scoop her up again and help her fight, and instead he ran like a coward. He was going to propose to her today. How can he ask for a commitment like that after what he's done?

"What do I do?" he begs Hugh.

"Seriously, bro?" Hugh cocks an eyebrow. "You don't know how this ends? You go after her. Tell her you're sorry and make sweet, sweet love. The end."

Briggs checks the time. It's two minutes to ten. He's supposed to meet Maeve today. It's in the datebook. He can't be late.

"You're a good mate, Hugh. The best."

Hugh waves away the compliment. "Yeah, yeah. Name a kid after me."

Briggs is in his car in seconds, barreling down the winding road back to town, driving at speeds he hasn't attempted since he was seventeen. He flies around a bend and almost runs into a flock of about a hundred sheep crossing the road. He slams on the brakes and grips the steering wheel. He'll send her a text. Tell her he's late but on his way. He reaches into the front seat where he keeps his phone, but of course, he left it at home. He had wanted to brood in private. Bloody idiot!

He lays on the horn and inches his way through the sheep. Finally through, he gasses it, speeding toward town. In the village, he has no choice but to slow down. Tourists are everywhere, jamming the streets with cars, bikes, or on foot. Why is all of Europe on vacation right now? He's better off making a run for it.

His doctor won't like him sprinting, but if there was ever a time for risk, it's now. Briggs double-parks the car and leaves the keys on the front seat. He'll apologize later, after he's done groveling at Maeve's feet. And he plans to grovel. If it takes the rest of his life to prove how much he loves her, he'll spend every day showing her.

Briggs takes off down the street in his flip-flops but quickly tears them off, gaining more ground barefoot, as fast as his legs will let him go toward the Moorings on the other side of town. He weaves through the crowd, stepping on toes and narrowly avoiding knocking an older woman over.

And then he sees the pub, just down the road, practically calling him. People linger outside, taking pictures. His heart pounds from exertion, but just a little farther and he's there. With tired legs and overworked lungs, he sprints the last few blocks. As he approaches, people turn in his direction, no doubt wondering what a crazed man is doing running at full speed through the street. Briggs vaguely hears someone say, "Isn't that the Murphy guy? Ireland's Most Wanted Potato?"

Briggs speeds around back. He doesn't bother knocking and takes the stairs three at a time.

"Maeve!" he yells. "I'm sorry I'm late, but I'm here!"

He bursts into the apartment. The table is still set, though the dishes have been cleaned, the pots and pans put away. Nothing is out of place. He can barely catch his breath as the bedroom door opens.

"Mae—"

But it's Barb who greets him, her lips pulled into a thin line, arms crossed over her chest. New images come to light now. Maeve's knitting bag is gone. Briggs's eyes fly to the mantel. The stick-figure drawings are still there. For a second, he's relieved . . . but then he notices that the elephant is gone.

"You're too late, Briggs," Barb says, her New York accent harsh. "She's gone."

His head spins as he searches for any trace of Maeve, his chest constricting in pain. He winces, his blood pounding too hard, his heart squeezed like a balloon. And then over in the corner, tucked away, he notices a karaoke machine. Maeve must have gotten it for the party last night. A surprise. No wonder she wouldn't tell him her song. She wanted to show him. And now he'll never know.

Briggs walks to the mantel, lightheaded and sweaty. He touches the drawing of Maeve, her bright eyes drawn in the color Bluetiful, and collapses.

20

Allison Y.
Spokane, WA
8/10/2023

★★★★★

Did anyone else see that?

So I'm standing outside the Moorings taking pictures with my sisters when this insanely gorgeous
man comes racing down the street like his ass is on
fire and he's Jack Ryan about to save the earth from
a bomb that's been planted in the pub. And then
I notice this isn't just some random hottie super-
hero. This is Briggs Murphy. Ireland's Most Wanted
Potato. So I snap a pic of him because who doesn't
want that eye candy for later (winters are long in
Spokane). Not that he notices. He's all yelling some
girl's name like he's Romeo trying to find Juliet. And
then he just disappears into the pub.

And all I could think at that moment was . . . Damn.
I hope a man runs after me like that one day.
#starcrossedloversofinishglass

Maryann and Keith are at O'Hare when Maeve arrives. Her suitcase may be heavy, but it's nothing compared to her heart. She prepared herself throughout the entire flight for the disappointment on her parents' faces, but when she comes through the arrival gate, Maryann exhales like she's been holding her breath since Maeve told her she was coming home. No disappointment, only relief. Seeing that, Maeve cracks, breaks into a run, and falls into their arms.

"It's OK. You're home. We've got you," Maryann says, her floral smell so familiar, it eases the ache in Maeve's chest. She must think Maeve wants to be here. That this is her daughter's home. That Maeve wants this.

Maeve doesn't have the guts to tell her mother how she really feels, to break her heart after she caused so much anxiety. She's too tired even to consider what will happen next.

"We missed you, kid," Keith says as he takes her bag.

"I'm sorry I ruined your cruise."

He waves away the apology. "You did your mom a favor. She wanted off that boat about two weeks into the trip. Turns out, Maryann Kaminski isn't really a cruise person. You gave her the excuse she needed to cut the trip short."

Maryann swats Keith's arm, like he's divulging a secret, but she doesn't correct him. "I'm a doctor. I should have known traveling around on a floating cesspool wouldn't be for me. No matter how nice it is."

Maeve has missed her family's banter and energy, her parents' familiarity. But as soothing as it is, it's not enough to fill the hole in her core. She clutches the elephant, trying to maintain an even keel when all she wants to do is fall apart.

Maryann notices the stuffed animal. "Reminds me of Bubbles, God, you loved elephants so much. Remember the petition you had people sign?" She laughs as Maeve tries not to cry "Did you pick that up in Ireland?"

At that, the dam breaks, and Maeve crumbles. A single tear slides down her cheek.

"Oh, sweetie! What is it?" Maryann begs.

"There's something I haven't told you yet . . . ," Maeve squeaks out. "About Liam."

Maryann's eyebrows rise, and the smallest flash of fear crosses her face. "Let's get you home. And you can start at the beginning."

~

When Maeve finished college, she and Maryann cleaned out her bedroom and packed up her childhood treasures for storage. All that's left now is the string of fairy lights around the ceiling.

"Adults should have more twinkle in their rooms," Maryann says. "Who doesn't want to look up and feel like they're sleeping under a night sky? I bet they'd be happier."

Maeve curls up in her old bed, blaming two weeks' lack of activity on her jet lag. She has no job. Sonya's no longer at her apartment. Maeve literally has nothing in her datebook. There's no reason to get up. She doesn't check her phone. Physically can't. If she touches it, she'll go straight to her photos, and then to Instagram, and then she'll be in a downward spiral she won't come back from. So she focuses on the tiny silver lights overhead, waiting for them to work their magic and make her happier.

Maryann and Keith mostly leave her be. They bring food and check on her a few times a day. Maryann reminds Maeve to shower. But everything hurts, and when the pain does lessen for a time, it comes back eventually.

Maryann and Keith know everything: the pub, the list, the presents, the debt. They offer to pay off what Maeve owes, but she refuses. Spencer is Maeve's problem, and she'll fix it. She tells her parents about everything, except Briggs. She aches just thinking of his name.

On day fifteen of her seclusion, Maryann tells Maeve she needs to wash the sheets. She suggests that Maeve go for a walk, get some fresh air. So Maeve wanders down the street toward the lake and onto the bike path. Lake Shore Drive is packed with cars and buses. Maeve puts her feet in Lake Michigan, hoping that might ground her. Boats pepper the water, their occupants enjoying the late August sunshine. Chicago is never more alive than in the summer. Maeve waits for the heartbeat of the city to jumpstart her own, but a plastic water bottle washes ashore at her feet, and there's broken glass everywhere, and graffiti mars the park bench behind her. The noise and exhaust make her head hurt. So she walks, eventually making it to Lincoln Park Zoo. She wanders the exhibits, hoping to see the elephants, but the zoo hasn't had elephants since 2009.

She walks again the next day, and the next. She walks like she's on a scavenger hunt, searching for the love she once had for Chicago. She walks until her legs hurt and her eyes burn. But the city smells like rotting garbage and dog piss, and the pavement radiates heat up her legs, making them sticky with sweat. Every dirt particle clings to her skin.

On her fourth straight day of walking, Maeve comes home, showers, and is about to climb back into bed when Maryann enters the room carrying a shoe box. She sits at the end of the bed and says, "I saw your grandparents today."

"I'm sorry I haven't visited them yet."

Maryann bats away the apology. "I was there looking for something." She taps the box.

"What is it?"

"Pictures. Back in the day, you had to get them developed," she jokes. Maeve tries to laugh. "This box is from when I traveled in Asia." Maeve sits up. "A few days ago, I remembered something about Liam.

We were sitting at the bar, and he said we should take a picture to document the night. He picked up my disposable camera and snapped a selfie of us. We didn't call them selfies back then. I remember when I got it developed, I laughed. He captured only a small bit of my face and all of his. So I went through the box today and found him. Do you want to see? It's a little blurry, but . . . it's him."

Maeve feels her first jolt of energy in three weeks. Maryann opens the box and takes out the picture. And there he is, smiling. Liam is young, with dark hair and bright blue eyes. He seems so happy. Even through the fuzziness, he radiates, like he's having the time of his life.

"His eyes were the first thing I noticed about him," Maryann says, barely above a whisper. "They were so beautiful. I was so happy you got them." Her voice shakes.

"Mom? What is it?"

"I hardly knew Liam, but I could tell, with just one night, how much life he had in him. He was someone you wanted in your orbit. Some people are just built with a gravitational pull." She looks down at the picture. "It's hard to believe that he's gone. It doesn't seem possible."

"He talked to me when I was at his grave," Maeve says quietly. "I know it doesn't make any sense, since I never met him or heard his voice, but I know it was him."

"What did he say?"

"'Thank you.'"

Maryann rests back against the wall. "He told me about his family's pub. He resented his father for forcing the place on him. I remember him saying that. He felt trapped in a future he had no say over. It's one of the reasons I never pushed him to take responsibility for you. I let him off the hook because he was already on one. I didn't want you to be another person he resented. I just can't figure out why he would leave the pub to you when he never wanted it in the first place. Why pass that pressure on?"

Maeve shrugs, knowing there will always be questions about Liam that will never get answered. "Can I keep this picture?"

"Of course." Maryann scoots off the bed and heads toward the door. She turns before she leaves. "But the island couldn't have been that bad. You liked it, right?"

Maeve admits, "I loved it."

"So maybe in the end, his life wasn't so bad there. Maybe he ended up loving it more than he thought."

"My friend Barb told me he had a motto at the end of his life," Maeve says. "'Enter laughing.'"

Maryann smiles. "I like that. He had a great laugh." She lets that lie, but adds, "Maybe that's the lesson here. Even in the bad times, if we search hard enough, there's always a reason to laugh, and if we can just hold on to that, maybe it won't hurt as bad."

So the next day, three weeks after coming home, Maeve decides to go looking for laughter in a familiar place. The garden apartment, which she's shared with Sonya since they graduated from college, is stuffy from being shut these past few months. Maeve opens a window, letting in a warm breeze. She plops herself on the couch where she and Sonya spent countless hours drinking wine, laughing, and planning their futures together. She waits to feel the slightest bit of joy from those memories, but all she registers is her best friend's absence. Maeve is alone. Again.

She hasn't contacted Sonya since she returned. There's just so much tension between them right now that Maeve doesn't even know where to start. But maybe it's time she tries.

So she texts: Remember when we convinced Victor Beale that after a woman has a baby an umbilical cord grows out of her belly button and for the rest of her life she has to trim it every month?

Sonya replies right away with a laughing emoji. You told him when women breastfeed, they flip their nipples down and spouts come out for the baby to drink from. And he believed you because your mom's a doctor. DYING.

Maeve laughs out loud for the first time in weeks. She sends three more laughter emojis. They go back and forth, rehashing old memories, Maeve giggling until her stomach hurts.

God, I missed you, Sonya finally texts.

Me too.

Maeve stares at her phone, wondering what will come next.
And then Sonya writes, Will you come over Saturday night?
Maeve doesn't reply right away. Can she go to Melanie's apartment, like nothing happened? Or is she so stubborn that she's willing to give up Sonya? Then again, Maeve's planner is dreadfully empty, and she needs to start filling her life up again.

Sure. What time?

Yay! 6 p.m. Sonya sends her the address in River North.
Maeve adds the details to her planner, and before she knows it, she's flipped back three weeks to the day she was meant to meet with Briggs. The day he was going to ask her to marry him. Now she'll never know if he would have gone through with it. She was prepared to say yes, even after the dinner-party nightmare. But when he never showed, she knew it was over. He would never be late.

She spends the rest of the day at the apartment and texts Maryann that she's staying the night. She orders from her favorite Thai food place and binges *Friends*. It's an improvement over staring at the ceiling in her childhood bedroom, at least. At some point, she'll need to get another job and find a new roommate.

The next morning, Maeve decides to reorganize her closet. She takes everything out and lays it around the room, but as she stands in front of the empty closet, no vision comes to her. No structure. No plan. Worst of all, she feels no excitement. Not like she did when she fixed up Liam's place. She looks at her bookshelf of rosewood-pink planners, shelved in chronological order with her initials on the spines. Her diaries of a control freak. The girl who wrote in them doesn't exist anymore.

Maeve puts on her Cubs jersey and favorite cutoff shorts, thinking that might help put her in the mood. Nothing. She leaves the clothes strewn about and ends up back on the couch watching *Grey's Anatomy*.

On her third day at the apartment, Maeve wakes up, still in her Cubs jersey and cutoffs. She emails her landlord, giving him a month's notice. She may not know where she's going right now, but she knows she can't live here anymore. This place was hers *and* Sonya's. Without Sonya, it's too empty. Hopefully Maryann and Keith won't mind if Maeve squats at their place for a bit longer.

And then right as Maeve is about to leave, there's a knock on the apartment door. For just a second, she thinks maybe it's Sonya, wanting to move back in. It's ridiculous, Maeve knows, but a lot of unexpected things have happened over the past few months.

It's not Sonya at the door. It's the last person Maeve expects, and she almost launches herself on him. She can't believe what she's seeing. He's actually here, standing in the doorway, sheepishly smiling, like he's here to rectify the biggest mistake of his life. It takes all of Maeve's strength not to wrap her hands around his neck . . . and throttle him.

Fucking Spencer.

He looks the same: Midwestern gorgeous, preppy, well-built, his sandy blond hair shaggy but acceptable at a country club. He rubs the back of his neck as he stands there, waiting. "Hi, Maeve."

For months Maeve has envisioned what she would say to Spencer if she saw him again, what she would do. Put him in a headlock. Break his nose. Spit in his face. Hold him hostage until he gives her every last dime to his name. Kick him in the balls. Or better yet, cut them off. But now, with the moment upon her, she's frozen. No words come. She's choking on them.

"Can I come in?" Spencer asks.

Maeve manages a nod, though her heart is screaming for her to poke his eyes out with a fork. Spencer enters hesitantly, like he's waiting for the roof to fall on his head. Seeing him in here, time seems to jump back one year. Spencer sits on the couch, and it's like a painting Maeve has looked at a million times. He fits in here, like the picture on the coffee table of Sonya and Maeve at a Cubs game. Like the ancient tea kettle in the kitchen. Like the Willis Tower magnet on the fridge.

Spencer rests back on the couch, his arms wide like he expects Maeve to fall into them. Like she might wipe clean what's happened in exchange for good sex and an apology. She stands across the room, her arms crossed. Spencer takes the hint and leans forward, his elbows resting on his well-tanned knees. His whole body glows summer bronze. No doubt he spent most of it lounging on a boat or at the pool, not at a desk indoors, working.

"Where's Sonya?" he asks.

"She doesn't live here anymore."

"Holy shit. I thought you two would live together forever."

"Things change." Maeve counts her words, promising herself to speak only the bare minimum.

Spencer runs his gaze up and down her body. "Yeah, they do. You look good. Really good."

"What do you want, Spencer?"

He runs a hand through his hair and swallows hard. "You wore that same outfit the first night I met you. Are you going to a game?"

"None of your business," she says curtly.

He raises his hands in surrender. "I get it. I wouldn't want to see me either after what I did."

"Then why are you here?"

He glances at her with a broken expression and sad brown eyes. "Because I'm sorry. I royally messed up. I hurt you and disappeared."

"I know all of that. You didn't have to come here to tell me."

"I know . . ." His jaw clenches. His hands do, too. "I'm here because I'm a coward, Maeve. OK? For the last nine months I've been living in my sister's basement, working at her local country club to earn the money to pay off the debt."

"You're working at a country club?"

He nods. "Landscaping. Cutting the grass. Maintaining the greens. I've even been bussing in the restaurant at night. I'll take out the garbage if it'll earn me a few extra dollars. But I like the landscaping bit. I'm actually good at it. They just offered me a full-time job."

Well, that explains the tan. "Good for you, Spencer. I'm glad you found your passion. I wish I cared, but it still doesn't explain why you're here."

He reaches into his pocket and pulls out a wad of cash. Hundred-dollar bills, a whole lot of them. "I'm here to pay you back. Every cent I spent on that credit card, plus interest." He counts the money on the coffee table: ten thousand dollars. "I know it's not everything I owe, but it's what I've made so far. Consider it a down payment as I earn the rest."

Maeve can't believe it. It's too good to be true. "Why should I believe there's more coming?"

"After what I did, you shouldn't, but maybe I could explain *why* I did it, and then, maybe, you'll trust me enough to know I *will* pay you back."

The coil around Maeve eases a bit. She sits in the chair across from Spencer, holding her posture strong. "I'm listening."

"You were the first girl I ever loved," he starts.

Maeve scoffs. "You had an odd way of showing it."

"I know," he says. "Just hear me out. I loved you. Like *really* loved you. From the first night I met you. You did something to me I'd never felt before. It was like . . . I was pulled into your orbit, and I couldn't get out. You had a hold on me like I'd never experienced with anyone else. And that scared the shit out of me."

"I had an orbit?" Maeve says. Just like Maryann said about Liam . . .

"You still do," Spencer says, looking embarrassed. "And the fact that you don't know it makes it even stronger."

"So it was all my fault because I sucked you into my orbit and made you love me? And you decided to ruin what we had because you were frightened of your strong feelings? I've heard this story before, Spencer, and it's bullshit. When you love someone, you don't leave, no matter how scared you are."

"No!" Spencer furrows his brow. "No, the opposite. I wanted you so badly I was scared you'd leave *me*. I wanted to impress you. I was afraid you'd leave when you found out what a loser I am. So I pretended not to be. Turns out, not being a loser takes a lot of money. I figured I'd just max out my credit cards, but I couldn't keep up. And since your credit was good, I opened a card in your name, justifying that every penny would be spent on you. I know, my logic was fucked up, but at the time, it made sense. I was desperate. I reasoned that it wouldn't be that big a deal when I eventually told you because I wanted to spend the rest of my life with you. I thought you'd think it was . . . sweet, actually."

"Sweet?"

"I know . . ." Spencer rubs his forehead. "Even well-intentioned lies are never justified. I know that now. I should have just told you the truth. We'd still be together if I had. Instead, I ruined us."

"And you left me to deal with it alone."

"By the time I realized how badly I screwed up, it was too late. I couldn't pay my bills, the rent, let alone the credit cards. My roommates kicked me out. I knew you'd wonder why, and I had already lied so much. You'd dump me. Hate me. I couldn't face that. I was ashamed and embarrassed, so I ran like a coward. I went back to Michigan and moved in with my sister. But I always planned to pay the debt back. I just needed to earn enough money to prove to you that I'm serious. I've been trying to see you for almost three months now. I've come here at least ten times, but you're never home. And I knew if I texted, you might not believe me. You might think it was another scam. I needed to see you in person."

Three months . . .

Maeve glances at the ten thousand dollars on the table. Is that enough money to forgive Spencer? Is there a price tag on forgiveness?

"I swear, I never meant to hurt you. I really did love you, Maeve. I just didn't love you the way I should have. I'm sure these past few months have been hell, all because of me. You deserve better. I knew the first night I met you I was playing well above the rim."

It would be so easy to let him off the hook. Maeve believes his confession. Why come back and lie to her now, after all these months? Everything he's said—about taking the credit card out in her name so he could take her on an extravagant trip to Mexico—makes sense. The pieces fit. And these past few months haven't been hell. They've actually been the best of her life. In the oddest way, if Spencer hadn't left her in debt, she might not have gone to Ireland because she wouldn't have needed Liam's inheritance. In the most twisted way, Maeve found Briggs because she loved Spencer first. Maybe he deserves her thanks for that.

Or maybe he fucking doesn't.

Maeve swipes the money off the table. "This is a start, but I expect more every month until it's all paid off. No exceptions."

Spencer nods. They come up with a system: He'll Venmo her, and she'll use the money to pay down the credit card. Any money she's already paid to debt collectors, he'll pay back, too. And all the interest. In the end, they shake on it. Spencer looks at their interlocked hands and smiles. He used to be so familiar to her. She knew the first sound he made in the morning and the last sigh before he fell asleep.

Maeve clasps her hands in her lap. "Well, that's it."

"That's it," Spencer agrees, his eyes downcast. Maeve ushers him to the door, but before he leaves, he says, "You might be dressed the same, but you're different. You're not the same girl I met at the bar."

"Sorry to disappoint."

"Disappoint?" Spencer says, his eyebrows raised. "I can't believe I let a girl like you get away. Biggest mistake of my life. Just know, whoever you end up with, Maeve . . . I fucking hate him."

~

Later that night, back with her parents, Maeve gets an email from Eoin.

Kaminski—

Rumor is you're back in Chicago. No goodbye kiss? You left before I could give you this (see attached). Also, I just received the offer from Henry for the Moorings. It's generous. I'm forwarding it to you now. The decision, ultimately, is yours.

Please advise.

—Asshole

The attachment is a scanned letter. Maeve recognizes the handwriting immediately.

Dear Maeve,
If you're reading this, you've completed the list, which means it's high time I explain myself. Why would I make you do those foolish things before you could take owner-ship of the pub? You probably assumed it was my way of convincing you not to sell it. If I could hold you hostage on the island long enough, you'd fall in love with the place, right?
But the thing is—I don't want that for you.
Why the hell did I make you do it then? The answer is simple. So you could walk away without any regrets. I wanted you to experience the island, the people, your family, so you could leave it behind and not wonder if you made the right choice. I know that kind of regret and it's bloody awful. I don't want that for my daughter.
So, I have one last request: Walk away. Go live your life somewhere else. Sell the pub knowing it was the right decision and I'm glad you did. I want a big life for my

little girl. Go find it. Don't limit yourself to our tiny island. You've experienced the best of it. Now put it in the past. It'll always be there for you if you want to come back and visit.

Be bold, Maeve. Take risks. Life is shorter than you think. Don't waste it. And when it's finally time for us to meet in the afterlife, I'll be waiting. I hope you enter laughing.

Love,

Da

Maeve reads and rereads the letter, sobbing in her bed, but this time Briggs isn't here to hold her. She's dreadfully alone, with no idea what to do next.

~

Sonya opens the door, shocked. "You're late, Maeve."

"Sorry." Maeve lugs herself inside.

"You're never late. I thought maybe you weren't coming."

"I lost track of time."

Sonya notices Maeve's poorly painted nails. "Oh my God." Then she takes in the wrinkled outfit that Maeve slept in. "Oh. My. God." She launches herself at Maeve and runs a hand up two weeks' worth of hair growth on her unshaven leg. "*Oh. My. God.* What the hell is happening?"

"Wine," Maeve whimpers. "Don't bother with a glass."

"Melanie!" Sonya yells toward the kitchen. "We have an emergency!"

An hour later, Maeve is reclined on the couch like she's in a therapy session. Half the bottle is gone, and the whole story's out in the open.

"That Eoin sounds like a real dick," Melanie says. "And I should know. Being a dick was my specialty."

Melanie is different than Maeve remembers. Softer. And the way she looks at Sonya, like she's gazing at the most precious piece of art in the whole wide world, tells Maeve everything she needs to know. She should have trusted her best friend. Sonya may be wilder than Maeve, more willing to take a chance, but she's smart. She knows bullshit when she sees it.

"I can't even blame Eoin," Maeve says. "I'm the one who lied to Briggs. Eoin just capitalized on it."

Sonya sits at the end of the couch, Maeve's feet in her lap, and speaks for the first time since Maeve started into the story. "I'm confused. Why are you here?"

Maeve sits up a little, her brain light with alcohol. "Because you invited me."

"No." Sonya waves the words away. "I don't mean *here*. I mean in Chicago."

"Briggs didn't come, Sonya! I waited, and he didn't come. I got my answer."

"Um, no, you didn't," Sonya says.

"How do you figure?"

"He never said he didn't want you."

"He was supposed to show up and *propose*," Maeve says forcefully. "He obviously changed his mind."

"Or he got caught up with something. People are late all the time, Mae."

"Caught up in what?" she counters.

"I don't know . . ." Sonya shrugs. "Traffic?"

Maeve is about to tell her how ridiculous that notion is when she remembers Eoin . . . her first night on the island . . . his excuse for being late. *Traffic.*

The sheep.

Maeve stands up in shock, her head spinning with wine and revelation, and immediately sits down again. "But he hasn't contacted me at all."

"So?" Sonya says. "Neither have you. And you left, Mae. I mean, what is he supposed to think?"

Maeve can't believe what she's hearing, and yet it makes perfect sense. Her words to Spencer come back to haunt her. *When you love someone, you don't leave, no matter how scared you are.*

She did the very thing Spencer did to her. She left without a word. She abandoned Briggs without explanation. And here she is, sitting in Chicago, acting like it's his fault.

"Fuck!" Maeve yells. "What do I do?"

"Are you seriously asking that question?" Sonya says. "Come on, Mae. Give yourself a little credit. You're the girl with a plan. If there was ever a person who knows what to do with a mess, it's you. Now go back to Ireland and clean this up."

Maeve launches herself at Sonya and Melanie, hugging and thanking them both. "I need to buy a plane ticket," she says, her mind swirling.

Melanie raises her hand. "I can help with that." Within minutes, she has Maeve booked on the next flight out, tomorrow afternoon. Business class.

"Seriously?" Maeve asks.

"As a thank-you," Melanie says. "For giving me a second chance." She smiles at Sonya, and Maeve sees it again. Real, raw love.

Maeve opens her email and sends a response to Eoin.

Hey Asshole,

Tell Henry I'm not selling.

Maeve

PS. Don't even think about walking into the Moorings ever again or I'll tell the whole town what you did to Aoife.

When she gets back to her parents' house, Maeve tells Maryann and Keith everything, including about Briggs.

"So the rumors are true?" Maryann teases. "You and Briggs Murphy. I was wondering when you were going to come to your senses."

"How do you know about him?"

"After you told us everything, I did a little digging." Maryann touches her daughter's cheek. "Babcia's pierogi. A culinary hit in Ireland! Who would have thought? I'm so proud of you, honey."

"You're seriously OK with this?"

"It doesn't matter if I'm OK with it," Maryann says. "It matters that you are. It's cliché, but Keith and I just want you to be happy. Plus, now that I've read so much about him, I need to meet this Briggs. He's quite the legend."

"Don't believe everything you read, Mom," Maeve says. "But in Briggs's case . . . it's true."

The next morning, Maeve heads to O'Hare. She sits in the back seat, fidgeting, running her hands up and down her smooth legs. When her phone chimes with a text, she's excited to see Barb's name on the screen.

You need to come back, Maeve.

Barb only has one tone. She's not reaching out because she misses Maeve. Something has happened.

Is it Niall???

No.

Maeve exhales some of the tension from her shoulders, but then another text comes through, and she gasps.

It's Briggs.

21

Millsie N.
Sussex, England
8/25/2023

✪✪✪✪

Silence.

Is anyone else concerned that neither the Moorings
nor the Thatch has posted anything on Instagram in
weeks? We were on the island just a few days ago
and the place was quiet. Too quiet.
Please tell me this story isn't over.

No one knows the exact origin of the grudge between the Dohertys and
Murphys. Some say it was a fight over land. Some say it was over sheep.
Some say it was as fickle as Mrs. Doherty excluding Mrs. Murphy from
a tea party. But most say it started over love. Two boys in love with the

same girl. Two girls in love with the same boy. Unrequited love. Star-crossed love. Forbidden love.

Because only one thing can ignite a passion so deep that it burns this long. If you're lucky love works in your favor. If you're not . . .

Five days after Maeve left Inishglass, a doctor cracked open Briggs's chest, stopped his beating heart, and removed a piece of it forever.

Briggs thought he was dying that morning in Liam's apartment. As his eyes went fuzzy, his hands tingled, and his legs gave out, he had a moment of clarity, but it was too bloody late. How could he have been so stupid? How could he have been so weak, so distracted, so blind? He'd seen firsthand how fast life ends, how fast one's planned future can shatter. He thought dying would be easier without love. Die with as few connections as possible and you'll leave the world a better place. He knew it, and yet he ignored it, convincing himself that falling in love was as good as heart surgery.

Briggs was not ready to die. No, Briggs was pissed.

"Cut the goddamn dramatics," Barb had yelled at him as she pulled him up off the floor. "You're wasting time. She left with Linda, fifteen minutes ago, for the ferry. If we drive fast, you might be able to catch her."

But as fast as he and Barb drove, it was too late. Maeve was gone before he got there.

As Briggs walked back to the car, defeated, Barb barked at him. "What the hell are you doing? You have a phone. Call her!" But Briggs had left his phone at home, and reception at the dock was shitty. "Fine. If you won't, I will."

Even then, Briggs stopped her.

"But you love her," Barb pleaded. "Why are you letting her go? Please tell me you aren't stupid enough to believe she doesn't love you back."

Briggs knew Maeve loved him. She may not have said it yet, but he knew.

He had made a decision when he woke up on the apartment floor. He may only have fainted, but it was too close a call. He had escaped death, but only for now, and if he wanted to love Maeve the best way he could, it was only fair to heal himself first. Scared as he was, it was time to mend his broken heart.

~

Twenty-four hours after surgery, Briggs is in the ICU. His mom, Isla, and Aoife rotate visits. Hugh runs the pub back on the island. After the first night in ICU, Briggs is moved to a general hospital bed. Forty-eight hours later, he starts to walk on his own. The doctors and nurses are impressed with his quick recovery, but he stays in the hospital for three more days, just in case, before moving to his mom's townhome in Cork to recuperate for the next week.

By the second week, Briggs is going crazy. His back and chest throb. Worse, he's anxious to contact Maeve. He wants to fly to America, to tell her what he's done, to touch her, kiss her, love her, convince her that he's sorry. Every mistake he has made is like a splinter he can't get out until he sees her, and they're starting to fester. But still, he waits. He returns to Inishglass, and his energy starts to come back. He walks around his house. One day he walks to his art studio, where he promptly lies on the couch and falls asleep, smelling Maeve on his blanket. He can't find the energy to paint and has to ask Hugh for a ride home.

Recovery would take weeks, the doctors had said, and Briggs finds it frustratingly true.

A few days later, he wakes up and walks to Aoife's meditation class. He walks home and takes a two-hour nap. The next day he does it again, this time needing only a thirty-minute power snooze. The day after that, when he gets home, Hugh is sitting at the kitchen table, sipping coffee and shaking off a late night at the pub. Briggs pours himself a cup and sits. He's not tired.

"I bought my ticket home," Hugh says. "I leave next week."

Briggs nods. "That's good, because you'd be out of a room soon. I'm selling the house."

Hugh chokes on his coffee. "What? When?"

Briggs tells him about a couple from France that he met back in July. "They mentioned wanting to buy a place in Ireland, and we kept in touch."

Hugh sits back in his seat, gobsmacked. "Wow. Does this mean we're like . . . fucking adults?"

"Aye. I believe it does."

"Well, this is a problem." Hugh rests his coffee cup on his stomach. "Who will my family make fun of at Thanksgiving now?"

Briggs chuckles. He'll miss Hugh more than he's willing to admit right now, but he's happy for him.

"Where are you gonna go once you sell this place?" Hugh asks.

Briggs sets his mug on the table. "I have a few ideas. It's time to make some changes."

"But you still haven't contacted Negroni?" Briggs shakes his head. "What the hell are you waiting for?" Hugh presses. "You had the surgery. You look relatively good, considering your beard resembles 1970s pubes."

"Piss off."

Hugh laughs. "Seriously, bro. Grapefruits like hers don't come around that often. If you don't lock her down, someone else will. You might be every girl's sexy Irish fantasy here, but your stiffest competition is a portly American who can't grow one scraggly chin pube, let alone an actual beard. But in Chicago there are guys in suits who own boats and have lots of money, which is a helluva lot sexier to some women. It's charming that you can make a fancy cocktail, but drinking them is a lot more fun, especially when someone else is paying. Have you seen a fit guy in a well-tailored suit? Eggplant city."

"If I wasn't incapacitated right now, I'd punch you in the face."

"Why do you think I'm saying it now? I know you can't come at me." Hugh leans forward and rests his elbows on the table. "Have you considered that the longer you wait, the more she might think you don't love her?"

Briggs has considered a lot of things these past few weeks. And while his lack of initiative might seem insane to Hugh, it's calculated. Because what Hugh doesn't know is that Briggs is selling his house so he can move to Chicago.

He has been selfish with Maeve. What he saw as holding on to her was actually holding her captive. If he wants to love her right, he has to compromise. If she wants Chicago, he'll go.

Briggs stands and puts his mug in the sink. "What's Thanksgiving like?"

Hugh shrugs. "It's mostly food, football, and familial shaming. But it's the only day of the year when you can eat stuffing and not feel guilty, so we put up with it."

"Must be some great stuffing."

"My mom makes it with sausage," Hugh says, and wipes his bottom lip like he's drooling. "It's fucking tits."

"Maybe I could come one year."

Hugh cocks his head. "Where are you going?"

He might suspect Briggs's plan, but now isn't the time for confessions. "I have something I have to do."

$\sim$

Briggs hasn't been to his father's grave in years. He has terrible memories of the day Joe Murphy was buried. The wet manure smell of the fields. The damp rain. The strong perfume of the older ladies in attendance. Smiling and thanking people for coming when really he wanted to scream and hide in his room. How unfair that on the worst day of his life, he had to be polite. It took years to get over it. Being back in the graveyard stirs it all to the surface, but this time it hurts a little less. He kneels down in front of Joe's grave, noting the dates of his life and wishing there wasn't an end, but ends are inevitable, and that's exactly why he's here right now.

When Briggs moves to Chicago, he won't be able to take the collage wall with him. His favorite picture of his father will stay cemented there, and he'll start a new collage in America.

It's funny that Briggs would love this picture of his father as much as he does. You can't see Joe Murphy's face well at all. It's a profile shot. He's kissing his wife. But what made Briggs love the picture so much was just that, that instead of smiling for the camera, Joe is kissing his wife, as if somehow, he wanted to be remembered not as a man who turned toward a flash, but who always turned toward love.

"It took me a while, but I finally get it, Da," Briggs whispers. "This will be my last jump."

Joe Murphy whispers back, "That's my son."

Briggs messages Barb: Text her now.

~

Briggs stands at the edge of the water in swim trunks and flip-flops. The late August sun warms his back when it manages to peek through the clouds. His hands tingle. His knees bend slightly with the urge to jump in. Around him, the water churns and slams against the rocks, but the pool just below is calm and deep. Safe.

Just today, his doctor gave him the OK to drive. He got in his Jeep and came here, the swerve of the roads so familiar, his body leaned into them like a choreographed dance.

Briggs peers over the edge, and for just a second, he thinks he'll jump. Three months ago, he would have. Three months ago, he would have seen it as a challenge. Three months ago, he would have seen it as a way of proving he was strong.

Three months ago, Briggs Murphy had a broken heart.

"Don't jump," a voice begs from behind him.

Briggs smells her before he sees her. He inhales her sweet scent, letting it flow into his lungs, feeling the blood flow more freely through his heart. Then he turns.

Her eyes home in on the scar on his chest like a beacon, and her mouth parts slightly. This creature he's wanted to devour for weeks stands before him, but the man she left isn't the same. He's scarred, and he's lost some weight in recovery. For just a moment, Briggs worries she'll be turned off by him. Disgusted at the mark that will follow him for the rest of his life.

Maeve approaches gently, her eyes on his chest. He wants to reach out, grab her, press her to him. It's been too long since he touched her, felt the soft skin of her thighs, the friction of their bodies. Every part of him quivers with desire and need. When her finger touches the sensitive skin of his scar, shivers crawl down his arms and his groin tightens. A breath he didn't know he was holding cascades out of his mouth as she traces the scar, slowly, as if memorizing it with her finger.

"Does this hurt?"

He shakes his head and grits his teeth. "Quite the opposite. But be careful with me, Maeve. They said eight weeks before I can shag again, and I promised I'd be a good lad."

Her finger moves from the scar to the left side of his chest. She places her whole hand on his heart. "How do you feel?"

"Relieved."

She nods, understanding. "Were you scared?"

Briggs shakes his head. "There are worse things than open-heart surgery."

"Why didn't you tell me?" She looks up at him, her brow pinched in confusion.

"Because I didn't want you to come back out of obligation or fear."

"But I—"

Briggs holds up a hand. "I had to prove how serious I am about you, Maeve."

"You could have sent a text," she jokes. "I would have believed you."

Briggs shakes his head. "I never should have walked out of that party. I should have stayed, because that's the kind of man you deserve, but I was a coward. I didn't want you to come back to that man. I wanted you to come back to someone better, someone worth spending your future with. I had to offer you the best version of myself. So this"—he places a hand on top of hers on his chest—"this is my way of making that a promise to you. I will take care of myself so I can love you better every damn day of my life. I won't leave again. I'll stay. Wherever you are in the world, I'm there, too. And if that's Chicago, then I want to come."

"You'd move to Chicago?" Briggs holds her gaze, putting all his confidence into his nod. "What about the Thatch?"

"Isla can run it."

"She's majoring in fashion design. She doesn't know how to run a pub."

"Then I'll sell it."

"But you love it."

He does. The Thatch is in Briggs's blood, as much as his father's DNA is, but he's part Peggy Murphy, too. "My mother moved to Inishglass for my father. If I have to move to Chicago so that you can be you, it's worth the sacrifice."

Maeve chews on her lower lip. Briggs waits, a part of him still nervous that she's only here to say goodbye, that his apology won't be enough, that leaving her once will still ultimately push her away.

"That's too bad," she says. Briggs inhales, preparing for the blow. "Because I don't live in Chicago anymore."

"Then wherever you are in America is where I want to be."

"I hate to disappoint you . . ."

Bloody hell, Briggs thinks. Hugh was right. He took too long.

"I'm not living in America anymore," Maeve continues. "And if you sell your pub, then who will my pub compete with?"

My pub. "You're not selling?"

She shakes her head. "How could I sell? I have a championship to protect."

Briggs laughs, and the tension in his chest that has lingered since his surgery evaporates. "Are you sure, Maeve? I don't want you to do this just for me."

"No, I'm doing this for me. Because I love you, Briggs. And I love this island. And I plan to stay right here for as long as you'll . . . fight with me." Her growing smile brightens the green all around them. "But I *do* have something very important to tell you."

"What?" Briggs pleads. "Whatever it is, I can handle it."

She takes a breath and locks her gaze on his. "'Hold On.'"

Briggs lifts one eyebrow, unsure what she means. "Hold on for what?"

"'Hold On' by Wilson Phillips."

"Maeve, what the hell are you talking about?"

She reaches onto her tiptoes, wraps her arms around his neck, and pulls him close. "That's my karaoke song."

~

Eight weeks to the day after his surgery, Briggs wakes up in bed next to Maeve. Hot, pulsing need radiates through him, like he's sixteen again and on the verge of having sex for the first time. He's so hungry for her, he can taste it.

He watches her sleeping deeply, wishing he could wake her up but not wanting to ruin her slumber. They both worked late last night. Tourists are still trickling onto the island, but it's finally slowing down a bit. With Hugh gone and Isla back at university, Briggs is busier than he's been in a long time. But he's enjoying the pace, and the customers, more than he ever has, thanks to the woman lying next to him. He no longer wakes up every morning anxious to jump. No, he's more than happy to stay right where he is for as long as he can.

But this morning, Briggs needs a distraction, so he rolls out of Maeve's bed and tiptoes to the shower. The weight he lost is back. The scar on his chest has faded some, along with his back pain, and while he still gets a little winded from time to time, he breathes easier now than he ever thought possible.

He takes his time in the shower, trimming his beard and manscaping. When he emerges from the bathroom in a cloud of steam, the faint sound of music comes through the closed bedroom door. He smiles and walks, towel around his waist, across the living room toward the noise, noting the stick-figure drawings and elephant on the mantel. He has a list of places in mind for their honeymoon, all destinations where Maeve can see her beloved elephants in the wild. Now if he would just ask her to marry him. The ring his mother gave him is tucked away in a drawer at the art studio. But he's not in a hurry like he was a few months ago. For now, he's enjoying their life just as it is. Someday, he'll get down on one knee.

Someday . . .

Briggs chuckles at the song as he quietly cracks the door to find Maeve in nothing but a **SAVE FERRIS** T-shirt, dancing ferociously to "Shut Up and Dance." She thrashes her head back and forth, throwing her hair in all directions. Her hips circle and pump, not to the beat, but to whatever rhythm she imagines in her head. She spins in a circle, tossing her hands in the air and singing the lyrics at the top of her lungs.

She turns and sees him in the doorway and pauses, her breath heavy, hair in her eyes.

Briggs leans on the doorjamb. "Should I get a spoon?"

Maeve smiles and blows the hair from her face. "It's been two months," she says. "I thought this day would never come."

"Aye," Briggs says, in awe of this woman. Thank God she left that damn red door open. "Me, too."

Maeve bounces across the room, pulls him toward her, discarding the towel on the floor, and together, they start to dance.

EPILOGUE

Dear Liam,

It's been almost a year since you died, and just in case you've missed a few things happening down here on Earth, I thought I'd write with an update since you seem so fond of letters.

First of all, Barb wants me to tell you that you're still a real son of a bitch for dying, and she hasn't forgiven you. In fact, she plans to hold it against you for the rest of her goddamn life. Her words, not mine. As you can see, she hasn't changed one bit. She did, however, start a new knitting group that's really taken off. It was actually Linda's idea, but we don't mention that. Inishglass now has its own chapter of Knitted Knockers, the organization that made Barb's prosthetic breasts! Ten of us meet every Thursday morning at Stitches and Bitches. So far we've donated over fifty prostheses for breast cancer patients and survivors. Thanks to your list, with my new hobby, I get to do good things for other people. And I'm not half-bad! Though Barb still says I'm only one step above shit, which is actually quite the compliment, coming from her.

And speaking of Stitches and Bitches, I officially have a job! I'm their "design specialist," which is just a fancy way of saying they pay me to organize the store and decorate their front window every month. But word got around the island, and I've become a sort of home-edit consultant. I'm scheduled out through the summer. Turns out, most people don't like organizing their houses. I know! Crazy! Apparently they find it overwhelming. Briggs says he always knew my control-freakish nature was really a superpower. He thinks I should grow the business off the island, to Cork and beyond. We've been throwing around a few names. So far, I like Mae I Help You the best. Isla's boyfriend is designing me a website and everything. But we'll see. There's enough to do here for now.

And don't worry. I haven't neglected the Moorings. It's doing better than ever. Thursday night karaoke has been a huge hit! Practically everyone on the island shows up! It's become a sort of community event. Derry thinks we should put a playlist on Spotify of all the locals' kara-oke songs, so tourists can follow it. I couldn't believe he even knew what Spotify was, but as you know well, peo-ple will surprise you. And the Irish Times *wrote a whole article about the #irelandsmostwantedpotato debate! The journalist loved my pierogi. She also loved Briggs, so the debate continues.*

The Thatch isn't doing half-bad either. Briggs started an "art walk" on the first Friday of every month so people can exhibit and sell their work at the pub. You wouldn't believe all the underground artists on this island! But again, people will surprise you.

And speaking of surprising people, you'll be happy to know Eoin is gone. He left the island after I decided not to sell the pub. Word is he quit the practice in Cork, too. No one knows where he's gone. I heard a rumor he's in LA, but I have a feeling no matter where he is, he'll leave again soon enough. I never did get to the bottom of why he did what he did. I think it was all about money. He wanted me to sell so he got a cut of the deal. Briggs thinks it was pure revenge. He wanted me to sell the Moorings to screw the Thatch, payback for Briggs siding with Aoife all those years ago. Aoife thinks Eoin felt left out, and show-ing up at the party was his way of throwing a tantrum. (I think she's being too nice.) Barb thinks some people are just assholes, and we shouldn't care what their motivation is because that only feeds their ego. The more we talk about him, the more power he thinks he has.

I think we're all probably right in some regard. But as much as I want to hate Eoin for what he did, I don't. In fact, he may have saved Briggs's life, considering the fallout from that night forced Briggs to have heart surgery. So in the end, I'm grateful. Though if I never see Eoin again, it'll be too soon.

And guess what? Sonya and Melanie are engaged! Their wedding is next fall in Chicago. A proper city wed-ding with a big ceremony at Fourth Presbyterian Church on Michigan Avenue and a fancy reception at the Field Museum. Briggs and I already have our tickets booked. And let me tell you, does that man look good in a suit. Hot damn! I didn't think we'd make it out of the store (but I won't go into those details in this letter).

And Maryann and Keith are coming to Ireland this summer! They'll be here for the Annual Football Rounders Grudge Match. I thought living an ocean away from each other would be hard, but it turns out technology is awesome (when the Wi-Fi is working) and we FaceTime as much as we can.

Hugh is coming back for the game as well! WITH HIS GIRLFRIEND. Briggs and I almost fell over when he told us, but apparently being an adult is super fucking sexy to women. According to Hugh, if he had known that, he would have grown up years ago.

And Aoife just came back a few weeks ago, too, after spending the winter in India on a meditation retreat, more mindful than ever. She was positively radiant. Something tells me her destiny isn't on Inishglass, but for now I'll take all the girls' nights I can get with her . . . just without the wax.

Now for an update on Briggs. No, I'm not pregnant. Maybe someday, when we're ready to take that step. For now, he's busy working on the art studio. After he sold his parents' home, he wasn't sure what house to buy on the island. And I suggested he not buy a house at all but add on to the art studio, since he loves it so much. He took the idea and ran with it. The addition should be done at the end of the summer. But not to fear, I'm keeping your apartment. The popularity of the island is only increasing, and we need as much summer help at the pub as possible. My plan is to house seasonal workers there for free. I thought you'd approve.

Which brings me to another bit of news with Briggs. We're getting married! The proposal wasn't anything extravagant, just the two of us one night at the art studio, him painting and me watching. He looked at me and said, "Marry me," and I said, "OK," and he said, "When?" and I got out my planner and flipped to November and said, "How about my birthday?" and he said, "Perfect." Then he pulled his mom's wedding ring out of a drawer and slipped it on my finger. It fit perfectly.

The whole island is going to shut down for the wedding. No tourists allowed all weekend. We're doing the ceremony at the Thatch and a bigger reception at the Moorings. Barb is officiating. And of course, there will be karaoke.

I'm sure you're wondering how we're going to keep up the feud, but it turns out, people don't really want Romeo and Juliet *to have a tragic ending. The story is so much better when it ends happy. Tourists have as much fun trying to snatch pictures of Briggs and me together as they did when we were feuding. We're all over social media, and it's a boon for the pubs! But of course, we're still fighting. Just last week, I plastic-wrapped all the toilets at the Thatch, just to remind Briggs who's boss. And get this—some Hollywood producer was just out here, talking to us about our very own reality show. Can you believe that? I don't think we'll do it, but it's fun to consider. The people in Inishglass would make quite the story! Can you imagine Barb on TV?!*

One last thing about the pub. I thought it needed a small change on the outside. I hope you don't mind. As a reminder to anyone who walks in the red door, there's now a sign that reads ENTER LAUGHING.

Which brings me to the main reason I'm writing this letter. I know you wanted me to sell the pub, and I appreciate what you said in your last letter. But living in a big city doesn't mean you have a big life, just like staying in a small town doesn't make your dreams tiny. I know you wanted me to explore the world, and I still might, but I've realized that what makes a life big isn't the number of stamps in your passport or the size of your hometown (or village). It's love. The more you have, the more you share, the bigger your life gets. So thanks for the fatherly advice, but in proper kid fashion, I didn't take it.

Thanks to you, I am living the biggest life on the tiniest island. And it's perfect.

Love,

Maeve

PS. Tell Niall we miss him, but I'm glad he's finally home with you.

ACKNOWLEDGMENTS

This book was truly a group effort from the start. Thank you to my acquiring editor, Carmen Johnson, for championing this story from its inception. It is a pleasure to write books for you.

To Renee Nyen for putting all the pieces together and for brainstorming with me these past six years. You weren't just my agent, you were so much more, and I'll be forever grateful.

To my incomparable editor, Jason Kirk. You're responsible for this wild ride, but what I'm most proud of, after six years and seven books together, is our friendship. You've brightened my life in more ways than just words on the page. I'll never forget the day Renee called and said you wanted *The Odds of Loving Grover Cleveland*. I may have gotten a book deal then, but my real prize was you. Thank you.

To my beloved friend Katherine Harvey for changing the direction of this book and insisting I write chapters from Briggs's perspective. Thank goodness for our crazy huskies that force us to walk them together every damn day.

To Jill Fons for running hundreds of miles with me (literally) while I talked through ideas for this book. We got there eventually! Only one person is more insane than me when it comes to running . . . and that's you. I'm so blessed you're my friend.

To everyone at Amazon who spends countless hours making books shine, from covers to marketing copy to promotional support. Thank you from the bottom of my heart.

To my team at kt literary and UTA, especially Kate Testerman and Addison Duffy. Through all the ups and downs of this year, thank you for not only picking up my calls, but picking me up when I needed it. Knowing you have my back is everything.

To my girls, Drew and Hazel, who have read all of my books. You have no idea how happy it makes me to see my stories in your hands. For you, I'll write forever.

And to Kyle. Always. It's you and me.

ABOUT THE AUTHOR

Photo © 2023 Kate Testerman

Rebekah Crane is the author of nine novels, including *June, Reimagined*; *The Upside of Falling Down*; and *The Odds of Loving Grover Cleveland*. She lives in Colorado with her husband, two daughters, and their rambunctious husky, Grover. For more information, visit rebekahcrane.com.